PILGRIM THROUGH THIS BARREN LAND

A Novel

CARY McMULLEN

Paperback ISBN 979-8-218-68763-2

E-book ISBN 979-8-218-74864-7

Printed in the United States of America

Cover art by Grace McMullen

Photograph by Cindy Skop

*For the extraordinary Evelyn
and her remarkable family,
joyful servants*

PROLOGUE:

COVER

ONE

The mallard descended in a diminishing spiral toward the gray lake. Through the thin mist above the water, he had seen the brown form of a female, and now he glided toward her, lowering his tail and feet to settle down near her. He paddled closer with a guttural muttering, a greeting that might receive a favorable response for mating, but the decoy was lifeless and there was only silence in the cold air.

The bird paused for a few moments, gulped some water and shook the rest off his head. He paddled closer to a patch of tall reeds in search of minnows. Watching intently in the blind, the hunter shifted his weight. The duck sensed danger and instantly beat his wings to get clear. He was strong, and in seconds he was fifteen feet above the water, accelerating.

MacKendrie had stood up the same instant the mallard began its flight, shotgun at his shoulder, tracking the bird. It was moving in a smooth arc, and a less experienced hunter would have aimed just ahead on the same plane, but with instinct he anticipated the duck would turn upward. He raised the gun slightly, squeezing the front trigger as he did so, and his shoulder was jolted as the weapon went off, sending a shocking *pow* though the still morning, startling nearby nesting birds.

The lead pellets ripped through the mallard's head and neck, and it fell straight down into the lake. In another moment, the shot's echoes died away, and all was silent again. MacKendrie lowered the gun, smoke wisping from the left barrel, and watched the spot where the bird floated. Satisfied, he broke open the shotgun, a 1937 Parker double-barreled 12 gauge, removing the spent shell and putting it in a pocket of his vest. A low whistle made him half-turn to his companion.

"Pretty damn good shot, if a preacher would pardon the expression," said the gray-haired man who stood up and gazed out at the duck. "Remind me to stay on this side of your shotgun."

"Thank you, Eli. Let's go get it."

The men climbed into a skiff hidden in the reeds.

"Well now, I don't know why so many of my shots miss," Ross said, unsuccessfully masking exasperation and envy. "Maybe if you'd let me use that fine old gun of yours, I'd have better luck."

"They have a saying in the military—it's not the gun, it's the gunner," MacKendrie said. "You're trying to correct your aim and jerking the gun."

"So you've told me, I believe," Ross replied shortly.

MacKendrie paddled the boat forward, collecting the decoy, and stopped beside the duck. Ross extended a net, lifted the body into the boat, and passed it back to MacKendrie, who examined it. The head was ruined, so taxidermy was out of the question, but the bird was magnificent, young with colors that were vibrant even in the dim light.

He rarely felt regret at his kills, but as he held the still-warm body, he experienced a moment of sadness at the order of creation. To live, one must kill other creatures. He didn't know why, but it couldn't be helped.

He turned the boat for shore and put the duck in his bag. He expected it would be tasty.

TWO

Smoke lay draped across the street like a dirty veil. Wang removed his glasses and rubbed his eyes. The racket from a passing pushcart had smothered his question, and now he repeated it. "Number fourteen?"

The old woman impatiently waved the back of her hand at him in the general direction of a row of low wooden buildings down the street. "Well, over there, young man! I mean, comrade." She saw he was not interested in the watches she showed him, even though she insisted they were not stolen, which was dubious. Annoyed as any salesman who has lost a customer, she turned her back.

Wang knew perfectly well where number fourteen Peng Zhen Street was, but he had stopped at the woman's booth as a ruse to surveille the street. Owl had schooled him strictly on that point. If there were signs the shop was being watched, he was to walk in calmly and place an order using a code word. He scanned the narrow street once more. It was cold for April, but he felt a trickle of sweat inside his thin jacket.

Two agents had disappeared in the past six months. The iron discipline that had been as valuable to the Party as guns was being turned upon an unruly China. The First Bureau, the intelligence arm of the Central Defense Ministry, looked for dissidents and counter-revolutionaries with astonishing fanaticism. Wang lived in constant fear.

He saw only bustle. After almost twenty years of war and five years of Communist rule, Shanghai was no longer the Paris of the East, yet here was a scene of traditional commerce—food sizzling on charcoal fires, people jostling each other looking for bargains. Above it all was the din of merchants hawking wares of all kinds. Two nearby had stentorian voices.

"Try my dumplings, best in Shanghai!" "Fine rugs, low price!"

Thirty meters ahead, a muscular man with close-cropped hair and sturdy shoes sauntered into a shop, and Wang kept his eye on the spot. The man came out again and was swiveling his head left and right as he talked to the owner. As Wang watched, the man turned and walked slowly away. In a moment he was lost in the crowd. If he was with the First Bureau, he was clumsy. Wang sighed. His mind was playing tricks again, he thought. He made his way to the shop.

He didn't look back at the street. If he had, he would have seen that the man with sturdy shoes was at a stall, pretending to examine an orange but watching Wang.

PART ONE:

THE DUCK HUNTER

THREE

The day dawned muggy and warm, too warm for March. There had been a string of them. False spring, some said. Anyone who ventured a remark about planting was promptly warned. Too early. Been frosts as late as May. You want to kill half your crop, go right ahead. But this warm spell was different, as if winter were a rebellious son who left home with no intention of coming back. Boys took their baseballs and gloves out of their closets, but the klatch of men standing outside First Presbyterian Church cursed silently. Their livelihoods depended on farming, one way or another, a warm spring might mean a dry summer, and the men fretted and made black jokes like a prisoner awaiting his fate. Perspiration was already beginning to stain their suits, and the farmers scowled at the prospect of working that afternoon. They viewed the Fourth Commandment as a luxury for old women and the affluent, even as they envied the prospect of resting on the Sabbath.

"Y'all hear about that teacher over to Whiteville?" one said suddenly with a crooked grin. "Got caught in back of a pickup with the principal. Had to leave town real sudden like. Family ee-mergency." There was low laughter, the men not wanting to seem too much like they were enjoying lewd thoughts in the shadow of the church.

Sunday morning gossip was segregated by gender in Kirkwell, as it was in hamlets across eastern North Carolina. The women had their visiting inside the sturdy red-brick sanctuary. Outside the men smoked, shuffled their feet, fussed about crop price forecasts, and made disapproving remarks about Negroes in Raleigh calling for the right to vote.

"Vote. Shoot. Not one of 'em got a lick of sense. Who they gonna vote for anyway?"

"It'll be one of their own kind, I imagine. They get to vote, they'll be running for office."

"Hmp! That ain't never gonna happen 'round here."

"It might if the gov'ment says we have to let 'em run."

"They can't do that!" It came from a rawboned young man whose gaunt face might have appeared in a Matthew Brady print.

"They did once before." Heads turned to a tall, thin man with gray hair. "After the Civil War. I taught you that in tenth grade, Dick Follett, you mullet head."

The men guffawed, and Follett grinned. "Aw, you know me, Mr. Eli. I wasn't too good at history. 'Sides, the Civil War, that was a long time ago."

"Well now, it is the year of our Lord nineteen hundred and fifty-three. Your Grandpa Follett probably remembers seeing Union troops on the streets of Wilmington when he was a boy. Ask him whether they let the coloreds vote." Yankees, someone murmured. Won't let that happen again, no sirree. Ross continued, "You all know the pastor's grandfather had something to do with that. He helped the Yankees run the state during Reconstruction."

Follett frowned. "What you mean?"

"The MacKendries came from a rich family around Wilmington that didn't want secession," Ross said. "When the war was over, they gave Hezekiah MacKendrie a place in the government. The pastor sees things a little different than most of us."

A grizzled man with a lined face nodded toward Ross. "What about you, Eli? Where's all this headed?"

Ross paused and spoke deliberately. "Change is in the air, gentlemen, whether we like it or not. The army's been desegregated. From what I hear, some of those colored boys are doing pretty well over in Korea. They're already hollering about equality. We just need to figure out how to slow things down. If we don't watch it, some judge is going to take the Negroes' side, and we'll have 'em moving in next to us."

The talk warmed as quickly as the air, but the sight of an unfamiliar black late-model Buick driving slowly along the street caught their attention. The men in town knew each other's cars by heart, and they fell silent as it pulled into the nearest spot at the curb. A short, stocky man in a gray suit and dark felt hat got out and made his way toward them. He was around fifty, they judged, with a square unlined face, an erect walk and an air of unperturbed confidence. Follett, who had been a corporal in the European theater, instinctively stood up straighter as he approached. The stranger stopped in front of them and looked them over.

"Morning, gents."

"Morning," they murmured.

"Warm today."

Yes, sure is, they agreed.

"I'm looking for Reverend MacKendrie. This is his church, isn't it?"

The men exchanged glances. "What you want with him, mister?" The question, from a fat, red-faced man in an ill-fitting suit, brimmed with territoriality.

"He's an old friend of mine," the stranger said, unruffled. "I was in the vicinity and thought I'd come see him. I figured I'd be sure to find him here on a Sunday morning."

No one spoke. The gray-haired man stepped forward, extending his hand.

"I'm Eli Ross. I'm an elder here. Jim MacKendrie is our pastor. He's finishing up a Sunday school class right about now. You need to speak to him right away?"

"No, no. I can wait."

"Church starts in about ten minutes. If you'd care to worship with us, I imagine he'd be glad to speak to you after."

"That's good of you."

"Let's go on inside where it's cooler." Ross stepped toward the church. "How do you know Pastor MacKendrie?"

"Mac and I were in the Navy together."

"Mac?"

"We called him Mac. Everyone has a nickname in the Navy."

"Jim doesn't talk much about his time in the war. Just said he was a chaplain in the South Pacific. That where you met him?"

"Yeah, at a base on Tinian. He was a good chaplain. Helped a lot of men."

"I can believe that. I was too old to go," Ross said. "I didn't get your name."

"Sorry. Harry Cohen."

Ross stopped. "Well now, I knew a fella named Cohen. At Chapel Hill. Jewish. That your persuasion, Mr. Cohen?" At the man's expression, he hastily added, "No offense."

Cohen returned evenly, "None taken. And call me Harry, please. It is my persuasion, but I don't practice much these days."

Ross cocked his head. "Well, we don't get many Jews around here, but you're mighty welcome. Let's go in."

They walked through a small vestibule into a plain sanctuary with dark wooden pews and half-paneled walls inset with four stained-glass windows each bearing likenesses of Christ. Cohen tried to ignore them. They approached a cluster of women arranged on a pew, and Cohen grasped they were debating the merits of brands of shortening. Ross pulled on the sleeve of one and reluctantly she stood, a plump woman with wavy hair that was the color of an old trumpet. She was heavily made up, Cohen observed—too much powder, excessive lipstick—and she wore a frilly dress that boasted turquoise polka dots the size of the dial on his watch.

Cohen held his hat against his chest as he took her hand. Gladys Ross batted her eyes at him. "How d'you do, Mr. Cone. Are you from around here? We know some Cones over to Jordanton. You related to any of them?"

Her husband spoke up. "Gladys, the gentleman's name is Cohen. Co. Hen. You're not from around here, are you, Harry?"

"Afraid not. I'm from New Jersey."

"Oh, my. I don't think I've ever met anyone from New *Jer*sey. 'Cept there was that one fella who came through selling what was it, some floor waxing gadget? He had a funny accent. Harriet—that's my friend Harriet Cunningham—she said she thought he was foreign, but I said no, that Charlene Hudson had talked to him and found out he was from Boston or Philadelphia or somewhere. Have you ever been to Boston, Mr. Cone?"

Cohen's reply was cut short by tinny chords from an upright piano played by a determined-looking woman with gray-streaked hair. The men from outside began to saunter inside, seeking out their wives. A side door adjoining the sanctuary opened, and people from a classroom beyond edged their way in, stopping to chat as they made their way to their usual seats. The clans of Connors, Campbells, Guthries and other natives of the sandy soil of Eastern North Carolina clustered and arranged themselves in the pews, slowly transforming themselves into a congregation, a cloud of atoms coalescing into a planet revolving around a distant sun.

As they settled into a pew, Cohen turned to his host.

"Is Mac—Reverend MacKendrie—a good preacher?"

Ross pondered a moment. "Have you ever studied Latin, Harry?"

"No. A little Hebrew when I was bar-mitzvahed."

"I suppose it's the same. Listening to Jim MacKendrie is a little like studying one of those ancient tongues. It's hard work, but you usually come away edified. Now, most of these folks," he glanced around, and his voice dropped to a murmur, "aren't too interested in working that hard when it comes to listening to a sermon. Jim gets complaints."

"But people like him?"

Ross's eyes narrowed. "Oh, sure. He can be a little preachy sometimes. I've told him he needs to loosen up about people smoking."

Cohen recalled a line from a personnel report that MacKendrie had been warned about making too many disapproving remarks about smoking. The door beside the chancel opened, and Cohen got his first look at MacKendrie in almost eight years. They had parted, none too amiably, on Tinian in 1945. Now he saw that MacKendrie had not let peacetime make him soft. He had the same high cheekbones that gave his face an angularity. MacKendrie's hairline was thinning, exaggerating his expansive forehead. You could show a movie on that, Cohen thought.

MacKendrie mounted the steps, placed some papers and a Bible on the pulpit and went to an elaborately carved chair with a red velvet seat. Before sitting down, he turned and looked out over the congregation, surveying the people steadily and methodically. When his gaze reached Cohen, he gave a small, involuntary movement. He stared for a moment, and a crease appeared between his brows. He sat down abruptly.

Throughout the worship service, Ross was solicitous, handing Cohen a shabby green hymnbook open to the proper page, offering a quiet explanation about the recitation of a creed or the singing of a response. When wooden plates were passed down the pews, Cohen fished a ten-dollar bill out of his wallet, tossed it in and saw Ross's look of surprise. He glanced around. Cohen wasn't interested in the fine points of anyone's belief, but he couldn't help notice that some around him, like Ross, were bright-eyed with devotion while others, like his wife, sat with fixed smiles and lowered eyes. It was the same everywhere, he decided. True believers side by side with those just passing time.

Finally, MacKendrie stood at the pulpit and announced he would read from Exodus. Cohen vaguely recalled hearing it before, something about Moses pleading with God not to abandon the Jews in the wilderness. Later, Cohen reflected that Ross was right about MacKendrie's preaching. It was Shakespearean.

Standing erect, MacKendrie declaimed, "Moses and the people must decide whether they will dare to walk beside a fearful God whom they have seen wipe out an army and whose demands are uncompromising, or whether they will journey across a perilous wilderness without the comfort and protection of that same God. How often in our lives do we plead with God to come and walk with us and deliver us out of some trouble we're in? And yet we fail to grasp what this means. For when God comes to us, it is not only with his power, it is with his holiness as well. When the Lord reaches down to pull us up out of the mire, his hand is aflame with righteousness. And we must ask ourselves whether we will reach up and take that hand, which will burn away the pride and falsehoods and vices that we love all too well."

Cohen was surprised to find himself offended, although he couldn't say why. MacKendrie preached for precisely twenty minutes, gave a nod to the pianist, and crashing chords from the piano shattered the reverie that lay over people. A stanza caught Cohen's attention.

Guide me, O Thou great Jehovah,
Pilgrim through this barren land.
I am weak, but Thou art mighty,
Hold me with Thy powerful hand.

Jehovah sounded old-fashioned, like something from the seventeen hundreds. Cohen remembered that Jews didn't dare to pronounce the name of God. Feeling a bit foolish, he coughed as the congregation sang the word, blotting it out.

MacKendrie pronounced a benediction, strode to the rear of the church and began shaking hands with people as they walked out. Cohen followed the Rosses, and as they waited in line, he could hear MacKendrie talking to the fat man who had challenged him when he first walked up.

"No, Joe, I don't buy that. It says in Genesis that all men are created in the image of God, and I don't see anything in there about only white men." The man went wide-eyed and started to raise his voice, but MacKendrie cut him off. "We've got some folks waiting. Why don't you come by sometime when we've got more time to talk about it?" He pivoted to speak to the next in line, and the man gave a slow stare and moved away but his voice carried inside the church.

"You hear what he just said? What he said 'bout— Ain't right..."

Ross stepped up and MacKendrie frowned.

"What have you been telling people, Eli? Joe Stallings asking about Yankees and race relations and if I was a Negro lover."

"Well, aren't you?" said Ross with a wide smile.

"I think you meant that as a joke." MacKendrie impassively turned to Cohen and held out his hand. "Well. Hello, Harry. You sure surprised me today."

"Hello, Mac. How are ya? I heard you had settled in here, and I thought I'd drive down and see you."

"Mac. I haven't been called that in a while. You're bringing back all kinds of memories."

Ross looked from one man to the other, offered his hand to Cohen with an invitation to come back anytime, and herded his wife out the door. The sanctuary had almost emptied. An elegantly dressed woman and two children stood a respectful distance away, while an elderly black janitor went from pew to pew, checking for anything left behind.

"Come and meet my wife," MacKendrie said. "Helen? Helen, do you remember me telling you about Harry Cohen that I met in the Navy? This is Harry."

Helen MacKendrie was slightly taller than Cohen, and she spoke in a refined drawl. "Why, how do you do, Harry. This is an unexpected pleasure. Jim certainly spoke about you a lot. These are our girls, Dorothy and Priscilla." They were shy, properly dressed, about seven and five, Cohen guessed. He bent forward and spoke to them, and the older one looked at him and smiled. The younger buried her face in her mother's dress.

"They're dolls, Mac. I wasn't around much to see my own kids grow up. You're a lucky man."

MacKendrie's smile was thin. Helen asked, "Did you come just to see Jim, Harry, or are you on a trip?"

"To see Jim. I thought we could get reacquainted."

"Of course. Won't you join us for lunch? It's nothing fancy but we'd love to have you."

"I'd love to join you, thanks."

"Wonderful. Jim, dear, I hope you don't mind, but I brought the girls in the car. It was so warm this morning. I'll take them on home and you two can join us."

MacKendrie signaled Cohen to follow. They walked down a short hallway into the pastor's study, which was small, spare and tidy, with full bookshelves, a desk, an extra chair, and a diploma on the wall. The one decorative object was a large stuffed duck sitting atop a bookshelf. MacKendrie went to a coat rack, divested himself of his heavy robe and exchanged it for his suit jacket. The sound of a struck match made him turn to see Cohen lifting the flame to a cigarette.

"Not in here, Harry."

"Hm? Oh. Sorry." Cohen waved out the match and looked for a wastebasket. "Bad habit. Tried to kick it, but it helps keep the weight off."

"You haven't changed much. But I almost didn't recognize you in civvies."

"Oh, I still wear the uniform occasionally. I'm mostly behind a desk these days." He gestured to the duck. "That's a nice bird. You bag it?"

MacKendrie nodded. "About a year ago. I got several nice birds that season."

"You were a pretty good shot. I remember that now. Everyone wondered how a chaplain could be so good with a gun."

MacKendrie shrugged. "My father taught me. We had lots of practice in China. Shall we go? It's not far to the manse, but you should drive your car over."

"Manse?"

"The Presbyterian term for the parsonage. Comes from the Church of Scotland, I think."

As they drove, Cohen mentioned a couple of men they had known in the Navy, but MacKendrie just nodded without comment.

Helen MacKendrie laid a generous lunch that included slabs of ham. Cohen didn't worry about kosher, especially in the interest of a mission, and ate every bite. He noticed that MacKendrie said little.

"Helen, this is delicious. I love coming to the South just to eat the food here."

She beamed. "Why, thank you, Harry. Do you get down this way much?"

"Every now and then. I'm based in Washington, but I sometimes make the rounds of the Navy bases—Norfolk, Jacksonville, so on."

"What made you stay in the Navy, Harry?" MacKendrie asked.

"Too lazy to get a real job, I guess." Helen laughed. "No, I like the Navy. I was offered a job at the Pentagon, and it was too good to pass up."

"Mr. Cohen?" Everyone turned to Dorothy. "Did you shoot anybody in the war?"

"Dottie! That is not a polite question for our guest," MacKendrie said sternly. The girl looked as if she might cry.

"It's okay, Mac." He addressed the girl. "No, Dorothy, I didn't have to shoot anybody. And it's a good thing, too, because I'm a very bad shot. Not nearly as good as your father."

Dottie smiled, Helen laughed, and even MacKendrie managed an amused look.

After a dessert of lemon meringue pie that Cohen gushed over, Helen asked the girls to help her with the dishes and shooed away the men. They made their way to a cozy study. MacKendrie brought in the chair that stood next to the telephone in the hall but Cohen remained standing, examining the books on the shelves. He was dying for a cigarette, but he knew better than to ask.

"I hope I'm not interrupting any plans," he said.

"We sometimes get visitors on Sunday afternoons. Old Southern custom, paying your respects to the pastor." MacKendrie stretched his long legs and stifled a yawn.

"You seem content here," Cohen remarked.

"It's peaceful, at least compared to the last dozen years."

"Cute kids you've got. Didn't you have a son? With your first wife? Richard, wasn't it?"

MacKendrie shifted in his chair. "Yes. He was a supply officer in the war. He's a lawyer now. But I don't think you came here to chat about family. What is it, Harry?"

Cohen smiled and sat down. "Direct as always. Your personnel reports mentioned that."

"So you've been checking up on me. I should have expected that from a former naval intelligence officer. Or is it former?"

Cohen shook his head. "Asian Operations."

"I see. Only now you're spying on the Communists instead of the Japanese."

"Peacetime intelligence is a different ball game. We have to be a lot more careful. Can't risk diplomatic incidents. We're having trouble right now getting good information from China."

"I figured this might have something to do with China."

Cohen leaned forward. "Mac, we may need your help."

MacKendrie frowned. "What kind of help?"

"Your advice, mostly. We've got an operation going on around Shanghai."

"Shanghai? What do you need me for? There are plenty of people who know more about Shanghai than I do."

"Well, the operation extends upriver. Up around Bai Miao. Your old stomping grounds. There aren't too many people who know that area as well as you."

Cohen had mispronounced the name badly—as *bay me-oh*—indicating he had not bothered to learn much of Chinese language and culture. MacKendrie was annoyed but didn't bother correcting him. He studied Cohen for a moment but could read nothing in his face. "No. All that's old history now. I'd rather not dredge it up."

"It's important, Mac. China's closed now, you know that."

"I can't help you."

Cohen's jaw clenched. "I hear they've turned your old mission station into a pig farm."

"Don't try to provoke me, Harry. It won't work."

Cohen leaned back. "Suppose I told you this involves someone you used to know?"

"Someone like who?" MacKendrie said skeptically.

"Does the name Wang Wenzhe ring a bell? I think you knew him as Paul."

"Paul—" MacKendrie started, then shook his head. "He's just a boy."

"Boys grow up."

MacKendrie stood up, agitated. "Are you trying to tell me Paul Wang is working for you? It's preposterous. He went to California. We got him into college. He was studying science, for God's sake."

"When was the last time you heard from him?"

MacKendrie paused. "A few years. Why?" Cohen didn't answer, and MacKendrie slowly sat down again, trying to keep his temper. "What do you want to know?"

"There's no rush. I came just to give you a heads up."

"You're scouting me." Cohen shrugged. "Advice. That's all?"

"Any information we can get is like gold."

MacKendrie slowly nodded. "All right. I don't know what I can tell you."

They stood. "That's great, Mac. I'll be back in touch when we need you."

"I don't doubt it. But Harry—" MacKendrie's voice dropped and Cohen was startled by a gleam in his eye. "Keep me informed about Paul Wang. All right?"

Cohen nodded. "Sure, Mac. I'll be off now. Let me say goodbye to your lovely wife."

"You better. Helen is a believer in etiquette."

Cohen fidgeted with a button. "Mac, about Nathan... I'm sorry. We were wrong. He was a good man."

MacKendrie put his hands in his pockets. "When you showed up, I thought that's what you wanted to talk about. It's okay, Harry. It's what happens in war. But I still think about him."

Later, as the children were napping, Helen found MacKendrie in his study, sitting and staring. "Well. What was all that about?"

He stirred. "Oh, not much. Harry was just doing a little sniffing around." She shook her head, puzzled. "The Navy likes to stay in touch with people that might be useful to them."

She was wary. "Useful how?"

"Harry thinks I might know some things about China for one of their...I don't know, surveillance missions."

"Oh. Well. You certainly do know a lot about China." She meant it as a good-natured jibe at MacKendrie's habit of talking about his days in the mission field. But he didn't seem to hear her. After a moment, she said, "What's bothering you, Jim?"

He shook his head. "Seeing Harry brought back some bad memories."

"You can tell me." She sat down on the empty chair.

MacKendrie was silent for a moment. "You remember me talking about Nathan Considine?"

"He was your friend. He was killed, you said."

"We were on Tinian. He was an Army pilot. Big fellow from Louisville, friendly. A fine Christian man, and there weren't too many of those out there. He flew transport planes. One day he was assigned to fly some supplies to an outpost. Routine stuff, but they always worried they'd run into a patrol. Those transport planes were no match for Japanese fighters. Harry Cohen was the naval intelligence officer on Tinian. He told Nathan there was no enemy activity on his flight route. He was wrong. The radio operators heard Nathan call in a mayday, but there was nothing anyone could do. The last words they heard him say were, 'Jesus, save me.'"

"Oh, Jim. How awful."

MacKendrie nodded. "It took me a long time to get over it. I know we're supposed to forgive, but every time I saw Cohen, I wanted to hit him and keep hitting him." He looked up to see a shocked expression on Helen's face. He leaned over and took her hand. "I'm sorry if this upsets you. War does that to men. Makes them hard, fills them with rage. I saw it over and over again. I was there to direct their hearts to God, but in that case I couldn't find my own way." He shook his head. "Physician, heal thyself."

Tears shone in Helen's eyes. "Jesus said that as a rebuke," she whispered.

Gratitude flooded him. He stood, pulled her up and held her. She shook a bit, and he shushed her.

"It was a long time ago, now. It's all right, Helen. In a way, seeing Harry today was a good thing. It helped me realize how much has changed."

Helen stepped back and sniffled. "I'd better go wake the girls, or they'll never get to sleep tonight."

MacKendrie dreamed that night he was on Tinian. He was in a bunker and bullets were whizzing around him, but he decided his duty was to go to the hospital. He stood up and walked with complete serenity as bombs went off and men around him cursed and fired up at the planes. A big man stopped in front of him, fired a rifle, then looked at him. A bullet hole as big as a fist appeared in his middle. There was no blood. He said, "Jesus, save me," then dissolved into a mist.

MacKendrie sat up, panting. Helen was still asleep. He ran his fingers through his hair, trying to get control of himself. When his breathing slowed, he lay back down, staring up at the dark.

"Christ," he whispered.

FOUR

April passed under a white glare with barely two days of rain, and people whispered "drought," as though it were a plague word, something that could be spread if spoken of openly. Tobacco planting was underway in the dust-dry fields, and farmers grasped a spider silk of hope that late spring rains would arrive and give life to their seedlings. But the dread of what lay ahead if there were no rain soon set people on edge.

A low current of irritation ran through MacKendrie's congregation—bickerings about petty matters, like the choice of a hymn. There was a dip in offerings, as if people were starting to hoard their earnings. Gossip reported arguments between friends. Despite MacKendrie's best efforts to make it joyful, Easter had been a listless occasion at First Presbyterian.

It affected his own household as well. As they sat at the breakfast table, Priss made a rude comment about Dottie's dress, and Dottie dumped Priss's oatmeal in her lap, setting off a wail that could be heard two houses away. Helen jerked Dottie out of her chair and was about to spank her when MacKendrie intervened.

"You take care of Priss. Dottie, come with me." She followed him slowly into his study. MacKendrie sat down and ordered her to stand in front of him.

"Look at me." Her dark eyes flickered up. "I'm not going to spank you because I don't want you going to school crying. Your mother and

I will discuss your punishment later. But I want you to know something. You thought you were getting even with Priss, but it never works that way. When someone has done you a wrong and you get back at them, it doesn't settle things, it only keeps it going. Priss is not going to remember why you dumped oatmeal in her lap. She's just going to want to get back at you for that."

"But she started it," Dottie protested.

"I know. You think she got what she deserved, but all she did was make a mean remark. I want you to go straight in there and tell Priss you're sorry and that you won't do that ever again."

"But she…"

"No buts. Let us worry about Priss. You apologize. Then get ready for school. Go on."

The apology had been grudgingly given, and Priss sullenly made no reply. Helen MacKendrie was pale with anger. She believed consequences should follow swiftly upon wrongdoing.

On Friday, the church's janitor arrived as usual to clean. Ulysses Brown, known to the white townspeople as Ug, had worked for First Presbyterian for nearly a generation. No one knew his age. He was muscular from years of hard labor, and his complexion was dark, like the color of the church's old hardwood floor.

MacKendrie once asked him about his unpleasant nickname. His grandfather had been a slave at a plantation outside Vicksburg, Mississippi, Brown said. The army of General Ulysses Grant had beaten the Confederates and freed the slaves thereabouts. Years later, the grandfather insisted that his first grandson would be named Ulysses Grant Brown. White folks didn't much like the name, Brown said with a grin, and called him U.G. instead, which became Ug. Doesn't it bother you, MacKendrie asked.

"No, sir. Ever' time they says it, reminds me I ain't a slave like my granddaddy."

In his study, MacKendrie was worrying over a phrase in the sermon when he glanced up and saw Brown standing in the doorway, holding a broom.

"Oh. Hello, Ulysses."

"Afternoon, sir. Mighty fine day, ain't it?"

"Sure is. We need the rain but I hope it will be nice on Sunday."

Brown shook his head slowly. "Won't be no rain next day or two, Pastor."

"No? Now how do you know that?"

"Can always tell. My leg act up on me. And today is layin' still."

"I've heard about that, folks that can tell when it's going to rain that way."

"Yessir. Ever since I hurt it, it tell me ever time when they's a change coming."

"How'd you hurt it?"

"Was a long time ago. I's unloading a bag of cotton in a wagon, and somethin' spooked the mules. Wheel knock me down, then ran over my leg and broke it. Broke it bad, too. Bone stick out like this." He held one hand level and the other angled up from it. "Couldn't go back to the field after that. Just as well, too." He smiled. "I don't miss picking cotton. Now this job here just about right for me. And I loves working in the house of the Lord."

"I feel the same way. The psalm says, 'I had rather be a doorkeeper in the house of my God, than to dwell in the tents of wickedness.'"

Brown laughed with delight. "Yessir! That's right."

He didn't move. After a moment, MacKendrie said, "Did you need something, Ulysses?"

Brown nodded. "Yessir. Is about my nephew."

MacKendrie waited and finally realized Brown wanted permission to speak. "Yes, go on."

"He in jail, Pastor."

MacKendrie gestured to a chair, but Brown shook his head and leaned on the broom. "What happened, Ulysses?"

There had been a robbery at a gas station out in the county three nights ago, Brown said. The owner was closing for the evening when a young Negro wearing a bandana had robbed him at gunpoint. It was nearly dark, and the robber was gone in seconds, but the owner said he recognized him as Jeremiah Brown.

"Now my nephew, he's a good boy. Never been in no trouble. Respectful. Smart, too. Family was hoping he'd get into college. Move on up. But sheriff done arrest him."

"And he says he didn't do it."

"Yessir. Has hisself a alibi. Was over in the next town, working."

MacKendrie leaned forward. "He was working at the time the robbery happened?"

"Yessir. His boss told the sheriff, but sheriff say it don't matter cause they got a witness say it was Jeremiah."

MacKendrie stared down at the desk. This sort of thing had happened in China frequently. Grudges settled by false accusations, incompetent investigations, mistakes covered up to save embarrassment. This was the first time he had encountered it in the States.

"What would you like me to do, Ulysses?"

"Jeremiah need someone to talk to. He's a good boy, go to church regular like. We'd be obliged if you'd go see him."

MacKendrie hesitated. "Would they let me see him?"

Brown shrugged. "You is white."

MacKendrie was startled by the starkness of it, a whole universe summed up in three words. He considered saying no but found his conscience wouldn't let him.

"I can't promise anything, Ulysses, but let me see what I can do."

Brown regarded him for a moment and apparently decided MacKendrie could be trusted. "Much oblige." He picked up the broom and walked out.

MacKendrie sat still, irritated and not sure why. He sighed, picked up the phone and dialed a number. He asked for Sheriff Hoolie Dixon.

Dixon was a big man with a tender heart. He was known to overlook minor offenses committed in foolishness by both black and white alike. His law enforcement techniques were outdated and some of his deputies were unqualified men, friends of friends who had asked for a favor, but he was so well liked he kept getting re-elected.

Dixon rumbled a hello, and after some pleasantries, said, "What can I do for you, Preacher?"

"Sheriff, I understand you have a young man named Jeremiah Brown in custody."

"Yessir. Got him on armed robbery."

"He's the nephew of our janitor, Ulysses Brown, maybe you know him."

"Ol' Ug? Sure I do. He's been around here a long time. Never given us any trouble. Has he put you up to something?"

"Well, he wants me to come over and talk to the boy."

A few moments of silence passed. "Uh-huh. Just why, exactly?"

"Ulysses says the boy's never been in trouble before and he's scared. I'd be there to offer some comfort." When Dixon didn't respond, MacKendrie added, "Pastors do that with prisoners, Sheriff."

"Oh, sure. We get that a lot. Only...it's usual for the coloreds to have their own preachers come see 'em."

"Ulysses says his preacher holds down a job over in Wilmington and can't come over during visiting hours."

"Uh-huh. Well...as I say, it'd be unusual." MacKendrie waited. Dixon cleared his throat. "I reckon there's no harm to it. Can you come over in the next hour? We close up by five."

The jail was several blocks away, and MacKendrie walked in the muggy warmth. His shirt was damp when he arrived. Dixon had spoken to the desk sergeant, and he was taken back to the cells, a double row of steel cages, where it was dank and smelled of urine. A few men sitting on bunks looked up idly as he passed. The jailer stopped and tapped the bars. "You've got a visitor."

A tall athletic man with a broad, handsome face stood. MacKendrie judged he was no more than nineteen. "Jeremiah? I'm James MacKendrie. Your Uncle Ulysses asked me to come see you."

"Yes, sir. My uncle's told me about you."

MacKendrie turned to the jailer. "Can you let me in?"

The man shook his head. "Against the rules. You'll have to talk from where you are. Knock on that door when you're done."

Brown leaned against the bars, and MacKendrie spoke in a low voice. "Are you all right, son?"

Brown grimaced. "I don't know, sir."

"Are you hurt?"

"No, sir."

"Ulysses tells me you've never been in jail before. This would shake up any man."

"It's..." He shook his head and his voice turned pleading. "I don't know what's going to happen to me. I didn't do it, Pastor! You've got to believe me!"

A catcall came from the cell behind MacKendrie. "Hoo, boy! Nobody gonna believe you. They gonna send you away for a long time!"

MacKendrie stared at the white prisoner, who gave a smirk and turned away. He returned to Brown. "Your uncle tells me you have an alibi. Who's your boss?"

Brown was breathing heavily. "It's Lawson Ford. He has a little place where the River Road crosses the highway to Wilmington. A restaurant. I run the register."

"This Ford, is he white?"

"No, sir. We mostly serve black folks." MacKendrie's heart sank, but Brown went on, "There was a white man who saw me, though. We do get a few white customers, and one stopped by that evening."

"Do you know him?"

"No, sir, but he and Mr. Ford said hello to one another, friendly like."

MacKendrie thought for a moment. "Do you have a lawyer, son?"

"The family's trying to find one for me."

"All right. Now listen, Jeremiah. You've got a lot of people praying for you, and that includes me. My advice is not to cause any trouble while you're here. Let's hope the sheriff will keep looking for the real culprit." Brown shook his head. "I'll have a word with him." The young man looked up in surprise.

"You will?"

"Yes. Try to keep your courage up. That and your faith are the things they can't take away from you."

Brown seemed to relax, and he nodded. "I'll try, sir."

"Good. If I can, I'll come see you again."

"Thank you, sir. I mean it."

MacKendrie knocked on the door at the end of the corridor and told the jailer he wanted to see the sheriff. Dixon admitted him to his cramped, musty office.

"Sheriff, I don't mean to interfere, but are you sure about this? The boy does have an alibi."

"Yeah. We talked to Lawson."

"And?"

"Well, you know, they do stick up for their own kind."

MacKendrie suppressed his first response. He said casually, "Jeremiah says a white man did see him that evening."

Dixon's brow furrowed. "Did he now?"

"He says it was a customer who seemed to know this Lawson Ford well. I'd hate to see an innocent man put away, Sheriff." Dixon grimaced, and MacKendrie decided to bluff. "Jeremiah's lawyer would be sure to put that witness on the stand in a trial."

Dixon looked down at his desk for so long MacKendrie wondered if he had dozed off. Finally he gave a heavy sigh. "Ahright. Guess we'll have to look into it."

MacKendrie nodded. "It's the right thing to do."

The sheriff slowly shook his head. "I heard that before."

FIVE

At midmorning, MacKendrie joined John Wesley Jones, the pastor at First Methodist, for coffee at the Pine Bough Café. They met each Tuesday to unburden themselves of the trials of small-town pastors. Jones was silver-haired, folksy, and suave. Years in the Methodist system had given him uncanny survival instincts, and he could spot trouble coming from far away.

"Jim, are you sure everything is okay at your place?"

MacKendrie looked up, surprised. "As far as I know. Why do you ask?"

Jones sipped his coffee and frowned. "Just something I heard the other day. You have a more progressive view of race relations than most folks around here."

"Oh, that. Well, I don't think the time is right for integration, but I suppose holding that Negroes are equal in the sight of God is a radical thought around here. When you live in the mission field you get used to dealing with folks of other races."

Jones leaned forward and lowered his voice. "Word's gotten around that you got that Brown boy off."

Irritated, MacKendrie said, "I didn't get him off. All I did was tell Hoolie Dixon about a witness he should talk to. I'd have done the same if the boy was white."

Jones nodded and said with emphasis, "Uh-huh."

"Hoolie did the right thing letting Jeremiah go." He paused. "What else have you heard?"

"One of the local farmers. Something to the effect that Jim MacKendrie was too friendly with...well, coloreds. There was a comment like, 'Next thing you know he'll be letting them in church.'"

They sat in silence for a few minutes and MacKendrie set his cup down with a clatter. "What do you think I should do?"

"Once something like this gets going, it's hard to stop," Jones reflected. "You could go have a private chat with your elders. Try to reassure them you're not about to do anything drastic."

MacKendrie leaned back and sighed. "Of course I'm not about to do anything drastic. I'm just not as diplomatic as you are, John. I'd probably wind up making things worse by talking to these knuckleheads." A head turned at the next table.

Jones put his palm flat on the table. "Be careful, Jim. These folks can get ugly if you get on their bad side."

MacKendrie waved a hand. "I went through a civil war in China and was a combat zone chaplain in World War Two. That's a lot of ugliness. I doubt if anything here is going to match it."

He walked back to the church along the main street. Men removed their hats and wiped the inside bands with white handkerchiefs, and women fanned themselves with whatever came to hand.

His study was not hot yet, but stuffy, and he took off his coat and turned on an oscillating fan. His leather-bound Bible sat on his desk, and he opened it to the flyleaf and read the familiar inscription: "To our son, Rev. James Jonathan MacKendrie, on the occasion of his graduation from Union Th. Sem., May 17, 1924. With much love, Papa and Mother."

Shortly after the turn of the century, Dr. David MacKendrie went off to China with his young wife to establish a hospital in Bai Miao. James MacKendrie and his brother had been born there.

Life in China was a constant test of principle. The unequal treaties that allowed Western companies to exploit China's wealth meant foreigners were hated and feared, even the ones like his father who came with the best of intentions. They endured the repeated epithet of *sei gwei lo*, white devil. The children were tormented by the peasant boys, who threw rocks and laughed at them. Almost daily Papa and Mother reminded them they were not to retaliate. It was not Christian, they said, and they had to show their faith by example. They were made to repeat "Whosoever shall smite thee on thy right cheek, turn to him the other also" until they said Jesus' words through clenched teeth.

His mind wandered back to Jones' advice. A few men were outspoken about segregation—Percy Weir, the biggest landowner in the county; Dick Follett, who had come back from the war a harder man than the easygoing teenager who enlisted; Joe Stallings. MacKendrie left the church and walked home to get the car.

He turned west onto the main highway out of town. At this time of year, without any tobacco plants in the fields, you could see almost to the horizon.

He listened to the radio for a little while, one small-town radio station after another, full of farm news and country music. He despised sentimentality, yet he had a fondness for operettas—von Suppé, Lehar, and especially Romberg. He would drive Helen and the girls to distraction playing his records of *The New Moon* or humming the drinking song from *The Student Prince*, although the only alcohol he had ever touched was a glass of wine at a fraternity mixer at Davidson, which he disliked the minute he tasted it.

He turned onto an oiled dirt road between fields. The Stallings farm was wedged in between a couple of larger ones, and he had to slow down to look at the mailboxes to find the entrance. He headed down a half-mile drive, pulling into a wide, packed-dirt yard that was littered with two junked and rusting trucks, some sort of tractor attachment, and a dented, faded blue pickup that he recognized as Joe Stallings' Chevy. Opposite sat a high square barn with big double doors that stood open. On the left, the yard was open to the fields beyond.

The house had been white, but the paint was peeling off the weathered plank siding. MacKendrie noticed as he parked that one window was missing a screen and a corner of the porch was sagging. Joe Stallings and his brother inherited the farm from their father, but the two didn't get along, and the brother left. Joe didn't have his father's knack. He struggled on, losing ground each year. There were no children.

MacKendrie mounted the steps to the porch and knocked on the door. "Hello, anyone home?" After a minute, he saw a pale round face appear briefly at the window overlooking the porch. More seconds passed, as if in hope he would go away. With a reluctant tug, the door opened, and a silent, almost shapeless figure stood on the other side of the screen, a ghost in an old print dress.

"Good afternoon, Edna," he said, removing his hat. She was a strange one. Edna Stallings came with her husband to church but didn't socialize with the other women. She rarely shopped in town except for groceries and would barely speak when spoken to. She reminded MacKendrie of some men he had seen in the hospital on Tinian. Shell shock, they called it. Seemed to be out on their feet all the time, just going through the motions.

She nodded but said nothing.

"I'm looking for Joe. Is he around?"

More silence, and he thought he would have to ask again, but she lifted a hand in the direction of the barn. "Try out back," she said, and looked down.

"Thanks, I will." As she reached for the door, MacKendrie spoke on impulse. "Edna. Edna? Are you all right? Is everything okay?" She stared as if he had spoken in a strange language. "Edna?"

Suddenly her gaze shifted and she seemed to snap out of it. "There," she said, speaking past him, and closed the door. MacKendrie turned and saw Stallings walking around the corner of the barn. He was examining some mechanical part and muttered "piece o' shit" just before he looked up, startled, to see MacKendrie standing there.

He grinned at Stallings' embarrassment. "Hello, Joe."

"Well, Preacher. Sorry about that." Stallings right cheek protruded from a wad of chewing tobacco as if mumps had afflicted one side of his face. He held up his oily right hand to indicate he would have extended it otherwise.

"I've heard worse. Having some trouble there?"

"Aw, this g—, this goll-darned fuel pump. Stu Jimson sold it to me. Know him? Well, don't let him sell you nothin'. He's a gyp. Second time he's sold me a bad part. Shoulda known better." Stallings pulled a grimy rag out of a rear pocket of his soiled overalls and wiped his hands. "What brings you out here?"

"Just came out to say hello. I can come back if you're busy."

"Naw, it's all right. I gotta take that part back but it can wait. Let's go sit where it's cooler."

Stallings put the part down in the bed of his truck, and they walked up the steps to the house.

"Kind of warm for this time of year, isn't it?" MacKendrie said.

Stallings shook his head. "I been prayin' for rain, Preacher. We don't get some, it's gonna be a right hard year." They sat down at a small table in a corner of the simple kitchen. MacKendrie noticed the sink was full of unwashed dishes. "Don't it say in the Bible somewhere that God can make it rain if he wants?" He reached for a cup sitting on the table and spit into it.

MacKendrie's stomach turned. He hadn't gotten used to the habit.

Stallings was staring, waiting for an answer. What was there to say to men whose homes and farms depended on a few inches of rain? "Sure it does, but it's one of those things I've never understood, Joe, why nature goes wrong sometimes."

Stallings' face fell. "Just not knowing. I could take it a little better if I knew why, you know?"

"Yeah, I do. During the war, lots of times I asked God why—"

"Now ol' Yancey Finney, farms over there a ways, he goes to that little Baptist church on Reedy Creek Road, y'know? Anyways, he says his preacher said it's a judgment on us."

"A judgment? For what?"

Stallings shrugged. "Letting the coloreds run wild, maybe. Next you know they'll be in the schools and ever'thing."

MacKendrie shook his head. "I don't know about that."

Stallings eyed him. "You're a preacher. Thought we was paying you to figure out what God's up to." He spit into the cup.

MacKendrie said stiffly, "No, Joe, you're paying me to preach the word of God and tend this flock. As your pastor, I'd say we just have to keep on asking and praying for God to give us rain. Maybe there's a lesson for us in that."

Stallings slapped a big hand on the table. "I don't see much of a lesson in a man losing his livelihood."

"Is it that bad for you?"

"Damn right." This time he didn't apologize. "We don't get rain this year, I might as well burn this place down. And I will, too, before I see them bankers take this place my granddaddy built."

"The bank's been after you?"

Stallings nodded heavily. "Yeah, an' the farm bureau says they ain't gonna give me no more loans after this. This year's it, Preacher."

"I see. Well, Joe, if there's anything we can do..."

Stallings waved a hand. "I never took charity, an' I ain't about to start."

"Sure, Joe. But you know folks would help you out if you needed it." Stallings looked sullen and said nothing. "Well, I'll let you get back to work."

Stallings walked with him out to the car. MacKendrie opened the door, then turned and said, "Joe, last Sunday, you asked about whites and coloreds. Negroes have their ways, and we have ours, and those ways don't mix very well, but I think they're children of God like us and ought to be treated with respect."

Stallings was quiet a moment, turned and spat. "You do, eh?"

MacKendrie kept his eyes fixed on Stallings and nodded.

"You learn that from your granddaddy?"

"What? Oh, my grandfather. I see Eli's been talking to you. I barely knew him. All that was a long time ago. I'm a lot more concerned with what's going on now."

Stallings looked bored. "Well, I'll tell you, Preacher, any colored tries to act like he's same as a white man 'round here's gonna find out different real quick like." He turned and trudged back toward his truck.

MacKendrie called after him, "I'll see you Sunday." Stallings didn't turn but lifted a hand and let it fall. He drove back to town, wondering if he had done any good.

After he and Helen were in bed that evening, he told her of his encounter with Stallings.

"I'm surprised you're worried about Joe Stallings," she said at last. "Just look at him and Edna. Everyone feels sorry for them."

"I know, but he's under a lot of pressure, and men in that situation can do foolish things."

Three weeks after Easter, spirits were lifted by a violent thunderstorm. The interior of the church had been slowly darkening, and the children's choir was part way through a song when a deep rumble momentarily smothered the soprano voices. No one could concentrate during the remainder of the service. Each flash filtered through the stained glass and the crescendo of thunder caused a small sensation. Wind-driven rain rattled the roof and the windows. People exchanged broad smiles and murmurs. By the time the service was over, the worst was past, but the vestibule became a kind of staging ground for people to brace themselves to plunge into the cold wind and rain, which they did with shouts and screams of exhilaration. Those waiting their turn laughed at the noise and the sight of women, their light dresses plastered to their skin by the time they reached their cars.

That night, after the children were in bed, the wind still swirled and sang in the pine boughs. Helen sat for a while at his feet as they listened to music on the radio. On impulse, he stood and pulled her to her feet and they danced awkwardly for a bit, swaying and making missteps. At last he clasped her against him and then kissed her deeply.

"Oh, Jim, yes," she murmured.

They went into the bedroom, closed the door, undressed in the dark and made love quietly as usual, stifling their moans and cries. Helen was still in her thirties, and MacKendrie would have been surprised to learn how often she yearned for him.

Everyone was hopeful the rain had quelled the drought, but it was soon evident that nature had teased them. The noon farm report on the radio stated that just a little more than an inch of rain had fallen, not nearly enough to make a dent in the dry spell. The temperature climbed, and spirits drooped as quickly as they had risen.

Two days later, MacKendrie left the manse precisely at eight to walk to the church and noticed the car was sagging to one side. He looked closer. A flat tire. No, two flat tires, the front and rear driver's side. He knelt by the front tire and examined it. There was some sort of tear in the sidewall. Strange, he didn't remember hitting anything. He looked at the rear tire and found a nearly identical tear. He looked closer. It was a clean cut, made by a blade.

He went back inside, looked up a number, and picked up the phone. Helen came into the hallway, surprised that he was back in the house.

"Jim?"

He held up a hand and dialed a number.

"Follett's Auto."

"Dick? It's James MacKendrie. How are things? Good, good. Dick, I came out this morning and found I have two flat tires. I only have one spare, so I'm going to need the car towed to your place." Helen was wide-eyed. "Yes. Thirty minutes. I'll be here."

He was pale as he hung up the phone. Helen said, "Jim, what happened?"

"Someone cut the tires."

Her hand flew up to her mouth. "Are you sure? Who would do such a thing?"

He shook his head. "John Wesley Jones told me the other day that people blamed me for Ulysses' nephew getting released." He glanced at her face and patted her shoulder. "This might have nothing to do with that. It could have just been some boys with nothing better to do."

He rode in the tow truck to Follett's Auto and watched through the glass in the office as the car was hoisted and a mechanic spoke to

Dick Follett, who had walked over to look at the tires. They grinned and the mechanic made some kind of gesture that could have been a stabbing motion. Follett turned away, still smiling, and made notes on a clipboard. The smile was gone when he came into the office and glanced up at MacKendrie.

"You need new tires, Pastor."

"They can't be fixed, Dick?"

"Afraid not. Not with the cuts on the sidewall like that. How'd that happen?"

"Well, it's pretty obvious, isn't it?" Follett didn't answer. "If I were the suspicious type, I'd say somebody might be sending me a message."

Follett frowned. "Aw, I don't know. Probably a prank."

"At my expense." Follett stared at his clipboard. "How much?"

"For two tires, balance, tax..." He totaled the figures. "Forty-eight fifty."

MacKendrie stared. That would take a bite out of their bank balance. "Didn't you have an ad in the paper for new tires for twelve apiece?"

"That was for a different tire. We don't have that one in your size." MacKendrie was silent, and Follett went on, "Normally we'd give you a pastor's discount, but with the crops and all..." His face was impassive.

MacKendrie turned to the door. "Call me at the church when it's ready."

The next day Eli Ross stopped by his study with an apologetic expression and an envelope.

"I'm sorry about those tires. There's nothing in the church budget to compensate you, but a few of us got together and thought this might help." He pushed the envelope across the desk. MacKendrie counted fifty dollars inside.

"That's very generous, Eli. This will help a lot. If it were just the money..." He put the envelope in his desk. "Do you think it had something to do with Jeremiah Brown?"

"Well now, there were some folks who didn't take kindly to that."

"What, to helping save an innocent man from prison?"

"I believe they saw it as interfering. Not something preachers around here usually do."

"Eli, this isn't going to get out of hand, is it?"

Ross looked surprised. "I don't see why it should, less you're planning on some other little escapade." He grinned. "I imagine things'll settle down. If you let them settle down," he added.

MacKendrie relaxed. "I'll behave myself, I promise."

Ross stood. "I'll just have a word with a few folks. Should be fine."

SIX

May passed into June, with its promise of unrelenting heat. Helen asked MacKendrie to buy talcum powder to ease her skin irritation, so he walked down the street from his office to Campbell's Drug Store. He was greeted from the front register by Cathy Campbell, dark-haired, heavy-set, who came forward to vigorously shake his hand. She burst out laughing.

"Whoo-oo! That sermon last Sunday was a doozy, Pastor. Gonna have to start getting down my dictionary and lugging it along when I come to church."

At first, he hadn't minded this sort of comment, but lately the joke had begun to wear thin. "How are things, Cathy?"

Her grin disappeared. "Well, we're managing, we're managing. Listen, Cy's in the back. Stop on by there, he wants to see you."

He made his way to the dispensary counter where Cy Campbell, in a white pharmacist's jacket, was counting pills into a bottle. Chubby and perpetually pleasant, he was a faithful member of the church, and stories abounded of how he fielded phone calls in the middle of the night from a frantic mother and went down to open up the store to dispense a remedy. Campbell looked up and smiled broadly.

"Jim. Just the man I want to see."

"Hello, Cy. Not interrupting, am I?"

"No, no, this is a good time. Why don't you step around here and we'll go in my office."

MacKendrie followed him into a cramped nook with just enough room for a desk and two chairs. He asked, "How's business these days?"

"Aw, we're so busy we just don't know what to do right now. Thing is, we're not making that much. Folks are having trouble paying. I'm not ever gonna let people go without medicine, but other things like aspirin and shaving cream, we're telling folks no more credit."

"That's a shame, but it sounds fair to me, Cy."

"You know, nobody's complaining. They know it's tough on ever'one till the crops come in again."

MacKendrie was afraid he was going to be asked about God and the weather. "What can I do for you, Cy?"

He leaned forward in his chair. "It's my daughter."

"Connie? She's not in trouble, is she?"

"No, least not yet. That's what's worrying us. She could get herself into trouble if she keeps up what she's doing."

Constance Campbell had not neglected her faith when she went away to college but had become more fervent. She was active in the Westminster Fellowship at the University of North Carolina, Campbell said, which delighted her parents at first, until Connie reported there had been long debates about the Christian position on integration. There had been meetings with students from North Carolina College, the black school in nearby Durham. Their stories made her indignant, then angry. Segregation should be abolished, she said, and that meant Negroes should be allowed to vote and elect people who would change the laws.

"Now Jim, you know me. Cathy and I try to treat ever'one fair. That's how we raised Connie and Bobby. But what these kids want is...I don't know what."

MacKendrie nodded. "It would mean a different world. But you know kids. They get excited about some idea but don't have the first notion of what to do about it. What's the harm in it as long as they're just talking?"

"If it was just talking, I probably wouldn't mind it. But they're past that. Those Carolina College fellas talked the Chapel Hill students into joining a voter registration drive in Durham."

"Did Connie help?"

"Shoot yeah, she did. Came home all excited about it. Told us how good it felt to help folks get a chance to vote who never had before. Said it made her proud to be an American. Don't that beat all?"

MacKendrie thought for a moment. "What are you worried about, Cy? That word will get around? Hurt your business?"

Campbell shook his head. "No sir, Durham's a ways off. If it stayed there, that'd be one thing. But they're talking about bringing this right in our lap."

"What? How?"

"This colored outfit, what's it called? N-A-C-P or something?" The N-double-A-C-P, MacKendrie said. "That's it. Bunch of radicals, if you ask me. They're saying colored folks ever'where need to be registered. Told those students they oughta go back to their hometowns and get registration drives going. So now Connie's determined to try to get the local coloreds registered to vote. They're talking about getting a drive going this summer right here."

MacKendrie imagined a young white woman traveling around the countryside in the company of black men knocking on doors, registering Negroes to vote. He sat back. "What do you want me to do, Cy?"

"Talk to her, Jim. She doesn't know you too well, but she grew up in this church, and she's always respected pastors."

MacKendrie hesitated, then said, "I don't know what good it'll do, Cy, but I'll be glad to talk to her. When is she going to be in town?"

"She'll be home next week."

"Tell her she can come by my study."

Campbell was visibly relieved. "I can't thank you enough. Cathy will be glad to hear it, too. She's been worried sick." He stood. "I think I've got a customer at the counter."

"Cy, Connie is a smart young woman. We may not agree with her on this, but you can still be proud of her."

Campbell turned, eyebrows arched. "You think she might be right?"

"I don't know. In the long run, maybe. But there's a time for everything, and I don't think this is it."

In the solitude of his study, MacKendrie found himself more and more dissatisfied with his sermons. He had been preaching on the Beatitudes, but Jesus' blessings seemed remote and detached from the growing crisis the weather presented to Kirkwell. He was pondering the problem when he heard some kind of noise in the sanctuary.

It was Ulysses Brown, he realized, humming something as he worked. At first, he was annoyed, but then he recognized the tune of a Negro hymn. He got up from his desk and walked to the entrance to the sanctuary. Brown was using an oil mop on the hardwood floors. MacKendrie stood and listened as he swung the mop to and fro. The deep voice suddenly changed from humming to singing.

Were you there when they crucified my Lord?
Were you there when they crucified my Lord?
Oh-ohh-oh, sometimes it causes me to tremble, tremble, tremble.
Were you there when they crucified my Lord?

MacKendrie stepped into the sanctuary. "Hello, Ulysses."

Brown straightened and smiled broadly. "Afternoon, sir. Mighty fine day, ain't it?"

"I'm afraid it's a little warm for me. How is your nephew?"

"He all right now. We sent him off somewhere till things they settle down like."

"That's a shame, but..."

"Yessir. He says to tell you he appreciated your help. Goes for me too."

MacKendrie nodded. "Ulysses, that song you were singing just now, that's a spiritual, isn't it?"

"Yessir. Sang it on Easter, so was on my mind."

"I knew I'd heard it."

"Is old. My grandaddy use to tell me they sung it when he was little. Said it was a favorite 'cause it helped 'em when they was suffering."

"When they were suffering. Helped them how?"

Brown studied him. "Well, sir, when folks got to work hard all day, and they ain't got no say about it. Maybe they wife or they babies got sold and they missing 'em. Maybe they master whip 'em. Well, then they sing about Jesus suffering and dying, and seem like he know what they feels. And it make 'em feel better."

MacKendrie stood lost in thought. Brown interrupted his reverie. "I almost done with the cleaning, Pastor."

"You go ahead, Ulysses."

He walked back to his office and tried to return to his sermon but found himself more dissatisfied than ever. Later, as he walked through the empty sanctuary, he glanced toward the chancel and saw the brass cross standing on the communion table. He gazed at it, hearing Brown's voice still reverberating in that quiet space.

Two weeks later, Connie Campbell showed up at his office, accompanied by a skinny, dark-haired boy wearing horn-rimmed glasses who appeared to be a few years older. MacKendrie was taken aback by how she had blossomed since last he saw her. She was tall, buxom, and had light brown tresses that gave her a natural appeal. She was not beautiful, but she more than made up for it in confidence, and she grasped his hand as firmly as any salesman might. He noticed she had lost some, but not all, of her Eastern Carolina drawl.

"Rev'rend MacKendrie, this is Walter Harper. He's helping me with...a little project."

The boy extended his hand. "Pleasure, sir. Call me Walt."

As they were seated, MacKendrie asked, "Are you a student at Chapel Hill too, Walt?"

"Graduate school, sir. Political science."

MacKendrie asked Connie about her studies. She was considering teaching or social work, she said. "You'd be good at either one, I'm sure. And I understand you've been active in the Westminster Fellowship."

"Oh, my goodness, I can't rightly tell you what that's meant to me. They're challenging us to really figure out what it means to follow Jesus. We're talking about real serious things and what we ought to be doing about them."

MacKendrie nodded. "Race relations being one of them?"

"Yes, sir. What with them about to integrate the university."

"Your father told me you're meeting with some Negro students."

She leaned forward and her voice rose. "Rev'rend, do you know what they have to put up with? I couldn't believe it when they told me. I mean, I knew they had to go to school separate and ever'thing and had to use different bathrooms, but I just never knew how humiliating it is. Getting insulted just for wanting to buy a cup of coffee at the diner. Those boys at North Carolina College, they're so smart and polite. And the girls, the stories they told about how they're treated by white folks. It just...it made me ashamed. And Rev'rend, they're *Christians*, just like us. They believe in Jesus just like we do." Her voice began to tremble. "How can we say they're not as good as us?" She fished in her purse for a hankie. "I'm sorry. It just makes me feel terrible when I think about it."

She had empathy. "It's painful to hear about the way people treat each other," he agreed.

She sniffed and wiped her nose. "And when I try to talk to the other students about it, they tell me I'm crazy. Or they get mad."

"Segregation has been around for a long time, Connie. Trying to change things..."

"Sir," Harper said, "we all know the South has to change. Some of us believe the time has come."

Connie said, "Rev'rend, I know why Daddy wanted me to come talk to you. It's about voter registration, isn't it?"

"Yeah. Your folks are worried."

"I've told them. Instead of worrying about me, they ought to be worried about making things better around here. What good's the Constitution if it's not for ever'one?" She looked at Harper. "Walter and I are helping with a registration campaign."

"Here, in Pender County?"

"Yes, sir. We've already started."

"Who's involved in this?"

Harper said, "The N-double-A-C-P chapter in Wilmington is overseeing it. Here in Kirkwell, it's being led by Reverend Evans."

"Who?"

Connie said, "It's Rev'rend Samuel T. Coleridge Evans. I call him Rev'rend Sam. He's pastor of a little church outside of town. Do you know him?" MacKendrie shook his head. "Oh, Rev'rend, you should meet him! He's the most eloquent preacher I've ever heard. Except maybe you," she said, flustered.

MacKendrie took a deep breath. "Connie, I've always believed that all the races are equal in the sight of God, and I've said so. But Negroes voting..." He threw up his hands. "You're talking about something folks aren't ready for, and they're going to fight back."

She lifted her chin. "We're ready to pay the price."

He shook his head. "I'm afraid if you go ahead with this, things could get out of hand."

"Out of hand, how?"

"What you're proposing is dangerous. There could be violence."

She was silent for a moment, then said, "You know, Rev'rend MacKendrie, one of the North Carolina College students I was talking to, his name is Cole, he told me he was walking down the street in Durham one day when a car full of white boys pulled up and said he didn't have any business being in that part of town. He tried talking to them, explaining what he was doing, but they grabbed him and started beating him up. Only thing that saved him from getting hurt bad was a white man came along and told those boys to stop. Cole, he showed us a scar on his face he got from that beating." She looked at him. "There's already violence going on, Rev'rend. The only way it's gonna to stop is if we get some laws passed, and that means Negroes need to be able to vote."

She was parroting someone, maybe this Evans fellow. "But Connie, that could happen to you. You and Walt here could get beat up, shot at, or, or worse. How do you intend to protect yourselves?"

She smiled. "Well, Rev'rend Sam says those who trust in the Lord shalt not be afraid for the terror by night, nor for the arrow that flieth by day..." she paused, trying to remember the rest.

"Nor for the pestilence that walketh in darkness, nor for the destruction that wasteth at noonday," he finished. "A lot of soldiers in the war had the words of the ninety-first Psalm on cards they kept in their pockets. A good many of them came home in caskets." The young people exchanged glances. He sighed. "I can see you're determined to go ahead with this. What exactly are you doing in this campaign?"

Harper leaned forward and spoke in a low, intense voice. "It has two stages. The first is education. We go around to the local Negro population and try to motivate them to register and describe the procedures. The second stage will be getting them to the county clerk's office and trying to overcome whatever obstacles are in the way."

Connie said, "Walter here has been helping with the education, telling folks how registration works. I've been helping Rev'rend Sam pick out the most likely people to try to register. We're expecting it might be a bit rough at first, and they want people who aren't gonna scare easy."

The Negro pastors were key to the effort, Harper said. If they could be persuaded to join the campaign, others would come around. Samuel Evans was lining up as many pastors as he could. Three meetings had been held so far, and two more were planned. The culmination of the campaign would be escorting dozens of Negroes to the county clerk's office on the eve of Independence Day to register.

"That's only a month off. How many have you signed up to register so far?"

Connie and Harper looked at each other. "It's been slow," Connie said reluctantly.

"How many?" MacKendrie persisted.

"Well, just one. Folks are scared," she added hastily.

MacKendrie nodded. "Understandably so. What will you do if you don't get lots of people to sign up?"

Harper said, "Then we'll go ahead with however many we have."

"Brave words," MacKendrie said. "I admire your desire to help these people. But don't be surprised if this campaign of yours doesn't yield the results you're hoping for. It takes an unusual person to volunteer for the front lines."

"Oh, we're not giving up," Harper said lightly. "We know it's going to be a long fight. Reverend Evans says so all the time."

Connie glanced at her watch and explained they had a family to visit. "Could you come out to Rev'rend Evans's church tomorrow?"

"What for, Connie?"

"He'd like to meet you."

"Why?"

"Well, you know, I've just been telling him about you."

"Connie, if you're trying to recruit me for this campaign, you're wasting your time. I have enough problems without adding this to the list."

A hurt look crossed her face. "I don't see any harm in just meeting him."

MacKendrie hesitated. He had raised enough hackles already around town, but someone had to keep an eye on this girl. "All right, Connie. What time?"

Left alone in his study, MacKendrie tried to turn his attention to his sermon, but he couldn't concentrate. Fragments of the conversation kept intruding in his thoughts—"change," "already violence going on."

SEVEN

The next morning at the post office, MacKendrie saw Percy Weir approaching. He and his sister, Cathy Campell, had inherited from their father the largest tobacco farm in the region, and several memorial plaques at First Presbyterian read "Given by Mr. and Mrs. Philandro Weir." Percy rarely attended but believed his family heritage meant deference was owed to him on any matter that affected the church. At forty, he was short and portly with a boyish face and was always seen in a short-brimmed fedora, a white shirt—short-sleeved when it was warm and long-sleeved when it was cold—and suspenders that held up dark woolen pants. He spoke without a greeting.

"Been hearing strange things about your sermons, Pastor MacKendrie. mighty strange things."

MacKendrie forced a smile. "Good morning, Percy. What have you heard?"

Weir was an excitable man, and now he gesticulated like a bird with a bad wing. "Well, now, I heard you said something about Jesus suffering on the cross and the folks around him suffering too, and uh, uh..."

"Well, that doesn't sound too strange, does it?"

Weir's hands fluttered even more wildly. "Aw, I can't remember ever'thing I heard, but it didn't sound right somehow."

"Percy, I don't know what you heard, but it sounds like whoever said it didn't get the whole thing. And you know how folks talk. Why, I don't believe a teensy bit of what they say about you."

"Just what have you—" Weir's flappings made him look like he was trying to take flight, then he saw MacKendrie's smile and wink. He grinned briefly. "Ahright, Pastor. Still, best be more careful. We took a chance bringing you here, you know, after what they said went on in China."

MacKendrie caught himself. He was about to say goodbye when Weir started up again.

"What d'you think about this weather?"

"Well..."

"Gonna ruin us for sure if it don't let up." His left hand waved back and forth as if shooing away flies. "We need rain bad. Maybe we ain't praying hard enough." He fished a pack of cigarettes out of his pocket and shook one free.

MacKendrie tried to hide his weariness. "Percy, we pray every—"

"Something ain't workin'." Weir stuck the cigarette in his mouth and flicked open a shiny gold-plated lighter. "God ain't playing with us, is he?" He struck the lighter and touched the flame to the cigarette. Smoke billowed upward around his hat.

MacKendrie faced him. "Playing with us. What do you mean?"

Weir removed the cigarette and raised his chin. "Don't know, but it ain't right. Somebody's being punished, don't you think?"

MacKendrie shook his head slowly. "You're the third person to say that to me this spring. God doesn't punish a thousand people for the sins of a dozen. What do you suggest, that we start exiling people from Pender County? Where would you start?"

"I can think of a few." He took a drag on the cigarette and blew the blue-gray smoke out of the side of his mouth. MacKendrie took a half-step back to avoid it. "I'm just saying. Something or somebody's to blame for this, and I'd like to know what."

"Well, let's see, maybe God's sending a message about growing the wrong kind of crops." He meant it as a good-natured jibe but instantly regretted it.

Weir leaned forward. "What's that?" He reached up and grasped his suspenders. "What about my crops?"

"Nothing, Percy, forget it."

"You saying something about growing tobacco?"

MacKendrie looked away. Feeling every inch the hypocrite, he said, "I wasn't serious."

Weir regarded him wide-eyed for a moment, then said slowly, "Lot of folks' livelihoods 'round here depend on tobacco, Preacher. Including yours. Don't you forget it."

After lunch, MacKendrie drove out of town, following the directions he had gotten from Connie Campbell. Mount Zion Missionary Baptist Church was several miles off a main highway, in a part of the county he wasn't familiar with. There were few farms out this way. It was wilder land, mostly full of pines and underbrush except for occasional clusters of rundown shacks. He passed houses with bare-dirt yards in which black children in tattered clothes stopped their games and stared or sometimes waved as he drove by. He waved back.

He almost missed the church. It was set back off the road, not much bigger than some of the houses around. There was no sign, just a small white wooden building with a squat steeple above the front door topped by a white-painted cross. Two cars were parked in front, one of which he recognized as Walt's dingy Chevy. The other was a sleek, black, late-model Mercury, freshly washed.

The front door of the church opened directly into the sanctuary, which was nearly square and plain, with a chancel elevated no more than six inches above the floor and a small choir loft beyond the pulpit. Standing in the center aisle were Connie and Walt and a man who stood with erect posture and an air of quick confidence. He was about thirty, MacKendrie guessed, with a hefty build, and he had a precisely trimmed thin mustache that ran along the contour of his upper lip. He was dressed in a nice gray suit that had a white handkerchief peeking above the chest pocket, a white shirt, and a royal blue tie secured with a silver bar.

Without waiting for an introduction, the man stepped forward and extended his hand. "Good afternoon, Pastor MacKendrie. I'm pleased to make your acquaintance," he said with careful enunciation in a raspy voice. His handshake was a tad more vigorous than necessary, and MacKendrie inhaled the strong aroma of cologne. A dandy, he thought.

"Good afternoon. You must be Pastor Evans. Connie has told me a lot about you."

"I trust she hasn't exaggerated," he said, turning and smiling. "Connie and Walter have been immensely helpful in our campaign. Come in, come in. You can sit in the front pew. Walter, would you be good enough to fetch a chair from the platform?"

MacKendrie and the young people sat in the pew, and Evans sat in the chair facing them. "You're named after a famous poet. Were your parents interested in literature?" MacKendrie asked.

"Ah, yes." He feigned a declamatory voice. "Water, water, everywhere, and not a drop to drink," then gave a stage laugh. MacKendrie noted the misquotation. "My mother was a high school teacher. I think she hoped my name would prompt me to become a writer, but alas, my imagination proved too feeble."

"Oh, nonsense," Connie exclaimed, and turned to MacKendrie. "You should hear him preach. There's nothing wrong with his imagination."

I would be interested to hear him preach, MacKendrie thought. A pastor's sermons unintentionally revealed all sorts of things. He said, "Pastor, I hope you'll excuse me for coming right to the point, but I have some concerns about this voter registration campaign of yours."

"Oh, it's not my campaign, Pastor MacKendrie. I'm merely a conductor on a train bound for freedom." He smiled broadly. Connie breathed a little sigh.

MacKendrie reflexively fell back on his missionary days, where politeness was the best practice. "No doubt it's a train Negroes have longed to see, but in my experience journeys like this are risky. I'm sure I don't have to tell you about the potential for danger. I'd hate to see anyone get hurt, and that goes for your people as well as Connie and Walt here."

"I share your concern about the danger," Evans said gravely. "What do you advise?"

"Isn't there some way to do this more gradually? It all seems so sudden. If you show up at the courthouse on July third, the results could be disastrous."

"Begging your pardon, sir," Harper said, "but I'm afraid there is no gradual way to register to vote. Sooner or later, Negroes will have to go to the county clerk's office and ask—or demand—to be registered, and we believe it should be sooner than later."

"You see, Pastor," Evans said slowly, "the burden of violence does not lie with us. Our intentions are entirely peaceful. We only wish to exercise our rights as Americans. It is not we who would inflict violence on anyone. To avoid any harm being inflicted, you must speak to those who would seek to inflict it."

It had a rehearsed quality to it, which annoyed MacKendrie for some reason, but he couldn't deny the logic. He was asking Evans to yield to threats. It was unfair, but this was not like standing up to a schoolyard bully.

Evans continued, "Indeed, Pastor MacKendrie, it is our hope that someone in the white community might speak out against any unnecessary confrontation. We are not asking for any white leaders to endorse our campaign, only to urge that we be allowed to pursue this course of action without harassment."

Connie spoke up. "If some of the white pastors could get together and write a letter to the editor or something, just asking ever'one to stay calm, it might help," she said in a manner so serious MacKendrie had to suppress a smile.

They were all looking at him.

"I see. Connie, you don't know what you're asking." He turned to Evans. "Tell me, Pastor, have there been many of the Negro pastors who have been willing to register, or to urge their congregations to register?" Evans let the question hang, and MacKendrie continued. "I thought so. And if I were to ask the white pastors to do what you're suggesting, I assure you I'd get the same reaction." He turned back to the young people. "You have to understand. These are men who have worked long and hard for years to get where they are. Their livelihoods and that of their families depend on the people sitting in the pews, and in some cases they hang by the slenderest of threads. Asking them to sign something like what you suggest would finish them."

Connie started to protest. "But what about—"

MacKendrie held up his hand. "Besides," he went on, "the greatest threat isn't from people coming to church on Sundays. The ones you have to worry about—"

Evans gave a mirthless laugh. "Are drunkards, rednecks, men who never darken the door of a church? I beg your pardon, Pastor, but do you recognize the name Harrison P. Mooneyham? He was the Grand Wizard of the Ku Klux Klan down in Conway, South Carolina, about ten years ago. *And* a deacon at First Baptist Church. His band of the

Klan terrorized black people down there for years. Now, I'm sure you have good people in your church, Pastor, but I think you see my point."

MacKendrie didn't answer.

"Isn't there anything you can do, sir?" Harper said.

"You realize," MacKendrie said, "that if I start talking to people, you will all be immediately at risk. Word will spread like wildfire. Not that it matters much." He nodded sideways at Connie. "There are rumors. The Campbells are telling people she's conducting research, but that's not going to satisfy people for very long."

"I see," Evans said. "Walter, do you recall the precautions we discussed? I believe it is time to put them in effect." He stood. "Pastor, we don't want to detain you any further. You have been most gracious with your time. I only ask that you pray for us."

MacKendrie stood and shook Evans's hand. "Of course I will." He walked a few paces toward the door, then turned back.

"I cannot be associated with your campaign, but suppose I were to go to the mayor and ask him to prevail on people to stay calm. Would that be satisfactory?"

He was sent off with smiles and handshakes and gushing thanks from the three, but as he drove back to town, a fateful feeling weighed him down. It reminded him of the time in Bai Miao just before he and his family left. Everyone knew war was coming, but no one could stop it.

MacKendrie didn't know Mayor Jimmy Ondrachek well, only that he owned Top Chek Appliances, Kirkwell's only appliance store, and was regarded as a shrewd businessman. As he stepped inside the store, he was greeted by a sharp ozone smell and rows of shiny white refrigerators and stoves. A salesman directed him to an office at the rear. The door was open, and Ondrachek, an athletic man in his late forties with tousled, jet-black hair, sat at his desk. He looked up and squinted at the knock, then bounded up and offered his hand when MacKendrie identified himself.

"We'll have to have you give the invocation at the city council meeting sometime," he said in a voice half again as loud as necessary, as if addressing an imaginary crowd. "Have a seat. To what do I owe the pleasure?"

"It's a delicate matter, Mayor. May I?" He rose and closed the door. Ondrachek's brows furrowed. MacKendrie spoke quietly. "I've learned about something I felt you should know. I'm sure we'd all like to keep the peace."

Ondrachek put his elbows on his desk. "What is it, Pastor?"

"Some of the Negroes in the area are planning to register to vote."

The mayor's eyes widened. "When?"

"According to what I've heard, on July third. They're planning to come to the courthouse."

Ondrachek's head and shoulders drooped. "Good God A'mighty. Well, now, won't that make for an interesting Independence Day."

"There's more. You know Cy Campbell? His daughter Connie is a student at Chapel Hill. She's helping them."

Ondrachek jerked upright. "She's what?"

"She and a graduate student named Walter Harper. The Campbells are members at First Presbyterian. Connie's been telling me about this. I have tried to talk her out of it, but she's determined to go ahead with it."

"Let me get this straight. We've got two white kids, one of 'em a local girl, who are helping coloreds line up to register to vote just before Fourth of July? Aw, that's just great. Who put her up to this? Not Cy?"

"No. There's a local Negro pastor who's heading it up. Name's Samuel Evans."

Ondrachek's brows knit together. "Evans. Seems like I know that name." He shook his head.

"Mayor, I'm mainly concerned about somebody getting hurt, especially Connie."

"They aiming to cause trouble?"

"Evans says no, that it's supposed to be peaceful. No, it's the Klan types I'm worried about. When they find out..."

Ondrachek shook his head. "There hasn't been any Klan meetings around here in a long time. Ten years or more."

"But there are some men hereabouts who might do something foolish."

Ondrachek nodded. "Could happen. What's a'matter with that girl anyway? Pretty damn fool thing to do, if you ask me, getting mixed up with colored agitators."

"Something she got exposed to at Chapel Hill. But I wouldn't go blaming this on outsiders. Evans is local. It was going to happen sooner or later, Jimmy, you know that. Question is, what can we do about it?"

"I don't know there's much we can do about it. They ain't gonna get registered, I can tell you that right now. Bob Crutchfield'll see to that." Crutchfield was the county clerk.

"He wouldn't set the police on them, would he?"

"Naw, nothing like that. We'll need to have 'em standing by just in case, but ol' Bob'll figure out a way to string 'em along. Tie 'em up in red tape till they get discouraged and give up. But like you said, there's a lot of folks that ain't gonna take kindly to this once they find out. Might try to discourage 'em."

"Jimmy, I kind of feel responsible for Connie since she's been confiding in me. Isn't there something you can do?"

"Like what?"

"People listen to you. Suppose you talk to folks, just informally around town. Try to keep things from escalating. Let 'em know you're aware of the situation and that nothing's going to come of it, that Bob Crutchfield will handle it. You could even say you're just letting the colored people blow off steam and then things will go back to normal. It'd make you look like you're in charge of the situation."

Ondrachek's brows worked furiously. Finally he said, "Might work. Can't promise anything, but might work. What about Connie? If she's standing up there with 'em, that's a whole other ball game."

"Let me worry about Connie. If I can't stop her from working on this, I think I can keep her out of sight."

Ondrachek shook his head. "All right, Pastor. Lemme see what I can do. I appreciate you coming to me with this." They shook hands. "Like I say, gonna be an interesting Fourth."

EIGHT

As if a biblical plague had descended on the fields of Pender County, the soil had turned to dust, and driving outside of town in any direction you could tell where the tractors were from miles away by the great clouds surrounding them. Men came home in the evening looking like apparitions, white from head to foot.

MacKendrie spent the next two weeks mending fences. Percy Weir was not one to keep a slight to himself, and soon explanations were being demanded from MacKendrie about his views on tobacco crops, from the church's elders, from a town councilman who owned a farm supply company, and from the chairman of the presbytery's committee on the ministry, who called him at home one evening. Helen listened to her husband's attempts at diplomacy.

"Yes, Arthur. Yes. I know that. Of course. It was a misunderstanding. Just a joke. I shouldn't have said it. No. No, I think things are settling down. I've made my apologies..."

Later, she sat next to him and took his hand. "I hate to see you being treated this way, Jim."

He looked at her gratefully. "It's my own fault, I suppose. I can't say I blame them. They're just trying to earn a living." He stood up. "I still think tobacco is a poison, but Percy was right about one thing. It pays my salary."

Word of the voter registration campaign had run around Kirkwell like an electric current. "The Negro vote" was the topic of every conversation wherever people gathered. A few loudly declared that any colored who dared to register to vote should be run out of the county, or worse. It was generally agreed among the white citizens that, fair or not, Negroes were not qualified to vote. This was confirmed by conversations with their janitors and maids and handymen, who allowed, glancing around to see who was listening, that they weren't much interested in politics.

Pastors were asked their opinions. The Baptists mostly followed the lead of Brother Josiah Shelnutt at First Baptist, who preached a sermon from the book of Ezra about how the scribe had forced the men of Israel to put away their foreign wives. Clearly this was a divine mandate about race mixing, he declared, something that allowing Negroes to vote would surely lead to. John Wesley Jones played it close to the vest, answering so broadly that parishioners walked away satisfied, no matter what their views.

MacKendrie didn't preach about the controversy, but he acknowledged it from the pulpit, praying for peace without mentioning names and urging calm. He told those who asked that the legal procedures ought to be followed. It wasn't untruthful, yet he felt vaguely dishonest. It didn't help that people smiled and shook his hand.

Eli Ross congratulated him. "It's the right answer, Jim. Let those lawyers up in Raleigh figure it out. That'll keep 'em busy for a while."

The real disapproval was directed at Cy and Cathy Campbell. They should never have let Connie get mixed up in all this, people said. Customer after customer expressed opinions about their parenting, letting her go off to college in the first place, what their tax money was being used for up at Chapel Hill, and a laundry list of other grievances about race relations, child rearing practices, and the sorry state of politics. Cy Campbell called MacKendrie to explain why they'd stopped coming to church.

"We're just exhausted, Jim. I've only lost my temper once, when some son of a gun implied that Connie was sleeping with Evans. I ran him out right quick. Cathy smiles and treats people nice no matter what they're saying, but brother, you ought to hear her after we lock the doors."

"How are things between you and Connie?"

Campbell sighed. "She and Cathy been fighting like Greeks and Turks. Cathy blames Walt for all this, and Connie won't hear of it. Cathy wants me to take her side, but I try to stay out of it. Thing is, I kinda like Walt. He's not a bad kid."

A few days later, MacKendrie heard Ulysses Brown puttering around the church. He went to a window and saw him returning the corrugated steel garbage cans to their place behind the building. He waited as Brown walked in the back door, wiping his hands with a rag, and asked him whether Negroes should vote.

Brown looked up at the ceiling. "Well, sir, voting is a mighty fine thing. White folks talk about it all the time, seem like. Election comes 'round and ever'body talking about who they's gonna vote for. People gets excited about it cause they knows it's important." He lowered his gaze to MacKendrie. "Black folks kinda get left out of all that."

"You think it's time they got to vote, too?"

"Been time for a long time, Pastor."

"Maybe you're right, Ulysses, but you know there are men who will stop at nothing to prevent it."

"Mmmm-hm." He shook his head, light reflecting off his glistening bald pate. "Is like my daddy use to say. White folks never gonna hand nothing over to the coloreds for free. Somebody's got to pay the price." He looked suddenly tired, like a man who has carried a heavy load up a long hill, and MacKendrie forgot what he was going to say.

"See, Pastor, when comes to folks getting hurt, depends on who it is. When it's white folks, they get all het up about *violence*. Don't want no *violence*. When it's black folks getting hurt, well, then it's just niggers getting what they deserve."

MacKendrie had no reply.

That evening, as the house cooled and creaked, the phone rang. He lifted the receiver. "MacKendrie residence."

"Reverend MacKendrie, I'm sorry to bother you at home like this, sir. My name is Lucas Vanderhoven. I'm a lieutenant in the Navy, based in Washington. I report to Captain Harry Cohen."

He was startled. "Lucas...did you say Vanderhoven?"

"Yes, sir."

"There were some Vanderhovens in Suzhou. Are you related to them?"

"Yes, sir. My father ran a school there. I was born in Suzhou."

"Good heavens. I remember him. John, wasn't it? He was from the Reformed Church in Michigan."

"That's right."

"Of course. I met him once or twice. How is he?"

"I'm afraid Pop died a few years ago. He had a bad heart. We left China in '35, before the war."

"Ah. I'm sorry. He had a good reputation among all the missionaries." Silence on the line. "Where are you calling from, Lucas?"

"I'm at Camp Lejeune, sir. Down here on an assignment."

"I see. And what can I do for you?"

"Sir, Captain Cohen would like me to have a word with you. About the matter he discussed with you before."

MacKendrie bit his lip. "Mm-hm. Well, go on."

"I'm afraid I can't talk on the phone about it. We're supposed to take precautions. It'll have to be in person."

Helen appeared at the end of the hallway, arms folded, watching. He gave her a glance, shook his head, and she retreated. "Well, could you come to Kirkwell tomorrow? We could talk in my office."

"I don't have access to a car, sir. Could you come over here?"

The Marine base was just outside Jacksonville, almost an hour's drive away. He tried to be patient. "Lucas, this isn't a very good time. We have some problems here in town, and I really can't spare the time to go all the way over there. I'm sorry, but if you want to talk, you'll have to come here."

"I see. Could you stand by for a minute?" It was closer to two minutes, and the seconds ticked by in the stuffy hallway. "Sir? I have a suggestion."

Vanderhoven said he could borrow a jeep. There was a diner on the outskirts of Wilmington. Could they meet there for breakfast tomorrow, about six-thirty? MacKendrie was nearing exasperation, but he had respected Vanderhoven's father, and the young man sounded earnest. He agreed. It was only a twenty-minute drive, and at least it wouldn't interfere with his day.

Helen was waiting in the living room, standing. "Jim?"

He sighed. "I have to go meet someone for breakfast, just outside Wilmington." She waited until he had to go on. "He's a young Navy officer named Lucas Vanderhoven. I knew his father a little in China. Lucas works for Harry Cohen. It sounds like they have more questions." Still she didn't speak. "It's nothing, Helen. We're meeting at six-thirty. I should be back here by eight, eight-thirty at the latest. It's a nuisance, that's all."

She shrugged, expressionless. "All right. One less plate for breakfast."

Vanderhoven was waiting for him when he walked in the diner. MacKendrie knew him at once. He was a Viking, tall, blond, and burly, dressed in a sport coat, white shirt and dark tie. They shook hands, exchanged pleasantries. A waitress appeared, and Vanderhoven told MacKendrie to order what he liked, that he would pick up the tab.

"Cohen's paying for it," he said with a grin.

As they waited for the food, MacKendrie asked about family, whether Vanderhoven's mother was still living, if they had any word from teachers or students at the school his father had run.

"At first after the war, we got letters. There was a student Pop was proud of. He was about my age, I guess. He stayed in touch. Then the civil war started, and the letters were less frequent. Then they stopped. No idea what happened to him."

MacKendrie sighed. "That happened a lot, I think. Anyone that had ties to America wound up dead or in hiding."

The waitress brought plates of eggs, sausage, and toast. As was his custom, MacKendrie bowed his head and silently gave thanks. When he looked up, he saw Vanderhoven had an embarrassed smile.

"I forget to do that. Pop would have a fit if he knew."

"It's hard to keep up habits, especially if you don't have someone to help remind you." He glanced at the young man. "You must miss your father."

The handsome face clouded. "Yes, sir. A lot. After I got into Annapolis, I kind of thought I was my own man, you know? Figured I had my own path ahead of me, didn't really need my parents to show me the way. Boy, was I wrong. Not a day goes by I don't wish I could call Pop and ask his advice."

MacKendrie winced. He rarely heard from his own son. Richard was an attorney, doing well in Richmond, or so he said, some kind of business law. He never quite understood why they had become distant from each other. Emily's death, his remarriage? Relations between Richard and Helen were polite but cool.

Vanderhoven leaned forward. "Sir, would you mind if we spoke in Chinese?" Seeing MacKendrie's surprise, he said, "There are a few things I need to ask you, and it's best if no one else knows." The diner was noisy, and they were in an out-of-the-way corner, but he glanced around to check.

MacKendrie smiled and said, "Well, I may be a little rusty, but sure, fire away."

Vanderhoven passed into fluent Mandarin, flecked with the regional accent MacKendrie recognized immediately. "This concerns your friend, Wang Wenzhe. We believe he is in danger. It may be necessary to bring him out of China."

MacKendrie frowned. "How can I help?"

For fifteen minutes, Vanderhoven queried MacKendrie about Wang's personality, the layout of the town of Bai Miao, whether there were people in the church there who could be trusted. Once, the waitress came up suddenly to ask if they wanted more coffee and was startled to hear them speaking an odd language.

Finally, Vanderhoven reverted to English.

"Sir, if we do succeed in recovering him, would you be willing to meet him when he gets stateside? Even if it means coming to California?"

"Of course. I think he's probably mad at me, though."

"Why?"

"Something happened after he came here to attend college. He had an attachment to me, and he wrote letters asking me to come see him, but it just wasn't possible. The letters stopped after a while."

Vanderhoven nodded and signaled to the waitress for the check. "Thanks, sir. This could help a lot."

"Well, I hope so. I'll pray for you and Wang. And Harry, too," he added.

Vanderhoven grinned. "He needs it. So do I."

The waitress appeared, and Vanderhoven gave her a ten, told her to keep the change. The men walked into the parking lot.

Vanderhoven said, "Oh, by the way, sir, you said on the phone there were some problems in town. Nothing serious, I hope."

MacKendrie grimaced and briefly sketched the rising tensions in Kirkwell. "I'm worried, Lucas. Feelings are running high. Things could get out of hand quickly. You're probably too young to remember what it was like during the warlord years in China."

"No, but Pop told me stories. It's that bad?"

"It's the same kind of hatred. The Negroes are on the wrong end of it." He gave a small smile. "I'm kind of in the middle."

The young man put a large hand on MacKendrie's shoulder. "Sounds like you're the one who needs the prayers."

NINE

Life began to evaporate in the heat. Tobacco plants that should have been a foot high were barely peeking above the dry ground. Flower gardens wilted. Fans ran in every room. Children had to stay indoors, babies suffered from heat rash, livestock sought out shade or stood still with heads drooping.

Eight days before Independence Day, Connie Campbell arrived in his office, looking sunburned and drawn.

"Connie, are you all right? You look worn out."

Her eyes filled with water and her voice trembled. "I am, Rev'rend. I'm so tired. I didn't know it would be this hard." She pulled a handkerchief from her purse and sobbed silently into it. MacKendrie waited.

When she regained her voice, she told him that the campaign had not been going well. There had been several meetings set up, only to have some canceled at the last minute or have just four or five people attend. The door-to-door work had yielded just one half-hearted commitment. The promised volunteer workers had not materialized. They had at most three people, including Evans, who were committed to show up at the courthouse to register.

"But the worst part," she said, tearing up again, "is what people've been saying. They've been calling me the most awful names. I'm embarrassed to tell you the mean things people are saying right to my face, people I've known all my life. That really hurts."

MacKendrie resisted the temptation to ask what she had expected. "What are you going to do?"

She looked surprised. "Why, keep going. We can't quit now."

He sighed. "All right. Tell me what's supposed to happen on July third."

Her determination returned as she talked. Bob Crutchfield would be notified that the Negroes who wanted to register would come to the courthouse at ten thirty. The police would also be told in hopes they would keep the peace in case of trouble. They didn't expect to get registered right away. It might take three or four trips, or more, but they would persist until they succeeded.

Summoning his sternest voice, MacKendrie said, "Connie, I want you to promise me something. Promise you won't walk into that courthouse with Evans and the others."

"What? Why not?"

"Do I really have to explain it after what you've just told me? The sight of a pretty white girl like you walking up those steps beside Evans is enough to drive some men right over the edge. It could make things a whole lot worse, not just for you but for Evans and his people, too."

Her voice rose. "But all that work! You're asking me to back out at the moment we've been working for?" Her eyes flashed at him. "I won't do it."

"Connie, please, think about this."

"No!" She stood up. "I guess I was wrong about you. You and all these so-called Christians been doing nothing but trying to stand in the way of justice for all these years, and now that we're just about to do something about it, you want me to be a good girl and stay home.

Well, I won't!" She stalked out of his office. He heard the door to the vestibule slam.

The next Sunday, Joe and Edna Stallings came to church, but MacKendrie saw something wasn't right. Joe swayed when he stood and emitted an audible belch in the middle of the sermon, drawing embarrassed titters. As MacKendrie greeted the worshipers after the service, Stallings ambled up, the smell of beer on his breath.

"What's 'is I hear about that Campbell girl helping 'em niggers vote?" he said, too loudly.

There were still several people waiting in line, who exchanged glances and edged their way out the door. Eli Ross sauntered over. MacKendrie said, "Joe, this isn't the place..."

"You gonna tell me 'bout it or not?"

"It's true. Connie Campbell has been working with a group of Negroes who want to register to vote."

He stared. "And you and her daddy let her do it?"

"Leave Cy out of this. He and I tried to talk her out of it. Besides, she hasn't been doing much. From what I hear, there may be only one or two who are going to try to register, and you know the clerk isn't going to let them do it. It's not worth getting upset about."

"Damn sure is. One or two this time, next time it'll be a hundred. If somethin' ain't done about it."

"Joe, I hope you're not thinking about causing trouble. The police are going to be there to see to it nothing gets out of hand."

"Hmp! Police can't watch 'em all the time." MacKendrie started to reply, but Stallings interrupted. "Hey," he said, looking past him. "Here now." A slow grin spread across his face.

MacKendrie looked over his shoulder and saw Ulysses tidying up the pews.

"Let's ask ol' Ug here what he thinks about it." He barreled forward, ignoring MacKendrie's pleas, and stepped quickly up to

Brown. For the first time, MacKendrie noticed that Stallings was not really fat. He was more like an out-of-shape athlete. Probably he had been a lineman on the high school football team, he thought.

"What you say, Ug," Stallings half-hollered, grinning.

Brown straightened, a paper bag he was using to collect trash in his hand. "Morning, Mister Joe," he said.

With a poor show of friendliness, Stallings said, "Preacher here'n me been talking about you and your kind. Haven't we, Preacher?" he called over his shoulder.

MacKendrie started to take a step forward, but Ross's hand shot out and held his arm.

"Now the Preacher, he says whites and, and—" he paused, leaning on the word—"Nee-groes is the same inside." He snorted. "I say if they was, what's the use in you being black and me white? Ought to be some difference, don't you think?" Brown stood still and said nothing. "Well come on, now. Let's hear it. What you say?" He wasn't smiling anymore.

Brown appeared to consider the question and slowly said, "I don't rightly know, Mister Joe. See, I never had much schooling." Stallings started to chuckle, but Brown continued, "That's why I leave it to someone is smarter'n me."

"Smarter. And who's that?" Stallings was almost giddy.

"Well, sir, smartest man I ever run across is ol' Paul."

Stallings' brow furrowed. "Paul who?"

"Apostle Paul. See, says in the Bible that Paul, he stands up and argues with men what sits around thinking all day long. Bound to be right smart, and ol' Paul, he tells 'em, 'God hath made of one blood all the nations of the earth.'" Brown paused and gazed at Stallings, who was gaping. "So see, I figure if Paul says we is one blood, must be so."

It took a moment before Stallings, his face flushed, jerked a step forward. His roar ruptured the quiet space. "Don't you lecture me, boy! I'll whip your goddamned black ass!"

MacKendrie threw off Ross's hand, which was still on his arm, took three fast strides, and swung around in front of Stallings.

"Enough!" Stallings looked up at him, his rage checked. "Look around you, Joe! Go on! Where do you think you are?" Stallings didn't turn his head but shifted his eyes one way and then another. "You're standing in the house of almighty God." He pointed down at the floor. "You will not take the name of God in vain here." He stepped closer. "There won't be any violence here, either." Stallings staggered a little but MacKendrie saw loathing behind his alcohol-clouded eyes. Without moving, MacKendrie said, "Ulysses, would you mind checking the wastebasket in my office?" He heard the rustle as Brown walked away.

Stallings said sullenly, "I ain't gonna be talked to like that by no nigger."

"Go home, Joe. Tend your farm. Nothing's going to come of this voting business, unless someone stirs things up. Eli, take his arm."

They got Stallings, still muttering and swearing, out to the truck, its metal skin radiating the midday heat. MacKendrie asked for the keys and handed them to Edna Stallings, insisting over Joe's protests that he was in no shape to drive.

"Give him some coffee and let him sleep it off. Call me if he gives you any trouble," he told her. Her only sign of acknowledgement was to glance at him briefly.

Ross walked back into the church with MacKendrie. "Well now, that was…diplomatic of you. Thing is, Joe was right. Ug shouldn't have embarrassed him like that."

MacKendrie stopped. "Embarrassed him? Joe embarrassed himself. And Ulysses gave one of the most apt uses of scripture I've heard in a long time."

Ross's eyes narrowed. "'God hath made of one blood all the nations of the earth.' You don't take that literally."

MacKendrie frowned. "I certainly do."

"Oh my." Ross looked away. "We'll have to have a talk sometime."

July Fourth fell on a Friday. Early in the week, patriotic bunting was strung across storefronts and flags were on display around town. There was to be a parade and a community picnic, but the preparations were carried out with anxiety. Harper, MacKendrie, and Cy Campbell had persuaded Connie to accept a compromise. She would go into the courthouse early and wait inside for Evans and the others to arrive.

At ten on Thursday morning, MacKendrie walked down to the courthouse. It was a plain but handsome stone building in neoclassical style with broad steps leading to the entrance. Already there were police officers milling around. He spotted Jimmy Ondrachek at the top of the steps, laughing and talking with a sergeant, and walked up.

"Morning, Mayor," he said, shaking hands. "Looks like you're ready."

"I imagine so. I just hope this don't drag on. This Evans fella, he gonna make a speech?"

"No idea. I wouldn't be surprised."

Ondrachek sighed and nodded to his right. Bud Carson, the editor of the *Gazette*, was checking his unwieldy camera with its flashbulb guard standing up like a radar dish. "Bud's been calling me every day, asking if I know anything. Hell, I don't know nothing. I told him he ought to be calling this Evans, but he says he can't reach him."

"Cy tells me he persuaded Bud to keep Connie's name out of it. Is she already inside?"

"Not as far as I know."

MacKendrie chose a spot about halfway up the steps, well to the side, and waited. As ten thirty approached, the police formed a corridor up and down the steps. Onlookers began to gather on the sidewalk and behind the cordon. When the appointed time arrived, there were about fifty people—all white—a mixture of teenage boys, businessmen, and a smattering of women, milling about. It was already above ninety degrees, and everyone was sweating. It wasn't long before the volume of the idle talk rose, becoming more raucous and vulgar.

"Where they at?" "Aw, they afraid to show up!" "They wanna vote, let's see their black asses!"

The clock on the front of the courthouse passed ten forty, then ten forty-five. MacKendrie had removed his hat and was wiping his face with his handkerchief and didn't see Connie Campbell slip up beside him. He nearly jumped when she spoke.

"Rev'rend MacKendrie?"

"Connie! What are you doing here? Why aren't you inside?"

She put both hands on his arm. "Rev'rend, I'm scared."

"Where are the others?"

"That's just it, I don't know. Walter didn't meet me this morning. And I haven't heard anything from Rev'rend Evans."

MacKendrie walked the girl down the steps and around an abutment where they were shielded from the crowd. "Tell me what you know," he said.

She took a couple of breaths, trying to control herself. "Walter was supposed to go meet Rev'rend Sam at his church at nine thirty. He was going to come pick me up, and we would all go to the courthouse. I waited and waited and Walter didn't come and nobody called. I didn't have a car, so I just started running over here. When I saw the crowd and heard 'em talking, I realized nobody showed up, and I got really scared. Then I saw you." She began to wail. "Oh, Rev'rend, what if they, they..." She buried her face in his chest.

MacKendrie grasped her shoulders and gently pushed her back. "Connie, look at me." Gasping and hiccupping, she looked up. "The first thing we're going to do is take you to your father's store. Then I'll get my car and go out to Mount Zion. Let's not jump to any conclusions."

They walked around the front of the courthouse, skirting the crowd, which was already starting to break up in disappointment. The Campbells rushed up when MacKendrie escorted her into the store, but he assured them nothing had happened. The four walked into the office in the back, where Connie promptly collapsed into her mother's arms, sobbing. "Shh, shh, it's all right, baby," Cathy Campbell soothed, rocking her daughter as if Connie were again six years old.

MacKendrie briefly repeated what Connie had told him. "I suspect everyone just got cold feet. I'll let you know what I find out."

MacKendrie told Helen as calmly as he could that no one had showed up at the courthouse and that he needed the car to run an errand. He drove as fast as he dared out of town and along the rural road to Mount Zion Missionary Baptist. He slowed, looking for landmarks, till he saw the clearing and pulled into the grassy space in front of the church.

There were no other cars to be seen. He walked up to the church and tried the knob. Locked. He walked around behind the building, looking for a window or a back door. There were none. He circled back to his car and looked around. The trees on either side of the clearing were still in the midday heat. There was no sound except for the whirring of cicadas. MacKendrie walked to the car and grasped the door handle, glancing back toward the road. A glint caught his eye.

He walked to the edge of the road. Broken glass lay scattered about. He bent and picked up a piece and examined it. Slight greenish tint, thick. A car window. He looked around. There was a set of tire tracks beside the glass, the grass dark and cut down from spinning tires, starting in the clearing and leading to the road. Fainter but still distinct, there was a second set, also leading out to the road. The tracks were fresh. MacKendrie looked around on the ground. He saw a shiny metal object and picked it up. It was a shell casing. Looking closely, he saw it was a .30-.30. He put the casing in his pocket and ran to his car. Avoiding the glass, he pulled onto the road in the direction the tracks led.

This time he drove slowly, looking carefully at the grassy shoulders and the trees and underbrush lining the road. There were no homes along this stretch. He had gone a mile and a half when he saw a tire track departing from the right edge of the road, making a long wavy line then joined by a second parallel track. They went on for a quarter of a mile, then abruptly turned toward the tree line and disappeared. MacKendrie pulled off the road and stopped. He walked back to the tracks and followed them to a wall of leafy bushes which appeared undisturbed. It was too perfect. He bent down and pulled on the lowest branch just above where the tracks disappeared. It gave easily, and he pulled it free. The end had been cut. He started pulling away the branches and saw the tail light of a car.

MacKendrie scrambled though the loose branches and ran to the driver's door of the Chevy. Walter Harper was leaning against the door, his head part-way out of the window. Carefully, MacKendrie opened the door and caught the boy as he slid sideways. There was a wound in his left side, and dark, sticky blood covered his middle and groin. As MacKendrie pulled him out of the car, Harper gasped and moaned. MacKendrie laid him on the ground, took off his jacket, folded it and put it under his head.

"Walter! Walter, can you hear me? Walter, it's James MacKendrie." He shook the boy's face, which was gray and had a streak of blood across the right cheek. His glasses were missing. MacKendrie saw he was in shock and had lost a lot of blood. Harper moaned again.

"Walter! Walter! Can you open your eyes?"

Harper's eyelids fluttered and half-opened but they didn't register that he saw anything. He said faintly, "Where..."

"You've been shot, Walter. Hang on, I'm going to get you to a doctor." He moved around to Harper's shoulders to drag him to his car.

"Ulysses," Harper said. MacKendrie froze.

"What did you say? Walter, what about Ulysses?"

"With...me. Ulyss..." He fainted.

MacKendrie sprang back to the car and looked in. On the back seat leaning against the door beside the shattered window was Ulysses Brown, his shirt a sheet of blood. Flies hummed. Ulysses' eyes were open. He was smiling.

TEN

"Let's go over it again, Preacher." Hoolie Dixon was sitting across from MacKendrie in the waiting room of the Cape Fear County Hospital in Wilmington. "If you don't mind, that is."

He repeated it. Evans and the campaign. Connie coming up to him at the courthouse. How he had gone to Mount Zion Missionary Baptist, found the broken glass and the shell casing, found the tire tracks and the car with Harper and Ulysses Brown inside. Ulysses was dead, so he left him there, dragged Harper to his car, and drove like mad to the hospital. As soon as Walter was taken into surgery, he had called the sheriff.

Dixon shook his head. "Pretty fair piece of detective work. If you ever leave the ministry, you can come work for me," he said with a smile.

MacKendrie gave a fleeting smile in return. "No thanks, Sheriff. I just hope you catch whoever did this."

Dixon shifted in his seat and looked thoughtful. "Well, sir, first we'll have to figure out just what happened. If that boy pulls through, he can tell us. But I'll tell you, Preacher, this one ain't gonna be easy."

"What do you mean?"

"Well, ol' Ug, ever'body liked him and all, but he was with a white boy on his way to register to vote. That ain't gonna set well. And the Harper boy, folks around here saw him as an outside agitator."

MacKendrie said nothing. He was half in shock, he realized. He hadn't even phoned Helen. He looked at his watch. Two thirty. She must be worried. He stood. "I have to make a phone call, if you don't need me for anything else."

Dixon stood. "No, no, you go ahead. We'll be in touch." As MacKendrie turned, Dixon continued, "There is one thing. Where was this Evans fella? He was supposed to meet Harper, but you didn't see any sign of him?"

"That's right. I don't know why he wasn't there, but considering what happened, I'd want to find out."

"Any idea where we can find him?"

"I understand he teaches at a Negro school. Connie Campbell probably knows the name of it."

MacKendrie found a pay phone, dialed the operator, and asked to reverse the charges. Helen answered.

"Helen, it's me."

"Jim, what on earth? Where are you?"

"I'm in Wilmington, at the hospital. No, don't interrupt. Just listen. Something terrible has happened." He gave her only the barest outline, leaving out the bloody details. He told her he would stay until he could get a report from the doctor about Walter Harper. "I want you to do something for me. Go down to Campbell's and tell them what's happened. See if they know how to get in touch with Walter's family. They need to know. Then go back home and wait. You'll probably start getting phone calls once word gets around. Just tell people I'm all right and that you don't know any more. I'll call you back once I hear about Walter."

He knew she was probably shaken, but her voice was firm. "I'll go to the Campbells right now. And I'll pray for the Harper boy."

MacKendrie returned to the waiting room and slumped in a chair. There were a few other people in the small room, and he realized they were looking at him with alarm. He was puzzled till he glanced down and saw why. Walter Harper's blood stained his shirt and pants. There was nothing he could do about it now, but he would have to figure out some way to get a change of clothes. He could hardly walk in the front door of the manse looking like a ghoul.

Good God, he was suddenly tired. The strain of the past month weighed on him all at once, and he buried his face in his hands. He leaned back and closed his eyes in fatigue. He must have dozed. A hand was shaking him, and he startled awake to see a white-coated doctor. "Excuse me, but I understand you brought in the boy with the gunshot?"

MacKendrie stood. "How is he?"

The doctor motioned for him to follow. When they were out of the waiting room, he said, "He lost a lot of blood. It didn't help that the weather was so hot. Another fifteen minutes and we would have lost him."

"He's alive?"

"Yes. Fortunately, the bullet didn't hit any vital organs. It passed through his side and just nicked an artery. We were able to cauterize it and stop the bleeding. He's weak, and he'll need a couple of more transfusions, but if there is no infection, he should be all right. We'll know within forty-eight hours."

"Thank God. Can I see him?"

"It's probably not a good idea. He's in recovery, and we have him sedated. Come back tomorrow and see if he has regained consciousness. Has the boy's family been notified?"

"We're trying to get in touch with them." He thanked the doctor and went back to the pay phones. Helen gave a sigh of relief at the news.

"The Campbells are going the call the Harper family," she said. "Connie was practically hysterical when I told her what happened. She wanted to drive right over there, but we talked her out of it."

"I'll call Cy and let him know the news. And Helen, do something else for me."

When he arrived in Kirkwell, it was after five, and there were few people on the streets. He was able to duck into the church without being seen. In his office a change of clothes lay on his desk. He took them into the men's room, stripped off his bloody clothes and washed his face and hands thoroughly. When he was dressed, he took the ruined clothing out back and put it into the metal garbage can. He held the round corrugated lid, looking at it. How many times had he seen Ulysses Brown carry that can around the church and lug it out to the street for collection. He slammed the lid down.

When he walked into the manse, Helen rushed to him and threw her arms around him, sobbing. "Jim. I'm just so sorry."

"Shh, shh. Come sit down. Where are the girls?"

"Upstairs in their room. I asked them to play quietly." She was still crying. "Poor Ulysses. And his wife. How's she going to manage?"

"I think their children are nearby. She has family."

"I just couldn't help thinking what I would do if you...if something..." He hugged her tightly. "Was it bad, Jim? What you saw?"

"Yes. Reminded me of the war. But this was different. You expect to see something like that in wartime. You don't expect to see it here. It was one of the most shocking—"

A solemn Dottie was standing by the couch. "Why is Mommy crying?"

MacKendrie had been dreading this moment. Ulysses always spoke to the girls and asked them what they were learning in school, and they loved his cheerful way of talking with them. "Dottie, we've had some very bad news. Go get your sister, and we'll talk about it."

He tried to explain as gently as possible. Someone had done something very wicked and hurt Ug with a gun so badly he had died, he said. Priss was silent, not seeming to understand. Dottie demanded to know why he had been shot and who shot him. As MacKendrie struggled to explain, the girl's face twisted and she burst out, "I hope they put him in jail! I hope they shoot him, too!" Helen's mouth flew open in shock.

"Dottie! You mustn't—"

MacKendrie put his hand across to touch Helen's shoulder as Dottie began to cry, and then as if it were contagious, Priss and then Helen joined in. MacKendrie found tears streaming down his face.

Helen stood up, wiping her eyes. "Come on, girls. Help me with dinner."

The phone calls started soon after, and continued on through dinner and into the evening. Some were well-wishers, expressing concern about MacKendrie and Harper.

"That was mighty brave of you, Jim," said Eli Ross. "Whoever did that could have still been around. I am sorry about Ug. He was a good colored man, only...well..."

Some callers were busybodies, angling for gossip. There were one or two like Percy Weir.

"Can't say I'm surprised, Pastor. I'm not saying Ug had it coming, but we just ain't ready for coloreds to vote."

Jimmy Ondrachek was one of the last to call. "I'm sorry about your janitor, Pastor. Hated to see it turn out that way. Did kinda solve our problem, though."

In the morning, MacKendrie had two visits to make, Walter Harper and Ulysses Brown's widow. Helen insisted on coming with him. She took the girls to a neighbor's house with a promise they would be back in time to take them to the Fourth of July parade.

Harper was sedated, but MacKendrie was allowed a brief visit at his bedside. The boy was pale but breathing easily. A bottle of blood hung above the bed, a red tube running down to the needle in his arm. The habits of his military chaplaincy returned. He leaned over, placed his hand on Harper's dark hair, and spoke softly in his ear, saying a brief prayer.

When he returned to the waiting room, Cathy and Connie Campbell were talking with Helen. Connie spoke rapidly when she saw him. "How is he? Was he awake? Did he say anything?"

MacKendrie put his hand on her arm. "He was asleep, Connie. He looks fine. He's going to be all right, but it's going to take some time." He turned to Cathy. "Is there any word from his parents?"

"They should be here shortly. They live in Shelby, out by Asheville. That's a long drive."

Connie started sniffling. "I'm just so sorry I've put everyone through this, Rev'rend," she quavered.

"Baby, we told you, it's no use fretting about it now," Cathy said.

"I should have been there with them," Connie said, looking for a handkerchief. "I let them down, Walter and poor...poor Ug." Her face crumpled, and she stifled a coughing sob.

"I never heard such nonsense in my life," Cathy said in a low, fierce voice. Sideways to MacKendrie, she said, "Will you tell her what would've happened to her if she'd been there? We been listening to this since yesterday."

"Your mother's right, Connie. Those men would have shot you without even thinking about it. Enough blood was spilled as it is."

"I just don't know how I can face Walter," Connie said, dabbing at her eyes.

"I wish to God you'd never met him," Cathy said. Connie's eyes flashed and in an instant she and her mother were talking fast and hot over each other. "Don't understand..." "No good for you..." "Best boy I ever..." "Ever see him again, I'll..."

MacKendrie took Cathy's arm and firmly steered her down the hallway, leaving Helen to take Connie's shoulder. Cathy Campbell was seething.

"It's that damn boy's own fault he got shot and Ug killed, an' I don't care who hears me say it. Putting my daughter at risk like that, I could go in there and wring his *neck*," she spat. MacKendrie said nothing, letting her get it out of her system. She was breathing heavily, and it took another few moments before she said, "When I think what could've happened... We're just glad it's over with."

"I don't think it's over," MacKendrie said.

She looked up. "What d'you mean?"

"Oh, it may be over as far as Connie's concerned. But it's not over."

Her eyes narrowed. "Well. She's all I care about."

On the return trip, MacKendrie turned off the main highway and began winding through narrow back roads. He had to slow the car down considerably on the one-track dirt road where the Browns lived. Along the road were tar-paper shacks. Some had been kept up a little, with a few chickens and a small garden to help fill bellies. Others were just a collection of splinters. MacKendrie could hardly believe his eyes. In China, this sort of poverty was the result of overpopulation and centuries of rigid Confucian rules about class. Here, he realized, it was something more deliberate, calculated.

They saw a cluster of people just ahead, and MacKendrie parked the car in the shade along the road next to the Browns' home. They were the only white people wading into a sea of black faces, but it was familiar to MacKendrie, who often had been the sole white in an assembly of Chinese. No one offered a hand, but men removed their hats as they spoke, and MacKendrie did the same. Helen, as a child of the South, moved easily among them, speaking the familiar and sympathetic words that whites had offered to their bereaved black servants for generations, a tacit concession that death held an equality that life did not.

Jeremiah Brown stepped forward. "Pastor MacKendrie. Thank you for coming, sir."

"Jeremiah, it's good to see you. But I'm a little surprised you're here."

"I had to come back when I heard about Uncle Ulysses. I'm glad to see you. I didn't get a chance to thank you in person for helping me out."

"I understand."

"Uncle Ulysses told me you had a hard time about that. He said it just went to show that you and Mrs. MacKendrie were good people."

"Well, we felt the same about Ulysses," MacKendrie said. "I rarely met a man who was as content with life. He was never bothered by what he didn't have."

This was met with murmurs of assent from those standing around. Brown said, "Yes, sir, that's the truth. He used to say to me, 'Boy, don't you worry about them folks with them fancy cars and clothes and such. Once they got 'em, it's all they think about.'" The MacKendries joined in the quiet laughter. Brown looked down and shook his head. "It was right hard, losing him that way."

"It was an offense against God," MacKendrie said with a force that surprised him and drew a commotion of near-shouts. "Yes!" "Yessir!" He put a hand on Brown's shoulder. "I promise you, I won't let this get dropped."

Brown held his gaze and nodded briefly. "Thank you, sir." He gestured to the house, which had the appearance of sturdiness although its vertical planks were the color of dirt. "My Aunt Essie, she'll want to speak to y'all."

The interior was dim and small and filled with people, but they parted when the MacKendries entered to make a narrow corridor leading to a corner where a spindly figure with white hair sat on a plain wooden chair, fanning herself, with younger women in attendance on each side. Pain ran through all the many crevices and wrinkles on her face like rivulets after a rainstorm.

MacKendrie stepped forward and bent forward. "We wanted to pay our respects, Mrs. Brown. Your husband was a fine, God-fearing man, and no matter what anyone else says, Helen and I respected him."

Essie Brown lifted her face and said softly, "Thank you, Pastor. I don't know why he had to go and leave me the way he did. It's a hard, hard thing. Mighty hard." She fanned more quickly, as whimpers and murmurs sounded around her.

"Yes, Mrs. Brown, I know it is. He was taken away too soon."

The talk went on this way. Helen asked if she were being taken care of and was told, yes, she had sisters and a daughter and grandchildren to look out for her. A son had left home and his whereabouts were uncertain. The hardship of the heat was commented on. Sensing they should leave the family to its grief, the MacKendries made their goodbyes.

As they descended the steps to the yard, a clipped voice behind them said, "That was kind of you, Pastor MacKendrie." They turned to see Samuel Evans on the porch. "It's good to see you again."

MacKendrie said, "Good morning, Pastor. I didn't expect to see you here."

"You probably have some questions for me. May I walk you to your car?" Evans stepped down beside them.

MacKendrie said, "Helen, this is Reverend Samuel Evans. He worked with Connie and Walter."

Helen said without warmth, "How do you do, Reverend Evans."

"Very well, thank you, Mrs. MacKendrie. Shall we?" They walked slowly, enveloped by the heat that radiated from all directions.

"What brings you here?" MacKendrie asked. He realized it sounded like a challenge.

"Oh, Ulysses belonged to my church. You didn't know? Yes, for a very long time, although of course, I've only been here two years. It was my duty to be here for the family."

"I see."

As they stood beside the car, MacKendrie suggested that Helen sit inside with the doors open to afford her some shade. He removed his jacket, and he and Evans walked a few paces away to stand under a tree.

"So Ulysses was the only one who intended to register. Is that right?" MacKendrie said.

Evans wiped his forehead with a crisp white handkerchief. "Yes."

"What happened to the others?"

Evans sighed heavily. "They were frightened. With reason, as we have seen. I tried to tell Ulysses he did not have to go through with it, but he said he wasn't going to be turned around anymore."

"And you? Where were you yesterday?"

Evans looked somber. "Thursday evening, Pastor, there was an incident at my home. I live in Wilmington, not far from Bethune High School, where I work. I was at home with my wife and children and we heard a hammering sound on the front porch. I looked through the curtain and saw fire in my yard and men getting into trucks and driving off. Those men had poured gas on my front yard in the shape of a cross and set it on fire. There was a note tacked to the porch." He reached inside his jacket and handed a sheet of paper to MacKendrie. In all capitals in block-letter printing, it read, "STAY AWAY FROM KIRKWELL TOMORROW IF YOU KNOW WHATS GOOD FOR YOU AND YOUR FAMILY."

MacKendrie handed it back. "Did you report this?"

Evans gave an ironic smile. "To whom? The police? I doubt I would have gotten a very sympathetic hearing."

MacKendrie was silent for a moment. "Pastor Evans, no one blames you for not coming to the courthouse. But why didn't you warn Walter? Call it off?"

"I did. I got in the car and drove over to the room Walter was renting. He wasn't there. So I wrote a note telling what had happened and that under no circumstances should he go to Mount Zion. I slipped it under the door. I expected to hear from him yesterday, but instead I got a call from one of my congregation telling me what happened." He said anxiously, "Have you seen Walter?"

"Yes. We just came from the hospital. He's weak, but the doctors think he's going to be all right. His family should be there soon."

"Thank God. I can't tell you how I felt when I found out what happened. I would have gone to see him myself, but, well...you know."

MacKendrie looked across the road, watching the dust motes glimmering in the sun. He said, "There's something that's bothering me. The arrangement was for you to meet Walter and Ulysses at your church yesterday morning, is that right?"

"Yes. At nine thirty. Walter was to go pick up Ulysses and meet me at the church, then we would go in together."

"Who else knew about this?"

"Ah, well, the N-double-A-C-P office—we always are supposed to let them know of our plans. A few of my family and friends." He looked up. "I see what you're getting at."

"Someone knew about your meeting place. If that scare tactic didn't work on you, they were determined to see to it that no Negroes registered to vote. But how did they find out?"

Evans shook his head. "I don't know. I warned Walter not to say anything to anyone, but..."

MacKendrie said, "Helen must be fainting from the heat." They started back toward the car. "I've promised Ulysses' family that I will not let the authorities drop this matter, and I mean it."

Evans stopped and faced him. "Pastor MacKendrie, you're a good man, and Negroes need friends like you. But there would be a price for speaking out on Ulysses' behalf. I think he sort of expected something like this might happen. We're going to remember his sacrifice. But none of the black folks around here will blame you if you leave this alone. It's not your cause."

"I'm not doing it for your cause, Pastor Evans. I'm doing it for Ulysses. And if I don't speak out, my conscience will bother me until the day I die. Goodbye." He extended his hand.

Evans smiled and grasped it. "Goodbye, Pastor. God bless you. We'll be watching."

ELEVEN

On Saturday, he and Helen put the girls in the car and drove to Wilmington. At the hospital, they were told Walter Harper had been moved to a private room. They sat the girls in a nearby waiting room and supplied them with coloring books. They found the room, knocked, and entered to find a tall, dark-haired, immaculately dressed woman sitting on the edge of the bed next to Walter, who was propped up in a reclining position. She stood, as did a sad-faced man in a linen jacket who was sitting in a chair next to the bed.

"You must be Walter's parents," MacKendrie said, extending his hand to the man. "I'm James MacKendrie, pastor of First Presbyterian in Kirkwell, and this is my wife, Helen."

"I'm Monroe Harper," said the man in a rich baritone. "This is my wife, Harriet."

Astonished, Helen said, "You're Monroe Harper? The singer?"

"I'm afraid so," he said with the barest of smiles.

"Oh, my word, Mr. Harper, we love your music so much. Jim and I listen to it all the time." To MacKendrie's amusement, his sane, unflappable wife turned into a teenage girl, all hands fluttering and nervous laughter. Monroe Harper was a crooner popular in the South, known for his polished delivery and powerful voice. He made frequent appearances at night clubs in Atlanta, broadcast live on WSB.

"You didn't know I had a famous father, did you, sir?" came Walter's voice from the bed, just above a whisper.

MacKendrie stepped forward and placed his hand on the boy's shoulder. "Hello, Walt. How do you feel?"

"Still pretty weak, sir. They say it'll be a few days before I can move around."

"You be sure and do what they tell you. We just thank God you're going to be all right."

Harriet Harper said in a refined Northeastern accent, "Walter has told us so much about you, Mr. MacKendrie. He says you...counseled him and the Campbell girl about their little campaign."

MacKendrie couldn't detect whether there was bitterness or gratitude in her voice. "Well, Walt and Connie have been very brave, braver than me, I'm ashamed to say."

Walt shook his head. "Not...true," he said. "You're...only one who helped."

"Easy, son. There'll be plenty of time later to talk about that. We're going to let you rest now. We just wanted to see how you're doing. We'll come back in a few days when you're stronger."

"Thanks, sir. Would you give Connie a message?"

"Of course, Walt."

"Tell her...sorry, but better if she doesn't visit for a while. Tell...I'll write."

"Okay, Walt. I'll make sure she understands. You just get better."

As they said goodbye, Monroe Harper offered to walk with them to the lobby. Once outside, he said apologetically, "Harriet doesn't really approve of the Campbell girl. She is protective of Walter, you see, and well..."

"Connie's a small-town Southern girl," MacKendrie said. "Well, perhaps it's for the best for now. Mr. Harper, a word of advice. Don't leave Walter alone, even for a minute. If you can hire a security guard, you should."

"My God," Harper said. "What have you heard?"

"Nothing. But the men who shot him might be uneasy about what Walter knows."

The MacKendries returned to the manse in mid-afternoon, and all appeared quiet. He dialed the Campbells' number and Connie answered.

"Oh, hello, Rev'rend." Her voice was distant, subdued.

"I just wanted you to know that Helen and I saw Walt today."

"Oh! Is he...how is..."

"He's awake but still weak. It'll be a few days before they let him walk."

There was silence, then a sob. "I've been praying for him, Rev'rend. I just felt so helpless, stuck here. Mama won't let me go see him anymore."

"I'm sorry, Connie. She's doing what she thinks best."

"She doesn't understand a thing. She thinks Walter got me into all this, but it was the campaign that got me and Walter together. We love each other, Rev'rend."

"I thought as much."

"Will you take me to see him?"

"Connie, Walt asked me to give you a message. He said to tell you that it might be best not to see him for a while. He said he'd write."

The girl's voice rose. "What? Why would he say that?"

"Connie, calm down. I think I know why. For one thing, Walt needs his peace and quiet right now in order to get better. That's what you want, isn't it? Well, then. Give things time. Let Walt write, and you can write him back."

He could hear sniffling. "Mama wants to send me up to my grandfolks' place outside of Greensboro for a while."

"That's not a bad idea. You've been through a lot, too. It wouldn't hurt to get away."

"Maybe you're right."

MacKendrie cleared his throat. "Connie, let me ask you something. You told me at the courthouse that Walt was going to meet Samuel Evans at Mount Zion, right?"

"Well, yeah. Walter told me they were gonna be there at nine thirty."

"Do you remember when he told you that?"

"I don't know, maybe two or three days before."

"Connie, did you tell anyone about that?"

"No."

"You're sure?"

There was a short silence. "No, I didn't say a word. Except to my folks, of course."

"Your folks?"

"Yeah, I told Mama and Daddy, but that was it. Why?"

"Oh, it's nothing, I'm sure."

In a low voice, Connie gave him the address of her grandparents and asked him to pass it on to Walter. After MacKendrie hung up, he whispered, "Connie. Stupid girl."

He had been preaching on the Beatitudes and already had a sermon written on the text "Blessed are the pure in heart, for they shall see God." Now, in the solitude of his study, he sat and prayed for a long time. Then he reached for his Bible.

That night, his preparations complete and the children in bed, MacKendrie sat next to Helen and took her hand.

"I just want you to be ready. People aren't going to like what I have to say tomorrow. They might make ugly remarks."

"You're going to preach about Ulysses?"

"Not about Ulysses. About what killed him."

"Well." There was no sound except for the occasional creak of the house settling as the heat subsided. Finally, she said, "Jim, are you sure about this? I know you think you're right, but no one at the church had anything to do with Ulysses getting killed. You're preaching to the wrong folks."

MacKendrie was gazing across the room. "I wonder."

She stared. "You're just going to stir things up needlessly. I'm worried for the girls."

He looked at her. "I've thought about that. But I don't want them to live in a place where men hate and kill and nobody says anything about it. I don't want them to be ashamed of their father because I was afraid to speak up."

"Are you afraid?"

He tried to keep his voice light. "Oh, I don't think anyone's going to take potshots at me, but I expect I'll be warned to keep my mouth shut. We just have to expect some kind of meanness."

Sunday's service was well attended. The sensation of the janitor's death drew people to the church, some because they were genuinely sorry, others because they didn't want to be left out of the talk about it. Every overhead fan was turning, and the ushers brought oscillating fans from home, placing them around the sanctuary to try to move the air, but it barely made a dent in the general discomfort.

When the offering plates had been brought forward and prayed over and the ushers retreated, MacKendrie opened his Bible. The lesson would be from Genesis, chapter four, verses eight through twelve, he said. "And Cain talked with Abel his brother: and it came to pass, when they were in the field, that Cain rose up against his brother, and slew him. And the Lord said unto Cain, 'Where is thy brother?' And he said, 'I know not: Am I my brother's keeper?' And he said, 'What hast thou done? The voice of thy brother's blood crieth unto me from the ground. And now thou art cursed from the earth, which hath opened her mouth to receive thy brother's blood from thy hand; when thou tillest the ground, it shall not henceforth yield unto thee her strength; a fugitive and a vagabond shalt thou be in the earth.'"

As MacKendrie closed the Bible and arranged his sermon, he was aware of uneasiness in the congregation. No one moved.

"I know that some of you wish that my sermons weren't quite so formal," MacKendrie began. "You've told me, 'Preacher, just say it plain so we can follow you.' Well, today you're going to get your wish. No formalities, no fancy words, just the word of God as plain as I can make it. And I'm not going to beat around the bush. Our lesson today makes it clear as glass. God hates murder."

He retold the story of Adam and Eve, how they were expelled from the Garden of Eden because of selfish disobedience to God. Self-centeredness, the root of all sin, had been passed on from parents to sons, he said.

"Now, Cain murders his brother out of jealousy. God had regard for Abel's offering and not for Cain's, so out of pure spite and envy of his brother, Cain hatches a plot. He lures Abel out to an isolated spot and ambushes him. It's deliberate, premeditated, and cold-blooded. A man he has known and loved from childhood he has now come to hate."

So far, they were with him. There were some arms folded in defiance and skeptical looks, but no one stirred.

"My friends, hatred is a poison that will seep out from the heart and mind and kill our souls if we let it. When we act upon hatred, we may think we are killing the thing we hate, but in fact we are cutting ourselves off from God and thus killing ourselves. When we kill out of hate, we are committing spiritual suicide."

There were stirrings and murmurs.

"Let's not fool ourselves. Our janitor Ulysses Brown was murdered. Just as with Cain and Abel, someone hatched a plot. They met Ulysses and Walter Harper in a lonely place and ambushed them. We can debate all we want to about whether Negroes should have the right to vote, but that doesn't change the fact that someone murdered Ulysses."

The rustling and murmurs grew louder.

"But we need to ask ourselves why he was murdered. It wasn't because he wanted to register to vote. That may have been the reason we tell ourselves, no doubt the reason the men who killed him told themselves, but the real reason was the same as Cain's: hatred. Ulysses Brown, a man many liked, even among us here, was killed because someone hated him. And you can be sure of a few things. One, God despises what was done to him. Two, God knows who did it. And three, if the men who killed Ulysses do not repent, they face the same fate as Cain—the curse of God. It would be better for them if a millstone were hung around their necks and they were thrown into the sea."

A general murmur broke out. MacKendrie pushed on.

"Now many of you may be saying, that's well and good for the killers, but we had nothing to do with that plot. We didn't drive out to Mount Zion Baptist Church. We didn't lie in wait. We didn't pull the trigger on that rifle. We didn't chase down Walter Harper's car and try to cover up the murder. Perhaps not. But as Jesus tells us, the man who hates his brother is just as guilty as the one who kills.

"So this is the challenge the word of God places before you and me this morning, right here. Have we been guilty of hatred? Has our envy, spite, jealousy, or prejudice caused us to hate another man? How often have we murdered another person in our hearts, even if we never used a knife or a gun to actually do the deed? The apostle John put it this way, 'Whoever says he loves God and hates his brother is a liar.' Ulysses Brown may not have been our racial brother, but he was our Christian brother. And I say that whoever killed him, if that man is sitting in a church somewhere this morning professing to love God, he is a liar!"

"You're the liar!" It came from the back, MacKendrie couldn't tell where. There were angry words he only half-heard. "Who does he think he is?" "Gone too far." "No right to say that."

Joe Stallings jumped up and edged his way to the aisle. MacKendrie watched as he took a step toward the chancel, then stopped. Stallings' face was red, and his mouth worked silently. He stared at MacKendrie, his eyes unblinking and filled with silent fury. Finally he said loudly, "You better watch your mouth, Preacher." He turned and barked, "Edna!" She scurried behind her husband as he stalked out of the sanctuary.

A stream of others followed, about half of the congregation. MacKendrie waited, mentally noting them. Gladys Ross was one, although Eli remained. The Folletts, the Whittiers and the Hendricks. To his surprise, Cathy Campbell walked out, leaving the rest of her family.

When they had filed out and some measure of peace returned, MacKendrie spoke calmly to the remnant. There was one last point, he said. God had showed mercy even to Cain. He did not take Cain's life, even though he deserved it.

"That same mercy is available to all of us, even to the ones who killed Ulysses. Perhaps some of you could convey that to our brothers and sisters who left early." He signaled to Andorra Scott, the accompanist, for the closing hymn.

The aftermath was everything he expected. The remarks from the remaining worshipers ranged from mild disapproval to a bitter "You're ruining this church." Connie Campbell tearfully said, "It was wonderful, Rev'rend." But her father sighed and said, "I hope you know what you're doing, Jim."

The phone rang constantly throughout the afternoon and into the evening. A few callers expressed admiration, regretting that they couldn't say so publicly. Some wanted to debate his interpretation of Genesis, saying there was nothing about hate in the text. One cursed him for a race mixer. The last call came after ten o'clock. Helen urged him not to answer, but MacKendrie picked up the receiver and said, "MacKendrie residence." At first there was only silence, and he said hello once or twice to make sure there was a connection. Then he heard breathing and background sounds, but whoever was on the line said nothing. He softly replaced the phone, and in response to Helen's look said, "The line was dead."

The following morning, the telephone rang only once, making Helen jump. It was John Wesley Jones, telling MacKendrie he wouldn't be able to meet him for coffee. MacKendrie detected an apologetic tone.

"This doesn't have anything to do with my sermon yesterday, does it, John?" he asked.

"Not directly, no. But you don't make it easy on your friends, Jim. From what I hear, you really put your foot in it. You sure you want to keep this up?"

"The only thing I'm sure of right now, John, is that a good man is dead, and if I don't speak up for him, nobody else will."

As the week went by, he sensed that something unusual was going on. He had been braced for tongue-lashings and worse wherever he turned, but instead there was a calm that unsettled him. As he walked around town, people returned his greetings but didn't linger to chat. Excuses were given of being in a hurry. There were nervous glances, embarrassed smiles, polite expressions barely murmured. Helen said she had noticed the same.

The following Sunday, he preached on "Blessed are the peacemakers." Attendance was a little below average, but it was as if the seasons had suddenly shifted from summer to winter. The congregation was stiff, unresponsive, in the recitation of the creed, in the singing of hymns, in flinty stares as he preached. After the service, no one spoke more than a cursory word to him. He noticed, through the open door of the vestibule, two or three knots of people on the lawn, talking.

The temperature peaked at a hundred and two on July twentieth. There were reports of an elderly lady succumbing to the heat. Diaper rash among newborns was rampant, and Vaseline sales were brisk in Campbell's pharmacy. Connie had gone to Greensboro, Cy told MacKendrie, and things were calmer at his house.

The next week, MacKendrie got a call from Monroe Harper. Walt was walking around, and the doctors decided he was strong enough to be released.

"We have a home in the Atlanta area, and we're going to take him there. We just thought you should know."

"I'm glad you did. Could I speak to Walt?"

There was a pause, then Walt Harper said, "Sir?"

"Walt, how are you feeling?"

"Pretty good, sir. My side is still sore, but they say that will go away."

"Good, good. Walt, the Campbells sent Connie to her grandparents in Greensboro for the rest of the summer. I thought it was a good idea. I have an address for you, but it sounds to me like her parents and yours aren't crazy about you two seeing each other."

The boy's voice dropped. "They can't stop us. Sooner or later, we'll see each other."

"Yes. Well. Walt, has the sheriff come to see you?"

"Yes, sir, a few days ago."

"Do you mind if I ask what you told him about the shooting?"

"Sure, I don't mind. I told him that morning I went and picked up Ulysses and we got to the church a little before nine thirty. He insisted on riding in the back because he said people wouldn't like it if they saw him riding in the front beside me. We pulled in front of the church and were just talking about the registration. I had parked facing the church, and all of a sudden I heard a bang on my left, coming from the woods. I didn't know what it was, but Ulysses started shouting at me to drive, drive. There was another bang and another, and I started the car and pulled around toward the road. Ulysses yelled for me to turn right, and just as I got on the road, I saw a man step out of the woods and point a rifle at us. It all happened so fast. I heard another bang and the window glass just went everywhere, and I thought Ulysses said something, but I was just trying to get out of there. When we were a little ways away, I asked Ulysses if he was all right. He didn't answer, so I glanced back and—"

MacKendrie said, "I know."

Harper's voice was shaky when he continued. "All I could think about was getting him to a doctor. I didn't even see them coming up behind me till they were right on me."

"Was it a pickup truck?"

"An old beat-up one. They got on my bumper and then tried to pull up beside me. I saw in my side mirror there was a fellow hanging out the passenger window with a rifle. I figured if I kept driving straight he'd get me for sure, so I swerved off the road to the right. I didn't hear the gunshot, but I think he must have shot through the car door. I felt this burning in my side, so bad I couldn't control the car. I remember coming up on the trees and stopping. I looked down, and I was bleeding. Then I saw the truck stop on the road and two men got out. I had no chance to run, so I figured I should just play dead. I smeared some blood on the seat and slumped over so they could see where I was shot. After a minute I heard someone say, right by the window, 'Looks like you got him.' The other says, 'Better make sure.' The first one said, 'Naw, if he ain't dead, he will be right quick. Let's get this car out of sight.' They opened the door and pushed me over and drove the car into the woods. I didn't dare open my eyes. I heard some rustling around and finally realized they were cutting branches and putting them over the car. After about fifteen minutes, I didn't hear them anymore. I waited a long time to make sure and was going to back the car up and drive back to town. But when I tried to sit up I was dizzy and weak. I thought I'd just rest a little to get my strength back, and I just... That's all I remember until I woke up in the hospital."

"So you never saw the men."

"Not clearly, no sir. The one with the rifle seemed kind of pudgy, but that's all I saw."

"You're a clever boy, Walt. Not many men would have had that much presence of mind."

"I didn't really think, you know?"

There was a brief silence. "Walt, I want to know something. Samuel Evans tells me that the night before you and Ulysses were shot, he and his family were threatened. He said he tried to warn you not to go to Mount Zion."

"Warn me? I never heard anything."

"He said he drove to the place where you were staying and you weren't there."

There was a pause. "No, I wasn't."

"You were with Connie, weren't you?" Harper didn't answer. "Walt, it doesn't matter. Just tell me the truth, son."

"Yes, sir, I was."

"All right. Don't worry, I won't say anything."

"Thanks, sir. I have to go. Could I get Connie's address?"

TWELVE

There was a slow decline in attendance, and in contributions. As he walked around town, he began to imagine he was the object of smirks, whispers, silent nods in his direction. At the bank, there was a problem with his paycheck. Funds wouldn't be available for a day or two, sorry for the inconvenience. Helen went to the grocery store and noticed she was overcharged for a roast, but when she complained, the manager coolly said the price had just gone up. A tail light on the car turned up broken one day, and the garage said they didn't have the bulb to replace it. A deputy stopped MacKendrie and gave him a ticket.

"Ten dollars!" Helen exclaimed, when MacKendrie told her how much the ticket cost. "Just for a tail light? Oh, Jim. They're turning against us, aren't they?"

"Some are, I suppose. It might be just a string of bad luck." He wiped his forehead. It was only ten in the morning, but the house was stifling.

"Maybe so," she said, without conviction. "Can you stay here with the girls for a little? I really need to have my hair done."

"Sure, dear. Anything to keep you looking beautiful."

She grinned. "That's enough of that, you. I'll be back in time to fix lunch."

He went into the girls' room and found Dottie reading and Priss playing with dolls. He sat down on the bed next to Dottie. "What are you reading, punkin?"

"Nancy Drew," she said, not looking up from the book.

"Oh, yes, the girl detective. She's pretty smart. Always figures out the mystery."

"I wish she was real."

"Why's that?" he asked, amused.

"So she could catch who killed Ug."

MacKendrie drew in his breath, then said, "Oh, honey, me too."

He went downstairs and dialed the number to the sheriff's office. A receptionist put him through to Hoolie Dixon.

"What can I do for you, Preacher?"

"I won't keep you but a minute, Sheriff, but I talked to Walter Harper the other day just before they released him from the hospital. He said you'd come to talk to him."

"Yessir. Had no idea he was Monroe Harper's boy. How about that?"

"Yes. Helen was thrilled to meet him. I just wondered if he gave you anything to go on."

"Well, afraid not. He told us what happened, gave us a partial description of those boys did the shootin', but it wasn't much."

"Walt said it was a beat-up pickup. And you've got the shell casing. That's something, anyway."

"Yeah, that's something. But you have any idea how many beat-up blue pickups there are around here, owned by fellas with .30-.30s? Be like trying to find the right frog in a frog pond. We'll keep on it, but it's gonna take some time."

As he hung up the phone, MacKendrie realized that Walt Harper had said nothing about the color of the truck.

Some of the farmers began to give up on their crops and plow under the withered tobacco plants that had managed to come up. Others desperately took to hauling in water, but it was a losing battle. As August crawled along, the heat was a prison they could not escape from.

One afternoon, John Wesley Jones showed up at his office.

"I didn't want to use the phone," he said. "Too many ears around."

"That sounds mysterious."

"Jim, you know folks are still mad at you."

"I figured they were, but nobody's talking to me. Helen and I are kind of getting the cold shoulder."

"Well, I think it's worse than that. Did you know about the meeting?"

"What meeting?"

"A secret meeting. Some of your congregation, and from what I hear, about half your elders. Met at somebody's home one evening last week."

"How'd you hear about this?"

Jones grinned. "Oh, you know. I hear things. Friend of a friend, that kind of thing." The grin disappeared. "Jim, this is serious. When these secret meetings start, it's real trouble. You might want to start thinking about another church. Pronto."

"What?" He stared at Jones in disbelief. "Just walk away? No. Even if I could find another position, it's..." He stood and walked a couple of paces. "It's cowardly. I can't do it, John."

"Jim, I've seen this before. It all goes downhill and there's no stopping it. If you won't do it for yourself, do it for your family. Your kids." MacKendrie gave him a sharp glance. "Oh, yes. They won't be left out of it." MacKendrie hunched forward, his face creased. "Talk it over with Helen, okay?" Jones stood up to leave.

"Sure, John, sure. Listen, do you know who was at this meeting?"

"No, but I know it was held at Percy Weir's place."

MacKendrie said nothing to Helen, but Jones's intelligence was right as usual. A few days later, as he sweated in his stifling study, he heard footsteps in the sanctuary and three men appeared at the door. It was Weir, Eli Ross, and Graham Guthrie, an assistant manager at First State Bank and the church treasurer, all wearing tense faces. Ross spoke.

"Jim? We'd like to have a word with you."

MacKendrie stood and eyed them. "Gentlemen, it would be a bit cramped in here. Let's go into the sanctuary." The three sat in a front-row pew and MacKendrie made them wait while he went to the back and turned on the overhead fans. He pulled out a chair to face them. "I suppose you're here to inform me what you've decided in those meetings of yours."

The men exchanged startled glances. He had them off-balance for a moment, but Ross said, "So you heard about that. Some of us are concerned about the way things are going, Jim." MacKendrie said nothing. "So...we just, ah..." He trailed off.

Weir nudged Guthrie. "The figures aren't good, Pastor MacKendrie." He extracted a ledger from a leather briefcase, opened it to a marked page, and peered at it. "Our income is down a little under twenty percent from last year at this time." He paused and looked up.

"I assume the drought has something to do with that," MacKendrie said mildly.

"I'm sure, although the last month we've seen about a forty percent drop in contributions," Guthrie continued. "Our balance is down to about five hundred dollars at the moment, which will barely get us through the month."

The men stared at MacKendrie.

"Well, we should pray that the Lord will provide," MacKendrie said. He waited, but no one spoke. "If there's nothing else, gentlemen..."

Ross stirred. "Jim, people are threatening to leave the church."

"Who is?"

"I've gotten five letters so far." As clerk of the Session, Ross was in charge of correspondence. MacKendrie prompted him for names, and Ross looked up at the ceiling, counting them off.

MacKendrie frowned. "None of those families are what I would call active members of the congregation."

"No, but they've been part of this church for a long time, and if they leave this church would be diminished." MacKendrie didn't reply.

"From what I hear, Pastor," Guthrie said, "there are a lot more that aren't going to bother resigning. They're just going to stop coming. And where does that leave us?"

"You mentioned four names," MacKendrie said to Ross. "Who's the fifth?" Ross's head turned to Weir, who let go of his suspenders and raised his hand a few inches. "I see." He leaned forward, put his elbows on his knees, and looked straight at Weir. "Your family's been part of this church a long time, Percy. You're going to leave just like that?"

Weir nodded and said slowly, "Yeah, we been here a long time. Daddy's money just about built half this building. But he wouldn't have put up with what's been going on here lately. And I ain't either." He crossed his legs. "Course, don't have to be that way."

Here we go, MacKendrie thought. "What do you mean?"

"I'd take back my letter and the others would too, if..."

"If?"

"I think you know."

"Spell it out for me." He was going to force them to say it.

"Be best if you was to resign, Pastor," Weir drawled.

MacKendrie looked down and shook his head.

"Jim, what did you expect?" Ross let out. "After that little performance the Sunday after Ug was shot? Did you really think you could just go on after that?"

"I know there are hard feelings about Ug and the sermon..."

"It's more than hard feelings, Jim," Ross said. "We all know this is about race relations. That sermon of yours just told everyone you're not on our side anymore." Guthrie and Weir nodded.

"I'm not on anyone's side here, Eli. I've tried to stay out of politics, you all know that. Unlike some other preachers here in town, I've never said a word from the pulpit about a party, a candidate, or an issue. And I don't know as I've changed my mind about Negroes voting, either, especially after what's just happened. No, gentlemen, as I said in my sermon, this is a simple matter of justice. A crime was committed against a fellow Christian, and it's our obligation to say that it was wrong and demand that the authorities find and arrest the murderers."

"And what if Hoolie don't find 'em?" Weir asked.

MacKendrie regarded him for a moment, then turned to Ross. "Do you think I should go, Eli?"

Ross folded his arms. "You've been a good pastor, Jim, but you might as well have taken a hammer to the stained glass windows. There's been damage, and I don't know as it can be repaired. For the good of the church..." He shrugged.

MacKendrie nodded, then sat up straight. "Gentlemen, I answered a call from the Lord to come here, and I'm not going to leave unless I have a sign that my work here is done. Besides, you know the way our system works. I can't just leave, even if I wanted to."

Weir squinted at him. "You want a sign? How clear's it have to be?"

The question hung in the humid air. Guthrie and Ross looked at Weir, who shook his head. They stood, and MacKendrie did the same.

"Jim, please think about this," Ross said. "Think about your family."

MacKendrie's eyes narrowed. "You're the second man to say something to me about the welfare of my family." As the three turned to leave, he said sharply, "Percy. I'd like to have a word with you in private."

The others hesitated, but Weir waved them off. When they were gone, he looked expectantly at MacKendrie.

"I had an interesting conversation with Connie the other day," MacKendrie began.

A sour look crossed Weir's face. "That crazy girl. You want to know who's responsible for Ug's shooting, it was as much her fault as anyone's and I told Cathy and Cy that."

"It just so happens I agree with you." Seeing Weir's surprise, he said, "But not for the reason you mean. You see, Connie said she told her parents when and where Walter and Ulysses would be the morning they were going to come to town to register. Now, we all know how Cathy likes to talk."

Weir reached up to grasp his suspenders, watching MacKendrie keenly. "Can't say I see your point."

"What I think, Percy, is that no one was supposed to get hurt that morning. Let's just say that Cathy gets to talking about where Walt and Ulysses were supposed to meet Evans. Some folks worry that maybe the county clerk won't be able to put them off and decide they need to be discouraged more persuasively. Evans gets a visit from some night riders at his house. Then somebody suggests a potshot or two at Walt's car the next morning out at Mount Zion would save everybody a lot of trouble. Not aiming to kill them, just scare them off. Maybe even get Walt Harper out of town and away from Connie. Only things get out of hand. Whoever gets tapped to fire a few rounds is a little too enthusiastic about the job and thinks why not just put a permanent end to this Negro voting business. Two dead bodies would send a pretty powerful message to anyone else thinking about it. But they didn't count on Walt Harper surviving, and they didn't know his father is a famous singer. One sentence from Monroe Harper on the radio, thanking people for their concern about his son, would be all it would take for the newspapers from half the South descending on Kirkwell. That would be mighty uncomfortable for the town's leading citizens."

The fans whirred overhead in the silence, and after a moment or two, Weir rocked back on his heels. "Quite a little theory," he said at last. "Always thought you had a real imagination, Preacher. Buuut—" he glanced down at his shoes, then looked up at MacKendrie with a grin—"I don't think we'll have to worry much about a bunch of attention from outside town. You see, Pastor, the businessmen that pay for Monroe Harper's shows, they're sensible. They know what folks like to hear when they tune in to hear him sing, and it ain't got nothing to do with coloreds voting." He lowered his voice. "And folks around here aren't gonna pay much attention to crazy ideas about who put who up to what." He slowly took a pack of cigarettes out of his pocket, fished in it before pulling one out, and stuck it in his mouth. He held the gold-plated lighter in his hand. "Take my advice, Pastor." He flicked the lighter into a flame and touched it to the end, making the brown tobacco flare and glow red. He blew the smoke up toward the ceiling. "Best for ever'one if you and your family just moved along. You're a little too smart for your own good." He knocked the ash off his cigarette as he turned away.

MacKendrie walked home through the shimmering heat. Pacing, he told Helen what had happened.

"Oh, Jim, how could they? This isn't just petty bickering. They're forcing you out without any kind of vote."

He shook his head. "The influential people in Kirkwell have decided I need to go, and they'd rather not wait to observe the niceties."

Helen took a deep breath. "Jim, I know you're in the right, but shouldn't we think about leaving? They're too strong, and you're all alone in this." Her voice broke. "I'm worried."

He took both her hands in his. "Me, too. Yes, we will need to leave, and probably soon. But I won't just walk away."

The next day he called Elmer Land, the stated clerk of Cape Fear Presbytery. MacKendrie regarded him as a sage. He had seen every imaginable problem a minister could deal with.

"I gather things are not good in Kirkwell," Land said. After MacKendrie described the events of the past few weeks, he said, "Well, Jim, I don't say you were wrong preaching that sermon. I just wonder if you were taking things out on your own people. We have to be careful about that kind of thing, you know."

"Elmer, you may be right, but people around here just saw it as a black man getting what was coming to him. But he was a fellow believer, murdered in cold blood, and I wasn't going to stand for it."

"And now they're after you?"

"There were some secret meetings, and now they want me to resign. Just leave, no vote of the church, nothing like that."

Land sighed. "It wouldn't be the first time. What do you want to do?"

"Elmer, I need a way out. Are there any openings you know of, here or anywhere else? I'd like to find another place as soon as possible."

"Well, the quick answer is no. All the pulpits of any size in our presbytery are filled. Only thing we've got is supply work, and that won't pay your bills. Now I can call around. You ought to do the same."

"All my connections were in the mission field. The ones stateside are on the west coast."

"Jim, I've seen these things wreck a man, ruin his family. I'd surely hate to see that happen to you."

"It's not going to, Elmer," MacKendrie said firmly. "It's wearing on us, but Helen's strong, and that's keeping me going."

Too upset to settle back down to study, he put on his coat and walked toward downtown with no particular purpose in mind. A Coke would taste good, he thought, and headed for Campbell's, which had a fountain. The bell on the door rang as he walked in, and he saw Eli Ross sitting at the counter, talking quietly but seriously with Cathy Campbell, who stood behind the counter, leaning forward on her hands. When they saw him, they stopped and looked at him warily. He briefly considered turning and walking out, but he strode forward and took the seat beside Ross.

"Good afternoon, folks," he said, as friendly as he could manage.

"Well, looky who's here," Cathy said, with barely a smile.

"How have you been, Cathy?"

"Aw, we're doing just fine, Pastor, just fine," she said flatly. How's Connie?"

Cathy Campbell's mouth stretched into a line. "She's doing fine at her granddad's place."

"Good, good, give her my regards." She said nothing. He turned to Ross. "Hello, Eli."

"Hi, Jim."

Cathy moved a cloth around on the counter. "What can I do for you?"

"I'll have a Coke, please."

She looked a Ross, who gave her a slight nod. "It's on me, Cathy."

As she pulled out a glass, MacKendrie said, "That's good of you, Eli. Thanks."

Cathy set the foaming glass down in front of him and said, "If y'all will excuse me, I've got some work to do in the back." She barged through the swinging half-door at the end of the counter.

"How have you been, Eli?"

"Oh, fine. I think the question is how you've been."

"We're managing," he said firmly. He wasn't about to show weakness. He waited for Ross to speak.

"Have you thought about what we said yesterday?"

"Of course I have."

"And?"

MacKendrie sighed. "I'm going to need a little time, Eli."

Ross shook his head. "Every day you stay is just going to make it worse."

"I am not going to leave with a tarnished reputation."

"It's been tarnished already by that sermon of yours."

"You know what I mean. I will not be made a coward and a quitter."

Ross said, "Well now, I never thought you were a quitter. That's kind of why we're in this situation."

"What do you mean?" Ross shook his head. "I see the handwriting on the wall. But I will not slink out of town in the night. I think I'm owed a dignified departure."

Ross smiled. "Heard a story once about a fella bein' run out of town tarred and feathered and put up on a rail. He said, 'If it weren't for the honor of it, I'd have just as soon taken the bus.'" MacKendrie's expression was blank. "Dignity can be a luxury for fellas in trouble, Jim."

"I hope that wasn't a threat," MacKendrie said in a tight voice.

He stood to leave and realized he hadn't even touched his Coke.

THIRTEEN

After church on Sunday, MacKendrie gathered the elders and informed them of his intention to leave in a month's time. There would need to be a congregational meeting to approve the resignation, but that could wait, he said. The men nodded and murmured it was for the best. Ross offered an embarrassed apology. "For how it all turned out."

Three days passed without incident. Helen began looking for boxes to start packing belongings. Dottie declared she didn't care if people were mad at them and wanted to leave right away. MacKendrie felt relief that the pressure was gone, but the future was a void. There was no place for his family to go, and his prayers felt more and more futile.

As July came to an end with no rain in sight, there were rumors that some farms were in danger of foreclosure.

In his study at the church, MacKendrie got a call from Elmer Land.

"Jim, I may have something for you. You know Lawrence Pope over at Bronson? Well, he had a heart attack a couple of days ago. Oh, he's gonna recover, but he told me he's decided to retire rather than go back to the pulpit, and I think that's the right thing for him. That's a fine little church there, and I think they'd like to talk to you. Could work out for everyone."

When MacKendrie told Helen, he said he felt sheepish.

She said, "For heaven's sake, why?"

"I guess I didn't trust God to get us through this."

"Oh, honey. I didn't want to say it, but I didn't either."

He would keep the news to himself until he talked to the elders in Bronson. Taking the afternoon off, he helped Helen sort through belongings in preparation for moving. It was nearly dusk when the phone jangled. There was an agitated voice on the other end.

"Pastor MacKendrie? It's Jeremiah Brown. I didn't know who else to call."

"Jeremiah, what—what is it?"

"There was—it was an accident, or, or it was—I didn't really hit her."

"Slow down, son. Start at the beginning."

Brown was driving a delivery truck for a local store owner. There was a glare on the windshield and he didn't see a woman—a white woman, he said—stepping into the street. He swerved at the last second, and she fell on the pavement. He stopped and helped her up, but she cursed at him, and a crowd of whites quickly gathered and started shouting that he had deliberately tried to run her down. One or two men tried to grab him, but Brown managed to get away.

"Sir, I'm at the store now, and there's a crowd of men out there. I swear I didn't hit that lady, but I'm afraid they're going to come in and get me."

"Is there any way you can escape?"

"No, sir. Please, I need your help!"

MacKendrie paused. "Hold on for a second." He stood with the receiver against his chest. He knew his next words would be fateful. There was no time to think or even to pray. He lifted the phone to his ear. "Where is the store?" Brown gave him the address. "All right, stay there."

He broke the connection and dialed the sheriff's office. The rings went unanswered. He glanced at his watch. It was after five.

He hung up the phone and stood without moving.

"Jim?" Helen was pale.

"There's trouble." He went to her. "I have to go."

She was trembling, said nothing, but nodded.

"Listen, keep the doors locked and the lights low. Don't answer the door unless it's me or the authorities. I'll be back soon."

Before he got in the car, on impulse, he grabbed an electric camp lantern from the garage. The store was south of the courthouse, a section of town where black homes and businesses clustered. MacKendrie had been this way only once or twice. It was not quite dark but getting hard to see. As he rounded a corner, he found the store. A block away, spilling into the street, about fifteen men were milling around. MacKendrie pulled up at the curb near the store and stepped out. He saw heads turn and stare at him. The hubbub died down.

In an instant, he was back in China. It was the twenties, and warlords were fighting for control of the country. Bai Miao was held by the forces of General Zhi, but a rival, Chun, wanted the strategic spot and besieged the city. Artillery and machine gun fire blasted at the walls. The mission station and hospital, outside the city gates, were considered sanctuaries, and MacKendrie was constantly on duty, screening refugees. One of Zhi's officers appeared and asked to be escorted to the hospital. The general wished to give money to his wounded soldiers.

The other missionaries advised against it, but MacKendrie told the officer to walk behind him slowly and remain silent, no matter what. Holding up a white handkerchief, he stepped into the road. The hospital was a quarter-mile away, and before they had gone a hundred yards, thirty men stood up behind a low wall and aimed rifles at them. MacKendrie heard the bolts click. He stood still, signaling for the officer to do the same. After a few moments, a young man in a uniform with the badge of Chun's army on his sleeve approached MacKendrie. He demanded to know who they were and where they were going.

MacKendrie said carefully that he was escorting a man sent by General Zhi to give greetings and encouragement to the wounded at the hospital. "I humbly ask that you allow me to take him there."

The young officer looked contemptuously at Zhi's man. He said, "I will allow it, if you return with him this same way." He stalked back to his cadre.

As they walked slowly, slowly toward the hospital, the soldiers taunted Zhi's officer. "Coward!" "Come out and fight us!" "You hide behind this white devil like a woman!" But no one fired a shot. When the money had been distributed and it was time to return to the mission station, MacKendrie cautiously looked down the road. Chun's soldiers were gone.

Now, as MacKendrie stood beside his car, he decided not to wait for these men to make the first move. He retrieved the lantern, switched it on, and walked toward the mob. As he got closer, he saw that some of them had clubs and staves. Most were wearing hats, their faces hidden in shadow. When he was within ten paces, he saw Dick Follett near the front of the uneven line. His hands were empty, but there was an unmistakable bulge in his pants pocket. MacKendrie made straight for him, stopped a few feet away, and held up the lantern. Follett squinted at the brightness, his face a mixture of anger and astonishment. No one spoke.

"Good evening, Dick." Follett only stared. MacKendrie looked left and right. "It looks like you and your friends here are upset. I hope you're not thinking about doing anything foolish."

Someone a few rows back shouted, "That nigger tried to kill Eunice Thornton!" It woke the crowd. There was a clamor of angry shouts. MacKendrie held up his hand and tried to talk, but they ignored him and kept shouting. "You better go home, Preacher!" "Stay out of this!" There was a momentary lull, and MacKendrie raised his voice.

"Did Eunice Thornton call the sheriff?" The hubbub died down. "Did Hoolie Dixon come out to arrest anyone? If there was a crime, the police need to handle it. You men are taking the law into your own hands!"

"We don't need the sheriff!" The clamor returned, angrier now. "We know how to handle his kind!" "We ain't gonna let you get him off this time!"

Several men in the front row moved forward, and MacKendrie involuntarily took a step back. But he swung around to Follett, blocked his path, and said loudly, "What about you, Dick Follett?" The men who had moved forward paused at the sound of the name, and the shouts fell to a grumble.

Follett regarded MacKendrie. "What about me, Pastor?"

MacKendrie found himself angry. "I know you, Dick! You fought for your country! You're a leader in this town. For God's sake, man, don't throw that away!"

For a moment Follett didn't reply, but then he said in a low voice, "I ain't throwing nothing away. You're the one doing that."

The faces reflected in the light were sullen, and the low grumble was starting to escalate again. Follett turned and was about to give a signal for the mob to move forward, and MacKendrie realized they were on the point of running over him.

"Just a minute!" Follett glanced back at him. "Dick, come with me! The rest of you men, stay here!" No one moved. "Dick, are you coming or not?"

Frowning, Follett stepped forward. "What you doing?"

MacKendrie turned his back to the crowd so that only Follett could hear. "You don't know what's in that store. Maybe they have guns. Some of these friends of yours could get shot. If you come with me, we can solve this without anyone getting hurt."

Moments passed. "All right, Pastor, but that boy ain't getting away with this." Follett turned to the mob. "Y'all wait here!"

MacKendrie led Follett across the street. The store was dark, but he banged on the door. "This is Jim MacKendrie! Open up!" Silence. He banged again. "Jeremiah! Open the door!"

A light appeared in a window, and a lock clicked. The door creaked open, and a middle-age black man peered out. "You is Pastor Mac?" He looked nervously at Follett.

"Yes. We need to talk to Jeremiah. It's all right. Tell him he can stand right here in the door."

The man disappeared, the door opened, and Jeremiah Brown stood in the doorway, his right hand holding a revolver. He looked from one to the other. "I ain't gonna let them take me, Pastor." Follett tensed.

"Easy, son," MacKendrie said. "You're not hurt, are you?"

Eyeing Follett, Brown said slowly, "No, sir."

"Jeremiah, there's no need for guns." He turned to Follett. "Suppose I take him in to the sheriff first thing tomorrow. I promise, this time I'll let Hoolie handle it."

Brown said, "You'd turn me in! You know what they'll do!"

Follett retorted, "They'll put you where you belong, boy!"

"That's enough, both of you!" MacKendrie said. "Jeremiah, what choice do you have? If I walk away now, you know what'll happen. If I take you to the sheriff, you have a chance to tell your side of the story. If Eunice Thornton wasn't hurt, there's not much of a case. And you'd still be alive." He turned to Follett. "What do you say, Dick?"

Follett looked at Brown and suddenly grinned. "Sure. Why not? Long as you just drop him off at the sheriff's and let it be."

MacKendrie said, "Jeremiah? Son, don't make this any worse."

Brown looked over at the still-grinning Follett and then at the mob across the street. He shook his head. "That's my jury over there. I'm sorry, sir."

He disappeared inside and the door slammed. Follett started to sprint across the street, shouting over his shoulder at MacKendrie, "Get out of here!"

It only took a few seconds after Follett reached the mob. They surged toward the store, yelling and cursing like banshees. MacKendrie hadn't moved, but now he was roughly pushed away by a succession of hands and bodies. The men set upon the store with their clubs, smashing the front window. A percussive *bang* caused everyone to flatten, but only for a moment. MacKendrie saw muzzle flashes as shots were unleashed into the store. A man ran up with something burning. A streak of flame sailed straight into the store, and a great cheer went up. The men started falling back, waiting, shouting, and within minutes smoke started pouring out of the broken window, followed shortly by flames.

The store owner came out first, running, his hands up in the air. One of the mob ran to meet him, club in hand, and MacKendrie watched in shock as one blow, two, three, struck the man down. In an instant, the fallen man was surrounded by a knot of kicking, sweating, swearing men, striking him with fists, feet, and clubs. MacKendrie was about to rush to the man's aid when Jeremiah Brown staggered through the front door of the store, coughing, his shirt smoking. There was a moment's pause, then a roar as the mob started for him. Brown didn't run but raised his hand holding the pistol. A volley of bullets reached him before he could aim. The impacts spun him around, and he fell face down.

A low-throated sound—humming? growling? no, laughter, MacKendrie decided—rose from the mob, which advanced, avoiding the heat from the store, by now a bonfire. They stood around Brown, insulting him, mocking him, as if death were no barrier to their rage.

"Let's take him and string him up!" someone shouted. There was a chorus of "Yeah!" and the circle began to close around the body when MacKendrie pushed aside someone in front and walked to where Brown lay. He knelt down, turned Brown over, and checked his pulse. Then he placed his palm over the face and bent his head, eyes closed, lips moving. He stood and faced the circle, their faces illuminated by flickering light from the fire. The heat in their eyes was almost greater than the flames next door.

"He's dead," MacKendrie announced. The low sound died away, and the men stood silent now. "You've done what you came to do. It's over." No one moved. MacKendrie's anger flared. "No one's going to touch this man! You got what you wanted, now go home, all of you!"

Glances were exchanged. One turned away. Then another. Within minutes, MacKendrie was alone with the remains of Jeremiah Brown. In the distance, he heard a siren.

He reached home about ten. He was calm, a little too calm, as he briefly told Helen that Brown had refused to surrender, fired first, and was killed by the mob. That was what he had told Hoolie Dixon as well, refusing to go into details or name names. Neither Dixon nor Helen believed he had told everything, but both accepted it without question. Dixon said, "Well, Preacher, you're the only witness we got." Helen wept, and said only, "This awful place."

MacKendrie sent her to bed and stayed awake for a long time, sitting in a chair in the living room. He thought about the guns sitting in a locked case in his study.

The next morning, Helen found him asleep in the chair and was frightened by his reaction when she touched his shoulder.

MacKendrie leapt up with a shout, his arms flailing. He was still panting as she pulled him into her arms to quiet him.

"What's going to happen to us?" she quavered.

"Nothing's going to happen to us." He was decisive now. "Try to act as normal as possible with the girls. After breakfast, take them to Wilmington for the day. Go shopping, go to a movie, anything to keep them occupied. No—" he anticipated her objection. "I need to stay here to talk to a couple of folks. After you get back, we'll talk about what to do."

After they drove away, he called the sheriff, who sounded exasperated. "You get yourself into more trouble than any preacher I ever met."

MacKendrie asked about the store owner.

"Ol' Zeke? Well, he was in pretty bad shape. Probably ain't gonna be the same." Dixon paused. "And you say you didn't recognize none of those fellas last night?"

"Let's just say there were some familiar faces, but I couldn't give you any names."

"Hm. Well, that may save us all a lot more trouble."

"Sheriff, it sounded to me like there were several different guns that shot at Jeremiah."

"Yeah. Had about four holes in him. Looked like different size bullets."

"Including a .30-.30?"

"Might've been. Have to wait and see what the coroner says. Looky here, Preacher, I can't tell you what to do, but if I was you, I'd get myself and my family out of town soon as possible. Those boys that killed Brown might come after you."

"I know. I'm going to send my wife and daughters some place safe. I have to stick around a few more days."

He busied himself by packing things into boxes. About mid-morning, he heard the low sound of a truck engine. Standing back from the front window, he saw a recent-model pickup, bright blue with gray trim, idling in the street. He couldn't make out the driver. The truck sat there for a few minutes, then slowly moved off. An hour later, the truck reappeared, this time cruising slowly past.

In the afternoon, he walked to the church, carrying a couple of empty boxes. He noticed that on the surface, things seemed to be carrying on as usual, but people were subdued, spent. No one returned his waves.

Just as he reached the door to the sanctuary, he saw the blue and gray truck parked a block away in front of the Pine Bough Café. Dropping the boxes, he walked over to the truck and was looking it over when Joe Stallings walked out of the café, keys in hand. He looked like a bumpkin on his way to his own wedding. His hair had been cut in a whitewall with what was left on top slicked down and parted, and he was clean-shaven. He wore a fresh white shirt and a gold ring flashed on the middle finger of his left hand. A mixture of cologne and cigar smoke hit MacKendrie's nostrils. Stallings blinked at the sight of MacKendrie, and he gave a crooked grin.

"Well, howdy there, Preacher."

"Hello, Joe. You look pretty spiffy today. What brings you to town?"

Stallings shrugged. "Just business."

"And a nice new truck, too. You must have figured out a way to beat the drought."

"Maybe I'm smarter than you give me credit for," Stallings said defiantly.

"Joe, one thing I never thought was that you were stupid. Foolish sometimes, but not stupid." Stallings tensed. MacKendrie ran a hand over the truck's fender. "How'd you manage this? Last time we talked, you were afraid the bank would take your farm."

Stallings shifted his feet. "I don't know that's any your business."

MacKendrie played a hunch. "Percy didn't have anything to do with this, did he? Did he give you an offer on your place? Maybe one too good to pass up?"

Stallings started, and for a second, MacKendrie thought he was going to take a swing. "Who told— How the hell—" he bellowed. His face was flushed, and he stared, then he slowly relaxed and the grin returned to his face.

MacKendrie pressed his advantage. "What I wonder is why Percy would want your place. Why would he be so generous to you? Unless maybe you did him a favor. Must have been a mighty important favor."

Stallings' grin slowly faded and he looked straight ahead.

"Well, as you say, that's none of my business," MacKendrie said casually, stepping away. "Still, you know how folks talk. By the way, was that you driving by the manse earlier?"

"Aw, I just wanted to make sure y'all was all right. Can't be too careful these days, you know. Specially with these riots going on." His grin returned. "Your wife and them girls of yours, they's mighty pretty. Better keep an eye on 'em."

MacKendrie walked back to the manse. Helen and the girls returned at four, and he took her arm, guided her into the bedroom and closed the door. She emerged five minutes later, her face wooden, and ordered Dottie and Priss to pack suitcases. She was taking them on a bus trip to see their Aunt Lily in Virginia. Priss was excited, but Dottie was suspicious.

"Why aren't you coming, Daddy?"

"I just have to stay here a few days, and then I'll come and join you," he promised.

She burst into tears. "I don't want to go! I want you to come too!" Helen put her hands over her face.

With a supreme effort, MacKendrie kept his emotions in check and smiled. He knelt before the girls, took one of their hands in each of his, and shushed Dottie. "It's all, right girls, my dear girls. You like to visit Aunt Lily, don't you?" They nodded, sniffling. "Sure, you do. There will be lots for you to do there. And soon we'll be back together."

When MacKendrie returned from the bus station about nine o'clock, the house was dark and quiet. He put a record on the stereo and, feeling a bit foolish, sang along loudly with Nelson Eddy: *"Give me some men who are stout-hearted men, who will fight for the right they adore..."*

He went into his study and unlocked the gun case.

FOURTEEN

It was late afternoon when Harry Cohen pulled into the drive of the—what had MacKendrie called it?—the "manse." There had been no one at the church, and he just remembered the way to the house. The response to his repeated knocking was a long pause and a muffled voice from inside.

"Who's there?"

"Mac? It's me, Harry." Another pause. "Harry Cohen."

There was rattling as locks were undone, the door opened a quarter, and MacKendrie peeked around the edge. "Harry, what in God's name are you doing here?"

"Hi, Mac. Sorry to just drop in like this, but something's come up. Can I come in?"

MacKendrie stared, not moving, until Cohen began to shift his feet. He said curtly, "This isn't a good time, Harry."

"This won't take long."

MacKendrie still didn't move. Finally, he relaxed and opened the door. To Cohen's surprise, he saw MacKendrie holding upright a shotgun that had been concealed by the door.

"Mac, what the hell is going on?"

"Come in, Harry."

MacKendrie couched the gun in the crook of his arm, snapping on the safety, and led Cohen into the living room. He laid the weapon on a bureau.

"Mac?"

MacKendrie motioned him to a chair and wearily recounted the past months. "I've told the elders I'm resigning, but it's way beyond that now."

"Why?"

"The riot, Jeremiah's murder...even the sheriff advised me to get out of town. Now Joe Stallings has been around, driving past the house. Gives me chills."

"One of those rubes hanging around your church the first day I showed up?"

"He may not wear a two-hundred dollar suit like you, but he's not a rube," MacKendrie snapped.

Cohen held up a hand and saw MacKendrie relax. "You think this Stallings had something to do with your janitor's death?"

"He was involved, I'm sure, but he didn't plan it. Someone else is pulling the strings."

"And the local cops?" When MacKendrie didn't answer, Cohen nodded. "I get it. Someone gives them the word and they disappear." His habit of assessment kicked in, and he began asking questions. "Where are your wife and kids? Not here?"

"No. I sent them to Helen's sister. She has a farm in Virginia."

"Why didn't you go with them?"

"I couldn't just leave, Harry. I'm waiting to hear from another church." Seeing Cohen's expression, he said, "I won't run away."

"So in the meantime you're sleeping with a shotgun next to you?" MacKendrie lifted his chin. "I don't know if you're brave, stubborn, or stupid. Maybe all three. One of the first rules of combat is if you're outnumbered and you've got a way to retreat, you take it."

"Harry, this isn't—"

"A battlefield? Looks like one to me." He paused. "Why don't you get in my car? I'll take you someplace safe."

MacKendrie appeared to waver but said, "No. Somehow I need to finish this."

Cohen shook his head. "You're the one that's going to be finished." He stood up. "All right. I need to move my car somewhere out of sight. Then I need to use your phone."

MacKendrie stood. "Why, what...what are you doing?"

"I'm sticking around. You need help." As if a thought just occurred to him, he reached inside his coat, pulled out a revolver, and opened the cylinder, checking it.

MacKendrie's eyes were wide. "Harry! You can't...this isn't..."

"Isn't my fight? It is now. You think I'd run out on you? Navy men have to stick together," he said with a grin, replacing the gun in his shoulder holster. "Besides, you're too valuable. I need you."

"Need me?" MacKendrie was still trying to grasp what was happening. "For what?"

But Cohen, car keys in hand, was out the door. He was all purpose and command now, in a theater of operations. He had been in quiet office suites and conference rooms for so long, he had forgotten the taste of adrenaline. Now he surveyed the house's interior strategically, ordered MacKendrie to help rearrange a table here, a stuffed chair over there, figuring entrance points, angles of attack.

"Who else has keys to this place?" he demanded.

MacKendrie stammered, "Uh, well...the clerk of Session, I think..."

"Who's that?"

"Eli. Eli Ross."

"Ross. I remember him. You trust him?"

MacKendrie hesitated. "Yes, but...I don't really have any friends around here right now. But he wouldn't..."

"All it would take is him handing that key to someone else." When MacKendrie looked shocked, Cohen said, "Can't help it. I get paid to think like the enemy."

Twilight was slowly settling over Kirkwell as Cohen decided they were ready. MacKendrie scrounged in the kitchen and came out with sandwiches and coffee. They ate in silence until Cohen broke it.

"Why'd you leave China, Mac?"

MacKendrie stopped in mid-chew. "That's a strange question to ask right now."

"We've got time. C'mon. How come? It was sudden, right?"

MacKendrie leaned forward. "How do you know that?" Then, "Don't answer. You've been checking on me. Now you need to fill in a gap in your files, is that it?"

Cohen shrugged. "Did the commies threaten you?"

MacKendrie looked at Cohen for a long while. "No. It wasn't the Communists. Nothing that dramatic. It was more...personal."

"It had to do with that kid, didn't it? Wang? The one you called Paul?"

MacKendrie nodded. "There were rumors."

"That you were his father?"

MacKendrie paused. "His mother came to the church in Bai Miao. Her husband was a brute. He died just as she found out she was pregnant. I tried to help her and the boy, that's all."

"Who started the rumors?"

Irritated, MacKendrie stood up and paced. "It was all just jealousy, Harry, nothing more."

"No truth to them?"

He rounded on Cohen. "No! What do you take me for?"

"I've seen it happen. To men you'd never suspect."

MacKendrie stopped and sighed. "Yeah. I know. But I loved my wife far too much for something like that to happen."

Cohen waited, then pressed on. "So why did you leave?"

MacKendrie slowly looked up as if seeing something far off. "Hm?" He waved a hand. "Oh, it was one of the church's elders. His son and Paul both applied to a private school in Shanghai. Paul got in, the other boy didn't. The father felt dishonored. He started complaining about me to the other elders. It was better for everyone if I left."

"You took the fall? I don't get it. It wasn't your fault the kid didn't get in."

MacKendrie shook his head. "Harry, how can you have worked in the Orient as long as you have and not understand the way it works over there? The elder was a good man, but he had lost face. And in China, you can live without food easier than you can live without honor." Cohen nodded. "Anyway, it was just as well. Within two years, the Japanese invaded. And Emily got sick. Even with the care she got in the States..."

As gently as he could, Cohen said, "Cancer, wasn't it?"

Without a word, MacKendrie began collecting the plates and mugs. Cohen stood. "I need a smoke. Don't worry," he said to MacKendrie's look, "I'll do it out back. It's dark enough now that no one will see me."

The spacious den, adjacent to the kitchen, opened onto the back porch, and Cohen opened the door a few inches, looked cautiously, and stepped outside.

When he came back, MacKendrie was putting away the last of the dishes. "Okay, Mac, here's the deal. There might be more than one of them. And they probably aren't going to just knock on the front door. They'll come in the back. But just in case, you cover the front, I'll take the back. No matter what, stay put, unless you hear me say 'ten.' That's your cue to come in on my left. That way we'll flank 'em."

MacKendrie listened with alarm to Cohen's tactical briefing. He hadn't dreamed of a shootout in his den, and he felt himself shaking. Helpless, he nodded.

"Harry, what if no one shows up? What if the morning comes and we're both here just looking at each other? You can't hang around here indefinitely."

"Then I'm getting you out of here, even if I have to knock you out and throw you in my car."

MacKendrie reflected. "All right. If nothing happens, I'll pack my car and leave. You have my word."

"Good." Cohen checked his watch. "If they're coming, it'll be middle of the night. You take the first watch. I'm gonna catch a few winks." He switched off the lights, settled into a chair in the den and put his revolver on the table beside him. He tilted his head back, folded his hands, and closed his eyes.

MacKendrie stood looking at him for a moment, then picked up his shotgun. There was a wide case opening from the kitchen into the dining room, and beyond was the front hallway. He pulled a chair next to the hallway, sat down, and laid the gun across his lap.

In the long silence, MacKendrie relived the past over and over. The war. Emily's death. His son Richard. The last four months—had it only been four months? Ulysses' death, and now Jeremiah's. He had put Helen and the girls in danger. How would she manage if something happened to him? How would his girls grow up without a father? His anxiety rose to a panic. What was he thinking, inviting a murderous assault? Cohen was right, he should have left town. He should leave now.

He looked at his watch. It was not too late. He stood and walked into the den. The sound startled Cohen, who jerked and snatched up the revolver. When he saw MacKendrie, he glared.

"Goddammit, Mac, don't sneak up on me like that! I could've done those guys' dirty work for them." He replaced the gun on the table. "What time is it?"

"Eleven thirty. Sorry if I surprised you, but look, Harry, I've decided you're right. We should just go. Now. I'll settle things from some place that's safe."

Cohen stood. "That's the first smart thing you've said since I got here. Okay, get what you need, and—" He held up a hand.

MacKendrie shook his head. "What—"

"Shut up," Cohen hissed.

The slightest rustle in the back yard. MacKendrie could just sense it too—there was someone moving out there. Then there was a brief murmur of voices, not more than thirty feet away. Cohen stepped close and whispered in MacKendrie's ear. "Go back to the front and wait, just like we planned."

Panicked, he whispered back, "No, I'll talk to them! I'll tell them I'm leaving—"

Cohen gripped his arm and said in a calm, low tone, "It's too late. They won't let you leave now. Go." When he didn't move, Cohen gave him a shove and a muttered command. "Go!"

He backed away, saw Cohen in the dim light pick up his revolver and station himself behind the chair where he had been sleeping. MacKendrie went back into the dining room at the entrance to the hall. As he stood trembling, he remembered his shotgun had the safety on. He clicked it off, and his glance landed on the hall table where there was a framed photo of the family—him, Helen, and the girls, all smiling. A low anger welled up. He would not let anyone keep him from seeing them again. He gripped the gun, his Browning Auto-5, held it level, his finger inside the trigger guard, and took a deep breath.

Moments passed. Then from the den, he heard the click of the back door lock and the slight creak of the hinge as the door opened.

Silence, then a thump as someone walked into a piece of furniture.

"That's far enough." Cohen's voice, clear and firm.

A startled clatter. "Shit!"

MacKendrie wasn't surprised, but his heart sank.

Cohen said, "Hold it right there."

More thumping. The intruder was stumbling into things in the semi-dark. Then silence. "That you, Preacher?" The words were slurred and leering. When Cohen didn't answer, Joe Stallings said in a low tone, "Who the hell are you?"

Cohen said, "Just take it easy. Don't make any sudden moves."

Silence. "Where's the preacher?" Stallings demanded.

"He's safe. If I were you, I'd just go back the way you came."

More silence. Stallings was confused, but he blustered, "Not till you tell me where—" When he spoke again, it was knowing, amused. "Wait just a minute. I seen you before. You're that Jew fella. You come around here a few months back." He let out a high-pitched giggle. "Hoo-eee! The preacher got him a Jew to stand up for him." He was laughing now. "What you say, Jew-boy? You gonna stick your nose where it don't belong? Get your head blowed off?"

After a moment, Cohen said, "Why don't you move along, Stallings?"

There was more giggling. "Well, guess if I can't get a preacher, might as well get a Jew. Just one more."

MacKendrie quickly moved through the dining room to the door of the den. "Joe! Don't—"

He saw Stallings raise the rifle and swing toward him. He ducked and as the rifle blast percussed his ears, a chunk of the frame above him ripped away.

Cohen's revolver went off but Stallings pivoted easily back and fired. Cohen's left shoulder knocked back, and he spun in a circle and sagged, his left arm useless.

"Harry!"

In one motion, Stallings pulled the bolt of the rifle back and forward. A spent shell pinged on the floor. He held the rifle at waist level, glaring at Cohen, but instead of aiming, he uttered a cry of rage and started walking forward. Cohen raised his revolver and fired two rapid shots. MacKendrie saw Stallings swat at his throat as if stung by a wasp. His body seemed to relax, and the rifle slipped from his hands. He fell forward, squirmed for a moment, and was still.

Cohen slumped to the floor.

"Harry!" He had only taken a couple of steps when the hinge of the back door creaked, and Eli Ross walked in, carrying a shotgun.

The two men stared at each other and at the same instant raised their guns to their shoulders. MacKendrie saw Ross blink. Without lowering his gun, he said, "Eli. My God, what have you done?"

Ross didn't answer. He glanced right and left, taking in first the body of Joe Stallings and then the unmoving Cohen. Keeping the shotgun aimed at MacKendrie, he lowered it to chest height. "Well, now. This is quite a mess. We didn't imagine you'd bring in reinforcements."

MacKendrie kept his gun at his shoulder. "I didn't call him. He showed up unexpectedly."

Ross shrugged. "I guess we'll just have to change our story."

"Story, what story?"

"The story we tell the sheriff. 'Course ol' Hoolie would go along if I told him men from Mars had killed you with a ray gun."

MacKendrie lowered his gun to waist level, still aimed at Ross. "But it's going to be you who kills me, isn't it, Eli?"

After a moment, Ross nodded slowly. "Yes."

MacKendrie was amazed at the anguish in his own voice. "Why, Eli? Why?"

"You know why!" Ross was furious. "You know damn well! You couldn't leave things be! First there was you taking up for Ug's nephew. We could've let that go, maybe. Then Ug. Oh, you had it figured out, I give you that. We were just trying to scare off him and the Harper boy, but Joe had been drinking and there wasn't any holding him back. But once it was done, that was going to be the end of it. Then you come along with that sermon, and pestering the sheriff and what all, and when we gave you and your family the cold shoulder, you still wouldn't take the hint and leave." He paused, breathing heavily. "Then you told Percy what you knew. That was a big mistake, Jim. And that business with the Brown boy the other night. You saw Dick Follett and a dozen others there. I'm sorry, but you know we can't just let you leave now."

"You keep saying 'we.' Who else is in on this?"

Ross gave a thin smile. "Never mind about that."

There was a rustle to MacKendrie's right, and Cohen gave a low moan. As much as MacKendrie wanted to go over to him, he didn't dare move. He said, "He's still alive. Are you really going to shoot a wounded man?"

Ross's eyes flickered. He didn't answer.

"What are you going to tell the sheriff?"

Ross sighed. "Oh, I don't know. Something about how you and I were cleaning our shotguns and mine went off accidentally. We'll have to haul Joe and your friend Cohen off somewhere and let Hoolie try to figure out what happened."

"No one will believe any of that, Eli."

"Maybe not. But no one's going to make a stink about it." He sighed again. "I'm sorry, Jim." He raised the shotgun to his shoulder.

In an instant, MacKendrie did the same. He noticed the barrel of Ross's gun was wavering. The two men stood still. Ross said, "I don't think you're going to kill me, Jim."

Seconds passed, and slowly MacKendrie lowered the shotgun, couching it in the crook of his left arm, the barrel pointing at an angle down. Ross was shaken to see the calmness in his face. MacKendrie nodded. "No. I won't kill you."

Ross grimaced. "That was charitable. I told you once I wouldn't want to be on the other end of your shotgun. Goodbye, Jim."

MacKendrie watched as the barrel of the gun wavered, then jerked as Ross tried to force his aim.

Harry Cohen was drifting in and out of consciousness. He knew he was hurt, and he knew he was in danger, but he couldn't summon the strength to stay awake. He heard voices, one of them familiar...

He was jolted by two gun blasts in rapid succession and a scream of pain. Mac, he thought. Mac needs my help. He had a pistol somewhere. He willed himself to open his eyes and began groping around the floor. Then someone was standing next to him, someone holding a shotgun.

Damn, he thought. Go through a whole damn war only to wind up dead on a floor in goddamn North Carolina. He waved a hand weakly, trying to say go on, get it over with...

"Harry! Harry, can you hear me?"

MacKendrie knelt next to Cohen and examined the wound. It was in the upper left chest, serious but not critical. He fished a handkerchief from his pocket, wadded it and pressed it against the spot. Cohen jerked back and gave a sharp yelp. His eyes opened wide and he stared, blinking against the pain.

"Mac? What the hell—damn, that hurts."

"Sorry. Just trying to stop the bleeding. There."

"What—what happened? I heard—"

"Yeah. It's okay. For now. I'll fill you in later. We need to get you to a doctor. I hear sirens, so the sheriff can get an ambulance for you. Just take it easy."

Cohen relaxed but reached out and grabbed MacKendrie's arm. "Are you okay, Mac? What about—"

"I'm okay. Stallings is dead. And Eli—well, he's going to have a limp, and he's mad as a hornet, but I've got his gun and he's not going to hurt us. Just rest."

* * *

Hoolie Dixon was known for a wide smile that seemed perpetually affixed to his face, but he was not smiling as he faced MacKendrie, who was becoming agitated.

"Sheriff, he needs a doctor, now. That's a rifle wound, and he's in shock. Call in an ambulance."

Long moments passed before Dixon rumbled, "We'll get him an ambulance directly. First I want to hear what you've got to say about this...this mess."

"I'm not saying a word until you call that ambulance." When Dixon didn't respond, MacKendrie added, "It won't look very good if he dies because he didn't get medical attention."

Dixon's jaw clenched, and he shifted from one foot to the other before he turned and barked at a deputy. "Johnson! Call Haines and tell 'em to send an ambulance over here. Fact, tell 'em to send two. We're gonna need one for Joe Stallings." He glowered at MacKendrie. "All right, Preacher. Let's have it."

"Sheriff, there's just one thing all this is about, and that's the shooting of Ulysses Brown and Walt Harper. If you test Joe's .30-.30, I think you'll find it's the rifle that did it. Harry Cohen just happened to drop in on me today, and if he hadn't, it would be me lying there instead of Joe. Maybe that would have made some people happy around here, but not my wife and daughters!" His voice rose at the end, and it was his turn to glare at Dixon, whose expression didn't change.

"Go on."

"I thought they were just going to try to scare me, but Harry knew better."

"Uh huh. And you're saying this Cohen fella killed Joe in self-defense."

"Joe fired first. First at me, hit that door frame, then wounded Harry, before Harry shot him."

A deputy walked up to Dixon's shoulder. "Sheriff—"

"Not now, Johnson. And what about Eli? How'd he get that buckshot in his foot?"

"If I told you he was aiming his gun at my head, would you believe it was self-defense?"

Dixon paused, and the deputy spoke up. "Sheriff, there's—"

"Just hold your horses, Johnson. Well, I'll tell you, Preacher, I'm gonna have to arrest you both."

MacKendrie almost laughed. "On what charge?"

"In your case, aggravated assault for a start. DA may want to up that to attempted murder. In that Cohen fella's case, I believe we'll start with murder two."

MacKendrie was calm. "Sheriff, you know those charges won't hold up."

"May be. That'll be for the DA to—what *is* it, Johnson?" He rounded on the deputy, who had now wedged himself between the two men in agitation.

"Sheriff, there's two men here to see you. Says they're from the FBI."

Dixon stared at his deputy as if he hadn't understood a word. "The FBI. Now what would— Where're they at?"

Before Johnson could reply, two athletic men in black suits entered the room. One strode up to Dixon and said briskly, "Sheriff Dixon? I'm Special Agent Dan Foster with the Raleigh office of the FBI. This is Special Agent Roberts." Foster flashed an ID card.

Dixon hooked his thumbs into his belt, trying to maintain his authority. "Well, now, Mister Foster, what can I do for the FBI?"

"Special Agent, if you don't mind. We received a call that a federal officer might be involved in an incident. Captain Harry Cohen of the U.S. Navy. Is that right?"

"Well, now..."

MacKendrie broke in. "Special Agent Foster, that's Captain Cohen there. He's been wounded and needs immediate medical attention."

Foster took one glance at Cohen and rapped, "Roberts." The other man moved quickly, menacingly ordered the deputy standing over him to move aside, and knelt beside Cohen, checking his pulse.

"He's alive, but he needs help now."

Foster faced Dixon. "Sheriff, this is now a federal crime scene. We're in charge of the investigation."

MacKendrie had never seen Dixon excited, but the sheriff protested, "See here! You can't just come in and—"

Foster cut him off. "We expect you and your men to cooperate fully. First we're going to get Captain Cohen to a hospital. Do you have an ambulance on scene?"

When Dixon fumbled, MacKendrie said, "Special Agent, I'm Reverend James MacKendrie, and Captain Cohen came to see me here at my home. I've had trouble persuading the sheriff about the urgency of Harry's condition. I doubt if an ambulance will be arriving soon."

Foster turned to Roberts. "Get him in our car. You," he said, addressing the slouching deputy nearby, "give him a hand." The deputy sullenly complied after it was hinted he was obstructing a federal investigation.

Foster said, "Reverend MacKendrie, you come with us."

Dixon raised his voice, red-faced. "Now you just hold on, dammit! I'm charging this man with aggravated assault. He's my prisoner!"

Foster reached into his suit and produced a card, thrusting it into Dixon's fist. "He's a material witness in the investigation. If you want to fight over custody, call the number on that card."

Dixon stared down at the card. "Who is it?"

"The U.S. District Attorney for Eastern North Carolina. In Raleigh. Now if you don't mind, Sheriff, I'd like your men to leave this crime scene as it is. We'll be back to look it over. I'll give you a call when we're in town."

As Dixon continued to stare at the card, Foster turned to MacKendrie. "Sir? If you'll follow me."

FIFTEEN

Fall's rains had finally dispelled the drought that oppressed the eastern seaboard, and winter made the heat an unpleasant memory. MacKendrie's blind was enveloped in a cold mist.

The marshy flats of the Tidewater were not that different from eastern North Carolina. The sky was the same gray, the mid-winter air just as sharp, his Parker 12 gauge was familiar in his hands. But MacKendrie had no partner with him. When he had hunted with Eli, they used his skiff. This one was rented. Somehow his decoys—some of them expensive—had not shown up among the belongings moved out of the manse, so he was relying on luck that the ducks would come close to the blind.

Now one did, a mallard swimming twenty yards away. He waited until the duck decided to take wing, stood, tracked the bird, squeezed the trigger and felt the recoil. But he missed. After a few hours, he went home empty-handed. It was the second time this winter his hunt had been unsuccessful.

After he had stowed his gear and changed, Helen set a mug of coffee before him and asked about his morning.

"I think I'm losing my touch," he said. "Maybe I'm starting to feel my age."

"Nonsense." She sat beside him at the kitchen table. "You've said yourself, if you come home with a duck once out of every four times, you're doing well."

He didn't argue. "There's something I've been meaning to tell you." She waited. "There's a new group organizing here in Norfolk. White and Negro clergymen, a few civic leaders. They're meeting to talk about improving race relations. I intend to join them."

At first, he was afraid she would object, but she simply said, "I think that's a fine idea." She went to a side table and returned with a letter addressed to Reverend J. MacKendrie. "This arrived this morning."

It was from John Wesley Jones, who began by apologizing for not doing more to help him out of "your predicament." The letter asked about him and his family and then went on in gossipy fashion about the aftermath of that night at the manse.

"Cy and Cathy forbade Connie from returning to college in the fall, but one day in September she went missing. Her parents were frantic, naturally, and the sheriff had his deputies scour the area. Well, you guessed it, she and the Harper boy had eloped. Cathy was fit to be tied, said it'd be a cold day in the nether regions before she'd talk to them, but I suspect that'd change if there's a grandbaby to cuddle.

"Things got back to normal pretty quick after you left. You probably heard your old church has a new pastor. Young fellow right out of seminary, God bless him. Those elders are going to lead him around like a poodle on a leash. I haven't talked to Eli. Word is he stays at home a lot. No charges ever filed in Jeremiah Brown's death.

"Strangest thing was Edna Stallings. She inherited the money Joe got for his farm, and no sooner was Joe's funeral over than she sold off the rest of what they owned, rented a little place in town and just kind of came alive. Started showing up around town, joined the Garden

Club, donating to the PTA, just as gracious as you please. I said it was like a resurrection..."

He showed Helen the letter, and she became agitated.

"If there were any justice, the ground would open up and swallow that town!" she said, slapping the letter on the table.

"Now, Helen..."

Hearing her anger brought his own dangerously near the surface. He had fought it ever since he left Kirkwell, but it flitted like a moth, settling briefly here and there—on Joe Stallings, Eli Ross, Connie Campbell and Samuel Coleridge Evans, even on Ulysses Brown, for drawing him into a controversy he didn't want any part of. He hated to admit it, but most of all he was angry at God.

He looked at Helen and impassively quoted the psalm, "Fret not thyself because of him who prospereth in his way, because of the man who bringeth wicked devices to pass."

She gave a sharp look, then sighed. "I know. It just makes me mad to think about it, that's all." She had changed since they moved to Norfolk, and he couldn't decide if it was for the better. She was stronger, more resolute, but sadder somehow.

MacKendrie went to the record player and put on *The Student Prince*. Helen made a face and left the room.

On Tuesday, MacKendrie dismissed his late-afternoon class—REL 102 Introduction to the Bible—and sauntered down the hallway to the administration office to pick up his check. He was an adjunct instructor at Tidewater Junior College. It was the only job he could find.

The elders at the church in Bronson had signaled to Elmer Land they would not be contacting MacKendrie. Even Land hinted there was nothing more he could do for him. He had gone from protective custody in Raleigh to reunite with a nearly hysterical Helen at her sister's place. After two weeks, he had borrowed a truck and ventured down to Wilmington to make arrangements with a moving company to retrieve the car and their belongings. He ran into a fellow pastor who was sympathetic and knew the dean at Tidewater Junior College. Three weeks later, they moved into a rented house in Norfolk.

His pay was meager, but MacKendrie rarely worried about money. Helen had taken a part-time job with the school district to help make ends meet. He had wanted the job as a way of staying busy, but he found that teaching didn't really suit him and missed the ministry. His students were mostly men just out of the service, secretaries, and tradesmen, trying desperately to move up in the world. The Bible classes were rumored to be easy electives. MacKendrie tried not to be too hard on them, but he also was determined not to shortchange the study of the scriptures. He gave out a lot of C's.

He went into the office and waved to Andrea Tapper, the dean's secretary. She was a buxom brunette, twenty years his junior, and she smoked constantly. But she seemed exotic to MacKendrie, and instead of repulsing him, the cigarettes added to her sultriness. He had never known anyone named Andrea. It sounded continental, although her face was pure Appalachia, round with a wide mouth. She evidently found it amusing to flirt with MacKendrie, which made him blush and laugh nervously, like a freshman in the presence of the campus beauty queen.

Andrea's eyes twinkled as she drawled, "Why, hello, Jim. How're you?"

"Good morning, Andrea, I'm fine, thanks. You look nice today." He rarely said that to Helen.

She tilted her head back. "Well, aren't you the charmer."

He gave a nervous giggle. "Just being honest. Anything new?"

"Not really. The dean keeps talking about building a gym, but the state won't give him the money." She picked up a cigarette, and

MacKendrie watched as she put it between her lips and left it unlit. "I keep telling him he ought to send me up to Richmond. Just give me a few minutes with the governor." She gave him a sly smile.

MacKendrie was sure he was blushing. He looked down.

"I almost forgot, I have a message for you." She leaned forward, retrieving a slip of paper from a tray, her loose blouse momentarily falling open. She smiled as she handed the slip to him. "This gentleman called earlier."

In a daze, he said "Thank you" without looking at the message. When Andrea turned back to her typewriter, MacKendrie glanced down and winced.

"Andrea, I need to use your phone, please."

Twenty minutes later, he walked into the lobby of the Washington Hotel, where Harry Cohen, dressed in Navy blues, his left arm in a sling, was waiting.

"Morning, Mac. Thanks for coming."

MacKendrie shook his head. "Harry, you're like a bad penny. You just keep turning up."

Cohen forced a smile and led him to the coffee shop. When they were seated and ordered, MacKendrie asked about his shoulder.

"Slow going. Docs say it'll never be a hundred percent, but I should be able to use the arm. If that guy Stallings had been sober, I'd have been a goner. I nearly was anyway. The FBI sure took their time getting there."

"I figured out later that's who you called when you asked to use my phone."

"Yeah. I have a buddy in the Bureau. Told him we were in a jam. Good thing they sent Foster. He's not from the South. Saw what that hick sheriff was trying to do and decided to do an end run around him."

MacKendrie laughed.

"What's funny?"

Still laughing, he said, "You should have seen the look on the sheriff's face when those agents told him they were taking us out of there. I've never seen Hoolie Dixon hopping mad before."

Cohen grinned. "I hear they dropped all the charges against you."

"Yes. Thanks to that lawyer from Arlington you sent down. It was a deal. He would speak to the FBI about dropping their investigation into your injury if they would drop all the charges against us. I think he threatened to subpoena anyone who might have had something to do with Ulysses Brown's death. Officially, the DA said self-defense in your case and accidental discharge of a firearm in mine. I'm obliged to you, Harry. I wouldn't have stood much of a chance in court in Kirkwell."

"So what exactly happened back there, Mac? While I was uncnscious."

MacKendrie took a sip of coffee. "Just after you shot Joe, Eli Ross came in with a shotgun. He's really a mild-mannered fellow," he added apologetically. "I didn't think he would shoot me. But the more we talked, the more I realized there was something at work in him. In all of those people, really. It's a sickness, Harry. They all have it, it's like an epidemic. Hatred of Negroes is just the symptom. They're at the mercy of things out of their control, and it's like they're burning up with fever for, I don't know, some kind of dream, some paradise lost. Every day they wake up and see they don't have it, and it makes them bitter and angry. It's deadly." He nodded. "A disease. I don't know if Christ almighty could heal them."

Cohen lit a cigarette and waited.

MacKendrie coughed. "Anyway, Eli knew I wasn't going to kill him. Although it crossed my mind." He gave a fleeting smile. "No, I knew I couldn't do that, even in self-defense. But I wasn't going to let him kill me, either. I lowered my gun but made sure it was aimed at his leg. Eli was jittery. His gun was wandering all over the place. He tried to force his aim, and I knew that's when he was going to shoot. I squeezed the trigger and caught him in the foot. It made him miss his shot. He went down and I grabbed his gun. You know the rest."

Cohen shook his head. "I guess I was partly right. You are brave. And stubborn. But not stupid."

"I don't know. I know I'm not a very good Christian."

"What?"

"When they helped Eli into the ambulance, you know what he shouted at me? 'Turn the other cheek! Turn the other cheek, damn you!'" Cohen looked puzzled. "The saying of Jesus, you know. 'Whosoever would smite thee on thy right cheek, turn to him the other also.' I didn't exactly turn the other cheek, did I?"

They were silent until Cohen said, "You know, Mac, it's me that's obliged to you. If you had let Ross kill you, I'd have been next."

MacKendrie nodded. "I know. I thought of that. By defending myself, I was also defending you. Jesus didn't really say anything about that—harming others in defense of the helpless, so I guess we have to figure that out on our own. I'm just not very good at that kind of moral arithmetic."

"Well, from my seat, you got it right."

MacKendrie gave a small smile. "Sure. It's just...I never suspected Eli."

"It's always the ones you least suspect."

He shook his head. "Now he's gotten away with it."

"What's that? Gotten away with it?"

"There were others, too, but Eli was the one behind it all along—the vandalism on my car, terrorizing Evans, Ug's death. And the plot to get rid of me. I didn't see it until the very end, and then it was plain as day. He's clever, determined, the worst kind of fanatic, a quiet one. He doesn't stand up and give loud speeches. He just has a word with someone. Three men dead, others wounded and injured, livelihoods ruined, and he just walked away."

"With a permanent limp, thanks to you. Maybe that'll give him something to think about."

"Oh, he'll probably wear it like a badge of honor. His wound in the war for the soul of the South. People will say, there goes Eli, he took a shot for our way of life."

Cohen tapped his cigarette ashes. "You want me to have a word with the U.S. District Attorney? Maybe they could come up with something. Conspiracy."

MacKendrie shook his head. "Ah. No," he said suddenly, "I've got to let it go. I suppose sometimes you have to let people live with their consciences. But Harry, something's been bothering me. You said back in that house that you were sticking around because I was...valuable, or something. That you needed me. What did you mean?"

"Glad you mentioned it. I've got a job for you. No, wait." He held up a hand to stop MacKendrie's objections. "Hear me out."

Later that evening, after the girls were in bed, MacKendrie said, "Helen, I had a visit from Harry Cohen today."

She looked up from her magazine. "Harry Cohen? Is he all right?"

"Still on the mend, but he's going to be okay."

"Oh, that's good. What did he want?" Her husband hesitated, and Helen MacKendrie's voice turned lower. "Jim? What did he want?"

"The Navy wants my help."

She started. "The Navy! Oh, Jim. You're not going back into the service." It was both a question and a statement.

"No, no, nothing like that. They just want me to give them some advice. About China."

"Oh. No harm in giving advice, is there?"

His reply was a little longer in coming than Helen liked, but he said with a smile, "No. No harm. Harry wants me to drive up to Washington next week for a meeting."

"Well. Maybe that will do you good. Give you a little project," she said, and went back to her magazine.

He gazed at her for a moment, her hair lit from behind as if she wore a nimbus. In the midst of all the uncertainties around him, he was certain that without Helen, he would be dead, or at least his soul would be lifeless. For a brief instant, the picture of Andrea Tapper leaning over the desk, revealing her pendulous breasts, crossed his mind. It was a snare, he thought, and he smiled, amazed he was ever tempted.

He kept pondering the meeting with Cohen. He had the distinct feeling that something lay ahead. There would be some use for him after all.

That evening before bed, MacKendrie picked up his worn Bible from the night stand and opened it to the Psalms. He read, *"Be thou my strong rock, for an house of defense to save me. Pull me out of the net that they have laid privily for me..."*

He closed his eyes, made a short prayer, and turned out the light.

PART TWO:

CALL OF THE CUCKOO

SIXTEEN

The dilapidated building at number 14 Peng Zhen Street contained three small shops. A sign in front of the middle door said simply "Paper." Wang went in. Behind the counter, Feng was haggling with a customer, so he stood in queue. It had been a full year since he first came to this grubby little shop.

He had been smuggled over the border from Hong Kong. He would be contacted, they said. His papers stated Zhang Weijun was the son of a factory worker, parents and siblings deceased. Excellent student. Sent to study marine biology at UCLA in 1948. Hated the decadent capitalism he saw in America. Returned to China in 1952 to assist the Revolution. Letter of introduction by a cadre leader in Shenzhen who vouched for the family's loyalty to the Party.

Like most good cover stories, there were bits of truth to it.

He applied for a position at the provincial office of the Ministry of Agriculture and was hired at once. An anxious month passed. Then on a pleasant spring day a fat man walked up to him at a park and abruptly asked, "Do you like birds? I have a friend who deals in them. I enjoy hearing their songs."

Warily, Wang said, "Many birds have beautiful songs. Do you have a favorite?"

"Yes. The cuckoo."

He almost jumped at the sound of his code name but replied, "The cuckoo is found in many lands. I once heard it sing in a faraway country."

He went with Feng to a shop that sold paper for ceremonial scrolls where a tall, stern man of about fifty with a neatly trimmed graying beard took him into a back room. To the public he was Mr. Wen, the shop owner, but he said, "You will call me Owl." The code name suited the fierce chief of Network Aviary. Wang was not permitted to do anything until Owl was satisfied that he knew procedures, codes, fallbacks, and safe houses by heart. In his last lesson, Wang was given a pill to be sewn into the sleeve of his tunic, with the instructions that if he were arrested, he was to tear it out with his teeth and swallow it.

"It will be quick. Much better than the First Bureau's methods," Owl said.

Because he traveled the great Yangtze River freely, his task was observation. Mining operations, descriptions and movements of military boats, information about rice harvests, all went into his reports. It was routine, repetitive, tedious work, not at all what he had imagined. Only the fear of arrest and Owl's anger made him diligent.

The customer paid for his package and left, muttering. Feng shook his head and said with his usual cheerfulness, "Hello, are you well? Mr. Wen, our esteemed customer Mr. Zhang is here!"

"Hello, Mr. Feng. I am well, thank you. And you?"

His moon face crinkled, and he sucked in his breath loudly through his teeth. "Ohh, I do not know. My head hurts these days. I think it is because Mr. Wen makes me tally the receipts. I never properly learned to use the *suànpán*." He held up the counting frame and shook it, making the red wooden beads rattle. "It is a torture device!"

Wang smiled. Feng's code name was Raven, and to customers he was genial and slow-witted. It was a persona that effectively concealed a nimble and ruthless agent. Owl had told him that Feng once was detained for questioning but played such a convincing fool the police became exasperated and let him go. A courier was suspected of betraying them, and Feng had tracked him down. He was found in an alley with a single knife wound to the heart.

Now Owl emerged from the back room. "If you paid as much attention to the *suànpán* as you do to food, your head would not hurt and your belly would not get in your own way."

Feng grinned. "You see, Mr. Zhang, how he treats me. Perhaps I should denounce him publicly as an oppressor of workers."

Wang had never dared tease Owl, but he said with mock seriousness, "Well, perhaps you should. It is rumored that he is a friend of Rockefeller and Ford."

Owl impassively ignored Feng's laughter, and Wang followed him into the small back room. He handed the chief a coded report which he stashed under a loose board, and they spoke quietly while they waited for the tea to brew.

"The Birdcatchers have a task for you," Owl said. "There are reports of military activity around Bai Miao. That's where you are from, isn't it?"

Wang was startled. "Yes. What sort of activity?"

"Unusual numbers of soldiers. It could be nothing, but our friends would like us to find out."

"Bai Miao is almost a hundred and fifty kilometers from here. I will have to find an excuse to go so far upriver. Perhaps I could convince Leung to let me set up an additional fish farm."

"Send word when you are ready to depart."

Feng entered the room and helped himself to a cup of tea. "Perhaps we should ask Kingfisher to help Cuckoo," he said.

"Who—" Wang began.

"One of our agents," Owl said curtly with a look at Feng that sent him back to the front room.

Wang knew better than to ask any more questions. "I just recalled that it has been one year since I met you. Do you remember?"

"Yes. But it is best in our business not to remember too much."

He left the shop and turned toward the main street. Glancing over his shoulder, he caught a glimpse of a dark-clothed man moving his way. He might be the one with the sturdy shoes he saw earlier. Wang crossed the street and began to walk quickly. He didn't slow down until he had walked a dozen blocks through the congested streets and reached a small park. He stepped onto the grass, stopped and took off his glasses, pulling out a handkerchief to wipe them. He tried to breathe normally and looked about slowly, turning every few seconds to glance in all directions. People walked by or sat and read newspapers. Motorbikes, bicycles, and carts rolled past. Soldiers stood on the pavement nearby in their crisp, deep green uniforms, rifles slung, talking and laughing. No one so much as glanced at him. There was no sign of the man. He considered whether to go back to the shop and tell Owl that the shop might be under surveillance, but the chief already thought him too nervous.

He walked slowly to his apartment and stopped at People's Market Number 122, a few dozen meters from his door. He produced a ration book, and in return he was given a small package of rice, a bit of dried pork and a packet of tea for his evening meal.

Since the people's victory over the Kuomintang, private lands had been confiscated, agriculture centralized, and food rationed with the result that starvation was reduced at a stroke. The merchant class had been left alone, but now campaigns were underway. To take the capitalist road was fast becoming a serious offense, and shopkeepers deemed too successful were warned. At least the city was safer, and cleaner. The streets had been cleared of pickpockets, opium dens, and prostitutes, but also of litter. Even spitting was roundly criticized. The Revolution required people become orderly and civilized.

Before unlocking his door, he checked to see if his neighbors were snooping, then quickly bent over and removed the tiny slip of paper near the bottom hinge he had placed there that morning. His apartment was simple and functional, not particularly shabby—a single room with a low bed, a chair and a table and a nook for cooking and cleaning up. That he did not have to share it he attributed to his government connections. On a small kerosene burner, he cooked the rice, boiled the pork, pouring the broth over the rice, and brewed the tea.

His assistants had been puzzled by his solitary existence. He had no wife, no family? Wang put them off by saying the Party was the only family he needed. But he wondered how many more nights he would have to eat alone.

Next morning he rose early as usual, nibbled a bit of rice, dressed and mounted his bicycle. The aquaculture station was several kilometers away from the main commercial district, on a road running beside the bank of the Yangtze. This was the only place he felt happy. Here, science banished pretense and deception. The work also allowed him freedom to travel on the river unmolested, which satisfied his obligations to the network.

He supervised farms that raised carp—*Cyprinus carpio*—a staple of the diet. The practice of fish farming was ancient, and traditionally, the farmers fed them nymphs of dragonflies and the excretions of silkworms. Wang was experimenting with whether a type of meal he had devised might increase the carp's growth. His training at Pacific Reformed was paying off. The labs there were much more sophisticated, of course, but he had adapted his methods to the simpler resources at hand.

He donned boots and went out to the pens, where two assistants were preparing to wade in. They turned respectfully to him.

"Good morning, Comrade Supervisor."

"Good morning, comrades. How are our friends today? Waiting for their breakfast, I see. Proceed, comrades. Let's keep to our schedule."

After the fish were fed and had settled down, he netted and weighed a dozen specimens. He took notes, then went into the office to write a report, pausing only briefly at noon to eat a bit of leftover rice. After the afternoon feeding, he dismissed the assistants, worked another hour, and went home as the sun was setting.

In the morning, he rode his bicycle to the Ministry of Agriculture office to present a monthly report to Inspector Leung, a timid man with a nervous laugh. He entered a cluttered anteroom plastered with garish posters that glorified the Party, the revolution, and the Chairman. Leung's formidable new assistant, Comrade Li, dressed in an immaculate Mao jacket, told him he must wait. He watched as she sorted through reports, muttering dire remarks.

"Imbeciles. *Pa!* They will never make their quotas." She looked at him as if just noticing he was there. "Look at this, comrade! The new people's farm in Xiaosu has been given a quota of ten thousand kilos of rice this year. The supervisor says only two-thirds of the fields have been planted because they lack workers. What is to be done with such incompetents?"

"It is regrettable," he said. "But why does not the Ministry give him more workers?"

"Our education campaigns have not yet persuaded enough young people to go and work on the farms. The supervisors know this. They must reach their quotas with the workers they have. The Revolution requires extra work of us all to succeed, don't you agree, comrade?"

"Yes, of course."

She was about his own age, moved gracefully, and wore round black spectacles. She might be considered pretty, Wang thought, then checked himself. The Americans had warned him to stay away from women. Even a casual affair could distract him or worse. Honey traps were a favorite technique of the First Bureau. Besides, Party policy frowned on casual sex as an example of decadent Western values. In practice, it was common for Party officials to keep mistresses.

He glanced at her again. She had high cheekbones and even teeth, although she did not smile. Her hair was short, in the style he had heard called in America a page boy. The Party had insisted that the traditional braids for both men and women belonged to "the superstitions of a subservient past," whatever that meant, but this modern style became her. Yes, she would be pretty, but for her severity.

"What is your full name, comrade?" he asked.

She looked up, hesitated, and said, "Li Ying."

"You are new here?"

"Yes. I came here a month ago."

"And how did you serve the Party before?"

Gazing at him, she said, "You are inquisitive. Is that why you became a scientist?"

Wang smiled. "I suppose so. I meant no offense."

She waved her hand. "No matter. I assisted the comrades in the Coastal Defense Department. Comrade Leung was unhappy with his assistant and asked the deputy minister for someone else. He made some inquiries, and I was recommended."

"I'm sure Comrade Leung is much happier now. And you? Does this work suit you?"

She said primly, "We serve the people as the Party thinks best."

Leung appeared at the door and beckoned. As he passed, he gave a brief nod to Li, who made no response.

After the necessary greetings, Wang presented his report. Twice daily feedings of the meal had increased the weight of the carp an average of eleven percent above those that had received just the traditional food. Further study would be needed to determine the proper amounts.

"Excellent work, Comrade Zhang. I shall report to the deputy minister that your study is promising and you should be allowed to continue."

"Thank you, Comrade Inspector. If I may suggest, it would be easy to add another farm farther upriver. It would provide fish for the markets in upper Jiangsu Province."

Leung looked dubious. "Where do you suggest?"

"A good place would be Bai Miao. It is a strategic point." The deputy minister was from a small village not far from Bai Miao, he pointed out.

Leung nodded vigorously. "How soon can this be done?"

"It will take a few months to get it properly established. I would like to travel there soon to find a good place for the farm."

"I will have to get permission from the deputy minister to establish a new farm, of course, but I believe he will agree. In the meantime you may go to Bai Miao. Comrade Li will prepare the necessary papers. And comrade, be efficient. Do not get into mischief," Leung said, wagging a finger. He added with a laugh, "Not that there is any mischief to find in Bai Miao."

Li told him to return the next day to receive the papers. "You are very clever, Comrade Scientist," she said with a slight nod. She wasn't exactly smiling, but he saw a glimpse of those even teeth between her parted lips as he turned away.

As he undressed that evening, he thought of his mother in Bai Miao. She had a favorite passage from the Bible that he recalled.

The Lord is my shepherd,
I have all that I need...

It always provoked him to ask questions. "Oma, if God is great, why would he become a shepherd like a Mongol?"

"It shows that God is not too proud to come and take care of foolish sheep like us, my son."

He loved his mother, but her Christian faith, so foreign to Chinese ways, had caused great hardship. After the Mission School in Shanghai closed and he was forced to return to Bai Miao, his life became hell. His love of school turned to despair because of the torment he endured. He begged his mother not to send him anymore, but she said only that Jesus was walking beside him. He began to hate her Jesus for putting him through it all.

There was a gang of them. One boy, the ringleader, looked every afternoon for Wang. At first, they walked beside him shouting insults. "Your mother is a traitor! You are worse than white devils!" Oma had told him strictly he was to remain silent and not to return insults with insults. Like a cat trying to provoke its prey to run, the gang grew bolder. One day they surrounded Wang on his way home and began pushing him. He glared at them and would have grabbed the leader, but he kept his fists clenched at his side. The boy stepped up, inches from his face.

"Coward! You and your mother are cowards! Your Jesus was a coward!"

He pushed Wang hard and he fell. The boy was pummeling him, and the other boys joined in. They pulled off his bag, emptied it of his schoolwork and began trampling it in the dust. A rock lay on the ground next to his head, and Wang seized it. He brought it down hard on the foot of the nearest boy, who gave a yell and jumped back. It gave him room, and he sprang up, fist raised, holding the rock, looking straight at the leader. Wang took a step toward him, and he flinched.

"If you bother me again, I will find you when you are alone and use this rock on your head," Wang said desperately.

With murmured bravado, the boy and his pals slowly dispersed. He gathered his torn and dirty schoolwork, crammed it into his bag along with the rock, and shakily walked home. His mother cried when she saw him but said nothing and began tending his bruises and cuts. The gang kept their distance from Wang after that, resorting to insults shouted from a safe distance. Although he was ashamed, because he knew what Pastor Ma would have said, he kept the rock in his bag for a long time.

He rose before dawn to prepare for the trip upriver. In the dim light, a bit of white on the floor by the door caught his eye. He picked up the slip of paper, opened it, and scanned the columns of characters, which looked like gibberish. Digging in his pouch, he found a pencil and began to make light marks at key places on the paper. Decoded it read:

First Bureau agents raided shop. Raven dead. Use tea room and safe house as fallback. Advise on Bai Miao.

He burned the message. His hands trembled as he took a sheet of paper and coded a response. He would hand it off to a courier on his way to the docks.

SEVENTEEN

MacKendrie slept fitfully and finally got up about five. He made coffee, sat down in his robe, and picked up his Bible. He read, "God is our refuge and strength, an ever-present help in trouble. Therefore we will not fear, though the earth give way..." It had been the inspiration for Martin Luther, hidden in Frederick's castle, to write *A Mighty Fortress is Our God*.

Humming a bit of the hymn, he fished a frying pan out of a cabinet and rummaged in the refrigerator for eggs. The clatter brought a yawning Helen to the kitchen.

"Gracious, Jim, what are you doing?"

"Sorry, dear. I thought I'd fix my own breakfast."

"What time did Harry say to meet him?"

"Nine o'clock. Sharp, he said."

She checked the kitchen clock. "Let me do that. You go get yourself ready."

He returned in thirty minutes, shaved and dressed, to find a plate of fried eggs, bacon and toast and a fresh cup of coffee. He found he was ravenously hungry. Helen roused the girls, and he said goodbye to them as they sleepily nursed their cereal.

"Where are you going?" asked Dorothy, nine years old now. The MacKendries had shielded her and six-year-old Priss from the worst of the danger and trauma of their last days in Kirkwell, but she knew enough to be suspicious of anything out of the ordinary.

"Just to a meeting in Washington," he said, which seemed to satisfy her. "Be good in school today."

It was a one-hour drive from Norfolk. His mood swung between dread and anticipation. He wasn't sure how much he could trust Harry Cohen, with his cryptic comments, but Cohen had given dark hints about Paul Wang.

"Besides, you owe me. I took out Stallings, you know," Cohen said.

It was hard to believe eight months had passed since he left North Carolina behind. The days were warming again after a cold winter.

As he approached the capital, he pulled into a parking lot to reexamine the map. The Pentagon was just west of the river. MacKendrie was good with navigation, a skill he had honed tramping the rural roads and open country of China on foot.

He found the massive building and stopped at a gate, where a polite young marine directed him to a parking space and the main entrance. A receptionist took his name and spoke into a phone. She handed him a pass.

"Captain Cohen is expecting you, sir. If you'll have a seat, he'll be right down."

MacKendrie watched the coming and going in the vast lobby. Uniforms of every branch of the services, ranks from private to two-star general officer, rows of ribbons, a few of which he remembered—Bronze Star, Pacific Combat Badge, Purple Heart. He had earned a few ribbons himself, mostly for meritorious service. They were still attached to his old uniform, stashed in a trunk somewhere.

He suddenly was swept back to Tinian. He could hear the fighters buzzing overhead, the noise from the port, the trucks, men shouting, saw the looming gray warships. As much as he hated to admit it, it had been the most exciting time in his life.

Cancer had taken Emily in '40, his work in the mission field was gone, Richard was away at college, and he was a shell of a man. There seemed no purpose to anything. Then the war began, and he was obsessed with becoming a Navy chaplain. It was mad, for he was almost forty-five, but in the early months of the war the Navy was desperate for men to serve in any capacity, and his credentials were impeccable.

MacKendrie found the role suited him well. Mission work in China had taught him discipline, persistence and resourcefulness, and he knew instinctively how to deal with hostile commanders, indifferent sailors and riotous behavior. He got good marks on stateside bases and could have remained in San Diego, but he itched to be closer to the action. He applied for a transfer, hoping to serve on a ship. Instead, he was assigned to Tinian.

It was an Army Air Corps base in the Northern Marianas that had been captured just months before he arrived in October 1944, a twin island of Saipan five miles to the north. Occasional air-raid sirens sent them diving for the bunkers, but no Japanese planes ever showed up. MacKendrie saw the damage of war, though, in the sailors and marines who were brought in on the medical evacuation planes. He thought he had been prepared for it, after the glimpses he had seen in China during the years of the warlords, but this was like walking through a slaughterhouse. Miraculously, as he spoke to those mangled and dying men, from somewhere within came words that he hadn't known he had. He spoke to them confidently, asking what they believed, assuring them that they were in the hands of God, offering them forgiveness for the terrible things they had done. He was mystified in the midst of his horror.

He was still in reverie when Cohen's voice snapped him out of it. "Morning, Mac." He reminded MacKendrie of a bulldog, with the same pugnacity. Today he was in uniform khakis, silver eagles on his collar. "You're right on time. This way."

"Who's at this meeting, Harry?"

"Oh, just a couple of gents I work with."

"In Naval Intelligence."

Cohen glanced around. "Yeah."

"I'd like to know what you're getting me into."

Cohen stopped and turned to him. "It's like I said before. We've got an operation going on the Yangtze River that goes up to Bai Miao. We don't have much info about that part of the river. The only foreigners who spent time there before the war were missionaries, and you and your family were there the longest."

"And I'm the only one left in my family who was there. I'm beginning to see why you said I was too valuable to lose, back there in Kirkwell."

Cohen smiled. "Those yokels were out for your scalp."

MacKendrie nodded. "I just want to make sure I'm not going to ruffle any more feathers. I'm not, am I?"

Cohen shrugged. "We just need to ask you a few questions."

They walked up stairs and through mazes of corridors, finally turning into a small conference room where two men in khakis were looking over a map. One was Lucas Vanderhoven. The other was probably twice the young man's age, balding, with a pipe clenched in his teeth. A haze of smoke hung around the overhead light.

Cohen said, "Mac, I think you know Luke Vanderhoven." He gestured to the older man. "This is Commander Jerry Allen. Jerry, this is Reverend Jim MacKendrie."

MacKendrie shook hands with Allen, then with Vanderhoven, even more impressively tall and blond in his uniform, who said, "It's good to see you again, sir."

"Thanks, Lucas. Same here."

Cohen pointed MacKendrie to a chair and sat facing him, flanked by the others. He lit a cigarette and blew a cloud of smoke upward.

"I don't have to fill you in on recent history in China, Mac. Let's just say we didn't count on the Communists winning out. No sooner than we get the Japs taken care of, we have to worry about Mao's gooks."

MacKendrie still bristled every time he heard the slur but took a deep breath and shook his head. "Harry, that country is in a mess. The Mission Board sent me and a couple of others over there in '47 to survey the situation, and we couldn't believe the devastation. And that was before the civil war. The Communists aren't going to be doing anything but rebuilding for years."

Allen removed his pipe. "That's what we thought, too, Reverend MacKendrie. We didn't expect Mao to send the People's Liberation Army into Korea, but he did, and they damn near pushed us into the Sea of Japan. Thank God for Doug MacArthur. If it weren't for him, we'd have lost that peninsula." He pointed the stem of his pipe at MacKendrie. "Communism is bent on one aim, global domination."

"We don't trust them, Mac," Cohen added. "And now they've closed off the country. It's been seven years since you were there. We need to know what they're doing. Are they rebuilding their military? How many men do they have? How much rice are they growing?" He paused. "I suppose I don't need to tell you that all this is classified?"

"Go on."

Cohen took a drag on the cigarette. "We've got agents inside, mostly natives with a grudge or some loyalties to us."

"Like Paul Wang?"

Allen stared at him.

"You know Wang?" Allen said.

"I'm surprised Harry didn't tell you," MacKendrie said. "Yes, I know Wang Wenzhe well. I gave him his Christian name, Paul, when I baptized him at the mission church in Bai Miao. He was like a son to me."

"And how do you know he's one of our operatives?" Allen asked accusingly.

"I didn't know he was an *operative*, commander. The last time I heard from Paul, he was at Pacific Reformed College, studying biology. I only agreed to this meeting because Harry said it involved Paul."

Allen turned to Cohen, who said impassively, "It was necessary to mention Wang in order to secure Reverend MacKendrie's cooperation."

Allen's eyes gleamed with fury. "Against protocols, Harry?"

"Take it easy, Jerry. Now that he's here, he's bound to the same security rules as we are. Right, Mac?" He leaned forward on the table. "You keep your lips buttoned? Nothing to anyone, including your wife?"

MacKendrie nodded. "I understand."

Cohen went on as if he had not been interrupted. "We'd like your opinion about whether there's anything in the Yangtze River valley around Bai Miao we should know about."

MacKendrie eyed the three unsmiling men across from him and said, "First of all, it's pronounced *bye mee-ow*, like good *bye* and the *meow* of a cat." He glanced at Vanderhoven, who nodded as if to say "I've tried."

"Let's see your map."

It was a small town—maybe thirty thousand before the war—with an inauspicious name. Bai Miao meant "white temple." White was symbolic of death, he explained. Legend had it that in an old Buddhist temple, now long gone, a monk had worn white robes instead of gray as a reminder of his mortality. The other monks copied him, the color became associated with the temple, and the nearby town was called by the temple's name.

The river at that point was more than three miles across, he said, no bridges. It was hilly, rural territory, a lot of rice fields and hamlets. He pointed out possible vantage points of the river, especially some old forts outside the town that had been rebuilt and used during the gunboat era of the twenties. They were in ruins when he last saw them. For an hour he showed them roads through the valleys, points where there were ferries.

They had questions about the roads. Mostly unpaved, he said, hard to use in the rainy season. What were the sentiments about the Communists when he was there? About the same as elsewhere in China, he said—enthusiasm among the peasants, with landowners and merchants supporting Chiang Kai-shek's Nationalists, the Kuomintang. He shrugged.

"I don't think there's much there of interest, gentlemen, unless you're planning an invasion, in which case you'd want it to control supply routes or troop movements on the river from Shanghai to the interior and vice versa. I'll say this," he added, "if you wanted to hide somebody out, those reed marshes along the south river bank are a maze of canals. A man could get lost in there for days."

The men exchanged glances. Vanderhoven was rapidly scribbling notes. MacKendrie leaned back from the table. "Is that what you want to know?"

There were nods, murmurs.

"Well. If that's all, then..."

"I'll walk you out," Cohen said. In the lobby, he extended his hand. "Thanks, Mac. This was a big help."

"Harry, what about Paul?"

Cohen looked around quickly. "Keep your voice down. What about him?"

"You said he might be in danger."

Cohen shook his head. "Can't tell you about that, Mac. All I can say is he works for us."

MacKendrie eyed him. "If anything happens to him, I want to know about it."

"Sure, Mac," Cohen said. "We know how to reach you. Oh, and uh..."

"Yes?"

"Well, if we needed to borrow you..."

"Borrow me?"

"For a few days. Could you manage it? You know, on the QT. Keep it from your wife, that kind of thing?"

MacKendrie was glum as he drove back to Norfolk. He had a feeling he hadn't helped Paul after all.

Helen greeted him with an anxious kiss. "What happened?"

"There was nothing to it, really. We looked at some maps, and they listened to my tales."

"Well," she said, "that's a relief."

"Why? Were you worried?"

"I couldn't help it. I thought maybe they were going to shanghai you, or whatever they call it."

"Shanghai me? For what?"

"Oh, I don't know, some sort of secret shenanigans."

MacKendrie laughed. "Our side doesn't work that way. Besides, can you see me as a spy?"

They laughed so hard it brought Dottie and Priss running to see what was so funny.

EIGHTEEN

The merciless wind swept unrelenting across the deck of the launch, causing Wang to gasp. He was wearing only a light coat over his cotton shirt, and he was numb clear through. He had endured more than three hours of piercing cold already, and the launch was still ten kilometers from Bai Miao. The sun was setting, and it would be dark by the time they arrived. He had not eaten since breakfast, and the roar of the motor gave him a headache. He was only consoled by what he had learned.

Li had arranged for him to ride upriver on a military launch, but when he arrived at the dock, an officious attendant told him the departure was delayed. "The boat will leave when Comrade Colonel Hua arrives. You must wait," he snapped.

He would have caught a ferry instead but for the mention of this Colonel Hua, and he settled down to wait. He passed the time by thinking of Li. Did she ever laugh? He tried to imagine her in a different setting than the anteroom of Leung's office. It was a warm day in Los Angeles, and she was wearing a skirt. She was walking in a park and laughing.

The colonel arrived in the afternoon with a detail of three soldiers. He was a pig-faced man wearing a heavy wool coat and a fur hat with ear flaps and a red star above the forehead. They marched past him without a glance. A burly soldier prevented Wang from boarding, and he had to talk his way onto the launch, explaining to a lieutenant that he was on an urgent assignment for the Ministry of Agriculture and promising not to cause trouble.

"Very well, comrade, come aboard," the lieutenant said. "But don't bother these men. Sergeant!"

"Sir." It was the burly one.

"Keep an eye on him, understand?"

For more than two hours the sergeant stood unflinching at the bow, but finally the cold wind forced him to take shelter in the lee of the cabin. He slung his rifle over his shoulder and blew on his hands, hopping from one foot to the other. Seeing the opportunity, Wang stood and copied him, flapping his hands around his sides, and gave a sympathetic laugh.

"The wind is bad, eh? What I would give for some woolen gloves." No reply. "And to be sent to Bai Miao, that insignificant dump! Ah, well, I suppose we do what we're told, right?"

The sergeant gave a humorless laugh. "I hope your lodgings are better than the barracks. This is my third trip to Bai Miao in three months. It is a shit hole."

"That is what I've heard. Just a lot of rice fields and a few pathetic inns. Not much for the People's Liberation Army to guard. Surely there are better places to be sent."

"Right. I fought the Americans in Korea. That was real fighting. We pushed them south away from our border. But then we were withdrawn and sent home."

"I have read how bravely our army fought. So now you are an important man—in the personal detail of a colonel."

He scowled. "I'm a driver and a bodyguard."

Wang shrugged. "And here we are, freezing our asses on the way to a shit hole." The sergeant laughed, with humor this time. "Why should a colonel make so many trips up here anyway if it's so unimportant?"

The soldier leaned forward. "Big project. Very secret. Just outside of town."

Wang looked puzzled. "Well, it doesn't seem like the army would be interested in a lot of rice fields."

"Not in the fields, you idiot." He whispered, "On the river."

The cabin door opened and the lieutenant looked suspiciously at the two of them. Wang retreated to his seat.

The Yangtze River was narrower here, but it was still more than six kilometers wide. It ran from west to east, with Bai Miao on the southern bank. The valley was not flat but dimpled with low hills and ridges. Suddenly Wang saw a familiar sight that made him smile in spite of his discomfort. The launch was passing a reed marsh that ran along the south shore of the river. It extended twenty meters or more from the bank into the river, with tall, thick masses of reeds, almost three meters high in places. As a child, he and his friends had sometimes ventured here, looking for crayfish, and Pastor Ma would come to hunt ducks with his shotgun. Wang was fascinated by it and begged to let him hold it, but he always refused, saying that someday he would teach him to use it safely. Then Pastor Ma suddenly had left Bai Miao.

Wang was just twelve and never understood why he had to leave, but he knew that the missionary's family had been here for more than thirty years and had even adopted a Chinese name to spare the natives having to pronounce "MacKendrie." When Pastor Ma said goodbye, he tried to comfort a weeping Wang, calling him Paul and promising they would meet again.

The launch began to slow and landed at a dock just beyond the reeds, where the soldiers were greeted by an honor guard. An elaborate ceremonial cry rang out, the colonel was helped onto the dock, and they climbed into jeeps waiting on the road that ran along the river and roared off, leaving Wang alone in the dusk. Bai Miao was still a few kilometers distant. He remembered this road well and tried to count how many years it had been since he walked along it.

As he entered the outskirts, he wondered where he would stay the night. The commissar's office was supposed to arrange for lodging, but by now it would be closed. He was about to ask someone if there were an inn nearby when he spotted a low building ahead with the national flag hanging from the eave. It had been the home of a merchant, he recalled, but now it clearly was the Party office, and by good fortune, there was a light in a window. The door of the building was unlocked. To his left, a light shone through a partially open door. He called hello.

"Who's there?"

He opened the door and found a shabbily dressed, bespectacled man of about forty seated at a desk, pen in midair.

"We are closed, comrade. Bring your complaint back tomorrow," he said, weariness around him like a fog.

"Ah. I am not here with a complaint, comrade. I am from the Ministry of Agriculture in Shanghai. I was supposed to arrive much earlier, but the boat was delayed. The commissar was supposed to have a place for me to stay. I saw the light in your office."

The man's face brightened, and he stood. "Please, come in." Wang stepped into the small office, which had notebooks and papers crammed onto shelves everywhere. "You are from Shanghai?"

"Yes, comrade. I am Zhang Weijun."

The man nodded. "I am Juh Jingbao, secretary to the commissar. You say you were expected?"

"Yes, or so I was told."

Juh sighed. "I am not informed of such things. And I am behind in my work, as you can see." He spread his hands in a helpless gesture. "I do not dare disturb the commissar at this hour."

"Of course. Is there an inn nearby where I could stay?"

Juh looked dubious. "Well, there are such places, but they are quite rough. Soldiers stay there mostly. Lots of drinking and carrying on. And they are usually filthy."

Wang's disappointment showed on his face. Juh said, "Comrade, it will not do to have such an eminent visitor stay in an inn. My humble home is at your disposal."

It was a generous offer, but politeness dictated that he object. "Oh, no, Comrade Juh. That is most commendable, but I shouldn't inconvenience you."

"Nonsense. It would be an honor. Besides, the commissar would be very unhappy with me if I sent you to an inn."

"Well, we cannot have the commissar unhappy. Thank you, I accept your hospitality."

Juh locked the office and they walked through the dark streets.

"We do not get many visitors here. Well, we didn't until recently. We are seeing an unusual number of soldiers in the city."

"My boat was delayed because we were waiting for a colonel."

Juh nodded. "Important officers, too. And then there are the others."

"The others?"

Juh glanced around and lowered his voice. "Russians."

"There are Russians in Bai Miao?"

"One of them came to the office last week to see the commissar himself. He was not a soldier but appeared quite important. They talked for hours. We see many of them in the city. They buy rice wine and talk about how they long for—what is the drink?"

"Vodka."

"Vodka. They are quite rude."

"Why are they here?"

"Well, we cannot speak of it. Here is the house. Mei? We have a guest."

A thin woman opened the door and held up a kerosene lantern, peering at them. Without a word she stood back respectfully.

"This is Comrade Zhang from Shanghai." He threw his head in the woman's direction. "My wife, Meili."

There were inquiries into each other's health, and then Juh spoke to the woman briefly in a low voice and she disappeared. In a small bare room, he gestured for Wang to take the only seat, a low stool.

"We will have dinner shortly," Juh said. "It will be a poor meal for a man of your stature."

"I am used to simple fare. Is the food supply adequate in Bai Miao?"

The host gave a shallow smile. "We are grateful for what we have, comrade."

Wang learned that Juh had joined the Revolution after hearing a speech by Zhou Enlai himself and had proved better at writing pamphlets than carrying a rifle. After the war he was sent to Bai Miao.

"Mostly I take down complaints and write reports. Not stimulating, but necessary, I suppose. And you?"

"I conduct research on fish. We are hoping to cultivate them in large numbers. I was sent here to look for a good location on the river for a farm."

Juh's eyes widened. "But this is excellent news. It would be most beneficial to the people here. We will assist you. Tomorrow I will introduce you to the commissar."

Meili appeared and gestured for them to come and eat. The meal consisted of rice into which egg had been cooked. Wang was given a single dumpling filled with bean paste. He was famished and ate gratefully.

The following day, Juh proved as good as his word. He gave Wang ration cards, a bicycle, and a letter signed by the commissar guaranteeing free travel. He was also given the use of a small house along the river road not far from the dock where he had arrived.

"Oh, and comrade, if you go west of the city, be careful," Juh said, raising his hand for emphasis. "The army has closed all traffic along the river road, and the vicinity around there is forbidden. A man was shot at a checkpoint two weeks ago. He was trying to reach his mother's village and became angry when they wouldn't let him through."

"Well. Clearly something is going on."

Juh lowered his gaze. "It is best not to speak about it."

Wang pedaled his bicycle through the congested streets in the direction of the river. Soon it appeared, broad and shining, with low hills far beyond to the north. He turned west on the road, which was busy with traffic. Army trucks barreled past in both directions. The city began to thin out, and soon he was the only one on the road. Ahead lay a sharp bend. As he rounded the curve, he saw a checkpoint about thirty meters ahead. Three soldiers with slung rifles walked behind a lowered gate. There was a guardhouse surrounded by sandbags and barbed wire on either side.

Wang dismounted. The soldiers were alert, watching him. He walked the bicycle forward slowly until he was ten meters from the gate, when a soldier yelled.

"Stop! There is no passage through here."

He called back, "I am sorry, comrade. I am new here."

The soldier ducked under the gate and walked up to him. "What are you doing here?"

"I am from the Ministry of Agriculture in Shanghai. I am conducting a study on the fish here and I am examining the terrain..."

"Never mind! This area is forbidden. Clear off, now!" He put his hand on the strap of his rifle.

Wang turned the bike around and rode off. Glancing to his right, he noticed there was a ridge above the road that ran roughly parallel. Pedaling on for a kilometer or so, he saw a small dock jutting into the river and dismounted. A few fishing boats rocked at their tethers. He walked out to the end of the dock and looked upriver. At first he saw nothing unusual, but then along the near bank just before the bend of the river he saw a dark shape that was too big for a fishing boat or a launch. He shielded his eyes. The boat turned slowly, and the unmistakable barrel of a heavy machine gun protruded. In the middle of the river was another just like it. There would be no point in trying to find out what was upriver by boat.

Wang spent the next few days prowling the river and the city, learning his way around again. Occasionally he was startled to see a familiar face—a man who used to own a tea room, a woman who belonged to the church. No one recognized him, perhaps because he had changed during his years away. His mother was in this city, and he yearned to see her, but he knew that was impossible for now. He had written her shortly before Cohen put him on the plane for Hong Kong, saying that he was working on a special project and it might be months before he could write again. He was careful to avoid the district where his old home sat.

He talked to fishermen about what they had seen upriver and shared meals with Juh, but he learned nothing more about what lay beyond the bend of the river. He began taking walks along the road heading west toward the nearby hamlet of Xiagang.

The ridge he had seen above the checkpoint sloped down to the Xiagang road. If a man could climb up to the ridge, he might be able to see upriver. He studied the hilly ground. It was not steep but uneven, and there was little cover. In the daytime anyone on the ridge would easily be seen. An observer would have to try it at dusk, when there would be just enough light to pick out his way. He had seen few soldiers, occasional clumps of two or three trudging toward town.

Wang had more than enough information to satisfy Owl. He should return to Shanghai and leave it to the chief to send an experienced agent to find out the rest. His part had been risky enough as it was, and he did not consider himself courageous. But the same curiosity that burned inside whenever he was faced with a scientific problem would not go away. It would take weeks to get another man back here and show him what he had already learned. He was here now. He made up his mind.

NINETEEN

The next day he left the house a half hour before sunset, his binoculars in his pouch. By the time he had walked on the Xiagang road a couple of kilometers outside of town, the day's foot and cart traffic had died down. He waited until a man pulling a hand-drawn wagon was well past and turned off the road, making for the slope. On his left, the sun was beginning to go down beyond the great mountains in the far distance. He judged the ridge to be about fifteen meters above him. He began to climb.

It was painstaking, finding a path among outcroppings that obstructed the way. He wondered how he would manage to get back down in the gloom. Just below the top he stopped and looked down at the road. It was empty. He found the ridge top was just wide enough for one man to walk along if done carefully. He tried to keep low, but there were few bushes, and he was conscious every second how exposed he was. Dropping to all fours, he crawled forward for another twenty meters, and there the ridge stopped and fell away toward the river below. He was looking across a beautiful vista.

Bordered by the sloping hills on his side of the river, the Yangtze stretched away in front of him as far as he could see. The sun slanted almost horizontal and tipped the hills around with reddish gold. Wang was not an artist, but he was taken aback by the scene. Pride swelled in him for this land, which had sustained his people for three thousand years.

A cool breeze swept past, and he shivered. He pulled his binoculars out of his bag. To the right, the river curved lazily back toward Bai Miao. He looked carefully along the banks and saw nothing of interest. He swept his gaze back and forth across the river. He had suspected the military activity might have to do with laying mines, but he saw nothing in the river that resembled a mine. The gunboats made slow back-and-forth runs in the middle of the stream.

He trained the binoculars on the far bank to his left. Just beyond the bend of the river, he saw a clearing and lights. Something was under construction. Looking closely, he saw the frame of a large structure, at least ten meters tall. Workers pushed wheelbarrows back and forth, and sparks from a welder's torch sprayed down from the steel skeleton. Part of the building was already enclosed, and he could see standing next to it another partially built structure. The light was fading and it was difficult to see, but Wang could just make out a kind of hourglass shape. It was a tower, but for what purpose he couldn't imagine.

He studied the site. It was a plant of some kind that needed proximity to the river. A power plant? It would be an ideal location, but an ordinary power plant would be—how did the Americans put it?—no big deal. There must be some military use for it. He mused until a sound from the river jerked him back to his senses. The feeling he had discovered something of importance caused his stomach to flutter. Quickly he stashed the binoculars and backed away from the vantage point. He scrambled back along the ridge line, stumbling and stubbing his feet on unseen rocks. He was gasping and sweating despite the chill settling on the hills. It was getting dark.

He was desperately looking for the point to turn off the ridge and make his way back down to the road. A sound, somewhere ahead of him, made him stop. A voice? Nothing, then more distinctly, voices. Crouching, he pulled out his binoculars. In the fading light, he could just make out half a dozen men in uniform. A patrol was on the ridge about sixty meters away, heading his direction.

He looked down, saw a level spot and jumped, landing heavily. He began scuffling down the slope. The noise attracted attention, and Wang could hear shouts. The rocks tore at his clothes as he half-slid, half-climbed down. There was a shout from the top of the ridge and a few seconds later a percussive *bang*. He flattened in fear. Two more *bangs* quickly followed and he heard the bullets hiss by to his right. He began crawling forward on hands and knees, trying to find a way without being seen. Fortunately, the soldiers did not seem to have torches, and they were as much at the mercy of the terrain as he was.

He saw the ribbon of road below. He fumbled in his bag for the binoculars, threw them away and heard them shatter on a rock. He cleared the last few meters of slope and as his feet hit the road he began running to his right, keeping low. He could hear the soldiers still on the hill, shouting and swearing. On the other side of the road, the ground angled gently down to a rough field with clumps of tall grass. Wang dove off the road into the nearest stand of grass and began crawling on all fours. He found a particularly thick bunch and lay still, watching the road. The shouts were coming nearer. He touched his sleeve and fingered the bump where the pill was sewn.

Movement on the left caught his eye. A man was walking down the road toward the town at a brisk pace. Perhaps he was anxious to get home. Wang watched as he continued on, oblivious to the soldiers clambering down the slope. He saw what would happen before it happened. He would have stood and waved at the man, but his legs did not move. He would have shouted at him to go back, but his mouth did not open.

As the man passed just below the patrol, there was a shout for him to stop. Startled, he began to run. A command and a volley of rifle fire. In horror, Wang saw the man drop straight down like a nail struck by an unseen hammer and collapse into a heap, then lie still. The patrol surrounded him, turned him over and examined him. A low murmur of undecipherable talk drifted over the field. Brief laughter that sounded obscene. The patrol leader issued commands, and they began marching back toward Bai Miao, leaving one soldier standing next to the body.

Wang did not move an inch as darkness fell around him. He didn't know how much time had passed before a pair of headlights crawled over the road from the city and stopped, illumining the heap on the road and the soldier standing beside it. The motor hummed as men walked into the beam, grabbed the body, and lifted and dragged it to the rear of the vehicle. Doors slammed, the motor gunned, and the headlights swept over Wang's head as the truck turned and went back the way it came, receding and leaving him lying in the field in utter blackness.

He stayed where he was, lying still, shivering, not sleeping but seeing before him the same scene over and over again—the man walking, then running, then shot down. Night birds and insects whirred and clicked around him, marking the hours until the sky began to lighten. Before his staring eyes, he saw movement and started with a gasp.

A peasant getting an early start on his way to Bai Miao was given a fright when in the field beside the road a man suddenly stood up shouting, "No! No! Go back!"

"Well, what is it then?" he shouted back, but the man in the field just stood looking at him with wild eyes. "A madman," the peasant muttered to himself and hurried on.

Slowly Wang began walking like a man with no will of his own. He didn't think but simply walked, passing the place on the road with the dark stain, walking on through the first stirrings of the city, down the river road until he reached the house. Inside, he abruptly sat down on his bed, bent over, and vomited. The spasms kept on wracking his body until he doubled up on the floor.

The convulsions and the smell revived him, and he got to his feet. After a few moments he began looking around. He needed water to clean up the mess. Picking up the bamboo bucket, he walked toward the river. Edging down to the water, he dipped in the bucket and raised it to his mouth, rinsing out the sour taste. The light was harsh on the surface of the river, and there was a sudden roaring in his ears.

He dropped the bucket and waded into the water. It was cold but he didn't care. He walked in up to his neck, then plunged under the water, swimming as if he himself were a carp, swimming as far as he could till his lungs cried for air and he was forced to the surface. He sucked in a great breath and screamed with all his might. He slapped and thrashed the water, punishing the river and shouting wordless curses. He went on smashing his hands against the flat unfeeling water until he heard someone behind him, calling.

"Zhang!"

He turned and saw a figure on the bank.

"Zhang, is it you?"

He stared. "Who is it?"

"It is Li, Li Ying. Are you mad? What are you doing out there?" He couldn't answer. "Come in!"

"Comrade Li?"

"Come out of the water! You'll die of the cold!"

Slowly he began to swim toward her. As he walked out of the shallows and onto the bank, he began to shiver uncontrollably. She took one look at him and said, "Come with me."

She led him to his house. Once inside, she found a blanket, handed it to him, and put the kettle on the burner. "Take off those wet things and wrap yourself up. I will be back soon." Confused, he did as she said. She returned with boxes that she sat on the table. He watched as she wrung out his clothes and hung them on a line in the corner, then turned to the kettle and made tea. She opened a box and pulled out a dumpling and a rice ball and set them on a plate. She handed him a steaming cup of tea, and he would have gulped it all at once if she had not ordered him to drink it slowly. After he had finished eating, she made cups of tea for both of them. She sat down on the bed beside him and they drank in silence.

Finally she said, "Leung sent me to find you. Communication upriver is difficult."

He gulped the tea. "Why did he send you?"

"You are overdue. He is anxious to hear your report." She offered him another dumpling, which he accepted. "The commissar's office told me you were staying here. When I didn't find you in the house, I thought you might be at the river. I heard you shouting." She looked closely at him. "What has happened to you?"

He groped for an answer. "I, ah, I—"

"Tell me." Her tone was firm but not unkind.

His defenses dissolved like salt in water. "A man, a man is— What have I done?" He stood and put his hands on the top of his head. The blanket slid off, but he took no notice. "God, what have I done!"

That night Wang woke up in a panic, dreaming that he was being chased by a man bloody from many wounds. He sat up, panting, heart racing. When he calmed down, he would have stood and walked around to clear his head, but he noticed a dark heap of clothes on the floor. The heap moved, and he heard a sigh and a light snore. He looked more closely and recognized Li's face.

He lay down again and slept.

TWENTY

People jammed the deck of the ferry. Some were displaced workers looking for an opportunity in the city, others appeared to be merchants whose livelihoods had been seized or threatened, still others looking for family. Wang and Li had to sit on the open deck, hemmed in on all sides. The smells of the people and the motion of the boat made him fear he would be sick again, but having her next to him helped.

Threatening clouds turned to rain just before they arrived in Shanghai. Everyone scrambled off the boat, running for cover. He hailed a bicycle taxi, gave the address of his apartment, and they sat in the drenching rain as the driver wound through streets filling with rivulets. She offered to come inside with him. "You are still not yourself," she fretted, but he told her to go home.

"I will be all right. Tell Leung I will give him my report in two days. And Comrade Li," he said, "I don't know what would have happened if you hadn't—"

She flashed a brief smile but then scolded. "Go inside where it's dry."

He remembered to check and found the slip of paper in the hinge. The apartment was familiar and should have been comforting, but somehow everything seemed altered and odd. He doffed his wet things and laid them out on the floor, rummaged in a chest and found dry clothes. He sat down at the table, took a slip of paper and wrote out a message.

Urgent. Must speak to Owl. Critical information from Bai Miao. Cuckoo.

The rain had stopped, and he went down to the newspaper kiosk and saw to his relief the courier was there. He bought a paper, passed the message, and walked to a noodle stand, using a ration card he found in the apartment to buy a steaming bowl of spicy soup, which he gobbled standing up. He returned to the apartment and lay down on the bed.

After he had blurted out to Li that he had seen a man shot down, she left and made some discreet inquiries. The dead man was Min Bolin, a clerk in a shop in Bai Miao. He had been to Xiagang to visit a relative and was on his way home. There was no explanation for why he might have gone into a forbidden area, and the stricken family, not wishing to make trouble, politely suggested the account of the patrol leader might have been mistaken. Min was known to be Christian, but the army found no evidence of counter-revolutionary activity and concluded he had made a foolish mistake and paid for it with his life.

After delivering this news, Li had prodded Wang for an answer. "What happened?"

He had an explanation. He wanted a better vantage point of the river, to see where there might be features that would be most favorable for the fish farm. He didn't think the army would patrol such a lonely spot. When he saw the soldiers, he became frightened and ran, hiding in the field. The man on the road had come along just then.

"I wanted to warn him, but I was afraid." He looked away in shame.

She was impassive, and he couldn't tell if she believed this story, but finally she said, "His bad luck was your good fortune. We will say nothing to anyone."

He stared. "Why would you take such a risk for me?"

She said, "This research of yours could be an important means of feeding the people. We have few good scientists as it is. We cannot afford to lose you."

"I see. It's because I am useful."

"Yes." Then, for just a moment, her sternness softened. "But I..." She stood. "You must rest."

She had taken care of everything so efficiently he was awed. She gave no sign of affection, but she was a flame and he was a moth. He had never known a woman like this. He wouldn't mention her to Owl.

On the second morning after returning to Shanghai, he saw a cap hanging from a nail in the window of the newspaper kiosk. He walked up to the booth, offered a coin for a copy of the *People's Daily*, and said, "Here, buy your girlfriend a flower." The attendant handed him a folded copy of the paper and said, "I'd rather buy cigarettes for myself." Inside the apartment, he opened the paper and found the message inside. He decoded, *Tea room. 10 o'clock tonight.*

Wang caught a trolley to the Ministry office, where Li was busy in Leung's anteroom. She quietly asked if he was well.

"I am having trouble sleeping," he said in a low voice. "I keep remembering—"

Leung appeared in the doorway and waved him inside. Wang told him there were two locations that would be suitable for large fish farms, if the Ministry wished to proceed with the next phase.

"I have been given permission by the deputy minister. You may set up a farm in Bai Miao." Leung gave a nervous laugh. "Do your best, comrade. We do not want to fail."

The telephone rang, and Leung dismissed him. As he walked past Li's desk, she said, "I have written out a sleep remedy that my mother used. The ingredients are easy to find. It may be of some help." She held out a sheet of paper.

"Thank you. That is very kind." He grasped the sheet but Li did not release it at first, and he looked at her in surprise.

In a low voice, she murmured, "There is also an opportunity for you to show your thanks."

A clerk entered the anteroom, and Wang casually folded the sheet and said in a haughty voice, "In my experience, Comrade Li, these folk remedies are mostly nonsense. Very unscientific."

She looked down and said deferentially, "I'm sure you are right, comrade. It was foolish to suggest it."

After he stepped outside, he opened the sheet. On the top was a list of ingredients and a few lines showing how to combine them. On the bottom, he read, "20 Blue Sky Street, 8 p.m. tomorrow." He re-read the note and suppressed a smile. Only later did he have misgivings, remembering Carol.

She was a fellow biology student at Pacific Reformed. Carol was white, and he never understood why she was attracted to him. He didn't even speak English very well. The affair was intense, and he had asked her to marry him at the end of the term, but she simply shook her head and said, "I can't. It was a mistake." He thought about returning to China but threw himself into his studies instead. He still remembered the pain.

Wang waited in his apartment until nine then set out on his bicycle on the forty-five minute ride across the city to the tea room, which was used as a place to drop messages and packages. The windows were dark and the door locked, but he rapped three times and said distinctly, "I have a delivery of jade tea."

The owner, Shu, opened the door. He was a short, pleasant man with bad teeth. After locking the door behind them, he led Wang into a back room where there was tea and food waiting. A few minutes later, there was a carefully patterned knock on the back door, and Shu admitted a tall, clean-shaven man wearing a Mao jacket and cap who looked as if he had come directly from a cadre meeting. Wang almost uttered a surprised cry until he looked again and saw it was Owl.

"*Ni hao*," he said with relief. "Your disguise is good."

The chief didn't reply. They helped themselves to food and drink and ate silently. Owl turned his dark eyes on Wang.

"This is a risky meeting. Your report."

He poured out everything about the mission to Bai Miao. The presence of Russians in the area, his discovery of the plant, how the pedestrian had died. Owl interrupted with questions. Did he himself see any Russians? What were the dimensions of the plant? Was he sure he had not been followed back to Shanghai?

"You have done well," Owl said finally. "More experienced men might not have learned as much."

Shu said, "But this plant you saw, what is special about it? Why the security around it?"

"I don't know," Wang said. "The shape of the tower reminds me of a photograph I saw of an experimental station in America. An atomic reactor."

Shu sucked in his breath, and Owl leaned forward. "Are you sure? If the Russians are helping build such a plant, this information would be priceless."

"I am not sure. All I know is what I have told you."

Shu shook his head. "Why would the Russians help Mao build such a plant? They have nothing to gain."

Wang said, "Perhaps the Party promised them something in return. Food, for instance."

"No. Food is scarce enough here. Not even Mao is stupid enough to trade away what little we have."

Owl said, "We will have to get someone inside this plant. This will be the most dangerous operation we have tried."

Shu said urgently, "We need the Kingfisher."

For a moment, Owl seemed to take the suggestion seriously, then he said, "No. That is not possible. We will pass on the information to the Birdcatchers. They may have some advice. For now, we will carry on as usual." He turned to Wang. "We will need a courier, someone who can move between Shanghai and Bai Miao without arousing suspicion. Can you arrange that?"

He did not look at the chief. "Leung has received permission for me to set up a fish farm there."

Owl slurped tea. "Good. You are proving useful after all." He noticed Wang's distant look. "Something is bothering you. Out with it."

He knew better than to expect sympathy from Owl, but shock and fear had not left him in almost three days. He looked up to see the chief glaring at him. "The man who was shot. His death troubles me."

"He was nothing." It was said with a dismissive click of the tongue. "How many innocent people have died in the last twenty years? He was just one more."

"Yes, I saw many innocent people die," Wang said evenly. "But none of them died in my place. I don't want another death on my conscience!"

Owl slowly stood, and Wang saw contempt at the corners of his mouth. "Conscience, is it! A word for women and holy men. It means weakness, and I have seen what soft agents can do to a network." He held out his hand, flat and vertical, like an axe blade, a simple gesture. "You'll do as you are told."

Wang swallowed. "For how much longer?"

"Until we no longer need you. If you have thoughts of disloyalty, you should think about your mother."

"What about her?" he said sharply.

Owl raised his shoulders and let them fall. He turned and slipped out the back door.

Wang and Shu walked to the front. "Are you all right?" the little man asked.

"Raven, then this poor fellow. Two dead in two weeks. It's like during the war."

"For us, the war never ended."

Wang pedaled home in the dark.

TWENTY-ONE

The next day Wang sent his assistants home early and went to his apartment to change. Blue Sky Street was in the same district, a twenty-minute bicycle ride. Spring was changing to summer, and the day was warm. As he approached the building, he heard his name. He looked up, and saw Li waving from a second-floor window.

She stood in the open door of the apartment at the landing. "Greetings," he said, and held out a bouquet of flowers. She accepted them with a smile and beckoned him inside. Normally single women in the Party were housed in barracks. He wondered what strings she had pulled to have her own flat.

The smell of dim sum filled the apartment. It was northern cuisine, not easy to find in Shanghai. A low table was filled with dishes, plates, and bowls. She must have been hoarding ration cards—a forbidden but common practice—to get her hands on this much food.

She offered him a cup of tea. "Please sit."

He had not eaten this well since returning to China. It was glorious, and he became expansive as he ate, talking about the fine points of marine biology. Somewhat to his surprise, Li was a congenial conversationalist, quick to grasp a point or ask an appropriate question. He spoke of his frustration at being unable to do proper examinations of dissected tissue.

"I need a better microscope. Of course, our facilities here are not as advanced as in Calif—" He broke off and picked up his bowl.

She said easily, "You mean in California? I heard that you studied there."

"Yes. I did."

"Before the Revolution?"

"While it was going on. I regret that I did not help in the struggle, but after the people prevailed, I decided to return and put my knowledge to use in rebuilding the nation." Before she could ask anything else, he said, "What of you? Where are you from?"

"My story is not very interesting," she said with a deflective gesture. "My father was a teacher in Nanjing. I was just a girl when the Japanese invaded. We fled, and my father joined the Party. He survived the war but died last year of illness. My mother lives with my sister in Beijing. As I say, not very interesting." She went to a cabinet and produced a flask. "Plum wine," she said with a conspiratorial smile.

"And how did you acquire this?" he said with pretended sternness. Plum wine was a rarity these days.

She leaned forward and whispered, "Do not ask too many questions."

They laughed and drank to the health of Chairman Mao, to the Party, to the Revolution, and to Comrade Inspector Leung. Soon Wang felt as if he were floating.

"To the carp! To *Cyprinus carpio*!" he said, too loudly.

Li giggled, then shushed him. "The neighbors will be suspicious," she said.

He clapped his hand over his mouth and looked sheepish. They exchanged looks and began laughing again, laughing for no reason until he leaned back too far and slopped a bit of wine on his clothes. Li laughed, but Wang was annoyed.

"Ah! My shirt will be ruined, and I do not have the means for another," he fretted.

"Let me see," she said, edging around the table and examining the spot. "The shirt can be saved, but it must be rinsed at once. Take it off, and I will pour hot water on the stain."

He sat still, his head muddled. Li had gone to the kettle and glanced back. "Well? Do you wish me to take out the stain?"

Yes, he decided, that was what he wanted. He slowly began to unfasten the shirt, fumbling with the buttons. Li made an impatient sound, came over and quickly unfastened the buttons and tugged the shirt off. She placed a cloth under it and poured a bit of steaming water from the kettle onto the spot, then placed another cloth on top.

"There. We will let it dry," she said. She sat down next to Wang. "More wine?"

"I shouldn't. I think I am already a little drunk." He involuntarily leaned a little toward her and giggled.

She leaned toward him, touching her shoulder to his and said in a low voice, "I think we are both a little drunk."

He recovered his balance and gazed at her, watching as she slowly extended her hand toward his chest and felt her cool palm against his skin. It was as if she had applied a healing medicine that spread outward and took away the fear he had felt every day for a year. He saw her face, those even teeth, and leaned toward her. This time, he was aware of every touch, every movement.

It was unlike what he had known with Carol. She was always impatient, petulant. He thought that even her lovemaking was typically American. With Li there was a shared understanding about how these things are done. It seemed very natural, unhurried. They made love quietly, with only an occasional whimper or soft moan, nothing to attract attention.

Finally, they lay still together, exchanging smiles.

"You expressed your thanks most satisfactorily," she said, grinning.

"Ha!" He raised on an elbow and looked at her. Questions chased each other through his mind. He left them unspoken, not wanting to spoil what had just happened, but asked, "Why have you not married?"

She grimaced and shook her head. "Men are fools. Brutes and dunces. I have no interest in marriage if it means keeping house and being used to satisfy a man's drunken desires."

He nodded. "I have seen many such marriages."

"And you? Most men your age are married."

"Oh, I am too hard to please," he said dismissively.

"Have I pleased you?"

He looked at her. "I am happier now than I have been in a long time." He kissed her and would have gone further, but she interrupted him.

"It is late. You must go." She stood, retrieved a robe and put it on.

Reluctantly Wang dressed. When he was ready, he embraced her and kissed her again. She finally pulled back and said with a serious face, "We must be careful."

He knew this was true. The Party had decreed that all relationships were subject to scrutiny. The personal was also political, and Party members had to receive permission to "talk about love." It was part of the Revolution, to uproot entrenched traditions and render everyone, including women, equal. Carrying on an illicit affair was to risk loss of position, humiliation, and "re-education."

Nevertheless, he said, "I want to see you again."

"You will, but if word gets back to Leung, we will both be in trouble. Especially me."

At the door he turned. "How will we communicate?"

Li smiled. "Don't worry. We will find a way."

The weeks passed as if it were a matter of days. Li arranged for their meetings by slipping a message into dispatches from Leung. His work seemed a mere distraction, a way to fill time until he could see her again. His assistants noticed the change in him. He was not so serious, made jokes and smiled for no reason. They nodded to each other and made sly remarks behind his back. It could only be a woman, they said.

The preparations for establishing the new farm in Bai Miao took longer than Wang expected. Wire for the pen was in short supply. Li directed him to a certain warehouse, where the manager read his requisition form and sucked in his breath between his teeth. "It is impossible, comrade. The army has already ordered everything we have."

"I see. Well, I will have to inform Comrade Li you were unable to help."

The manager eyed him and turned his palm up. "Wait. Perhaps I was mistaken. I believe we have two rolls of wire after all." Wang promised to pick them up and transport them himself, afraid they would be stolen if he had them delivered.

By August, the river was swollen from rains that had drenched the Yangtze valley all summer. The work had been hard, and to his dismay, the farms were proving difficult to manage. The fish were kept in large open pens on the river, the current tugged at the wire, and it was difficult to contain the fish. Worse, despite the first encouraging results, they were not thriving. He traveled constantly, seeing to one problem after another.

It had meant lengthy separations from Li, which added to his misery. Their reunions were a riot of lovemaking that left him bleary and complacent. She became angry about it once as he lolled about her apartment naked. "You are becoming nothing more than a bourgeois householder. Look at you, demanding favors of me every time you show up. That's enough for tonight. Get dressed and go home!" But he smiled at her anger and rode his bicycle back to his apartment in a dreamlike state.

He had sent regular messages to Owl advising him of his travels up and down the river but got only an occasional terse acknowledgement. It suited him perfectly well, and he hoped that getting an agent inside the plant would prove impossible, but Owl's hatred of the Communists burned hotter than black powder and Wang knew he would not give up easily.

For his part, he had never felt any animosity toward the Communists. He knew of their excesses, of course, and thought their regimentation and bureaucracy ridiculous, but he also understood that the lot of common people had improved since the Revolution. It was unlikely that his work of raising fish to feed workers would have gotten much support had the Kuomintang prevailed.

Nostalgia sent him back to China. The American preoccupation with money and things was bewildering. His fellow students talked about parties and cars and were not interested in his accounts of life in China. His studies were scant consolation for the loneliness he felt. He could not get used to the food and dreamed of his mother's cooking. Yet her letters told of friends arrested for associations with America and urged him to stay in California. He could not return to China without coming under suspicion, and in any event, he had no money.

Then a professor had introduced him to a man named Cohen, who invited him to dinner. He worked for an organization that was interested in information about China, he said. Would Wang be willing to work for him?

"What sort of work?" Wang asked.

"I will be honest," Cohen said. "It will mean going back to China secretly, under an assumed name. You would be part of a network of...observers."

"Ah. You want me to be a spy. Against my country."

"Your country is run by ruthless men who have taken away the people's freedom. Surely you are not on their side?"

Wang didn't reply. It was strange how the Communists had used the same slogans to describe the Nationalists.

Cohen's offer was a way of going home, even if under a false identity. In the end, he agreed, but he hadn't realized that once he joined the network, there would be no way out. More and more he was coming to despise it and to sympathize with the people who were supposed to be his enemies. He had much more in common with Juh Jingbao, with whom he was becoming good friends, than with Owl. He was often tempted to withhold or alter the information he gathered, but he was afraid of what Owl would do if he found out. The chief had a grim motto, "We do not allow mistakes in this organization." He longed to be free of his double life, but he could not think of a way to do it without endangering his mother.

And now there was Li.

When he returned to Bai Miao, he avoided going into the city, still haunted by the night he went up to the ridge. He imagined someone would start shouting that this was the man who was responsible for an innocent person's death. At unexpected moments, the scene of Min Bolin falling under the soldier's bullets appeared before him. Once two cars crashed into each other nearby with a bang, and he threw himself to the ground, drawing stares from passersby.

He idly realized one morning as he prepared tea and rice that it was Sunday. As he ate, pictures from the past flashed through his mind and an impulse rose within him. Leaving the food on the table, he shouldered his pouch and walked quickly toward the city.

Bai Miao had grown in the years he was gone. It was a typical Chinese town, with ornamental gates at each of the four compass points. In the old days, the city was contained inside walls, but it had long ago spilled beyond them, and now the gates stood well inside the city's outer borders, serving as landmarks and signs of signs of civic pride.

He wasn't sure if the church was in the same location, and it took him a few tries to find the place, but he saw it, an unadorned square wooden building with characters painted on the door that read *Heaven's Way Church*. He noticed that a cross mounted above the door had been removed. It was still early. The doors were shut and no one approached. He found an empty vendor's stall that allowed him to observe the street and sat down.

In his childhood, his mother would bring him to this building an hour before services started so that they could go in as soon as the doors were unlocked. She adored this plain little place, and as he looked at it again, he grudgingly remembered that he had liked coming here. Here his mother was called "sister" and treated with a measure of respect and warmth. And here, when he was in town, Pastor Ma would never fail to kneel down and look him in the face and say hello and ask how his studies were going. A tall pale man with spectacles, a high forehead and a friendly way, whom he had followed around like a street dog hoping for a scrap of food. It was Pastor Ma who had taken such a special interest in him and his mother, ensuring they had enough to eat. It was he who gave him the name Paul and saw to it that he got into the missionary school in Shanghai, where he learned English and loved science. Perhaps he will become a doctor like the father of Pastor Ma, the adults said.

The memory turned bitter and he almost started to leave when he saw an elderly man approaching the church. It was the sexton, coming to unlock the building, and Wang smiled at his slow, bobbing walk. He usually hummed an old Chinese hymn, and watching him, Wang could hear it in his head. He closed his eyes, trying to recall the words.

Spring wind, summer rain, then the harvest grain;
Pearly rice and corn, fragrant autumn morn.
Though our work is hard, God gives us reward.

A hand on his shoulder made him leap to his feet, panicked. He was looking into a familiar face, though lined now and full of astonishment. They stared at each other, speechless, and then, his face transforming from surprise to joy, Pastor Dou exclaimed, "It is you. Wang Wenzhe!" The instant he spoke, Wang grabbed his arm, spun him around, and forced him to walk quickly around a corner to a spot between two buildings, growling in a low voice for him to be quiet.

When they stopped, Dou grasped his arms. "Wenzhe, what is it? Why are you hiding? Come, we must take you to see your mother! She will want—"

"Be quiet! Be quiet, do you understand? You must be quiet, or we will all suffer!"

Dou looked as if he had been struck. Wang looked quickly around. No uniforms in sight, only a few merchants chatting with idle customers, peasants carrying sacks. As he looked back at Dou, the pastor let go of his arms. "Wenzhe. It has been a long time. You were still a boy when you left here." He looked him up and down, beaming. "Now you are a man. And you have returned."

Wang felt naked, exposed, being addressed by his real name in the open like this, but he tried to speak calmly. "Pastor Dou, greetings. I'm sorry I spoke to you that way."

"Something is wrong. Tell me."

"I did not want to be seen."

"What is it? Are you in trouble? We can—"

"No, I am not in trouble. But it cannot be known that Wang Wenzhe has returned to Bai Miao." Seeing Dou's confusion, he said carefully, "The people I work for think I am someone else."

Alarm showed in Dou's eyes. He said, "Your mother..."

Wang nodded. "I came here hoping just to watch her go into the church, to see if she is all right." He asked anxiously, "Is she well?"

"Yes, she is well, but she longs to see you."

"And I long to see her. But we cannot yet meet openly. I was only able to return to China under a disguise. And I cannot be seen in the church. I do not want to put anyone in danger."

The pastor's face was grave, and he shook his head. "Wenzhe, what sort of business are you mixed up in? You were always a good boy, so smart."

"It is better not to speak of it. How can I get a message to you?"

Dou glanced around and spoke in low tones. "Go past the church two hundred meters. You will see a house with a sign out front that says 'Anchors repaired.' Knock twice and say, 'I need a new rope.'" Dou looked down the street. "I must go. I have to deliver some food to a widow. Her husband was killed by the army."

Wang began breathing heavily. "Why was he killed?"

"These are the people we are dealing with. He was shot for no reason while walking home from Xiagang. They accused him of entering a forbidden zone, but it is nonsense."

"When was this?"

"Three months ago."

"He had a wife? Children?"

"A wife and a small son." He placed a hand on Wang's arm. "You know her. She is the daughter of your mother's cousin."

Shock overtook him. "Yuming?"

Dou nodded. "Grief has made her a living corpse. She barely speaks or eats. Her mother has to care for the little boy, who is too young to understand."

"My cousin." He remembered Yuming well—a plain, submissive girl. Whenever his mother brought him to visit, she watched silently as Wang played with her brothers, wanting to join in but not daring to. When she came of age, his mother began to talk to her cousin of a marriage between the two of them. Wang objected that he did not want to marry such a dull girl, but his mother insisted that he must marry a fellow believer, and there were few other choices. But as did many Chinese who professed Christianity, Yuming's mother also relied on tradition. She consulted a matchmaker, who declared the match inauspicious and marriage talk ended abruptly. When Wang left for America, she was still unmarried.

"Is there something you wish me to tell her?" Dou asked.

Wang shook his head. "Go. Please say nothing to my mother yet."

The pastor placed a hand on his shoulder. "God be with you."

Wang turned and went back to the house, where the tea and the rice were cold.

TWENTY-TWO

Cautiously Wang began to venture into Bai Miao again. Still afraid that he would be accused of causing Min's death, he had kept to himself in the house and at the farm, going into the city only to purchase what was needed. He had avoided the Party office, but he missed his conversations with Juh. He liked this humble man whose simple life Wang envied. On impulse, he walked into Juh's cluttered office and asked him to dinner.

"Allow me to repay you for your past generosity," he said.

Juh smiled broadly. "It would be an honor to dine with you, Zhang, but really, you do not need to repay me."

"Nonsense. Without you, my life here would have been dreary. Allow me to show my appreciation."

They agreed on the following evening. He went to a nearby inn and arranged to have food and wine delivered to the house. Juh was amazed when he arrived to see the feast spread before them.

"All this? Have you been hoarding ration cards?"

Wang grinned. "It is impolite to ask such a question of your host. Come, a toast to our friendship."

They gorged themselves and drank flask after flask of rice wine. Juh was not his usual modest self but instead garrulous, roaring with laughter and making rude comments about women in the city. Then suddenly he fell silent.

Wang leaned forward. "Is something amiss?"

Juh shook his head. "I have been thinking about the war. Those were great days, glorious days. The Party was united, all the comrades fighting together against our enemies. Now..." He waved a hand as he would to get rid of a fly.

"Now?"

Juh shook his head. "Now we are no more than petty bureaucrats, fighting among ourselves for a little better position. We won great victories over the Japanese emperor and the Nationalist tyrant Chiang. For what? So we could write five-year plans and congratulate ourselves? Bah!" He took a long drink. "The Party has lost its soul."

Wang nodded and sighed. "It is the same everywhere. My supervisor is a fool. At least your commissar is a competent man, yes?"

"The commissar! What a joke. He got this position because his wife is the sister of a provincial minister."

Wang spread his hands. "And you such an able and diligent worker. It is an injustice."

Juh nodded emphatically. "He would be helpless without me. Why, just yesterday, that jackass, the plant supervisor, came around. He wanted—" Juh checked himself.

"It's all right," Wang said casually. "Everyone knows something is being built upriver."

Juh lowered his voice. "He was complaining about the food supplied to the workers. Food is short. He knows this, but he demanded double rations and threatened to create a big stink about it. The commissar should have thrown him out. Instead he said, 'Of course, comrade, of course. We will see to it at once.' He ordered a reduction in the number of ration cards distributed in the city. It is criminal, I tell you!" Juh leaned forward, slopping some of his wine. "He entrusted that task to me, his stooge."

"You are no stooge. Surely there is something you can do to correct this wrong."

Juh exhaled loudly and said, "The plant is being built under the authority of Beijing. There is nothing I can do."

"Beijing?"

"I have seen the dispatches."

Wang tried to sound judicious. "Even the Party is not always right. You said yourself it has lost its soul."

Juh looked up. "Perhaps I have said too much."

He had to help Juh walk home and turned him over to Meili, who offered him brief thanks and silently took charge of her husband, trundling him into the bedroom. She was such a mouse. Most wives would have complained and scolded, Wang reflected as he walked home.

The intelligence was valuable, but he waited a couple of days before going back to the Party office. Juh greeted him with an embarrassed smile. "*Ni hao*. Are you well?"

"I am well, but you do not look good."

"I am all right." He lowered his voice and spoke urgently. "I beg you, please say nothing to anyone about...what we discussed."

Wang hoped his lie was convincing. "Of course."

Juh looked relieved. "The best mirror is a friend's eyes," he said, quoting the proverb. "If my words were rash, it is just that we are under pressure now to see to it—" He dropped his voice. "—that all goes well." He tilted his head in the direction of the river and held up a fistful of papers. "Directives. Quite explicit about the consequences of failure. We are—"

A man appeared at the entrance to the office. "Comrade Juh, apologies for the interruption. The commissar wishes to see you."

Juh stood and placed the papers in a drawer. "Excuse me," he said to Wang. "Come again soon."

Exchanging good wishes, they walked out of the little office, and Juh closed the door but didn't lock it. Wang stepped outside the building, counted to ten and walked back inside. No one was watching and he went inside Juh's office, closing the door behind him. Quickly he went to the desk, opened the drawer, and pulled out the papers.

From the time he was young, Wang had a photographic memory. It was one reason he had done well in school. Memorizing Chinese characters, mathematical formulas, chemical charts, all had come easily to him. Now he quickly leafed through the papers, reading and committing them to memory. There were routine requests for information from the Central Defense Committee, reports on deliveries from the Ministry of Industry. Others were letters from obscure bureaucrats addressed to the commissar, directing him to give full cooperation to the People's Liberation Army. Feverishly he scanned the documents. The word "Politburo" caught his eye. It was a letter to the commissar.

> *The Politburo of the Communist Worker's Party cannot emphasize strongly enough, Comrade Commissar, the importance of this project. The successful completion of this manufacturing plant will further good relations with our brothers in the Union of Soviet Socialist Republics. It is therefore essential that the electronics engineers from Russia be shown every courtesy. The specialized transistors this plant will produce are intended for use in missiles that will defend the U.S.S.R. and the People's Republic of China from threats from America and the imperialist West.*
> *You are hereby directed—*

Footsteps sounded outside the door and he froze, but they receded again. Wang replaced the papers, went to the door and opened it a crack. Two men stood talking several meters away in the hallway. Wang opened the door and said distinctly, "Thank you, comrade, that is most useful." They ignored him. He walked quickly back to the house, where he committed to his notebook everything he remembered. He tore the pages out and stuffed them into a small pouch that he slid inside his waistband.

He knew he should return at once to Shanghai and give the information to Owl, but if it were intercepted and traced back to Juh... There had to be another way, but there was no one he could turn to for advice.

He walked back into the city, past the church, and found the shop with the sign "Anchors repaired." Inside he was met by a large man.

"I need a new rope," Wang said.

The man looked at him warily. "Who are you?"

"I am a relative of Sister Lin. Pastor Dou said I could get a message to him here."

"I am Qin," the man said. "Can you wait?"

He showed Wang to a back room. Hours passed, with Wang pacing, sweating, thinking of his choices. At last, the door opened and Dou entered.

"Wenzhe, greetings. I am glad to see you."

"Greetings, Pastor Dou. Ah, excuse the question, but were you followed?" Dou hesitated. "It is important."

"I am sometimes followed, and our services often are watched, but I do not think I was followed here."

"You are under suspicion?"

Dou sighed. "All Christians are suspected of connections to the West. And pastors have been arrested for preaching our loyalty is to God alone."

"I do not want to get you in trouble."

"*Ai*, Wenzhe, what is the matter? Why are you here?"

"Well, we cannot speak of it. But I would like to see my mother. Is it possible for me to meet her in private?"

Dou thought for a moment. "We have a prayer meeting tonight. Your mother always comes. There is a room in the back where you could meet. Come to the alley behind the church. Look for Qin."

He returned early that evening, well ahead of the prayer meeting, and found Qin waiting in the alley. The big man opened a door into a small anteroom. It was not long before Wang heard singing in the adjoining sanctuary, low at first, then louder as more people arrived. The door to the room opened, and his bewildered mother walked in. They had not seen each other in five years, but the shock of recognition struck them both at once, and she shrieked as she rushed up to embrace him. The singing drowned most of her cries, but Wang still had to shush her.

"Oma, please, you will disturb the meeting." Tears blurred his sight. "It is all right now."

"Wenzhe, son, you are here! Let me see you. Ah, so skinny! You have not been eating."

He laughed, dashing away his tears. "I have not found anyone who cooks as well as you."

She beamed at him. "Wenzhe, you have returned. God has answered my prayers. Come, I must give my testimony—"

She started for the door, but Wang seized her wrist. "Oma, wait! I must talk to you." He pulled her onto a bench and sat next to her.

"Wenzhe, why did you not tell me you were coming? Have you finished your studies? What—" She broke off at the look on his face.

"I do not have much time. You must tell no one that you have seen me. No, listen! My life and yours and Pastor Dou's depend on this. As far as you know, I am still in America, you understand?"

Her face fell. "*Ai*, Wenzhe, what have you done?"

"I came back to China in secret. I...I have done some wrongs, but I am trying to make things right."

She shook her head. "You were safe in America. Why have you come back?"

"I was unhappy. I thought I would never see you again."

Tears welled in her eyes. "But you are not yourself. And now you cannot stay."

"No, but Oma, have patience. It may be possible for us to be together again soon. I just need some time to—"

Her upraised palm stopped him. The singing in the church had turned to chanting a psalm. She was calm and firm. "You are all I have left. I have longed to see you, but as my own son. I think you have done a foolish thing in coming back to China. You were safe, but now you are in danger."

He stammered, "Oma, I..."

She stood. "I must join the service." As if a thought had just occurred to her, she said, "Pastor Ma. Have you seen him? Is he well?"

He avoided her eyes. "I have not seen him in a long time. I believe he is a pastor in America somewhere."

"Will you go back to America?"

Now he stood and faced her. "No. Not if I can stay. I will see you again soon."

She turned away, shaking her head. "I will pray for you. Farewell, my son."

Before he could reply, she left the small room. He watched from the door, the giant Qin walking next to her tiny frame.

TWENTY-THREE

The next day Wang boarded the ferry for Shanghai.

All was in order at his apartment. He coded a message for Owl and hurried down to the newspaper kiosk. As he rounded the corner, he saw with a start that it was empty. He strolled by, glancing at it as he passed. It looked abandoned. He walked on and caught a crosstown trolley, alighting at the stop nearest Shu's tea room. He walked to a corner fifty meters away from the building and stood watching for several minutes. No one entered or left. As he approached it slowly, his heart began to pound. He tested the door knob, but it did not open. There was damage around the frame. Turning around, he saw a boy of about twelve watching him with curiosity.

"You there, boy," he said in a friendly voice.

"*Ni hao*," the boy replied.

"I often come to this tea room for refreshment, but it is closed today. Do you know why?"

The boy shook his head. "I think it will be closed forever."

"What's that? Why? Speak up." The boy looked nervous, as if he might run. "Here, I have a few coins for you if you will tell me why it is closed." The boy fidgeted but took a step closer as Wang fished in his bag and held up two silver coins. The boy's hand reached, but he closed his fist. "First tell me."

He spoke in a low voice. "The owner was arrested."

"Arrested? Are you sure?"

"I'm sure. The police came and broke the door in. There was shouting and then they dragged Mr. Shu out and put him in a car and drove off. Since then the place has been closed."

"Did you see this?"

The boy nodded solemnly. "Can I have the coins?"

Wang held them up and said, "When did this happen?"

"Yesterday."

He dropped the coins in the boy's hand. He had to think. He went to a nearby inn, asked for a seat, and ordered tea. His hands shook as he lifted the cup to his mouth. Protocol called for him to fall back at the safe house. Owl might be in hiding there. But what if the First Bureau knew everything? The place would be a death trap. Yet he had only one other option, which he had not yet fully worked out.

One of Owl's strict rules was to assume at all times that he was under surveillance. In the weeks he had traveled up and down the river, Wang had been careless. The villages and landmarks had grown familiar, and even some of the people on the ferry were the same. Now he looked around, fully alert. People drank tea, talked quietly with others, read newspapers.

He paid for the tea and left the inn, turning onto the nearby boulevard, surrounded on all sides by the bustle of the city. At an intersection, he stopped with the knot of people waiting to cross. The late afternoon was hot, tropical, and he half-turned as he wiped his forehead. A man twenty meters behind him in a gray shirt was leaning against a building.

Wang crossed the street, walked two more blocks and turned left. As he rounded the corner, he saw the gray shirt behind him raise his hand to his hair. He walked with the flow of pedestrians, turning back to the right at the next block, then right again, went a hundred meters and stopped in front of a store window. To his right, he saw a young man with close-cropped hair wearing black pants and shoes slow his pace and stop to pull a cigarette out of his pocket. He resumed walking.

Just ahead, a man pulled his bicycle off the street, leaned it against a store front, and walked inside the shop. When he reached the bicycle, Wang took the handlebars and with two quick steps pushed it into the street, mounted it, and began pedaling fast. A narrow alley appeared on his right, and he barreled into it, barely missing people on either side. He looked frantically for some opening, but there were only blank walls and small doors. A glance back over his shoulder showed some commotion at the entrance to the alley.

He dodged a pushcart, swerved around two cooking stalls. Still pedaling fast, he saw up ahead what he had hoped for, a busy street. He rounded the corner without looking, almost colliding with a jeep. He crossed in front of a taxi that screeched its brakes and blared its horn and turned right at the next corner onto a twisting road.

He was near the Huangpu River, the tributary of the Yangtze that ran through the city, and he veered that way. He pulled up at a water taxi stand and gave the boatman the fare and an extra twenty yuan with a few words. He climbed in, lay down in the bottom, and the boatman threw a filthy cloth over him. The motor sputtered and hummed, and he felt the boat pull out into the river. After ten minutes, he lifted the cloth, looked around and told the boatman to put in on the west bank at the nearest dock. He was sure he had shaken the surveillance, but he still took precautions, changing directions and checking behind him.

Wang hailed a bicycle taxi, and said, "Revolution Square." It was a small, pleasant park halfway across the city, always crowded with pensioners, lovers, street merchants, and the occasional policeman. Wang directed the driver to circle the park slowly, explaining that he was looking for someone. As the taxi rolled under a row of trees,

Wang told the driver to stop and paid him well. He walked casually from tree to tree, reversed his track and circled back to a monument on the south side of the square, rendered with melodramatic heroism, commemorating some little-remembered cadre's victory. He walked on past the square to a nearby street, turned a couple of times and paused. The street was busy, but no one was following him.

He approached an intersection where on the opposite side of the street stood a nondescript cottage. Next to the door hung an unlighted lantern. Wang stood on the corner, watching. His heart throbbed, but he dared not stand too long. Finally, seeing nothing suspicious, he crossed the street. Tensed to run at the first sound, he walked around the corner of the house to a small garden, counted the stones bordering it, lifted the ninth, and found the key. He went back to the door, sweating. He took down the lantern, put the key in the lock and forcefully shoved it open in case someone was waiting behind it. The curtains were drawn, and it was dim inside, but there was only silence and emptiness. He locked the door behind him. The house was musty, the boards creaked under his feet. Anyone stepping inside would think the place was abandoned, but Wang knew the appearance was deliberate.

He hissed, "Are you there? It is Zhang. Hello?"

He was taken from behind, with silent swiftness, a hand over his mouth, a knife at his throat. A moment's pause, and Owl said, low and intense, "Were you followed?"

Wang tried to answer but Owl's hand squeezed his mouth tight. He managed to shake his head and after another moment, the hand and the knife were gone. Wang panted as Owl stepped to the front window and stood looking. "There was someone," Wang gasped. "At the tea room."

In two quick steps, Owl loomed over him. "The tea room!"

Wang held up a hand. "I didn't know. I was going to send a message, but the courier's booth was empty. I went to the tea room, and a boy told me what happened to Shu. I thought someone, maybe two people, were following me, but I eluded them. No one was watching when I came here."

"You are certain."

Wang had caught his breath and straightened. "Yes."

Owl sheathed his knife and led Wang over to a low table where they sat on cushions.

"What if Shu tells them about this place?" Wang asked.

"Shu is dead. He took the pill before they could interrogate him."

Wang stared, then frowned. "How do you know?" Owl didn't answer. Wang shook his head. "How is this happening?"

"We are up against a cunning foe." For the first time, Owl's face seemed to soften. "I did not tell you because you are new to all this. I didn't want to frighten you. The First Bureau has a top counter-intelligence agent. We know him only as The Archer. He has been systematically uncovering our networks. I thought Aviary was secure, but The Archer has found a weakness, somehow. For some time, I suspected you were the weakness."

"Me? But I don't...I haven't..."

Owl waved a hand. "No matter. We will have to disband. We need to get you out of China."

"Out— Where?"

He shrugged. "Where do you think?"

"America." Wang was silent for a moment. "Listen. I have some information. There is a clerk named Juh at the Party office in Bai Miao. I have become friendly with him. He told me the plant is being built on orders from Beijing. He says he has dispatches."

Owl sat forward, tense now. "Did he say what was in the dispatches?"

Wang met Owl's eyes. "No."

"This Juh, what do you know of him?"

"Merely a humble clerk. Unhappy with his superior, but loyal to the Party."

"No chance he would help you?" Wang shook his head. "Do you know where he keeps the dispatches?"

"I think so."

Owl was silent for a long time. At last he said, "Very well. You will have one more assignment."

Owl insisted that Wang stay that night in the safe house before returning for the last time to Bai Miao. He could not sleep, thinking about Owl's terse command: If you cannot get the documents secretly, do it by force. Kill Juh if necessary.

He knew now what he wanted.

When he woke, the house was empty.

He made for the Ministry. An alley ran behind the building, and he followed it to a small rear entrance, which was locked. He had to knock repeatedly until an angry clerk opened it and demanded to know what he wanted. Wang talked his way inside with a story about being late for a meeting. Desperately hoping that he would not run into Leung, he walked quickly into the anteroom where Li looked up in surprise and would have said his name, but he shook his head vigorously and motioned to her. With a look toward Leung's office, she slid from her chair and he led her down the stairs and into the alley.

She looked at him sharply. "We have been trying to reach you. Leung is demanding to know the results from the farms. What is wrong?"

"Something has happened."

"What?"

"Not here. Can you meet me later?"

She hesitated. "All right. Come to my apartment—"

"No. Not your place."

Her eyes narrowed. "Where then?"

He gestured. "Go east down the main boulevard, then north at the Long March monument. Two blocks, turn right. The Double Happiness Inn."

"I know it."

"Can you come at six?" She nodded. "And Li? Bring food. I'm starving."

She slammed the door behind her.

It was half past six when she arrived. She called his name, and he opened the door to find her laden with boxes. Wordlessly she set the food out on the floor.

"Were you followed?" he asked tersely. She shook her head. "You're sure?"

"I'm sure of it." They ate without talking until finally she said, "What is this about?"

He had decided to tell her a version of the truth. "I am being extorted. I don't know who they are for certain, but I think they are Nationalists, counter-revolutionaries."

Li went rigid. She placed both hands on the floor. "What do they want?"

"They want me to work for them, find out things about the military, gather intelligence. They are following me all the time. Yesterday I managed to shake them off."

"When did they first approach you?"

He hesitated. "Perhaps a month ago."

"How many are there?"

Irritated, he said, "I do not know, but they are dangerous!"

She spoke carefully. "Have you told the authorities?" He shook his head, and she looked down. "They have threatened you?"

"My mother. She lives in Bai Miao."

She frowned. "In your file, it says Zhang Weijun has no living relatives."

Now he was flustered. "I lied when I applied to return to China. I didn't want to put my mother in danger, in case I came under suspicion. But they know about her. They are using her to force me to work for them."

In a remarkably calm manner, she said, "So. Counter-revolutionary spies have learned that you have a weakness, one you lied about to our government, and they are exploiting it to recruit you. Yet you do not want to report this to the authorities, which is itself a counter-revolutionary act. And not reporting all this would make me guilty of a counter-revolutionary act." She regarded him for a moment. "What are you going to do?"

He hesitated. "I want to get away and start a new life in another city. I would like you to help me."

She stared, stood, paced, then began to laugh, which irritated him. "You make it sound easy," she said. "Forge the right papers and just disappear. And hope no one comes looking for you. You must be mad." She laughed again.

He raised his voice. "It is not funny!"

She rounded on him. "What do you think would happen if you just drop out of sight? Leung would report it. The authorities would suspect right away that you are engaged in something criminal, or worse. They would start poking around. Eventually they would find your mother. That is, if these counter-revolutionaries don't find her first. Then what?"

"Don't you think I've thought of all that?" He paused, breathing hard. "The only way to save my mother and get away is if Zhang Weijun is dead."

Li blinked, then nodded. "I see. An accident, perhaps, while you are on the river, tending the farms? They find an empty boat with your effects in it?"

"Yes. Something like that."

"So the Nationalist spies have no reason to harm your mother, and you send her a letter saying you are living in such-and-such city under such-and-such name. And you want me to help. Provide you with papers, a new identity as, what, a low-level bureaucrat, nothing that would attract attention? Arrange for an introduction in a new city?" He nodded, not meeting her eyes. She came and sat down again, facing him. Finally she put her face in her hands. "Zhang. *Ai*, what a mess you've made."

He waited, then asked eagerly, "Could you do it?"

Her head snapped up. "Could I do it? It is not a question whether I could do it. The question is whether you are determined to go ahead with this madness. Suppose you bungle some part of this scheme and are discovered? Think of the risk—to you, your mother. Me."

He hesitated, then said, "I have made up my mind."

"What of your work?" she said.

"One of my assistants will have to continue it. I will make sure all the notes are left behind."

She asked pointedly, "And what of us?"

He looked down. "You know how I feel about you. I could have tried to leave without telling you, but... Ying, come with me."

At first he thought she was going to laugh, but she placed a hand over her mouth, and he could see she was near tears. There was a long silence. She said, "You don't know how much you are asking. I have duties here."

He scowled. "The Party. You would put that ahead of our happiness?"

"Sometimes...the greater good..." she said without conviction.

"You talk like a petty bureaucrat."

"Where would we work? How would we live?"

"You are very resourceful. It would not be so bad..." he began.

"Please! Don't try to tell me how easy it will be, how we will live out our days in contentment! You know that is not true."

"It would be hard. But not impossible."

She started to reply, then looked down. "No. I can't go with you."

"I knew you would say that." He looked up to see her frowning and felt as though a curtain had fallen between them.

She stood. "I cannot give you an answer now to your...plan. You must carry on as if nothing is wrong. Prepare a report for Leung and bring it to the office tomorrow. Then go to Bai Miao. I will send word or come in person."

"How long?"

"A few days at most." She turned to leave.

His heart ached. "I have been happy when I am with you, Ying. If I do not see you again..."

She looked back and they stood in awkward silence. He wanted to go to her, hold her tightly but she said, "Farewell."

She reached for the door and did not look back.

TWENTY-FOUR

Lucas Vanderhoven's heels made a staccato pattern on the stone floors as he walked briskly down the long corridor of the Pentagon's C ring. He stopped at the dark oak door stenciled with the words *Deputy Chief, Asian Operations*, rapped three times and walked in without waiting for a reply.

Harry Cohen looked up from a desk littered with dossiers. He squinted against the smoke from a cigarette drooping from one side of his mouth.

"What ya got, Luke?"

"Morning, sir. It's a message from China."

Cohen stood and held out a hand. "Which network?"

"Aviary."

Muttering a curse, Cohen snatched the paper, scanned it quickly, then sat down and read it again slowly. "Christ," he said softly. He looked up at Vanderhoven. "When did this come in?"

"Oh six hundred. I know, three hours ago. Cryptography's backed up."

Cohen re-read the message. "Damn. The chief's going to have my hide."

"It's not your fault, sir."

Cohen knew he was right, but it was one more in a string of failures. The only consolation was that the guys at Langley weren't doing any better.

"What do you think, Luke? Is Hong Kong still an option?"

"It was still open as of a few days ago. We should double-check with our station there. If the network is kaput, the First Bureau might have the army seal the border."

"Yeah. All right." He picked up a pen and scribbled on the message *Reply: Message received, instructions to follow*. "Have this coded and sent, pronto. Tell the code boys it is A-one priority, and if it's not sent inside an hour, I'm going to personally come down and kick their asses."

"Aye, sir." He hurried out.

Reluctantly, Cohen pressed an intercom button. A voice replied "Yes?"

"Ann, it's Cohen. I need to brief the admiral on something that just came in."

There was a pause. "Is it urgent, captain? He's got a full schedule this morning."

"Believe me, he's going to want to hear this."

Five minutes later, he was admitted to the office of Rear Admiral Joe Flaherty, who did not offer him a chair. "Make it snappy, Harry. I've got some damn congressman coming to pester me about money."

"Sir, I just got a message from China. Another network is collapsing."

Flaherty's jaw clenched. "Which one?"

"Aviary."

The admiral stared. "Isn't that one run by...?"

Cohen nodded. "Yes, sir. Colonel Chen. He's down to two agents, and one of them is a guy we inserted. Not a professional. Chen says we need to get him out of there, or risk losing everything."

"What does that mean?"

"Chen knows a lot about our other networks, more than he should. If he's captured, they would be compromised too. He thinks this agent we sent, code name Cuckoo, is a weak spot. If we can get him out, Chen and the other agent can go underground. Lie low for a while until we can rebuild the network."

Flaherty stood and walked to a window. "How many networks have we lost, Harry? Two?"

"Three, sir, counting Aviary."

"How many networks left?"

"Two. But one of them has been steady, giving us good intel."

"One out of five."

"Actually, Aviary gave us good stuff, sir. Cuckoo performed better than we expected."

"And now we're shutting it down."

Patiently, Cohen said, "Admiral, the shelf life of these networks is pretty damn short. We're lucky if they last a year. That's about what Aviary lasted."

Flaherty persisted. "How many agents lost?"

Cohen knew but pretended to calculate. "Eleven confirmed dead, two or three others missing and presumed dead."

There was a long silence. "Jesus, Mary, and Joseph. Any explanations?" Before Cohen could reply, he waved him off. "Never mind. We need a new approach, but that'll have to wait. All right, Harry. Do whatever you have to."

"Aye, sir. Thank you, sir."

In his office, Cohen made phone calls. He summoned Vanderhoven. Inquiries were made. Reports were retrieved and reviewed. Orders ran down the chain of command. He stood at his desk, looking at scattered files.

"Any word from Hong Kong?" he asked Vanderhoven.

"Not yet. Sir, should we consider using the Falcon?"

Cohen shot a look at the young man. "You've been itching to try that, haven't you?"

Vanderhoven grinned, then turned serious. "Just as a backup. I mean, if we can't get him out over land, what choice do we have?"

Cohen exhaled loudly. "Yeah, I know. I thought about the Falcon, but damn, it's a long shot. All right, call San Diego and have them take it out of mothballs."

"Will do."

By the end of the day, Cohen was satisfied that a plan and a backup were underway. Something was missing, he thought. He snapped his fingers, startling a fatigued Vanderhoven, who was balancing two files on his knees.

"Luke, I need you to find a phone number. In Norfolk. Once we hear from Hong Kong, I need to call an old friend."

* * *

James MacKendrie had never been so bored in his life. As an adjunct at Tidewater Junior College, he was subject to the judgments of the dean, who had decided that the Bible classes MacKendrie taught would not be offered this summer.

He made discreet inquiries about openings at churches in the presbytery—permanent, interim, even occasionally supplying pulpits, he would take anything. It had been almost a year since he left Kirkwell, and he thought that the black mark against him might have faded by now, although even in his own memory, the events of last summer were still vivid.

What had happened wasn't a secret. Anyone who associated with civil rights for Negroes—or was suspected of it—was subject to a gentlemen's agreement. Sorry, the presbytery's stated clerk had told him, nothing available right now.

He chafed at the enforced idleness. He had run out of chores to do and couldn't stand to read one more book. He missed the ministry and longed to be useful somehow. He wondered if he and Helen would have to move the family farther north so he could join the more liberal-minded United Presbyterian Church. They were barely managing financially.

This particular morning, he was idly going through some old files from his days at Bai Miao. He picked up a report he had sent to the Mission Board, expressing his opinion that more responsibilities should be given to the Chinese pastors. One especially showed promise, he wrote, Pastor Dou Minyi. "We should not assume that we know best how to run the affairs of the church in China," he had written, "when its own leaders are capable and understand their own people better than us." What, he wondered, had become of Pastor Dou? He had seen him briefly in '47 during his survey trip, but that was before the Communists expelled Westerners and cracked down on churches. He had neglected to pray for him and the other pastors in China, he thought ruefully.

"Jim?" Helen's voice brought him back to the present. "Telephone."

He picked up the receiver of the hall phone. "James MacKendrie speaking."

"Mac, glad I caught you. It's Harry Cohen. Listen, how would you like to take a little trip?"

That evening, after the girls were in bed, MacKendrie told Helen about the conversation.

"San Diego!" she exclaimed. "What's in San Diego?"

"The Naval Station. It's a big one, like the one here."

"But why go all the way out there, when there's one right in our back yard?" She was trying unsuccessfully to hide some anxiety.

"It has to do with this project Harry's working on. You remember. I mentioned it after I went up to that meeting in D.C."

"But I thought you told him what he needed."

"I thought so, too, but there's some part of this he wants me to see, and it's in San Diego."

"But Jim..." He waited. Finally, resigned, she asked tartly, "How long will you be gone?"

"Harry said four days. It'll take the better part of a day each way just to get there and back." She didn't speak but looked sulky. "Look, Helen, I know this will be inconvenient for you, but the girls are no trouble and I'm not doing much to help around here right now anyway. Four days isn't that long. Besides," he added, "Harry has promised me a consultant's fee."

She looked up at that. "How much?"

"Five hundred."

Her eyes widened but her face remained blank. "Well," she said at last, "I guess it will be all right. I'm just not sure this fellow is telling you everything."

She doesn't want me to get in any more trouble, he thought. "He probably isn't," MacKendrie agreed. "But if he tries to pull anything on me, I'll just tell him to keep the money and come home."

She flashed him a serious look. "You better."

TWENTY-FIVE

For days, Wang waited at the house in Bai Miao without word. He tried to keep himself busy with the fish farm, but it was useless. Finally in a fit of impatience and anger, he tore down the wire pen and let the carp go back into the river. He found that he envied them.

Any minute he might be visited by agents of The Archer or by Li. He didn't dare visit Juh for fear of implicating him if he were to be caught. Occasionally he fingered the capsule sewn into his sleeve. Would he actually have the courage to use it, he wondered. He considered going to the nearest police station and simply giving himself up. He could confess everything, hope that they would understand he had a change of heart, that he wanted to stay, live a normal life in China. But he knew that even if they eventually believed him, it would mean terrible consequences in the short run for everyone he knew—his mother, Pastor Dou, Li. He even felt a twinge of regret for what it would mean for Owl and for the Kingfisher, whoever he was. He couldn't put them through all that. No, best for all if Zhang Weijun simply disappeared. That is, if Li agreed to his plan.

The nights were the worst. The summer heat was oppressive. He couldn't sleep, and with no one to help him pass the time, he stared into the dark, dire scenarios running through his head over and over.

Twice he dressed and went to taverns in town, drinking cups of rice wine while he watched others gambling and drunkenly carousing. On one of those occasions, he saw a cluster of white men at a table, carrying on in a strange language and bothering the women servers. So these are the Russians Juh told me about, he thought. More information that Owl would find valuable, if he ever did pass it on. He touched his waistband, where he still kept the transcripts of the dispatches he had seen in Juh's office.

On the fourth night, he was lying in the dark, debating whether to go back to the tavern, when a sharp rap at the door sent a bolt of panic through him.

"Who is it?" he cried.

The door opened, and short figure dressed in dark clothes slipped into the room. She spoke in the dark before he recognized her. "It is me."

"Li!" He sprang up and rushed forward, but she stepped back before he reached her. "Here, let me light the lamp."

"No. Leave the place dark."

Confused but excited, he said, "You've come. Now you will help me get away." She didn't answer. After a moment, he said, "Li? Is something wrong?" He had the feeling she was staring at him in the dark.

Finally she said stiffly, "Gather all your personal things. Leave behind your notes on the farms. Come with me."

He began to stuff his extra shirts into his bag. "Where—"

"Be quiet."

She went to the door, opened it and looked carefully around, then gestured for him to follow. They walked silently into the city, avoiding the main streets, walking through dark alleys this way and that, Li constantly looking around to see if they were followed. Finally they stopped at a nondescript house. Li rapped at the door twice, waited, then once more. The door opened and he followed her past a dark anteroom into a lighted space.

Two people stood. He couldn't make them out. One of them turned up a lamp, and to his utter astonishment, he saw Pastor Dou and his mother. Oma's face showed deep disapproval.

"Well, what— Oma—" he stammered. He looked at Li. "Ying—"

"You fool!" Li said, taking a step toward him. "Do you know what you're doing?" He had no idea what to say, and she glared at him in contempt. "Owl was right. You are an amateur."

"Owl! How—" In an instant, he saw the truth. "You're one of them. Or I suppose I should say one of us." He stared at her a moment and began to grin and pace in a little circle. "Oh, Ying. Don't tell me you're the damned Kingfisher." She didn't answer, and his voice rose. "You bitch! All this time..." He wanted to grab her by the throat and start shaking, and he took two quick steps forward. She pirouetted like a dancer, gave a little jump and her foot shot into his stomach, jolting him backward to land sitting on the floor. His mother covered her face but didn't move. He couldn't catch his breath, and Li walked over with an exasperated expression.

"Lie flat," she ordered, pushing his shoulder down to the floor. She knelt next to him. "This is why Owl gave me the assignment to watch over you. He never trusted you."

He looked at her face. She was still pretty, in spite of everything, he thought. Gasping, he said, "So, that's all I was. Your assignment."

She took his arm and helped him up. "At first that was all, but later... I grew fond of you."

"Does Owl know that?" She shook her head. He wanted to reach for her but saw his mother over her shoulder, watching intently. He went to a chair, rubbing his stomach, and sat down. The others joined around him. "Why are you here?" he asked Li.

"To save your worthless life." There was a hint of gentleness in the way she said it. "When you asked me to give you a new identity, I could have just told Owl. But you know what he would have said. And done. So I told him you failed to get the dispatches and we should proceed with your evacuation."

Desperately, he said, "But why not let me stay? You could—"

Li broke in crossly, "Do you really think we would have let you stay in China after this? You'd have been found out the minute you were on your own. Before he would let the First Bureau find you, Owl himself would have finished you off. We've sent word to the Birdcatchers. They'll have you out of here in a matter of days."

He lifted his chin. "What if I refuse to leave?"

"You are thinking of your mother." Li looked at her, and Oma lowered her eyes. She turned back to Wang. "You are the only one of us who has family. If the First Bureau learns who you are, your mother will be the first one they will arrest. Is that what you want?"

Desperately he tried to think. "You can give her a new identity, too. We can hide together."

"You are talking like a fool," Li said shortly. "Will your mother accept a new name, a new home? Will she give up being Christian in order to remain safe? Is that what you wish, Madame Wei?"

Wang already knew the answer. His mother wore a placid expression, and she spoke gently. "Wenzhe, son, you must listen to this woman." He started to protest, but she raised a hand and he fell silent, just as if he were a boy again. "I cannot go with you. You must go so that you can live. I don't know why you have been so reckless as to join these people. I taught you that our way is peaceful."

"I told you. I could not come home as Wang Wenzhe." He buried his head in his hands. "What will become of you?"

"I am in the hands of God, as you are."

Dou spoke. "We will look after her. It is better for her if you go, as Li Ying says.

Wang raised his head and looked impassively at Li. "All right. Have it your way. What do we do?"

"It will take a little time to arrange. This is a safe house. Stay inside, and we will send food. I will come back for you when we are ready." She paused and looked at him suspiciously. "Do you have anything I should know?"

Reluctantly he fished the pouch from his waistband and handed it to her. She stood and turned for the door. Dou said, "Go in peace."

Looking back, she flashed a smile. "Thank you. My grandfather was a pastor, you know." Then she was gone.

"We must go," Dou said.

"A word with you," Wang said, and took him aside. He whispered in Dou's ear for a long minute. At one point, the pastor stepped back and stared at him, but Wang gestured and stepped close again, whispering further. At last, Dou stepped back and nodded.

"I will speak to her," he said.

Wang took his mother's hand. "Oma, you must not try to see me before I leave. It is too risky now." He hung his head. "I have ruined everything. I'm sorry."

"I was angry at first when I learned the truth, but it is all right now. It will be all right." She stood on tiptoe and placed her hand on top of his head. "God bless you, Wenzhe. Goodbye."

He placed his cheek against hers. "I will write you from America. And Oma—pray for me."

During the next three days, Wang thought he would lose his mind with boredom. Li had forbidden him from leaving the safe house. The bear-like Qin wordlessly delivered food to him twice a day but refused all of Wang's attempts to talk. Once, desperate for some respite from the bare, cramped quarters, he had waited until dark and stepped outside. He would have walked around, perhaps to find a tavern, but he realized that he was in an unfamiliar part of town, and he might not be able to find his way back. Reluctantly, he retreated to the security of the house.

Thoughts raced through his mind. What if Owl had been captured? Or Li? They would kill themselves, as required. He would be cut off, on his own, with no way of contacting anyone in another network and no escape. He could return to Shanghai, continue working for the ministry as Zhang Weijun as if nothing were wrong. In some ways, it was what he wanted. But he would be stuck permanently with his false identity, unable to contact his mother again. And he knew he would live every day with the fear of a knock on his door in the middle of the night.

He could barely eat or sleep, sick with worry, anger, and boredom.

On the fourth morning, Qin found Wang huddled in a corner, talking to himself. Qin tried to speak to him but was ignored. He jerked Wang to his feet and shook him but got only incoherent shouting. Even two quick slaps only reduced Wang to laughing and then sobbing. He left and found Pastor Dou.

When they returned, Wang appeared to be sleeping. Dou told Qin to wait outside and cautiously approached Wang. He gently shook him, speaking his name, and Wang turned over, moaning slightly. Dou sat him upright and forced him to drink water. Wang choked a little, coughing, and looked blearily around.

"What are you doing here?"

"Qin said you were unwell."

Wang barked a short laugh. "Ha! I am unwell, yes. Sick to my soul, I believe you would say."

"I'm sorry. I wish I could do more, but this is a deadly business, Wenzhe. If it were known I am helping you, it would mean more than just my arrest. The authorities would say that Christians are imperialist puppets. Whatever goodwill we have would be discredited. More than lives are at stake."

"Ah, yes. The church cannot afford to be too political these days, eh, Pastor? 'Render unto Caesar that which is Caesar's and to God what belongs to God.' How convenient."

Dou stiffened. "It is hardly convenient to be harassed, your buildings defaced, your elders and pastors beaten and imprisoned. You are trying to avoid that same fate, I think."

Wang put his hands over his face. "I'm sorry. You're right. I am bitter that it has all come to this."

Dou put a hand on his shoulder. "It will be over soon. I have a message from our friend in Shanghai." He handed Wang a slip of paper.

Wang read, "After dark, walk to the house by the river and wait."

"So," he said, "you will be free of me tonight."

Dou stood. "We are all praying that you will be free, in body but also in spirit. Go in peace."

He left Wang to count the hours remaining in his last day in China.

TWENTY-SIX

Ambient sound filtered through MacKendrie's fitful sleep. A strong vibration below audible hearing, a distant *clank-clank*. Only half awake, he opened his eyes. There was just the barest amount of light, and he couldn't figure out where he was. It was a small, plain room. There was a chair, next to a table, something dark and shapeless on the floor.

Where was Helen? He bolted up, feeling next to him. It was a single bed, a metal-frame bunk. He remembered and relaxed, feeling foolish. He was in guest quarters at Naval Station San Diego. Fully awake now, he leaned back against the wall. The past two days had left him as disoriented as a child spinning around with his eyes closed until he was unable to tell up from down.

After persuading Helen to let him go, MacKendrie had called Cohen back and said yes. He was told to be ready at oh-eight-hundred Monday. A car would pick him up and drive him to Andrews Air Base outside Washington. A military transport plane would be waiting for him.

The flight was long. The plane stopped in the Midwest somewhere to refuel. It was a DC-3, comfortable enough but the drone of the engines was loud and there was turbulence that bucked the plane for an hour, making him queasy. There were only three others in the cabin, one a formidable-looking commander. Another was amiable enough, a lieutenant named Sellers, and he was on his way to an assignment as a signal officer on the *Bataan*, a light carrier. He was young, single, and carefree, and MacKendrie was surprised to find he harbored some envy. He loved his family beyond words, but he longed for the simplicity of Sellers' life at that moment.

Sellers casually asked, "What about you, Mr. MacKendrie? What's a civilian doing on his way to a Navy base?"

Cohen had given him a cover story in case he was asked. "Oh, I'm in the Reserve, and they want me to report to San Diego for a few weeks. That's the Navy for you. All those bases on the east coast, and they send me across the country."

Sellers laughed. He asked whether MacKendrie had been in the war, where he had served, what his duty had been. Upon learning he had been a chaplain, Sellers' face turned pale and he made some excuse about catching some shut-eye before they arrived. It was a common enough reaction. MacKendrie had encountered it especially in civilian life, where there were no insignia to tip people off about his vocation. A chill would drop over conversation like a north wind in autumn when he revealed he was a pastor. It was the natural self-consciousness of people who believed they were suddenly in the presence of holiness. Guilt over some secret sin, belief lapsed since childhood, or disappointments with God caused them to step back as if he radiated an unbearable heat.

The plane had touched down in San Diego in early evening, but he had by now spent more than twelve hours traveling and he was exhausted. He was met by a seaman in a jeep and taken to quarters. Cohen would come get him at ten-thirty next morning, he was told. MacKendrie had collapsed on the bunk without undressing.

Now he sat and listened. The noise was a ship, a big one, either getting underway or trying out her engines in the bay. He could hear distant cries of chiefs and officers at the base, ordering ship's work.

What time was it? His eyes adjusted to the gloom, and he saw his wristwatch on the table. He didn't remember removing it last night. His grip was on the floor. He got up and examined the watch. Almost nine. He considered whether to try to go back to sleep. His head ached, a sure sign he hadn't slept enough, but he was also hungry. With any luck, the mess hall was still open.

He opened the door, walked down a hallway and found the head. He used the toilet, washed his hands and ran the cold water over his face and hair, slicking it back. No one else seemed to be using these quarters. He stepped outside and felt warm sunshine and a light, balmy breeze, nothing like the oppressive stickiness of eastern Virginia. There was bustle all around him, sailors and officers walking in all directions and off to his right the sights and sounds of the ships at their docks. MacKendrie scanned the profiles—a destroyer, no two; a carrier, a big one; and a couple of smaller boats he couldn't make out. Since the end of the war, the Navy had decommissioned a lot of ships. He wondered if these were on their way to the scrap heap.

He looked at the buildings and spotted one about fifty yards away that instinct told him was the enlisted men's mess hall. The instant he stepped inside, he smiled. It was just the way he remembered it—the spartan furnishings, the heavy smells of the food, men with metal trays heaped with bacon and powdered eggs, ready to complain about how bad the food was but eating their fill of it anyway. He walked over to the massive coffee urn, filled a mug, and carried it over to the chow line. The cooks dished eggs, bacon, and toast onto his tray.

He found a spot at a long table a few chairs away from a group of three sailors who ignored him, laughing and joshing each other about the usual concerns of young men—girls, baseball, and finding a way to get out of work.

"I'm tellin' ya, Jonesey, forget her. She's too classy for ya," said a black-haired sailor with a roman nose, razzing a chubby, bespectacled sailor.

Another man gave the first one a light shove. "Whattya talkin' about, she's a cigarette girl at a dive, for chrissake. Luchese, you wouldn't know a classy girl if she ran up your ass with a jeep."

This was met with hoots and counter-insults. MacKendrie ducked his head to hide a grin. It had been a long time since he had been around this kind of unvarnished banter.

He gulped down the eggs, although they tasted terrible. The coffee was too strong, but he didn't care. Anything to get the grogginess out. After he finished his meal, he took the mug over and got a second cup. As he sipped, he felt a tingle of excitement.

Someone yelled "Ten-hut!" and there was a deafening clatter of chairs as sailors jumped to attention. MacKendrie's first instinct on hearing the command was to stand as well, but he sat still, looking around. Harry Cohen walked through the door, dressed in crisp khakis. He swept off his cap, stuffed it under his arm and said clearly, "As you were. Finish your breakfast." Chairs clattered again as men sat back down and resumed eating, the loud talk replaced with murmurs. Cohen made for the coffee urn, then took a chair opposite MacKendrie.

"Hello, Mac. Thought I might find you here. You don't look any worse for wear."

"I'm trying to shake it off. Three thousand miles in twelve hours is a lot."

They sat drinking coffee as the mess hall cleared. "You okay?" Cohen asked.

"Yeah. I'm thinking about Helen. It took some convincing for me to be here."

Cohen set his mug down with a clap. "You can call her later. I need your attention on this job. I'll come get you in your quarters in a half hour. Be ready." He picked up his cap and strode out of the room, men snapping to attention as he left.

MacKendrie went back to his room and checked his gear. Everything was in order. He took his toothbrush and shaving kit into the head and returned fifteen minutes later, feeling fresh. He had just zipped up his grip when there was a knock at the door, which immediately swung open. Cohen said, "This way. I've got a jeep."

MacKendrie had been here before, briefly as a duty chaplain and then on his way back east to be discharged in 1946. All he remembered was how big the base was. Now he saw it again, as Cohen drove along the streets, the sprawling expanse of buildings and Quonset huts, trucks and cranes, and always the sea close at hand. Cohen turned past the docks till he reached a secluded part of the base alongside the bay and pulled up at a couple of low, square buildings without markings. They walked inside the nearest, past an open room with desks occupied by men and women, some in uniform, some in civvies. He stopped at an empty desk, pulled out the chair, and jerked his head sideways. "Have a seat."

Cohen went into an office and walked out carrying a file, which he slapped down on the desk. "We have a briefing in half an hour. Read this first." He walked away, leaving MacKendrie staring down at the manila file, which had two lines typed neatly on the tab. It read, "Wang, Wenzhe" and below that an incomprehensible string of letters and numbers, some kind of filing code perhaps. MacKendrie hunched over the desk and opened the folder.

The dossier was thin, only a few pages. Clearly not the complete file. The first page had a small black-and-white photo of Paul staring straight into the camera. How adult he looked, with his wide-set eyes behind his glasses and his solemn expression. With a shock, MacKendrie realized he was twenty-five years old by now.

He scanned the opening lines, which had Wang's name, "a/k/a Paul," and his duty—field agent, status active, posted in Shanghai with Network Aviary, code name Cuckoo. More lines contained biographical notes on his date and place of birth, father's name Wang Jing, mother's name Wei Lin. A line caught his eye. "Educated at Shanghai Christian Mission School, 1934-1939. Assistance rendered by Rev. James J. MacKendrie, nature of relationship undetermined (cross-ref. GJ327-S/A)."

MacKendrie gave a start. Somewhere there was a dossier on him. Well, of course there was. He reread the phrase "nature of relationship undetermined," frowning. He had explained all this to Harry. Paul had been a protégé, nothing more, but his father-like affection for the boy was too simple an explanation for Cohen.

He closed his eyes and saw him, about six, pixie-like and earnest, with a bowl haircut and insatiable curiosity. He was MacKendrie's shadow, tagging along whenever he returned from his itinerations, pulling on his pants leg and asking questions.

"Pastor Ma, Pastor Ma."

"Yes, Paul?"

"I can count to ten in English."

"Go on and count, then."

The boy's face creased in concentration. "Wun, tyoo, ree, fo..." Soon enough he was doing simple math and reading the Mother Goose books Emily gave him. His mother began asking, shyly at first and then with more determination, about sending him to the Mission School in Shanghai.

"Sister Lin, he is too young. Let him attend the village school for a year, then we will discuss it."

"Pastor Ma, the village boys tease him and say terrible things to him because we are Christian. He would be happy at the Mission School. And the village teacher is incompetent, all the men say so."

She was petite, and the women in the church, laughing, called her Little Tiger for her fierceness in protecting her son. For months she persisted until MacKendrie relented and spoke to the headmaster.

He went back to the file.

Little known about activities during War. Re-established contact with MacKendrie 1947. Entered Pacific Reformed College 30 August 1948, studied marine biology.

MacKendrie recalled sending the packet, addressed to Pastor Dou, whom he knew he could trust, containing passage on a liner from Hong Kong to Los Angeles, two hundred dollars in cash, and a letter containing instructions on what to pack, what not to pack, what to say when asked certain questions, and introducing him to Rev. and Mrs. Chester Andrews, former Presbyterian missionaries to China, who would meet him at the dock and help him get settled at Pacific Reformed.

"I am sorry that I cannot meet you upon your arrival, Paul," he had written. "As you will learn, America is a very big country, and I am at the other end from where you will be. I have a new family now, and it is difficult to travel. I will write and try to come and see you when I can. You can always call the Andrews for help. I leave you in God's hands. Remember, 'All things work together for good for those who love God.'"

He felt guilty, not being there to welcome Paul in person, but Helen was due to deliver Priss any day, and Dottie was just three. There was a glut of ministers, many of them discharged chaplains, looking for positions, and he was scrambling to find temporary posts until he could receive a permanent call to a church. He got a telegram from Andrews, letting him know Paul had arrived all right. The letters from Paul that followed were polite but bewildered, asking for advice on all sorts of ordinary things. "When will you visit?" he pleaded. Then the letters became infrequent and dour, then forlorn, just before they stopped.

MacKendrie picked up the file again.

Notes on first contact by agency recruiter, Professor Jeremiah Hale, Pac. Ref. Coll., cross-reference etc. Contact by Capt. Harold Cohen, two cross-references, on 3 May 1951. Left Pac. Ref. without graduating. Given cover name Zhang Weijun, forged papers, smuggled back into China. Joined Ministry of Agriculture, Shanghai, on 13 March 1952, as marine biologist. Reports attached: observations on Yangtze River.

MacKendrie shuffled through the papers, but there were no reports. The final entry read: "Incident reports follow on critical discovery by Cuckoo—" He turned the page, but the dossier stopped there.

MacKendrie looked around. The people in the office sat typing, stood talking together, huddled at tables over papers they passed back and forth. Looking to his right, he saw Cohen in his office, smoking a cigarette and holding a manila file just like the one in front of him. MacKendrie leafed through the dossier once more, and he looked at Wang's black and white photo. An awful sense of dread settled over him.

"Oh, Paul," he murmured to himself. "What have you gotten into?"

TWENTY-SEVEN

MacKendrie closed the file just as Cohen walked up, and he handed it to him.

"Harry—"

"I know, I know, you got questions. Save 'em till after the briefing. Let's go."

They walked into a back room with a conference table covered with maps. Seated at the table were the straw-blond Lucas Vanderhoven and a lean sailor with weary eyes, graying temples, and a chief petty officer's insignia. They came to attention when Cohen entered.

"As you were. Luke, get the door, will you? You remember Jim MacKendrie?"

Vanderhoeven extended his hand. "Good to see you again, sir."

Cohen said, "Mac, this is Chief Jack Fletcher. He'll be helping us with this operation."

"Hello, Chief." As they shook hands, MacKendrie felt as if Fletcher were sizing him up. He responded only with a curt "Sir."

"Have a seat, gents," Cohen rapped. "I'll get right to this. A couple of years ago, we sent an agent into Shanghai, code named Cuckoo. He's a native but has some ties to the States. We recruited him while he was studying here." He gestured to MacKendrie. "Mac here knows him from way back. He's been working undercover as a marine biologist for the Chinese agriculture bureau, up and down the Yangtze. He's gathered some vital information, but we've had word that his cover is in danger of being blown, and we need to get him out of there. The usual overland routes are closed. That only leaves a pickup on the water. He can't get to the open ocean. The coastline is heavily patrolled, so a rendezvous anywhere north or south of Shanghai Bay is sure to be spotted. But there's a chink in the armor. The patrols are staggered. A small craft could slip by them and make it upriver. The objective of this mission is to retrieve our agent from a point on the Yangtze near Bai Miao."

Cohen paused. No one spoke. MacKendrie was incredulous but held his tongue.

"I don't need to tell you that this will be dangerous in the extreme," Cohen resumed. "We don't know how much the commies suspect. If the rescue team is captured, our government will completely deny any knowledge of the operation. They'll be on their own, at the mercy of the Chinese. Any questions?"

Again silence. MacKendrie couldn't keep quiet any longer.

"Are you telling me that you're going to send a boat into one of the busiest harbors in China, up one of its most vital rivers eighty miles, find one man, and get back out undetected?"

"Sounds nuts, doesn't it?" Cohen gave a mirthless chuckle, and Vanderhoven and Fletcher gave quiet little laughs.

"You're serious," MacKendrie said in astonishment.

Cohen's face turned angry. "You're damn right I'm serious." He leaned forward and jabbed a finger in MacKendrie's direction. "This man got us some real intelligence, and I'll be goddamned if I'm going to let him fall into their stinking hands. Do you know what they'd do to him? He'd never be able to keep from telling them everything. The whole fucking network would get rolled up like a cheap rug. He risked his life for us, now we're going to take a risk to get him out. Do you read me?"

MacKendrie was struck as if he had been slapped by what was at stake—not just Paul Wang's life but other lives and years of intelligence work. He saw perspiration beading on Cohen's forehead, and he gave a nod.

Cohen stepped back, pulled out a handkerchief and mopped his face. "Take a look at this map, gents."

They crowded around the table, which held a detailed map of the East China Sea. Cohen pointed out the main features. Shanghai was the point of a roughly equilateral triangle, about eighty miles on each side, with the southern tip of Japan to the northeast and the island of Okinawa to the southeast. A destroyer based at Okinawa would be standing by. On board was a specially equipped and camouflaged boat, designed to run fast and quiet. A two-man team would be flown to Okinawa, board the ship and be ferried to a point thirty miles due east of Shanghai, outside territorial waters and beyond the range of Chinese radar.

Cohen lit a cigarette. "Here's where it starts getting hairy."

On 3 September, under cover of night, the boat would leave the destroyer, travel across open ocean, avoid the coastal patrols and slide into Shanghai harbor. The estuary was enormous, thirty miles across, so there was a good chance the boat could maneuver through it without getting too close to another boat. It would then continue up river to the southern bank of the river below Bai Miao before daylight.

"The destination is the canals in those reed beds you told us about, Mac. The crew will have to hide out in those reeds during the day. We'll need you to figure out the best spot to avoid detection. The rendezvous with Cuckoo will take place after dark, at twenty-four-hundred hours. There will be a signal. Once they get him on board, they get the hell out of there, back through the harbor and out to the ship."

"We receive the signal by radio, sir?" Fletcher asked.

"Yeah, but except for that transmission you'll have to observe strict radio silence inside ten miles of the coast."

"What about weapons?"

"No weapons. You'll be wearing plain clothes, and we'll throw in some fishing gear. Your cover, if you're caught, will be that you were deep sea fishing off Japan and got lost. It's flimsy, but that's the best we can do."

Fletcher looked grim but said nothing.

MacKendrie asked, "Do you have a more detailed map of the river around Bai Miao?"

Cohen slid another map on top of the first. MacKendrie studied it. The river angled northwest from Shanghai, narrowing, then bent west. The map was incomplete. It showed nothing of the reed marsh just below the city.

"So you want me to map out those canals?"

"That's right," Cohen said.

"Harry, the last time I explored those canals was 1936. I can barely remember them, and God only knows if they're the same as then."

"We'll give you some time to think about it. Do the best you can. This is our only option."

Fletcher asked about food, navigation gear, other details. MacKendrie was suddenly curious.

"So the chief here is the pilot, is that right?" They looked at him. "Who's the other crew member?"

Vanderhoven spoke up. "That's me, sir."

MacKendrie nodded. It made sense.

Cohen read out the schedule. The team would board a plane at oh-five-thirty hours tomorrow. They would refuel at Pearl Harbor then go on to Okinawa. It would be twelve hours in the air, fourteen hours travel time, and about fourteen-hundred local time when they landed. They would spend the night at Okinawa to adjust to the time difference. The destroyer would shove off from the island at oh-nine-hundred the following morning.

"It'll take about four hours to get to the departure point. That'll give us plenty of time to make sure everything is in order. Weather reports indicate no storms in the area." Cohen checked his watch. "It's almost noon. Let's break and get some chow. This afternoon, gents, we're going to go over the timing of the operation again and again till you can recite it in your sleep." Cohen waved the three of them on, saying he had some reports to read. "Take them to the officers' mess, Luke."

As they stood and stretched, Cohen spoke to MacKendrie. "Sure you don't want to fly out with us to Okinawa? See how it turns out?"

MacKendrie shook his head. "Just send word to me."

They piled into a jeep, Fletcher driving. He wheeled back across the base near a set of buildings that appeared to be headquarters. They pulled up at a smart-looking building with glass doors. The officer's mess was refined, with tables for four and cloth napkins. They ordered steaks. The coffee was perfect and the food delicious.

MacKendrie eyed Fletcher, who was sawing away at his steak. "Where are you from, Chief?" he asked casually.

He looked up. "Tulsa, Oklahoma, sir."

"I've never been there. What's it like?"

Fletcher chewed a few moments, gazing at him. "It's in the foothills of the Ozarks. It's pretty around there. Lot of good hunting."

"It's an oil town, isn't it?"

Fletcher nodded. "Just about everybody there's connected with oil. My daddy was a roughneck who made it to foreman. Tough old bastard."

"You ever work in the oil field?"

He shook his head. "No, sir. Joined up so I wouldn't have to."

"Why the Navy?"

Fletcher gave a faint smile. "Aren't any Navy bases within a thousand miles of Tulsa. No chance I could be sent back there."

"The Navy must have suited you. You made chief."

He nodded. "First time I ever set eyes on a ship, I knew I was home. Been that way ever since."

"I heard a lot of men say that, during the war. I wanted to serve on a ship, but they sent me to Tinian instead."

Fletcher looked at him closely. "Captain Cohen said you were a chaplain, sir. That right?"

"That's right." Something in Fletcher's manner prompted him to say, "What's on your mind, Jack?"

Fletcher hesitated, then said, "Well, sir, nothing against religion. Just seems to me a carbine would be more use than a prayer in the situation we're going into. Begging your pardon."

Vanderhoven snapped, "Chief."

MacKendrie gave a short laugh. "I heard that a lot in the war, Jack. Had a commander once ask me to sing a verse of 'Praise the Lord and pass the ammunition.'"

Fletcher stammered, "Sir, I didn't—"

MacKendrie waved him off. "Only a man with the morals of an eight-year-old boy thinks God approves of us shooting one another. I spent my time in the Navy trying to help men find forgiveness for putting another man in the sights of a gun and pulling the trigger, but it wasn't my place to judge them for what they did. And by the way, Jack," he added, "a gun is just something made by human hands. Ever had one jam on you? Uh-huh. Me, too. A prayer doesn't jam, if you do it the right way."

Fletcher looked at him as if he had just spoken a strange language.

Vanderhoven glanced at his watch. "We'd better get moving." He stood and led the way through the doors of the mess, turned to say something to Fletcher, and missed the top step. He crashed down the stairs, tumbling, and there was a snap as his foot got caught between two treads. He let out a roar of pain.

Fletcher and MacKendrie were at his side in an instant, pulling him free of the stairs, but when they moved his leg, Vanderhoven let out another shout and a string of curses. With a sickening feeling, MacKendrie saw the ankle was bent at an angle.

He put a hand on Fletcher's shoulder. "Chief, go inside and call the base hospital. The lieutenant has a broken ankle."

TWENTY-EIGHT

At the infirmary, MacKendrie and Fletcher waited while the doctors examined a still-swearing Lucas Vanderhoven.

"I'd better notify Captain Cohen," Fletcher said, and went to find a phone.

It wasn't long before a nurse approached MacKendrie and said Vanderhoven wanted to speak to him. He followed her to a curtained exam room, where the burly lieutenant lay on a gurney, his exposed ankle purpling.

"Lucas, how's the ankle?" MacKendrie asked.

"They've given me something, but it still hurts like hell, sir. Doc says it might be broken in two places. Damn stupid of me. Funny, I played football at Annapolis, never got so much as a cut. Just as I'm about to go on one of the few peacetime missions on tap, I step off the stairs wrong, and I'm out. Stupid."

"It's a shame. You were ideal for the job."

"Sir, about the mission—"

"Don't worry about that right now. There's nothing you can do. Just focus on getting better."

"Yes, sir, but, well...Captain Cohen..." MacKendrie waited. "There was a backup plan you need to know..."

Rapid footsteps clattered behind them and Harry Cohen rushed into the exam room. "Luke! What the hell...?" He looked at MacKendrie, his face a mixture of confusion, anger, and accusation.

MacKendrie said, "I'll wait out front. Lucas, you be sure and do as the doctors tell you."

In the waiting room, he found a morose Fletcher, who gave him a questioning look.

"Broken ankle, all right," MacKendrie said. "He's going to be on crutches for weeks."

"Well, I guess there goes the mission," Fletcher said in a low voice.

"If it's as important as Harry said, they'll probably just delay it."

A few minutes later, a grim-faced Cohen strode past them, snapping, "Let's go." They got into a jeep and rode pell-mell through the base back to the office. As they made their way back to the briefing room, Cohen said, "Chief, wait out here, will you? I need to have a word with Mac." He waved MacKendrie into a chair and lit a cigarette.

"Mac, I'll give it to you straight. I need you to take Vanderhoven's place."

At first, Cohen thought MacKendrie had not understood. He expected an outburst, but instead MacKendrie's chin sank onto his chest, and he stared absently at the floor. Cohen waited, unsure whether to prompt him to say something, anything. He was just about to speak when MacKendrie looked up at him. Cohen couldn't read the expression. More than anything, it seemed sad.

"My God," he said at last. "You want me to get on that small boat with Fletcher, go back into China and fetch Paul Wang off the river like the baby Moses." He shook his head. "Harry, there has got to be another way."

Cohen nodded. "That's what we thought. At first, we were going to get him out by one of the land routes to Hong Kong. Then we got word they were closed. We went through several options. Nothing was working. The network chief asked if we could get upriver to make the pickup. We were already working on a small craft that could make these kinds of covert rescues, so we thought this was the time to try it."

"But Harry, there's got to be someone else, someone who's trained in this sort of thing."

"We don't have time, Mac. It'd have to be somebody who knows the river and speaks the language. I doubt there's three guys in all the intelligence services together that'd fit that profile, and it'd take weeks to find them."

"Just delay the mission."

"If we do, odds are good that Wang will be captured or dead before we get there. The net's closing in on him, Mac. We go now or your friend is finished. Vanderhoven wants to go anyway, but regulations say we can't send anyone into the field who isn't medically fit. Um, you can pass a physical, can't you?"

MacKendrie laughed, stopped, then laughed some more as Cohen grinned, watching him. "Too bad I can't use fitness as an excuse," he gasped, still laughing. He caught his breath and looked at Cohen. "What makes all this such a top priority?" Before Cohen could answer, MacKendrie cut in, "And don't tell me it's classified."

Cohen stood, walked to the end of the table, crushed out the cigarette in a tray, turned and came back and slumped next to MacKendrie. He suddenly looked haggard. "You grew up there. I don't suppose it would surprise you if I said that our operations inside China have been a complete flop? They've whipped us good, Mac. I've never seen anything like it. I thought Japanese counterintelligence was the best I'd ever seen, but the Chinese are better. We're down to two networks, our agents rounded up, most of them dead. We haven't gotten much solid information out of China in four years. The brass wants results, Mac. If the team's caught, if Wang misses the rendezvous, if the boat springs a leak, my goose is cooked. I'll be packed off to Miami with my pension."

"To say nothing of losing a man's life."

"A lot of men have lost their lives already."

"But this one's special?" MacKendrie pressed.

Cohen shrugged. "I suppose. One of our talent spotters at Pacific Reformed flagged us. When I read the initial report, I flew out to talk to him. I thought he was perfect. Trained in science, and the Chinese are short of scientists. Had a chip on his shoulder, although I never figured out why. Resourceful, and you can't teach that. I just had a feeling he wouldn't let us down. But I don't have to tell you. You knew him." He regarded MacKendrie. "You told me back in Kirkwell he's the reason you got kicked out of China."

MacKendrie stiffened. "I didn't get kicked out of China. I agreed it was best to leave."

"Because of the rumors that you were his father."

MacKendrie's voice rose. "A rumor started by an envious man and kept alive by chattering old women. I thought the situation would settle down, but it got worse."

"Why don't you go over it again?"

He took a deep breath. He and Emily hadn't been in China long. One day the pastor of the church in Bai Miao brought a young woman named Wei Lin to him. She was desperate. Her husband was a petty landowner, much older than her. He treated her badly, beat her often. One of Lin's relatives, a cousin, had converted and persuaded her to come to the church, where she was treated warmly for the first time in her life. Soon Lin herself converted, but her husband hated Westerners and regarded Christianity as alien to Chinese ways. He made it hard on her, but she persisted in visiting the church. Then he fell ill, and within days he was dead. His family was obligated to take

Lin in, but they blamed her for his death. They said she had learned witchcraft from the Christians and used it to kill her husband. She was afraid and fled. A family in the church took her in.

"Soon after that she fainted during worship. I took her to my father at the clinic, and he examined her. She was pregnant. I felt sorry for her and looked in on her often. After the baby was born, Emily and I saw to it that she had what she needed. He was a bright child, about the same age as my Richard. They became good friends for a while. I gave him English lessons, took him along when I went hunting. It was my idea to call him Paul."

"But?"

"An elder in the church wanted me to help get his son into the missionary school in Shanghai. The boy was a dunce, but I said I'd try. He didn't qualify. Big disgrace for the family. To make it worse, Paul was accepted. The elder blamed me. It wasn't long after that the rumors started in earnest."

"And you left even though you were innocent?"

"It was causing a division in the church, so I told the Mission Board it was best for me to leave. Besides, Emily was getting sicker by the day."

"Did you see Wang again?"

He nodded. "Briefly. After the war, on that survey for the Mission Board. Somehow Paul and his mother survived. Lin pleaded with me to send him to college in the States. I knew the provost at Pacific Reformed and made the arrangements. I got a few letters from him, but..." He turned to Cohen. "It is nuts, you know, Harry, this scheme of yours. It's a suicide mission."

"No, it isn't. Kamikaze is for the Japs," Cohen flared, then relaxed. "I know it's a long shot. But that's just it, they won't be expecting it. I've seen operations like this succeed against the odds. If it goes according to plan, it'll work."

"If. You're gambling more lives on a big if." Cohen didn't answer. "Harry. You know I can't do it." Cohen's head swiveled toward him and his eyes narrowed, as if trying to focus on him. "I can't get on that rescue boat. If I were single or younger, I'd risk my life to save Paul. But now I've got three good reasons why I can't go."

Cohen nodded. "Your family. I know." He let the silence settle for a minute. "Look, Mac, it's a tough choice. I can't tell you what to do. I'm only laying out the facts for you. If you're not on that plane tomorrow, Paul Wang is as good as dead."

"And if I go and wind up dead or imprisoned, what happens to my family?"

"The best I can do is promise they'll get what we would pay you."

MacKendrie snorted. "Five hundred dollars? Not much of a compensation."

"Oh. Guess I didn't mention it. You'd be considered a contractor on a covert operation. Your fee would be twenty-five thousand."

MacKendrie sat up. "Twenty-five thousand!" It was seven years' salary in Kirkwell. He stood and paced. He hated the thought that he was being tempted by the money. "I need time to think about this. An hour?"

Cohen looked at his watch. "Okay. No more." He left MacKendrie alone in the briefing room.

It was Kirkwell all over again. He was almost murdered in his own home, depriving Helen of a husband and his daughters of a father, all because of stubbornness and foolish belief in principle. Harry Cohen's sudden appearance had been like a miracle, he thought later, an angel with a revolver rather than a flaming sword. When he was reunited with his family, he swore to himself he would never put himself in that situation again. But now Paul's life was in danger.

He stood and paced. What did he know about Paul these days anyway? He clearly was not the boy he knew in Bai Miao. What had made him go back to China as a spy? And why should he now put his own life in danger for a man who was as good as a stranger? Patriotism? Nostalgia? They weren't good enough reasons. He was on the point of telling Cohen no, when a glimmer from something on the side table next to him caught his eye. It was a medallion of some kind. Idly picking it up, he read the inscription on one side:

To our beloved Harold, as you leave to serve our country

It must belong to Harry, he thought. He flipped it over. In the center were two Hebrew letters. Remembering the basic Hebrew he was required to learn at seminary, he recognized the letters *chet*, pronounced with a hard "ch," like clearing the throat, and *yodh*. "*Chet, yodh. Chai*," he translated, whispering to himself. "Life."

Carrying the medallion, he walked into the next room, where Cohen looked up expectantly.

"I think this is yours," MacKendrie said, holding out the medallion. Cohen stood and tentatively took it. "All right, Harry. I'll do it."

Cohen looked down at the medallion and placed it on the desk. He gave MacKendrie an understanding look. "Thanks, Mac." With a gesture, he led him back into the briefing room, signaling Fletcher to join them.

"Chief, retired Lieutenant Commander James MacKendrie here will be taking Vanderhoven's place on this mission."

Fletcher, wide-eyed, said nothing.

"Let's get into the details, gents."

Cohen pulled out a map of the mouth of the Yangtze. The boat would do fifty knots at full speed, so it would take thirty minutes from launch to Shanghai. Reports indicated the coastal patrols' sweeps left a fifteen-minute window to get into the harbor. The crew would wait offshore, watching to make sure the patrols were following a regular pattern, then move in. Once they reached the mouth of the harbor, they would go slowly to avoid attracting attention. There would be no moon and city lights would be minimal that time of night. The boat had some gear to disguise it, and if they kept to the middle of the harbor, they might be regarded as just a fishing vessel. Once they were past the city, they'd make twenty knots upriver. Any faster and they might be noticed. It would take about three hours to reach the reed marsh.

"You'll have to get yourself into those reeds and concealed before it starts getting light, say by oh-five-thirty," Cohen said. "We'll launch you at oh-one-hundred hours, which gives you four hours to reach your destination with some margin for error. Once you're in the reeds, it'll be a long day of waiting and hiding, but you can take turns getting some shut-eye. You'll need it."

"No lights, right? It'll be pitch black. How are we going to find the canals and make sure we're concealed?" MacKendrie asked.

"We'll give you a couple of dark lanterns. They'll show you what's in front of you without throwing off a lot of light."

The pickup of the Cuckoo would take place at midnight the next night. The crew would move out of the reeds and upriver along the south bank till they located a dock. It was a half-mile below the city and used mainly for cargo. Fletcher and MacKendrie would wait about a hundred yards off the dock. There would be a radio signal: "The Cuckoo will fly now." MacKendrie would reply in Mandarin, "The cage is open." They would pick him up at the dock and proceed downriver at the same speed as before.

"What if we don't get the signal?" MacKendrie asked.

"You can wait up to one hour. After that, you risk being unable to get out while it's dark. One more thing, gents," Cohen said. "After you launch, the destroyer will not sit at anchor. If it was spotted by a plane, they'd figure something's up. The ship will make its way back to the shipping lane between Okinawa and Japan and cruise slowly, then after dark it will turn back and proceed to the point where we dropped you off. If you're on schedule, you should make it out of the harbor and back to the ship by oh-five-hundred."

"What if we're hailed by a patrol?" Fletcher asked.

"Cuckoo has a cover story. You'll have to hope they don't come too close to see you're Americans. Any other questions? All right, let's go over it again."

They drilled for hours, until Cohen was satisfied. He told MacKendrie and Fletcher their gear was being brought over to a barracks near the intelligence office, and they were to remain there overnight. MacKendrie would start work that evening on a map of the canals. Lights out would be at twenty-one-hundred hours, and they would be wakened at oh-four-thirty.

"Any problems, you come to me here. You've got an hour before chow. Stretch your legs. I'll see you in the morning."

MacKendrie walked outside. He was drenched in sweat, and his chest fluttered. He strolled toward the bay, and stood in a grassy patch watching the ships. It was late afternoon. What day was it? Tuesday. He walked back inside and into the briefing room, where Cohen was looking at a report.

"Harry, I want to talk to Helen before I leave."

He looked up. "Uh, no can do, Mac. SOP is no personal calls after you've been briefed. You might let something slip."

MacKendrie had anticipated this. "I think you'll make an exception for me."

"Why?"

"Because this is a special circumstance, that's why. And you know I won't say anything that will cause Helen to worry."

Cohen thought for a moment and nodded. "Okay, Mac. You can use my office."

It took several minutes for the operator to put him through.

"Hello, Helen? It's Jim." There was static on the line. He heard her saying "Who?" "Jim!" There was a burst of excitement on the other end of the line, with shrieks from the girls wanting to talk to him. Each had to have a turn, talking about school and friends. Finally Helen sent them in another room. She was cautious, asking how he was.

"I'm fine, dear. It's just that there's been a delay out here. I'm going to need to stay for a few extra days."

"Oh, Jim."

"I know. And Helen, I'm going to be unable to call you. I didn't want you to worry. No, I can't explain. It's all very hush-hush. You know how the military is. All I can tell you is just that we're working on a job, and they won't let me call till we're done."

"Well, that's just ridiculous," she said. "Not even your own family! Of course I'm going to worry, not hearing like that. Is it safe?"

"Oh, it's perfectly safe," MacKendrie said, glad that she couldn't see his face. "I should be able to call you by this time next week." He felt himself choking up again and knew he had to stop talking. "Helen, I have to hang up. I love you, dear."

She began to cry. "Jim, can't you come home now? I'm frightened. There's something you're not telling me. Come home, please!"

It was all he could do to keep from crying. "I...I can't, Helen. I wish I could, but..." He passed into helpless silence.

The time would go by quickly, he told her, and was in the middle of telling her again that he loved her when the line went dead.

That evening, in the small barracks, MacKendrie spread some paper on his bunk and tried to recall the times he had been duck hunting in the reed marsh. The canals were natural pathways that had been cut through the reeds over the centuries by traditional fishing boats. They were subtle and narrow, cutting into the marsh at an angle, so they were hard to see from the river. There was a landmark that marked a canal he always used. A tree, a stump? It was something that lined up with the entrance. After an hour, he gave up and sat back on his bunk. Fletcher, who had been poring over intelligence reports, looked up.

"How's it going, sir?"

MacKendrie shook his head. "I don't know, Jack. It's been a long time. There's a landmark that I can't seem to recall. If we were looking in the daylight, I could probably recognize it, but it's going to be black as the devil's heart on that river."

"You'll find it, sir." MacKendrie saw Fletcher was grinning. "It'll come back to you. I bet I could find my way back to my old high school in Tulsa, and I haven't been there in twenty years."

He played along. "You know, you're probably right. There were several canals in that marsh anyway, and we're bound to find one of them."

"Sure. Whattya say we get some shut-eye. Oh-four-thirty is gonna be mighty early."

MacKendrie was groggy, but before lying down, he fished in his grip and found his pocket-sized New Testament and Psalms, the same one he had used on Tinian in the war. As he turned to the back, by chance his eye fell on the opening verse of Psalm 144.

"Blessed be the Lord my strength which teacheth my hands to war, and my fingers to fight."

TWENTY-NINE

A man stood at the end of a long road before him. He had a familiar, portly figure, but his features were indistinct, and he was calling. MacKendrie couldn't make out the words and began walking toward him. He had white hair and wore authority as easily as his dark suit. MacKendrie waved at him.

"Father! Father, hello!"

Dr. MacKendrie was speaking in that measured voice his son remembered so well, but what was he saying? The closer McKendrie got, the less distinct his father seemed.

Turn... Turn what? Turn around?

–other... Turn another? MacKendrie began to run, but his father was coming no nearer. *...cheek...*

"Father, wait for me!" There was a light shining in his eyes. He couldn't see...

The overhead light snapped on and he sat up to see Fletcher in his skivvies making up his bunk. It hardly mattered what the bunk looked like, but it was automatic for Fletcher, the result of years of discipline. He glanced over. "Morning, sir."

"Good morning." MacKendrie was panting, as if he had been running a sprint.

A half-hour later they pulled onto the tarmac, where Cohen and Vanderhoven, his foot in a cast and hobbling on crutches, were waiting next to the plane, a converted DC-3. There was little conversation as they piled on board and strapped in.

After takeoff, Cohen passed out C-rations. MacKendrie had never eaten them. There were four small drab green tin cans, each with a key lightly soldered on the bottom. He pried the key off of the can labeled *M Unit—Chopped Eggs and Ham* and opened it. Inside was a pale mash of scrambled powdered eggs and bits of dried ham. Using the flat wooden spoon from the can of sundries, he dug out a mound and tried it. If it had been heated, it might have been tolerable, but this was slightly cool, making the tasteless and slimy stuff unpalatable. There was also a packet of instant coffee, and Cohen produced some warm water in paper cups. MacKendrie was glad to have it.

It would be another five hours to Pearl. Alert now, MacKendrie looked around and spotted Fletcher, happily gobbling the contents of his C-ration. He worked his way over to an empty seat next to him.

"How can you eat that stuff, Jack?" he said, shaking his head.

"This? I'm used to it. It's what we had in the war."

"I thought you were on a ship in the war."

"I was at the end, but I started out as a petty officer third class on a PT boat in the South Pacific. All we had were C-rations when we were on patrol."

"What was your duty?"

"Weapons, sir. Small arms, large caliber, torpedoes, you name it. Also the backup helmsman."

"I'm beginning to see why they picked you for this mission. You see much action?"

"We saw our fair share. Some run-ins with Jap patrols. We had better speed and firepower, but I was glad when I got on board a regular ship." They were quiet a moment and Fletcher said, "Sir, I— um..."

"You want to know if you can count on me in a scrape." He saw Fletcher's expression. "Right?"

"Don't get me wrong. You seem like a stand-up guy, and you know your way around the territory. But you've never been in a fight. Sir."

MacKendrie nodded. "You're right. On Tinian, I never picked up a weapon myself, but you should know this, Chief. I have my reasons for going on this mission, and they all have to do with getting Paul Wang, me, and you back here in one piece. I don't give a spit about fighting Chinese Communism, but I'm going to do whatever the job calls for to get back. There'll be time to worry about forgiveness later."

Fletcher gave him a long look, and a smile played at the corners of his mouth. Cohen wandered over.

"Hey, Mac. Do me a favor and save the chatter for later. Work on how to get into those reeds, okay?"

MacKendrie and Fletcher exchanged the look of men who have been given an order by a superior. MacKendrie stood.

"Aye, aye, Captain." Over his shoulder, he said, "Hey, Chief, when we get to Okinawa, maybe you can give me some pointers at the firing range if we have time."

Fletcher brightened. "That'd be great, sir."

He resumed his seat, fished the primitive map from his shirt and spread it on his lap. He tried retracing in his mind his hunting excursions. The drone of the engines had a hypnotic effect, and he closed his eyes, envisioning the scene. Upriver from the mission station was a jetty where he would hire a wide, shallow-drafted boat. The boatmen knew he would never pay more than thirty yuan, but they always haggled with him anyway.

They would drift downriver past the city. He could smell the heavy, fish-water scent of the river. How long would it take, he tried to recall. Fifteen minutes? Twenty? He could see the reeds, jutting into the river, thick and tall, eight feet above the water. Slow, he would tell the boatman, no paddling. Steer near the reeds. He was looking for something. They were drifting, drifting, five minutes perhaps, and ... here, here, he would say, steer right. They were gliding into the reeds, through a narrow corridor with them high on each side. But what had he seen? What had been the marker?

He opened his eyes and began to make a rough sketch of the river, the location of the city, and the marsh, but he was sure that the scale was all wrong, and he still had no idea where the canal was or what the landmark had been. He shook his head and stashed the map in his shirt pocket. He moved next to the window and looked out onto the cloud-scattered skyscape with the featureless dark Pacific underneath. The excitement he had felt early on was gone now, replaced by a low dread. He knew it would get worse. He closed his eyes and slept.

Someone was shaking his shoulder. "Sir?" He didn't want to wake up, but the shaking continued. "Sir, we're approaching Pearl." He squinted up at Fletcher. "You need to secure yourself."

It was overcast and a squall was threatening at Pearl Harbor, but when he stepped off the plane, the tropical wind felt fresh and warm. There were palms everywhere, and he saw mountains across the bay. He relaxed for the first time in days. Honolulu had been a paradise for him and Emily and Richard when they left China on their way back to the States. He had regretted almost everything about being forced from the mission field, but the week they spent in Oahu gave him hope that things would be all right. That was before Emily's diagnosis.

"There's chow and a head in the hangar over there," Cohen said, pointing. "Don't get too comfortable. We take off again in forty-five minutes."

The food was nothing more than coffee and hamburgers, but MacKendrie ate and drank greedily. He was contemplating a third cup of coffee when he spotted Cohen standing off to himself, smoking a cigarette. He sauntered over, and Cohen looked at him expectantly.

"I've been working on a map of that marsh." MacKendrie shook his head. "I've got part of it, but the details are fuzzy. There's a landmark that I can't recall. We're going to have to feel our way along."

He nodded. "Okay, Mac. I understand." They stood in silence, shifting from one foot to the other. Cohen blew a cloud of smoke and said, "You're not sore at me, are you, Mac?"

MacKendrie said distinctly, "Let not the sun go down upon your wrath."

Cohen's brow furrowed, then he nodded. "The Bible, right?"

"Ephesians four twenty-six. One of my memory verses as a boy. No, I'm not mad at you, Harry. It was my choice to be here."

Cohen was about to reply when he saw the pilot give him a thumbs up. He dropped the cigarette, crushed it, and shouted, "Let's go, gents!"

It was a long, dull flight to Okinawa, more than seven hours of doing nothing. Fletcher and Vanderhoven tried to lure him into a game of gin rummy, but they were betting, penny a point. There had been much debate among the missionaries in China whether it was a transgression even to play bridge. In the end, it was agreed that it might not be sinful, but they should avoid the appearance of gambling, especially since the Chinese were notorious for gambling on everything.

MacKendrie thought of Helen and the girls, wondering what they were doing. It was eight o'clock on the east coast. Soon they would be observing the rituals of brushing teeth and putting on pajamas. Cohen had warned him not to write any letters. If he didn't return, his effects would be sent home but letters would be confiscated.

MacKendrie realized he had an extra sheet of paper for drawing maps, and making sure Cohen wasn't watching, he pulled it out of his shirt pocket and began to write quickly.

My dearest Helen, Dottie, and Priss, he began, and tears stung his eyes. He gathered himself for a few moments, dashed a hand across his face, and kept going.

> *If you are reading this, you will be confused and very sad. I am sorry I couldn't tell you what I was doing. I would not blame you for being mad at me, but I can only tell you that I believed it was the right thing to do. Arrangements have been made to provide for you. Dottie and Priss, I wish I could be with you to watch you grow up into fine young women like your mother. She is wise, and you must always listen to her. I love you all more than I can say, and I wish I didn't have to go on this journey, but sometimes we are not able to choose the path that is safe and peaceful.*
> *God bless you and be with you always,*
> *Jim*

As he stashed the letter, he felt drained. He would have to find someone to mail it if the worst happened. He prayed, closed his eyes, and slept.

When they arrived at Okinawa, it was late afternoon although it seemed to him as if it were the middle of the night. Stay awake as long as you can, Cohen told them, it will help beat the time lag. Find something to do till chow time.

After their gear was stowed in a nearby barracks, Fletcher motioned to MacKendrie. They walked to the base firing range, where Fletcher spoke to the ordnance officer, and they were given what appeared to be two standard carbines and several clips of ammunition. They took a position on the firing line, and Fletcher showed MacKendrie the rifles.

The first was an M-1 Garand, the rifle used by the infantry and marines in the war. MacKendrie had seen plenty of them and had been given a quick course in their operation when he was in officer training school. He hadn't fired one since then, but it came back to him quickly. Push in the clip, release it to load the first round, release the safety when ready to fire. It was semi-automatic, one round with each pull of the trigger.

"Give it a try, sir," Fletcher said, handing it over.

Keeping it pointed downrange, MacKendrie weighed the rifle in his hands. It was pretty light, really, and he tried raising it to his shoulder a couple of times. The line officer called "Ready on the firing line!" He took a wide stance sideways to the target, raised the rifle, and braced his elbow against his side. He released the safety, and sighted the target. He let out his breath, let the target meander down to the sight, and squeezed the trigger.

The air cracked and the recoil jolted his shoulder, knocking a painful bruise on his collarbone. Hold it tighter against the shoulder. He looked for the marker on the target. One o'clock, outside the outer ring. He raised the rifle again, sighted, squeezed.

Again the crack and the jolt, but this time he was ready for it. Twelve o'clock, inside the outer ring. It was shooting high, he thought. An eagerness to master the weapon seized him. He aimed low, exhaled, squeezed the trigger.

Crack-jolt. Inner ring, six o'clock. He had overcompensated.

Aim, fire. Five o'clock, well inside the inner ring.

Aim, fire. Inside the inner ring, three o'clock.

Fire. Near-pinwheel at nine o'clock.

On impulse, he fired in succession, crack-crack. The clip ejected with a ping. The second shot was well off, the result of the recoil, but the first was another near-pinwheel at twelve o'clock. MacKendrie lowered the rifle and looked around to see Fletcher, wide-eyed.

"Captain Cohen wasn't kidding. That was pretty damn good shooting. Begging your pardon, sir."

MacKendrie flipped the rifle over and back, pretending to examine it to hide the fact he was pleased with himself. "Got another clip?"

He went through two more clips, practicing rapid firing, and learned how to keep it steady enough to produce a decent cluster around the inside of the inner ring.

"Try this one," Fletcher said, lifting the other rifle. "It's an M-2. Fully automatic."

It looked like the same rifle but used a thirty-round box magazine that made it heavier. Careful, Fletcher warned. It would go through that clip in less than five seconds. Gingerly, MacKendrie raised the rifle, released the safety. He sighted the target, exhaled, squeezed, and panicked as the rifle fired almost out of control. He had no idea how many rounds he had fired. The target showed two in the inner ring and a succession of shots running farther and farther out till they ran off the target. Fletcher laughed as MacKendrie lowered the rifle and held it away, in awe of the firepower.

"Don't be afraid of it, sir. You'll get used to it. Try it in short bursts."

Reluctantly, MacKendrie raised the rifle. Short bursts. Keep it tight. He aimed, squeezed and held the trigger for just a second. The rifle erupted like a chainsaw. He was still having trouble controlling it, the recoils coming quickly on top of each other, making it difficult to keep sighted. He inhaled, exhaled, fired again, just a quick squeeze of the trigger, with about the same result. One more burst and the rifle stopped, the magazine empty. He lowered the rifle, looking for the marks. They were all over the target, mostly around the outer ring with a few strays outside. There was only one in the inner ring.

"Don't worry about it," Fletcher said. "At a hundred yards, you put a lot of ammo in a small space. That's the idea with an M-2."

MacKendrie said nothing but felt a low horror. This weapon wasn't designed for the kind of precision needed for hunting, as he was used to. Its only purpose was for mowing down men, as many and as fast as possible. He held the rifle upright and gave it back to Fletcher, glad to be rid of it.

"Good shooting, sir," Fletcher said cheerfully, carrying the rifles as they walked back to the ordnance room. "Good to have you aboard."

MacKendrie managed a smile. "Thanks, Chief. Same here."

THIRTY

At mid-morning the next day, MacKendrie was standing at the rail of the destroyer's forward deck, looking over the uninterrupted ocean surface. The calm seas were like corrugated metal under a white-hot sky. This was what he had wanted to experience during the war, the mariner's thrill of riding the borderless waters, bent on a purpose, knowing and accepting the mortal danger the capricious sea held. The *USS Hawkins* was making about thirty knots, and the ocean breeze in his face was heavy and salty.

He looked off the port beam where just a few hundred miles away was the land where he had grown up, where his parents were buried, and where he would soon return, either briefly or perhaps to join them forever. He remembered the story of how some missionaries in the 1800s had been on their way to China when their ship was overtaken by pirates, who threw them into the sea. They had been deemed martyrs who gave their lives in the cause of the gospel. If he were killed on this mission, no such honor would be given to him.

He checked his watch. Eleven fifteen, local time. They would be near the launch point in a few hours. The sailors sauntered around the deck, in no hurry to carry out their duties. It was peacetime, and the ship was on a routine run, so the crew was under no compulsion to act smart. They had been told the mission involved intelligence and ordered under threat of court-martial to keep their mouths shut about what they saw and heard. But there was no prospect of action, only a forty-eight-hour cruise in the East China Sea, so the mood on the ship was light.

He saw Jack Fletcher walking toward him with a practiced gait on the rising and falling deck, not bothering to hold the rails. MacKendrie was not used to the motion of the ship yet. He had not been seasick exactly, but queasy, and didn't eat anything all morning, preferring cups of strong black coffee. Fletcher leaned on the rail beside him.

"Morning, sir."

"Good morning, Chief. Any news?"

"We're on schedule. Everything's square." They watched the sea for a while, then Fletcher turned to him. "I think I found someone who can help you with that letter of yours. There's a PO on board I used to serve with. Lewis. Good guy, I think you can trust him."

"Does he understand I just want him to hold it and only mail it if the ship goes back to base without us?"

"Yes, sir. He knows it's against regs, but he said everyone deserves to send a last letter home."

They watched the horizon silently. MacKendrie said, "What about you, Jack? Are you giving Petty Officer Lewis a letter, too? Someone you want to hear from you?"

Fletcher shook his head. "Nah. My parents are dead. Never had a wife. I got a brother, but we didn't get along. There's my sister. Sharon. She lives in Oklahoma City, got a husband, couple of kids. I visit her when I can. If we don't come back, I asked Captain Cohen to send my stuff to her."

"When can I give Lewis the letter?"

"He'll be off-duty about sixteen hundred. I'll bring him to our quarters later." Fletcher squinted up at the sky. "Doldrums. Seen it go on like this for weeks. Least we won't have a problem with the weather."

They split up, and MacKendrie returned to the tiny quarters he and Fletcher were assigned. The destroyer was not a big ship, and the quarters were just below deck, amidships. It was narrow and spartan, with two bunks and two lockers, just a place to stow their gear and catch forty winks if they had time. MacKendrie was used to living simply. In the mission field, the missionaries' homes were spacious compared to those of most Chinese families, but too many frills were discouraged on the grounds that they were there to share the lot of the poor. James and Emily MacKendrie had tried to keep their home furnished sparingly. He stretched on the bunk and felt the slow rise and fall of the ship. He hoped he would feel up to eating when it was time for chow.

He must have dozed. Fletcher was shaking his shoulder. "We've arrived, sir. We're at dead stop at the launch point. Cohen wants to see us."

He followed Fletcher to a small wardroom, where Cohen and Vanderhoven sat at a table.

"I just wanted to have a short briefing," Cohen said. "Luke, any signals from our network?" Vanderhoven shook his head. "So we're assuming the Cuckoo will be at the pickup point about thirty-six hours from now. You're both clear on the procedures?" They nodded. "Chief, if the worst happens and you're stopped, open the cocks and try to scuttle the boat. There's nothing top secret on board, but it'll give them less to go on. If you don't have time to do that, at least pitch the radio overboard."

"Aye, sir."

"We've got a few hours of daylight yet. Let's launch the boat and do a shakedown. Mac, you might as well go along."

They made their way topside and went aft, where a dozen sailors were standing around a boat sitting on the deck next to a hoist. As they got closer, MacKendrie looked at it with dismay. He wasn't sure what he expected, perhaps something armored and fearsome.

It was about twenty-five feet long and ten feet wide, sleek, with the front deck covering a cabin below and an open deck aft. The sides of the boat came up about waist-high on anyone standing in the rear, so that if you crouched down you wouldn't be seen. A flange ran down both sides of the inner hull, allowing a place to sit. At the tail of the boat was a big rectangular box that completely enclosed two inboard motors. The propellers, which were retractable, jutted below. The boat was painted gray.

So this was supposed to take them into the darkness and back. MacKendrie turned to Fletcher. "Have you piloted this thing before?"

He was smiling broadly. "Yes, sir. Or one just like it. You'll be surprised how she runs."

They walked around the boat, Fletcher describing it like a proud father. The boat was light and would only draw about two feet of water. Extra fuel would be stored in the cabin. There was a three-day supply of rations and a simple medical kit. A lightweight wooden frame fit into pre-drilled holes on the deck with a canvas covering to stretch over it that would make the boat vaguely resemble a *sampan*, a Chinese fishing vessel. The engines were twin eighty-horsepower motors that had specially designed mufflers, and the engine compartment was lined with sound-absorbent material.

"She could run right by you at full throttle, and you'd never hear the motors," Fletcher said.

Cohen walked over. "Hop in, gents, let's see how she does." He turned to a crew of sailors and barked, "Stand by the hoist, you men!"

The boat seemed even smaller to MacKendrie as he stood on its rear deck. There was barely enough room for two men to stand side by side. He took a seat as Fletcher stood grasping the wheel. Cohen continued to bellow orders, the fore and aft lines went taut, and the boat lifted from the deck. Slowly the hoist swung to the side, and MacKendrie's stomach fluttered as he looked down at the water twenty feet below. The hum of the hoist and the noise of the deck receded as they slowly lowered to the surface. Once they were floating next to the sheer steel hull of the *Hawkins*, Fletcher and MacKendrie unhooked the lines from the turnbuckles. Fletcher took the wheel. He flipped a switch, pushed a button, and MacKendrie felt rather than heard the engines come to life. The boat quivered with a light vibration, and there was a hum like a bumblebee worrying a flower.

Fletcher looked up and gave a thumbs-up sign, which Cohen, looking down from the rail, returned. The chief slowly lifted a lever and eased the boat about fifty yards away from the ship. He performed a couple of wide turns, first to port, then to starboard. He looked back at MacKendrie.

"Hold onto your hat, Skipper," he said, then pulled the lever straight up.

MacKendrie had barely braced himself and was nearly thrown back against the stern. The boat's bow rose and it shot forward as if it were thrown from a catapult. The wind roared in their ears as they dashed across the water, chopping every few seconds. They must be doing forty or fifty knots, MacKendrie thought. It was thrilling, almost frightening how fast they were moving over the water. He looked back at the *Hawkins* and saw it dropping back quickly. Fletcher moved the wheel slightly, and the boat turned to port, still running fast. They circled back toward the ship and shot past the stern, fleetingly seeing sailors crowding the rail and pointing. There was almost no sound coming from the engine compartment, but the boat was alive with the motors' fury.

Fletcher pushed the throttle down, and the boat's nose fell level. He executed a couple of sharp turns, the boat pivoting about so quickly MacKendrie was pressed against the side. The chief tried a few other maneuvers, turning slow and fast, accelerating and decelerating. Finally he throttled down to idle and turned to MacKendrie.

"What do you think, Skipper?"

MacKendrie wiped his forehead. "Mighty impressive, Chief." Then startled, he said, "What did you call me?"

"Skipper, that's what."

"Why'd you call me that? I'm not an officer."

"You used to be. Every boat needs a skipper, and I'm just a petty officer. That makes you the skipper."

MacKendrie opened his mouth, then shut it, having no idea how to refute this naval logic. Whether he liked it or not, it seemed he had been made the commander of a Navy spy boat.

Fletcher said, "Let me show you how it works, Skipper."

The chief showed him the controls. Ignition switch, start button. Throttle lever. Up for full, push right and down for reverse. Switch to raise and lower the props.

"That's it. Give it a try. Just don't make a sharp turn at full speed. You'll turn us flat over."

Cautiously, MacKendrie pulled up on the throttle, and the boat responded instantly. He tried a few turns and was amazed at the light touch it took to turn the boat. She had been well designed. He straightened out on a tack in front of the ship and slowly pulled the throttle up to full. He had to lean forward to keep his balance as the bow angled up. The pace was heart-stopping. They shot past the ship and in seconds were a hundred yards past. He throttled down to idle and circled the boat around. Fletcher, standing beside him, was beaming.

"You handled her pretty good, Skipper."

"Thanks, Chief, but I hope I don't have to operate her. She's yours." He stepped aside to give Fletcher the wheel.

There was a static burst, and the radio spoke. "Falcon, this is Hunt Master, how do you read? Come in, Falcon."

Fletcher reached just inside the cabin and grabbed a microphone. A couple of exchanges established that radio communication was clear. They were ordered to return to ship as soon as they were satisfied that the boat was operational.

"Roger, Hunt Master. We're coming in. Falcon out."

Fletcher eased the boat back alongside the *Hawkins*, where the crew was standing by above. The lines were lowered and secured, and they were slowly lifted off the sea, swung above the deck and lowered. MacKendrie's legs felt wobbly as he climbed onto the deck, and he tried not to show it. Cohen was laughing and clapping Fletcher on the shoulder.

"Let's go get some chow, gents," Cohen said. MacKendrie suddenly realized he was famished.

The food in the officers' mess was not as delicious as at the base in San Diego, but it was hot and filling. It was the old standard of the Navy and Marines—creamed chipped beef on toast. MacKendrie ate two helpings, washed down with strong coffee. It was crowded, with five men around a single table—Cohen, Vanderhoven, Fletcher, MacKendrie, and a junior officer. As if following some unwritten rule, no one spoke about the mission. There was talk of which was the better team, the Yankees or the Dodgers, and it was hotly debated whether the rookie, Mantle, might be a better centerfielder than DiMaggio. The ensign was teased about popping the question to his girlfriend. MacKendrie thought about Helen. The mess began to empty.

Cohen said, "Chief, did you get that fishing gear stashed on the boat?"

"Not yet, sir. I'll take care of it."

"Good." He looked at MacKendrie. "I'll see the two of you on deck at zero-zero-thirty."

After he left, Fletcher said, "If you'll go to our quarters, Skipper, I'll bring Lewis around."

There was something about Lewis that seemed trustworthy. MacKendrie handed over the letter and pointed out the address. Lewis nodded and stashed the letter.

"Don't worry, sir. Odds are it won't ever get mailed."

"Thanks, Mister Lewis. I'm looking forward to getting that back from you."

Fletcher said he wanted to check the boat one more time. When he returned to the cabin, MacKendrie was reading a psalm, and he climbed onto the top bunk without speaking.

MacKendrie put the book down, and leaned forward, elbows on knees, thumbs under his chin. Silently he prayed, "Dear God, forgive me. I don't know how I got here, but I can only get home if you help me. I don't deserve it, but please, please, for the sake of my wife and children, spare me, and Jack as well. Bring us, and Paul, out of the snake's den. Let there be peace, not violence."

When he finished, he realized the cabin was quiet and he glanced up to see Fletcher watching him. "That was a long prayer, Skipper," he said.

"I suppose it was. I lose track of the time when I'm praying sometimes."

After a moment, Fletcher said, "I guess I just don't get it, sir."

MacKendrie stood. "Why's that, Jack?"

Fletcher shook his head. "My grandma was a holy roller. Drug me off to this little clapboard church whenever she could get her hands on me when I was a kid. All I saw were people acting crazy, talking gibberish, preaching that went on for what seemed like days. Lot of hollerin'. I always thought it was just a bunch of racket. People making noise and they were the only ones listening."

"You still think that?"

Fletcher stared overhead. "I dunno. Saw plenty of things in the war that made me wonder where God was. Men dying, calling out for him. Didn't help. I asked myself what kind of God he was if he let a guy die who was asking for his help."

MacKendrie nodded. "I wondered the same thing sometimes." Seeing Fletcher's look, he said, "Oh, yes. On Tinian, in that hospital. You couldn't help but wonder where God was."

They listened to the faint sounds of the ship's creak and clank at anchor. Fletcher said, "But you still pray."

MacKendrie nodded again. "I still pray. See, Jack, it wasn't God pulling those triggers. It was men. We were the ones killing each other, making an unholy mess of things. He lets us do that, you know. Then when we run to him for help, sometimes it's too late."

"So where was he? God."

"Oh, he was there all along. With the suffering and the dying. That's where you'll always find him." Fletcher looked like a schoolboy who had been given a lesson almost, but not quite, beyond his grasp. "Try to get some rest, Chief. You'll need it."

"Aye, sir," Fletcher said absently.

MacKendrie stretched out on his bunk and closed his eyes, feeling the ship rock. He couldn't sleep, seeing scenes from the past, imagining scenes that might come to pass.

There was a knock on the cabin door. Come, he said. A sailor entered carrying a bundle of clothes.

"Mister MacKendrie? Captain Cohen sent these. Said you and the chief were to change into them. He also said to leave all your personal stuff with your gear."

Fletcher spoke from the top bunk. "Thanks, seaman. Set 'em down."

Wordlessly they stood and stripped down to their skivvies. The clothes Cohen sent were plain khakis without any markings or insignia. The shirts were long-sleeved, and they were the right size. Harry had done his homework. When he was dressed, MacKendrie folded his clothes and placed them neatly inside his grip. He left his watch on. They might need it if Fletcher's failed. Looking at his hand, he saw his wedding ring. Slowly he slipped it off and placed it on top of his clothes, then closed the clasp on the bag.

"Zero-zero-two-five, Skipper. Time to go."

"Lead on, Chief."

On deck, Cohen looked on as the crew made their preparations. Fletcher went on board to do a final check of the supplies. A sailor brought Cohen and MacKendrie paper cups of hot coffee, which they sipped as they watched. After awhile, Fletcher walked over.

"She's ready, Captain."

"Tell the officer of the deck we'll launch in five minutes."

"Aye, sir."

Cohen turned to MacKendrie. "Mac, I know I said no personal effects, but I thought you might like to have this." Out of his pocket, he pulled a small cross on a chain and held it out.

MacKendrie stared at it a moment, noting that it was actually a crucifix. "Where'd you get that, Harry?"

Cohen seemed a little embarrassed. "The chaplain at Okinawa. Anyway, I thought, you know…"

MacKendrie shook his head. "Thanks, Harry, but you keep it. If we're caught, I don't think it would be a good idea to have it with me. Besides, for the next thirty-six hours, I'd rather not think about the cross."

They walked to the boat. Fletcher was already aboard. Cohen said, "Good luck, Mac. I'll see you back here soon."

"Sure." He climbed aboard the boat and sat in the rear.

THIRTY-ONE

The boat was hoisted, swung over the side and lowered into blackness. It was worse this time, MacKendrie thought, because you couldn't even see the water below. When they were afloat, they released the lines, which disappeared above. Fletcher started the engines, then reached into the cabin and spoke into the microphone. Radio check, he said.

"We read you. Good hunting, Falcon."

Fletcher had a compass on a string around his neck, and he opened it. They would be bearing two-six-five, west-southwest. Without lights or better gear, navigation would be rough. They might miss the opening of the river by miles.

"Ready, Skipper? Here we go." Fletcher guided the boat slowly away from the destroyer, then gradually lifted the throttle. In seconds, the lights of the *Hawkins* receded until they were a small cluster. It was the only reference point in a sphere of utter blackness. They were hurtling straight ahead into darkness so deep you couldn't make out the bow. The boat was running almost full speed, and it was terrifying, not seeing what was in front of them. The steady chop-chop of the waves made it worse, imagining that any second they might strike an object, an unmoored buoy maybe, or a large sea creature.

After several minutes, MacKendrie realized the blackness wasn't complete. It was partly overcast, but there was enough reflected starlight that he could just see the surface. He stood up next to Fletcher and looked out. Far ahead, he thought he saw a faint glow above the horizon that indicated land.

Fletcher half-shouted, "There's some binoculars in the cabin. Keep 'em close and help me watch for anything ahead."

MacKendrie ducked into the cabin, bounced by the chop. He poked his head back up. "Need a light, Chief," he called out.

"The dark lanterns are on your left."

He found them, box-like devices with shutters in front that could be adjusted. He flipped a switch, and the cabin lit up. It was more spacious than he anticipated, and the supplies were neatly laid out. Fuel cans in the front, C-rations to the right, camouflage equipment to the side. The binoculars were lying on the canvas covering.

Standing next to the wheel, leaning forward against the tilt of the deck, he was glad he could act useful, but there was little to see. The *Hawkin*'s lights had disappeared. There were no other lights visible in any direction. He rested his arms on the top deck and let himself be carried forward. Neither man spoke. Fletcher occasionally held his watch up to his eyes, then did the same with the compass. MacKendrie realized he was navigating by dead reckoning, estimating the distance traveled by the time elapsed and keeping the boat as near on course as he could. MacKendrie checked his own watch. They had been away from the ship about twenty minutes. It might take another fifteen before they came near land.

It was closer to twenty-five minutes. The ship might have been farther offshore than they thought, but MacKendrie was becoming concerned that there was no sign of land. Suddenly he glimpsed something far ahead, a bare pinprick of light. Fletcher hadn't seen it. MacKendrie raised the binoculars and tried to get a fix on it. Between the bouncing of the boat and the distance, he couldn't keep the light in his sights, so he couldn't tell if it was a boat or the light from a dock.

Cupping his hand in front of his mouth, he said, "Light ahead, Chief." He pointed. Fletcher eased the throttle down to half. MacKendrie looked again through the glasses. It appeared to be a stationary light, probably a dock, but he couldn't tell. He looked left and right and saw no other lights, although the glow, ahead to port, had gotten brighter. Fletcher cut the engines to idle and asked for the binoculars. As he studied the light, he murmured, "I think we're a little north of Shanghai, Skipper. I'm going to run due south for a little while and see if we can see anything. I don't want to get any closer yet."

Consulting his compass, he made a quarter-turn to port and accelerated to half-speed. For ten minutes, the glow grew stronger, then suddenly an array of lights began to twinkle far ahead off the starboard bow.

Fletcher said, "That's Shanghai, right? On the south bank of the river?"

"That's it." MacKendrie realized they were rounding a peninsula that was formed by the mainland and the north channel of the river. He remembered the map. From north bank to south, the mouth of the Yangtze where it meets the China Sea is vast, thirty miles across. Chongming Island, eight miles wide and twenty-five miles long, divided the mouth of the river into a narrower north channel and the more heavily used main channel. The entrance to the north channel should be near, just the other side of the peninsula. He tapped Fletcher's arm.

"Chief, I've got an idea. The north channel is narrower, but it's not used much and there are very few settlements on either side of that branch of the river. We'd have to go slower, but it would mean less chance of being spotted. Once we get past Chongming Island, we'll be well upriver of Shanghai."

"Yeah? Sounds like a good plan, Skipper. Watch for the island."

MacKendrie took the glasses and scanned. He could just make out the features of the shoreline, clumps of trees and vegetation. Then he saw it, an expanse of open water, still wide, a couple of miles across, and the island beyond. He pointed.

"That's the mouth of the channel."

Fletcher nodded. He turned the boat toward the river and came to a dead stop. He checked his watch. It was a little before two. "Now we'll watch for patrols."

They were still far enough offshore that the boat wouldn't be seen from the river. An occasional fishing boat crept along. Fifteen minutes had passed when they heard an engine's humming to their left, and they saw lights much brighter than those of any fishing vessel moving steadily from the main channel northward. Fletcher was watching through the binoculars, and MacKendrie felt him go tense as it passed in front of them. All he could tell without the glasses was that the boat was bigger than theirs. It didn't slow and continued north up the coastline, disappearing around the headland.

Fletcher relaxed. "Didn't like the looks of that," he said quietly.

"What did you see?"

"It was about forty feet long, with a machine gun on a deck above the pilot house. She's probably faster than us. And if she had swung those search lights out this way, she'd have spotted us for sure."

"Are we going in now?"

"Not yet. It took about twelve minutes from the time we spotted her till she was gone. Cohen said the patrols were staggered. Let's see if another one comes from north to south."

They stood watching, as the boat rocked beneath them. Almost twenty minutes later, they heard the same throaty humming and saw the patrol boat's lights on their right. It made the same slow, deliberate pass by the river and moved off to the south, finally becoming another twinkling light among the others at Shanghai.

"Was it the same one?" MacKendrie asked.

Fletcher shook his head. "Markings were different. I don't read Chinese, but they were different. Let's go."

"What about the camouflage covering?"

"We can't wait. We've got to get into the river before a patrol comes back."

He started the engines and eased the boat forward. MacKendrie took the glasses and swept the coastline north and south as they approached the mouth of the channel. His khakis were wet with seawater and sweat. They glided into the river. No sign of boats of any kind, only a few barges tied up along the bank. They kept to the middle of the channel, with plenty of distance between them and the banks on either side. The engines were barely making a sound.

MacKendrie whispered, "Chief, bear toward the right-hand side. There's fewer villages over there, and I think there's a shoal right in the middle of this channel we'll have to get around."

"Sure, Skipper."

They were moving slowly, maybe fifteen miles an hour. It was hard to believe they were near one of the largest cities of a nation of five hundred million people. There was almost no sound and only an occasional small light to the right or left. The river was placid on the surface, but occasionally the current would catch them and shove them sideways. Fletcher fought the wheel and raised the throttle. MacKendrie pointed ahead at a bright spot in the river.

"There's the shoal," he whispered.

"Good thing we're only drawing a few feet," Fletcher said as he navigated around it.

"Up ahead, the channel narrows and takes a ninety-degree bend to the left. There's a village there. A little after that and it rejoins the river."

Fletcher followed the course of the channel, turning the boat to port. A few minutes later the island and the north bank dropped away, and they entered the wide Yangtze River. Downriver to the left were the lights of Shanghai. Fletcher turned the boat to starboard.

"We've got to move a little quicker, Skipper. It'll start getting light about oh-five-hundred, and that only gives us a couple of hours to go fifty miles."

"Okay, Jack, but you're going to have to slow down once we pass Nantong on the north bank. There are a couple of islands that take up most of the river."

For the next hour and a quarter, neither spoke. MacKendrie watched for patrols, but they passed only an occasional junk or fishing boat at anchor. The sky was still black.

The lights of Nantong came in view, and MacKendrie told Fletcher to bear left, along the south bank. He pointed up, where a light shone at the top of a hill whose black outline they could see next to the bank. He leaned in and said quietly, "Used to be a temple up there with a stone in it. People believed if you were bitten by a mad dog, you went up there and touched the stone. Supposed to cure you."

He could see Fletcher grin and shake his head, then immediately they staggered as the boat turned almost sideways. Fletcher twisted the wheel. "Son of a bitch!" he hissed. "Goddamn current." He opened the throttle and the boat shuddered, caught between the force of the river and the engines' surge. For a moment, MacKendrie was afraid the boat was going to spin around like a top, but just as suddenly, the current eased and the boat sprang forward.

"Jesus," Fletcher whispered. He glanced at MacKendrie. "Why didn't you tell me this river was so treacherous?"

MacKendrie put a hand on Fletcher's shoulder. "You're doing fine, Chief. It's not too far ahead, now."

He checked his watch. It was ten after four. They had been lucky so far, but MacKendrie dreaded what came next, finding the entrance to the canal.

At four-thirty, Fletcher whispered, "By my reckoning, we should be getting close. See anything familiar?"

"Not yet. Stay about a hundred yards off the south bank and cut your speed a little."

MacKendrie scanned the bank with the binoculars. Five minutes passed, then ten. He saw nothing. Then movement caught his eye just above the water. Reeds, in clumps at first, then more and more, an enormous expanse of them, six feet high or more, stretching into the river and as far as he could see westward along the bank. He pointed.

"There's the marsh."

Fletcher nodded. "What do we do?"

"Keep moving upriver. We're still several miles from Bai Miao."

Looking through the glasses, MacKendrie hoped to see some sign, some landmark that would jog his memory, but this part of the marsh was featureless, with nothing to see but bobbing reeds. They could just pick a place and try to get the boat into the reeds, but he remembered they were thick and it would be difficult in the shallows without the engines to force the boat into them. They could even get stuck.

"Skipper," Fletcher said. He jerked his head behind them. At first MacKendrie wasn't sure what he meant, but then he noticed that he could make out the outlines of the hills on either side of the river more clearly. The sky was beginning to turn from ink black to dark blue. Fletcher pointed out to the middle of the river. They could see boats starting to move slowly back and forth. None were near enough to see them yet, but lights were starting to appear along the banks. The river was awaking from sleep. He nodded back to Fletcher and resumed scanning the bank.

Nothing. Minutes passed. Then suddenly a dark mass rose behind the reeds. A hill, he thought at first, but no. It was too uniform, about fifteen feet high, level at the top. He remembered. Dikes. The rice farmers built dikes along this part of the river, with gates cut into them to let water into the fields. On the river side of the gates, inlets had been cut through the reeds. The reeds were thinner next to those inlets, and it had been a perfect place to wait in his skiff for ducks. There was a particular inlet that had been a favorite spot, with a pole of some sort, probably a totem commemorating an ancestor, stuck into the dike above it. The totem was surely long gone, but it didn't matter. Any one of the inlets would do.

"Chief, pull in a little closer, fifty yards or so, and go slow," MacKendrie whispered.

He checked his watch. Five ten. The sky was lightening noticeably. They had less than twenty minutes to get off the river. Fletcher tapped his arm urgently and pointed. A boat with a light on the bow was making its way downriver in their direction.

"Patrol?" Fletcher hissed.

MacKendrie watched it through the glasses. It was still dim, but he said, "No. Fisherman. But we better get down." They crouched below the top of the hull and waited, listening. MacKendrie faintly heard a voice. The Chinese language is musical, and he thought the man was talking, but then he realized he was singing to himself. It was an old folk song, one he hadn't heard in ages, and it made him smile in spite of their danger of being seen. The song faded as the boat passed on by. The fisherman was either not curious or too preoccupied.

MacKendrie stood and put the glasses to his eyes. Along the edge of the reeds he saw a break. Trying to control his voice, he pointed. "Pull a little closer to that spot, Chief." He looked again. He put his hand on Fletcher's shoulder. "This is it. It's an inlet. Should be shallow, about waist-high. When you get close, pull up the props, and we'll use the paddles."

Fletcher nodded, and spun the wheel, swinging the stern out and pointing the boat straight toward the inlet. He cut the speed to idle, then with twenty yards to go turned off the engines and they glided forward. Just before they reached the reeds, Fletcher flipped a switch, and they heard the propellers retract. They picked up the oars resting on hooks just inside the hull, and paddled, guiding the boat into the inlet. The reeds rose above them on either side, bobbing and rattling softly in the waves they made.

When the boat had glided about fifty yards down the inlet, MacKendrie said, "One of us will have to get out and shove her in among these reeds."

"I'll do it."

Fletcher took off his shoes and swung over the side. The water came just above his waist. He pushed the bow sideways, then moved to the stern. "Paddle, Skipper," he said, and shoved with effort. The boat edged forward among the reeds, then slowed and stopped. The rear half of the boat still protruded into the inlet. Someone passing nearby could see it.

"Let me get out, Jack. If it's lighter, she might go in. I'll pull, you push."

MacKendrie clambered over the side. The water was warm, and he felt the soft mud under his feet. There were splashes around him as water creatures fled, disturbed by the interlopers. He pushed his way through the reeds to the bow, where there was a line, and MacKendrie grabbed it. "Ready, Chief? One, two, *three*." The boat inched forward. "Again." Another six inches. Again and again, and then finally it slid in as if easing into a berth. MacKendrie pushed aside the reeds and moved to the stern, where even in the dim light he could see Fletcher standing in the water.

"You think she's out of sight?" Fletcher whispered.

"I think so. No one comes into these inlets this time of year, and anyone looking from the river wouldn't see the boat. Just to be on the safe side, we'll cut some reeds and put 'em around the stern. We ought to put up the camouflage, too."

Fletcher produced a folding knife, and cut armloads of reeds from the opposite side of the inlet, floating them over to MacKendrie, who stacked them up around the stern. He motioned to Fletcher, and they waded to the rear deck. Fletcher hauled himself on board, then pulled up MacKendrie. Soaked and panting, they sat side by side on the deck. The only sounds were the rattle of the reeds, the occasional croak of a frog, and the splash of a fish nabbing an insect. Still panting, Fletcher pointed up at the sky. It was blue with the promise of dawn minutes away. He grinned at MacKendrie and extended a hand.

"We made it, Skipper. You found the spot."

MacKendrie shook his head. "Not a minute too soon. I was getting worried we were going to have to sit at anchor in plain sight and hope no one bothered us."

When they regained their breath, they put up the camouflage canopy, which, MacKendrie said, would give them some shade from the sun without having to go into the stifling cabin. It's going to be hot and steamy, he warned Fletcher. Soon enough, they could feel the sun heating up the river, and they took off their shirts and sat down to wait.

They broke out C-rations and a canteen. MacKendrie was hungry, but even more he was bone-weary. He barely finished the ration and said, "Chief, if it's okay with you, I'm gonna get some shut-eye."

"Sure, Skipper. I'll take the first watch."

He stretched out on the damp rear deck. The boat sat mostly still. He could hear far-off sounds that he couldn't make out, voices perhaps, or a distant boat engine. He had lost track of time. He had no idea what day it was or what time back on the east coast. All he knew was that he was safe for now. He closed his eyes.

He was running across a big field. On the other side, he could see Helen and the girls, waving at him and smiling. He was shouting, trying to warn them of something, he didn't know what, but they couldn't hear him. People kept appearing, trying to stop him to ask him questions. Connie Campbell, wearing a blood-red dress, held out a piece of paper and pen. "Could you just sign this letter, Rev'rend?" Eli Ross appeared, smiling. "Let me use that gun of yours." Far ahead, he could see a blue pickup truck driving toward his family, speeding up, aiming right at them...

Someone was shaking him violently, and he lashed out, swinging his fists.

"Skipper! For God's sake, wake up! Skipper!"

He opened his eyes to a white glare and gasped as he realized Fletcher was talking to him.

"Easy, sir. Here, sit up," Fletcher said in a low voice and dragged him to a sitting position. "Sorry I shook you so hard, but you were yelling like crazy. Lucky no one's around or they'd have heard you for sure."

MacKendrie hung his head, still panting. "Oh, God, what a nightmare."

"Here, have some water." Fletcher passed a canteen.

The water revived him a little, and he looked around. "Thanks, Chief. Sorry for the noise."

"Forget it."

"What time is it?"

"Almost noon. It's been quiet. No problems. Keep hearing voices, though. Sounds like they're on the other side of this levee."

"Rice farmers. Lots of rice fields on the other side of this dike. They're getting close to harvest this time of year. Course, I guess the rice is going to the government these days."

"Want something to eat?"

"Sure. Let's see what Cohen packed for us."

It was some kind of tasteless stew and crackers. MacKendrie didn't care. He ate without thinking. They sat under the canopy, shaded, but the heat was oppressive.

"So you know people around here?" Fletcher whispered.

"I used to. There might still be a few around, but the war was hard on this country. Then the Communists relocated people."

They ate in silence until Fletcher spoke. "You think this guy, the Cuckoo, will be out there tonight?"

"I don't know, Chief. A thousand things could have gone wrong."

"Yeah. What if they picked him up and he spilled the beans about us?"

MacKendrie nodded. "I thought about that. I—"

An engine, a big one, approaching not far off. They crouched. They couldn't see the river for the thicket of reeds, but they felt the vibration of the big boat's engine. Then MacKendrie heard a shout over the noise.

"Corporal, see anything?"

The reply was too faint. The boat was moving slowly and seemed to be about a hundred yards away. It must have taken five minutes or more for the noise of the engine to recede. MacKendrie and Fletcher sat down again.

"It was a patrol," MacKendrie whispered. "Looking for something, but it could have been anything. A lot of smuggling goes on around here."

"Wouldn't that be a kick in the head. Get caught by a patrol looking for smugglers."

"Why don't you get some sleep, Chief. I'll take the next watch."

Fletcher curled up at the stern and soon was out like a light. MacKendrie sat on the deck, listening to the sounds around him. He could hear the indistinct voices of the rice field workers, occasionally catching a word or two. There were some sounds of river traffic, boatmen calling out and cursing, boat engines out in the middle of the water. Then there were the sounds of the marsh—the birds, frogs, and fish all looking for food. MacKendrie had been something of an amateur ornithologist when he was younger. He had made a study of the birds of this region, keeping a diary of his sightings, describing the species, some of which he heard now. Warblers, sparrows, cuckoos, all calling out in territorial warning or in hopes of finding a mate. The marsh was alive with the sounds of life, unconcerned with politics or war but only the simplicity of eating and mating.

The hours passed slowly. At one point, sweating, MacKendrie slipped over the side into the water to cool off, but it was like dipping into bath water. He looked at his watch. Four fifteen. They still had almost eight hours. He would feel better after the sun went down.

Fletcher woke up and gave a questioning look. MacKendrie shook his head. The chief went into the cabin and pulled out the fuel cans. He signaled to MacKendrie to lend a hand, and they unlatched the engine cowling and lifted it off. Fletcher topped off the fuel, and they replaced and secured the cowling.

They waited and watched as the sky went from white to blue to dusky and finally to black. They made one more meal of the C-rations, and MacKendrie hoped he wouldn't have to eat any more of them. Eight o'clock passed. Nine. Then ten. They felt the tension rising as the time stretched out.

"How far do you reckon we are from that dock?" Fletcher whispered to MacKendrie.

"Can't be more than a few miles. I think we're about eight miles below Bai Miao."

"It's almost eleven. It'll take us about twenty minutes to get out of this marsh and underway. Maybe another fifteen to find the dock. Let's shove off in about ten minutes. That'll put us in position early and we can observe the situation from the river."

"Okay. The radio's on the right frequency, isn't it?"

There was silence for a moment. MacKendrie wondered if he'd said something wrong, then Fletcher said easily, "Relax, Skipper. I double-checked. I've got the gain set low, but if this bird calls the way he's supposed to, we'll hear it."

At eleven ten, Fletcher tapped his watch. "That's it. Let's go."

They jumped in the water, MacKendrie pushing on the bow and Fletcher pulling on the stern. It took effort, but it was easier getting the boat out of the reeds than it had been getting in. They paddled the boat forward the fifty-yard length of the inlet, and Fletcher held up a hand. Cautiously they eased forward to the edge of the river, which stretched away before them. There were scattered lights on the far bank and a fishing boat here and there, but nothing suspicious. Fletcher signaled, and they paddled out another fifty yards. They stowed the paddles, and Fletcher flipped a switch. They heard the propellers drop. After another look around, he pressed the button to start the engines, and they felt the vibration as they came to life. The men looked at each other with relief.

Fletcher raised the throttle and they moved ahead slowly, staying about a hundred yards off the bank. MacKendrie reached into the cabin and brought out a dark lantern. He adjusted the shutters, turned it on, and aimed it toward the bank, sweeping back and forth. For a while there was only the marsh. A glow above the river told them they were getting close to Bai Miao.

MacKendrie saw a dark form ahead on the bank and turned the lantern toward it. The faint light showed it was a dock, about a hundred yards ahead. He pointed, and Fletcher nodded. He turned off the light, and Fletcher shut off the engines and turned the boat to face the dock. Noiselessly, he lowered a small anchor to keep them from drifting in the current. The two men stood side by side, looking over the forward deck, and waited.

There was no sound but the gurgle of the river. They strained to listen for a voice from the radio. Midnight passed. The tension grew as the minutes went by. Fletcher checked his watch again and again. MacKendrie wondered if he had taken this risk for nothing.

THIRTY-TWO

Wang passed through the city, looking longingly at each landmark, each inn. Bai Miao held much unhappiness for him when he was young, but now he saw only his home. He followed the river road and arrived at the dark house. Inside, he found the electric lantern.

He busied himself by going through the house meticulously, looking for anything that might be incriminating. He went through his pouch, but other than clothes he had only his identity papers and his field notes, written in a notebook. He sat on the bed and looked back through the notes. They represented countless hours of hard work, wading in the frigid river in the winter, standing in soaking rains and under a white-hot sun in summer. He leafed through the pages, which amounted to little good, he thought. He had failed as a scientist, failed to help the lot of the people. He reached the last page of his notes, jotted down just a few days ago. In the right hands, they might provide the basis for a capable man to carry on the work more successfully, but he knew if he left them behind they would be confiscated, examined for clues to codes or intelligence about the network, and then placed in a dossier in a First Bureau office somewhere. He tore the sheets out of the notebook, then placed them on the floor and dropped a lighted match onto them.

There was a soft knock at the door. "Who is there?" he asked.

"Li Ying."

He opened the door and saw Li wearing a tight-fitting black shirt and trousers and an impassive expression. They stood looking at each other until she made an impatient gesture. "Let me in."

She was carrying a wooden box, which she sat on the table. Working quickly, she unlatched the cover, and Wang saw it was a radio. Li turned it on, made sure it was working, and sat down on the divan. "Come, sit," she said in a clipped voice. "I will brief you." He sat facing her.

The escape would take place by boat. The Americans had a specially designed craft. He would give a radio signal at midnight and be picked up by the boat at the dock. "You will say, 'The Cuckoo wishes to fly.' If they are waiting and all is well, they will reply, 'The cage is open.'"

"So. They take me away and everyone is happy." She said nothing. "What about Owl?"

"He will carry on."

"But the First Bureau..."

"He has outwitted them for years. Don't worry about Owl."

Wang shook his head. "And you?"

"There is still work to be done. Owl needs my help."

He made a disgusted sound. "You know the Nationalists will never succeed. It is futile. Ying, you have a chance to get free of all this. You can join me. Come with me tonight."

For a brief moment, he thought he saw doubt in her face. "You want me to be your wife and live in America?" He looked down, imagining the absurdity of it. She leaned forward. "There is another reason I cannot come, but I cannot tell you now. You should ask the Birdcatchers." She checked her watch. "We have two and a half hours to wait." She reached into her waistband, pulled out a slender knife, and offered it to him. "Here. You may need this." He tucked it inside the sleeve of his shirt.

She extinguished the lantern, and they sat in the dark. She silently refused to answer any of his questions. Once, he moved next to her and tried to embrace her, but she threw up her arm. He tried to move it, but it was like a wooden beam. The heat of the day lingered and dampness gathered on every surface. The air was thick, and Wang's mind ran wild with dread and possibilities. Finally they began to stir, anticipating the moment to give the signal.

Two sharp raps at the door made him start. He didn't move, but Li noiselessly was up and standing near the door. Three more raps, insistent. A muffled voice said, "Zhang?" It was a man's voice. He walked carefully past Li to the door, listening. Pounding now. "Zhang! Are you there? It is Juh."

He felt relief but also confusion. He hesitated, then reached out to open the door. Li's hand stopped him. She whispered low, "Don't."

The pounding returned. "Zhang, I know you're there. Wake up! It's important."

He opened the door, and his friend stood on the threshold with an electric torch and an agitated manner. "You are here," he said eagerly. Wang did not offer a greeting and blocked the doorway. "May I come in? I have news," Juh said quickly.

"I have been asleep. Can't it wait?" He tried to sound cross.

"No. You must let me explain."

He thought quickly. Everything must seem normal. "Very well, come in." Li was seated primly on the divan, and when he saw her, Juh stopped short.

"*Ai-ya*. So, I have interrupted a private evening." He grinned at Wang. "A friend?"

"This is Comrade Li. She works at the Ministry in Shanghai."

"Ah, good evening, Comrade Li. Zhang has spoken of you, but he did not tell me that you were..."

"Never mind," Wang said. "You must tell no one about this. The Party would punish us both if it were known."

"Of course, of course," Juh said affably. "You can rely on me."

"I'm sorry I have nothing to offer. I—we—have just arrived from Shanghai." He tried to appear relaxed, but he could feel the minutes ticking.

"I have been waiting for you to return."

"Well, what is it then?"

"You must come with me. There is a meeting of regional Party officials in the city, tonight. They want to hear about your project." When Wang looked blank, Juh added with emphasis, "The carp."

"Yes, yes, the carp. They are meeting...tonight? And they want to hear about the fish farms?" It was odd. Rallies and banquets were sometimes held at night, but rarely this late. "Who is at this meeting?"

Impatiently Juh said, "Oh, the commissar, the plant director, the assistant to the regional supervisor...I can't recall the others. But they have heard of your great project, and they want to hear a report from you. It is a great opportunity."

Wang glanced at Li. Her face remained expressionless, but her eyes were fixed on Juh and her body seemed tense as a spring. Now Juh stood and gestured animatedly. "Come, we must hurry. The meeting will not last much longer." He reached down and grabbed Wang's hand, but Wang jerked it back. Juh's expression changed at once, and he glared at him.

Wang stood and Li followed suit. "I'm sorry, but it is late. I am weary from traveling, and I have caught a fever. Please give my regrets to the commissar, but I cannot come."

Juh's frown deepened. "One doesn't treat important officials like this, Zhang. It would be much better if you come with me."

He shook his head. "I cannot. Now, you must excuse me..."

Juh said, "It is a pity." He opened the pouch at his side, reached in and drew out a black pistol, which he pointed at Wang, who was irritated, thinking that Juh was playing a prank. He was about to make a dismissive remark, but Li was instantly at his side and gripped his arm.

"I am afraid that you will have to come with me, Zhang. We have been waiting for you." He looked at Li. "You will have to come also, comrade."

"Juh, what are you doing? What is this?"

"You can drop the pretense. We know everything."

"What do you mean?"

"We were told that the construction of the plant would likely attract counter-revolutionary agents. It was only a week later you showed up at the office. We put you at ease, let you feel secure, and fed you false intelligence." He laughed at the look on Wang's face. "That nonsense in the papers in my desk. We knew you would take it straight to your chief, but you slipped our surveillance. We continued to watch here on the chance you would be foolish enough to come back. And here you are."

Wang grasped his left wrist with his right hand, within reach of the knife. He was not a fighter, but perhaps he could take Juh by surprise. Slowly he began to slide his hand inside the sleeve. "But Juh, my friend, you are mistaken. All I have been doing for months is raising fish." His fingertips reached the hilt of the knife.

"It is no good, Zhang. We knew who you were the moment you returned to China. Wang Wenzhe left for America and returned as Zhang Weijun." Juh waved the pistol. "Of course, all spies have assumed names. You know me as Juh, the humble clerk. In the First Bureau—"

"Your code name is The Archer." Wang was almost blinded by the clarity of it all.

Juh laughed. "Very good! You led us to two agents and a courier. We only need to find your chief. And there is one other agent as well, a clever one. Now you will come with me and tell us where to find them. My ruse to capture you was not very clever, I suppose, but—"

Li suddenly rounded on Wang. "You!" she burst out. "You are not a scientist?"

He caught on at once. Moaning, he said, "Ying, I've done a terrible thing, asking you here." He turned to Juh. "Please, let her go. She knows nothing about this."

Juh shook his head. "It is too late now. I think you have been an innocent victim of this traitor, Comrade Li, but of course, we will have to question you."

Wang had his fingers around the hilt of the knife. "Where are you taking me?"

"There is a checkpoint about two kilometers away. I notified the patrol that I would be bringing a prisoner. They are waiting."

Li gave Wang a hard push, causing him to stagger. "Traitor!" she said in a contemptuous voice.

Juh said, "Yes, comrade, but we don't have—"

Li took a step forward. "You betrayed the people!" she shouted. "You betrayed me!" She reached down to the table beside her, snatched up a brass bowl, took a quick step toward Wang and raised it as if to strike him, then pivoted and threw it at Juh's head.

He reflexively raised the hand holding the gun to deflect it, and in a swift movement, Li leaped forward and trapped Juh's forearm. She threw her body weight forward, bringing his arm crashing against the wall and sending the gun flying. It clattered onto the open floor. Juh cried in pain and with his other hand smacked Li's face hard, causing her to stagger. Wang had watched, open-mouthed, as they struggled, but at the sight of Li recoiling from the blow, he became furious and pulled out the knife. Juh took a quick step in the direction of the gun, but Wang stepped in front of him, brandishing the knife.

Panting, Juh said, "You won't cut me, fish farmer. I'm a soldier." He feinted to his right, causing Wang to pivot. Juh gave a cry and dove headlong into his midsection, knocking him off his feet. He landed on his back and cracked his head on the floor, knocking him momentarily senseless. He heard shouts and scuffling and the sound of wood smashing and sat up to see Li and Juh lurching around the room, arms and hands both locked around the pistol. Juh was forcing her backward, backward toward a wall.

Woozy, Wang looked around. A piece of wood lay nearby, the leg of his table. He crawled over to it, grabbed it and tried to stand but collapsed from dizziness. Li cried out in pain as Juh bent her hand back. Staggering forward like a drunken man, Wang gave a yell and swung the club at Juh's head. He missed but barreled into him, sending Juh and Li sprawling in different directions.

He got to his feet to see Juh, kneeling, aim the pistol directly at his head. Wang instinctively threw up a hand to ward off the shot. There was a shrill cry and a grunt as Juh's breath was forced out by a blow. The percussion of a shot assaulted Wang's ears in the small space of the house, and his left leg was knocked out from under him. Suddenly there was silence. He felt an intense burning near his knee. He looked up and saw Juh lying face down on the floor. Li stood over him, Wang's knife in her hand.

He started to stand but cried in pain and rolled over. Looking down, he saw his trouser leg was soaked with a dark stain. He pulled up the trouser and stared at the gunshot wound, which was bleeding badly. Li was at his side at once and cut away the trouser with the knife. Blood was pulsing from the wound. She pressed her hands hard on the wound, sending waves of pain into his body, and he gave a sharp yell. "When I let go, put your hands over the wound," she ordered. He pressed down on the spot, feeling the warm ooze under his hands. Quickly, still panting from the combat, Li took the cut-off trouser and sliced it into a strip, then wrapped it twice around Wang's leg above the knee and began twisting it.

He gasped with pain as the tourniquet bit into his leg, but Li kept turning until the band was impossibly tight. The blood stopped flowing, and he saw the hole from the bullet, about three centimeters below the knee. Wang felt lightheaded and suddenly cold. He was going into shock.

"Here," Li said, and she took his hand and placed it on the twisted cloth. "Hold this." She looked around, found a sturdy piece of wood, and inserted it into the tourniquet, then tied another piece of cloth around the stick to hold it in place.

"That won't hold very long," she said. She checked her watch. "Wang, it is after midnight! We must use the radio to call the rescue boat."

Panting with pain, he said, "You said there was some reason you had to remain and work for Owl. What is it?"

Astonished, she said, "We do not have time for this!"

"Tell me what it is," he demanded. "I will not make the call until you tell me."

She glared at him. "All right! You might have guessed. I have known him since I was a girl. My father and Owl were Kuomintang officers and friends. My father was killed in a battle with the Japanese. Owl looked after us, protected us. After the war, my family was targeted by the Communists. He got them to safety in Taiwan, but I stayed behind." She stood over him and said angrily, "I owe him everything! Don't you understand, you fool? He's my husband!"

* * *

A single *bang*, faint but clear, pierced the thick air on the river, and both men involuntarily jumped. "Gunfire," Fletcher hissed. They listened, but heard only the sounds of the river. "Less than a mile away, by the sound of it," he whispered. "That wasn't target practice, take my word for it." They waited, but there were no more shots. Fletcher put a hand on MacKendrie's arm. "That's no coincidence, Skipper. Maybe this plan's snafued. What do you say we get out of here?"

MacKendrie had the same impulse, but something held him back. "Let's wait and listen for just a bit. If we see anything suspicious, we can shove off."

"I don't like it," Fletcher said. "Something's gone wrong, I'm telling ya, Skipper."

"Maybe. But we've come this far. We ought to give the mission a chance. Let's keep alert. If we see activity near the dock, we'll figure the jig is up and we can take off."

"If we wait till then, it may be too late," Fletcher said pointedly. "Let's get out while we can."

MacKendrie hesitated. Every instinct told him Fletcher was right, but Paul was near, he knew it. He said, "The mission is to get this man out alive if we can. You told me I'm the skipper, so here's my order, Chief—we wait and watch." He stared straight ahead to avoid Fletcher's look.

"Aye, aye, sir."

MacKendrie scanned the shoreline with the binoculars but saw no movement. For long moments, they heard and saw nothing, not even a fishing boat. Fletcher checked his watch.

"Zero-zero-three-oh, Skipper," he whispered. "Thirty minutes."

MacKendrie nodded. Fletcher was muttering under his breath. MacKendrie just caught "snafued." "Easy, Chief. We've still got time."

"Not much, we don't. If we don't hear—"

A muffled crackle came from the cabin. The radio spoke. MacKendrie just made out the Mandarin phrase.

"The Cuckoo wishes to fly. The Cuckoo wishes to fly."

MacKendrie looked up, dazed. "It's the signal. 'The Cuckoo wishes to fly.'"

Neither one moved. The radio crackled again. "Do you hear? The Cuckoo wishes to fly."

MacKendrie suddenly realized it was Paul's voice, and he began groping for the microphone. He pressed the transmit button and said in Mandarin, "The cage is open. The cage is open."

A moment's silence. The voice on the radio said, "The Cuckoo has a broken wing and cannot fly alone."

MacKendrie looked up. "He says he's hurt and needs help." Fletcher cursed softly. MacKendrie transmitted, "Where is the Cuckoo now?"

"What..." Fletcher asked.

"I asked where he's located."

The response came, "A house on the road above the dock. Three hundred meters west."

MacKendrie lowered the mic. "He's in a house about three hundred and thirty yards west of the dock. He says there's a road."

Fletcher's voice was firm. "Well, that's too damn bad."

"What do you mean? We can't leave him."

"Oh, yes, we can. This was not in the brief."

"Chief..."

"Listen!" Fletcher's voice was low and fierce. "Out here we've got a chance. You want us to put ashore and walk around, two Americans in civvies, a quarter of a mile on Chinese soil? Begging your pardon, sir, but are you nuts? It's a trap. The place is probably crawling with troops."

The radio crackled. "Can you help? Time is short."

MacKendrie held the mic helplessly. Then on impulse he raised it. "Can the Cuckoo say what was the favorite Bible verse of Pastor Ma?"

"What..." Fletcher demanded, but MacKendrie raised his hand. They waited.

Low and slow came the response, "All things work together for good for those who love God." Then, "Is it you?"

"Yes," MacKendrie said. "Does the Cuckoo have company?"

"A friend."

"Wait there. I am coming." He tossed the microphone into the cabin and faced Fletcher. "It's not a trap, Jack. It's him. He knew my favorite Bible verse and asked if it was me. I told him I'm coming to get him."

"Goddammit, Skipper, you can't! I won't let you."

"Jack, listen. You pull up to the dock and drop me off, then return here and wait thirty minutes. It's dark and quiet and deserted out here. Odds are I won't see anyone. I know, I stick out like a sore thumb, but I speak the language. If I see anyone I'll give them some kind of story about doing research. Not that they'd believe it."

"Russian," Fletcher said. "Tell them you're a Russian engineer. It was in my briefing but not yours. Russians have been sighted in the area. They'll believe that."

"All right. I'll pick up the Cuckoo and get him back here. Three hundred yards isn't far. I'll take a dark lantern and signal you from the dock. If I'm not back in thirty minutes, you can clear out. Go straight downriver and out into the sea."

"Like hell I'd leave you! If you're not back in thirty minutes, I'll go back into the reeds and we'll fall back same time tomorrow night."

MacKendrie put his hand on Fletcher's shoulder. "No, Jack. We get out tonight or not at all. Let's go. Now."

Wordlessly, Fletcher pulled up the anchor. He started the engines and glided the boat forward. They pulled alongside the dock, and MacKendrie, clutching the lantern, stepped up onto it. He looked down into the boat. "Jack..."

"Just go, Skipper. I'll be out there, waiting."

THIRTY-THREE

The moment MacKendrie stepped off the dock and glanced back to see the boat glide silently behind the veil of night, leaving him alone in the dark, he thought panic would paralyze him, and he wanted to scream, come back, come back. He had trouble catching his breath. He had no idea how long he stood, trying to gain control of himself. Suddenly from the reeds came the call of a bird. At first he didn't hear it, but it came again and then again. It was musical and familiar. *Klug-koo.* A cuckoo.

He stared down at the lantern in his hands, reached for the switch, and shone it about until he saw the borders of a road. He began walking quickly. The faint light was a bouncing dot on the dark ribbon of road, just enough in the blackness for him to make his way. He was fit enough thanks to his regimen of walking, but soon he began to pant, and he was aware of his rasping breath in the near-silence. Ahead he saw the glow of Bai Miao at rest. The road was straight and level, and MacKendrie was tempted to run, but he held back. If he tripped and sprained an ankle, it could doom him.

He must have gone two hundred yards by now, he thought, shouldn't be far. He angled the lantern up from the road and swung it side to side, but there was only open country around him. He lowered the lantern and kept walking. Fifty, sixty paces later, he raised it again. The faint light disclosed a black shape ahead on the left.

Another ten paces and he saw it was a house. MacKendrie slowed and started to walk as quietly as he could.

He was a few paces from the corner of the house and could see a window, a curtain illumined by a low light from within. His lantern showed a half-open door. He took a step toward it and said in a low whisper, in English, "Paul. Paul, are you there?" Silence. Another step. A little louder, he said, "Wang Wenzhe."

Through the door stepped a woman. She was Chinese, dressed in a black tunic and trousers. She had a plain face that wore a hard expression.

"You are Ma?" she said quickly in Mandarin. He was so startled, he said nothing and didn't move. "We have no time. You are here for the Cuckoo, yes? Come quickly."

She went to the door, stopped and looked back at him. When he still didn't move, she impatiently waved at him in the peculiar Chinese gesture that struck a chord of memory. Certain that he was walking into a trap but resigned, MacKendrie stepped forward into the house.

In the middle of the floor lay a man's body, and he almost dropped the lantern at the sight of it. He couldn't see the face.

"Here." The woman's voice made him jump, and he spun. She stood across the room, next to a divan on which a man sat, his right leg propped up with some kind of tourniquet around it, bloody from the knee down. In three quick strides he was next to the divan. The face was not the boy he remembered, but it was the same face.

"Paul!" They grasped each other's arms. "It is you."

"Pastor Ma. How can it be?"

"I cannot explain now. Are you all right?"

"I have been shot. I will need help." MacKendrie looked up at the expressionless face of the woman. "She is Li," Wang said.

"The boat is waiting. I will help you to the dock. Once we get to the ship, they'll take care of your leg." He stood, took Wang's hand,

and pulled him up, then said, "Put your arm over my shoulder. Good." Looking at Li, MacKendrie said, "It will go faster if you take the other side."

She shook her head abruptly, and Wang said, "She too must escape. She cannot help us."

The three moved awkwardly toward the door, edging around the body. The room was a smashed-up wreck.

"What happened here, Paul?"

"It was a trap. They will search for me soon."

MacKendrie gasped, "What?"

"There will be a patrol, but we can still get away if we hurry."

MacKendrie nodded. "Let's go."

Before they could move, a bright light shone on the window shutter and the half-open door, and a harsh voice shouted, "You in the house! Come out! We are looking for the traitor Zhang Weijun! We know he is here. You have thirty seconds or we will shoot!"

Li reached under her tunic and pulled out a black pistol. She checked it to make sure the safety was off and looked over at Wang.

"What are you going to do?" MacKendrie whispered to Li.

"We cannot be captured. I will kill him"—nodding to Wang—"then myself. You can do whatever you like." She took a step toward them.

Wang looked at MacKendrie, his face full of sorrow. "I'm sorry," he said. "If I had known it was you, I never would have sent the signal."

Li raised the pistol, aiming at Wang's head. "No, wait!" MacKendrie hissed. "Wait. We can fool them."

She looked annoyed. "What do you mean? They are waiting outside, ready to shoot."

The voice shouted, "You have fifteen seconds!"

Quickly MacKendrie said, "They are looking for a Chinese man. What if they were greeted by a Russian engineer fluent in Mandarin and his Chinese girlfriend who are using this house for a rendezvous? We could tell them we are alone and there is no traitor here."

Li and Wang exchanged quick glances. "All right," Li said. She threw Wang's arm off of MacKendrie, undid two of the buttons on his shirt, yanked his shirttail out, and draped his arm over her shoulder. "Hide," she told Wang, then turned to MacKendrie. "You must do the talking. Act drunk. Tell them Captain Yang has given you permission to use this house." She pulled him toward the door. "And use the word 'comrades' a lot." Keeping the pistol in her right hand, she put it behind MacKendrie's back.

Suddenly she burst into shrieks of giddy laughter and began to stagger as they reached the door. MacKendrie immediately caught on. He let out a roar of laughter, and he and Li stumbled forward through the door and into a flood of light.

"Comrades!" he bellowed. They took zig-zag steps forward.

There was a momentary silence, then the voice said, "Stop! Stop there."

MacKendrie and Li leaned against each other, staggering and giggling. He saw that the light came from a flashlight held by the patrol commander, a sergeant, who had a pistol in the other hand. It was hard to see beyond the glare, but he made out three more soldiers behind the one in front.

"Of course, comrade, of course," MacKendrie said, expansively but slurred. "We want no trouble. What are you looking for?"

The sergeant took a few steps, followed cautiously by the soldiers. They were about twenty feet away. "Who are you?" he barked. "What are you doing here?"

MacKendrie smiled as widely as he could. "Me? I am Karloff." It was the only Russian-sounding name he could think of. He doubted these men had ever seen American horror movies. "Soviet engineer. Here to help glorious People's Republic. Yes?" He guffawed, and Li tittered. She pulled his head down as if trying to kiss him, but he shook her off and said, "Later, dear, later."

"I asked what you are doing here." The sergeant was angry. He was in danger of failing his assignment and looking foolish in the bargain.

"Well, we are having a little party. Your Captain Yang gave us permission. I asked him, I said..."

"Captain Yang? He said you could come here?"

"Why, yes, comrade. I told him I met this girl, you see." He nodded sideways and gave a lewd grin. "Beautiful girl, eh? I told the captain we needed a little privacy. He said there is just the place. And here we are. Ha! We have wine, comrades, you want some?"

"No! We are looking for a man, a dangerous agent. A traitor to the people. This is his house." The sergeant lowered the light a little.

"His house? But—" MacKendrie slowly looked around as if confused. "But he is gone. We are only ones here. Aren't we, dear?" He leaned over and kissed Li's cheek, and she gave a little shriek.

The sergeant stood still for a moment. "There was a gunshot. In this direction."

"It came from over there," Li said, in a casual way that suggested it was of no concern to her and her would-be lover. She gestured vaguely with her free arm toward the open country.

The flashlight beam followed her gesture and darted back and forth, scanning the vacant darkness. Hope flickered in MacKendrie's chest. Then the light returned, shining directly into their faces as if looking closer. Slowly MacKendrie raised his free hand to shield his eyes and said, "Comrades..."

"I have orders." The sergeant half-turned to the soldiers. "Search the house!"

The next instant, Li's left hand shoved MacKendrie hard in his chest, and he fell backward. Before he hit the ground, he heard a rapid, concussive *pop-pop-pop-pop*. A soldier's body smacked down a few feet away and didn't move. A rifle clattered on the ground next to him. A loud *bang* and a muzzle flash, and he saw Li suddenly crouch, then raise her pistol and fire, *pop-pop*. Instinctively, MacKendrie reached forward and grabbed the rifle. The flashlight was on the ground, throwing light away from the house into the night. Crouching, he looked up to see the sergeant's body stretched out in front of him. Two more bodies were scattered about. A *bang* came from ahead to the right, and he saw at the edge of the light the fourth soldier, his rifle level at his hip, a frightened expression on his face.

"Shoot! Shoot him!" shouted Li. She was sitting on the ground, the pistol in her limp right hand.

At this the soldier began to back up, then he whirled and ran back toward the city.

"Shoot!" Li said angrily. "We can't let him tell what happened!"

MacKendrie stood and shouldered the rifle. He could just make out the fleeing soldier in his light khaki uniform. He looked down the sight at the man's back and fingered the trigger. Then abruptly he lowered the rifle and tossed it aside. He knelt beside Li, who was lying on her back, clutching her side.

"You're hurt," he said.

"Why didn't you fire?" The question was angry, but her voice was subdued.

"He slipped into the darkness. Here, let me see." He took her hand away. In the faint light, he saw the dark tunic glistening wet.

A noise made him look up. Wang hobbled forward and knelt down. "Ying," he said. He reached out and smoothed the hair from her face. She was staring straight up into the black sky.

"Go," she said faintly. MacKendrie and Wang looked at each other. Then she said, "Check the pistol. Is there one more shot?"

MacKendrie didn't move, so Wang reached over her and took the gun. He removed the magazine, then replaced it. "There are two bullets," he said.

"Give it to me." Wang placed it in her right hand. "Now go. While you can."

MacKendrie stood and picked up the sergeant's flashlight. He pulled Wang up, then put his arm over his shoulders. Wang looked down and said, "Farewell. I don't even know your real name."

In a faint but cross voice, she said, "Remember me as Li Ying. The one who saved your life."

MacKendrie said, "Paul, let's go." They began hobbling together down the road. They had gone less than fifty feet when there was a sharp *pop* behind them.

It was like running a three-legged race, a game MacKendrie never liked at the missionaries' picnics. They staggered and weaved across the road, throwing each other off balance and sometimes forcing Wang to put his weight on his bad leg, which caused him to cry out. Once they stumbled so badly that MacKendrie fell to his knees and Wang dropped heavily on his side. He pulled Wang up and they set off again, gasping. The effort had them drenched in sweat.

Behind them in the distance, MacKendrie thought he heard a noise, perhaps a voice or maybe a vehicle engine. "Quickly," he snapped.

The pace seemed excruciatingly slow. The noises became distinct. MacKendrie glanced over his shoulder and saw vehicles' headlights, moving in their direction. Panic began to rise in his chest, but he fought it down. "Come on. Not far now."

MacKendrie had no idea how much time had elapsed since he climbed onto the dock. Now as they hop-stepped along, he saw ahead in the flashlight's beam wooden posts that marked the dock. They surged forward and scuffled down the slight embankment to the dock. "Wait here," he said.

MacKendrie walked to the end of the dock and shone the light out onto the river. He and Fletcher had agreed on a signal: the Morse for "c"—long-short-long-short. He saw and heard nothing. He repeated the signal. Then repeated it again. Silence and darkness. Strangely, he was calm. He couldn't blame Jack. He had probably heard the gunfire and figured everyone was dead. He wondered if he should throw himself in the river and swim until his strength gave out. Would God forgive suicide to avoid torture? He glanced back at Wang. "Paul—"

He felt the engines rather than heard them. He turned and saw a dark shape gliding silently toward him with an arched covering above the deck. Speaking as loudly as he dared, he said, "Jack."

"Skipper," came the answer.

THIRTY-FOUR

Fletcher pulled the boat alongside and held the boat steady, MacKendrie lowered Wang into it, then jumped in. They gave the boat a backward shove, and Fletcher wheeled the boat about.

MacKendrie whispered in Fletcher's ear, "Get us away from the bank and I'll brief you."

When they were in the middle of the river, running slow, Fletcher said, "I thought you were dead, Skipper. All that shooting. I almost took off."

"Thank God you didn't. There was a patrol. Another agent, a woman, got three of them."

"Jesus. Where is she?"

"Dead. One of the soldiers got away, Jack."

Fletcher shot him a hard look. "Damn."

"It's worse. Paul says they're looking for him."

Fletcher whirled around and glared at Wang. "Tell us what you know."

Wang, sitting on the inside flange, shifted his leg and grimaced. He spoke in broken English. "First Bureau, they come to arrest me. Know everything, real name, network. They will look for me."

Fletcher said, "How much time do we have?"

"Do not know, but I think they know nothing of rescue."

"Damn it. They'll put everyone on alert. If I were them, the river is the first place I'd look."

"May have time," Wang said. "Their radio, phone—not so good."

Fletcher looked at MacKendrie. "Let's get out of here. The faster the better."

"Okay, but you're still going to have to slow down for the islands around Nantong." He held up his hand. "Just a sec before we take off."

He reached into the cabin and brought out a blanket and a canteen. He handed the canteen to Wang and wrapped the blanket around him. He said in Mandarin, "Hang on. We're going to go very fast."

Fletcher raised the throttle a little, guided the boat to the middle of the river, then gradually pulled up on the lever till the boat was running about two-thirds. The bow rose, and the boat flew down the river with little more than a purr from the engines. Fletcher swung the boat easily to avoid the occasional anchored or slow-moving boat, sending them jumping up and down in the wake. Every few minutes, the boat would fishtail as the current took it, and Fletcher fought the wheel to get it back on course.

MacKendrie stood beside him, straining to see any sign of danger. After twenty minutes, he said in Fletcher's ear, "Islands at Nantong ahead. Cut your speed." Fletcher looked at him and made no move. "Cut it, Chief, or we'll run aground!"

Reluctantly, Fletcher eased off the throttle. They could see the river channel narrowing, and the islands protruding into the river. Fletcher slowed some more, and they cruised, navigating the space carefully. The black mass of the second and bigger island was sliding past, and they could just see the channel starting to widen. Fletcher put his hand on the throttle and was about to pull it up when a bright light shone on the canvas canopy from the left.

"You! In the boat! Stop!"

MacKendrie whispered in Fletcher's ear, "Patrol. They want us to stop." Fletcher shook his head vigorously, and was about to yank the throttle up when Wang said quietly, "Stop boat. Let me handle." Fletcher and MacKendrie looked uncertainly at each other, then MacKendrie nodded. Fletcher hesistated.

The voice said, "Stop! Or we will shoot!"

At a quick sign from MacKendrie, Fletcher cut the throttle, and the boat slowed to idle. Wang stood unsteadily and kept his bloody leg behind the canopy. He faced the spotlight. "What do you want?"

"Who are you? Identify yourself!" The patrol had been hidden in the lee of the island, and now it glided forward, still about thirty yards away.

"I am Hsu Gongli. I work for the Ministry of Agriculture. We are transporting workers to Shanghai, comrade."

MacKendrie whispered to Fletcher, "If I give you the sign, go full speed." In response, Fletcher bent over and rummaged inside the cabin. What's he doing? MacKendrie thought.

The patrol commander barked, "Why are you traveling at night?"

"We were ordered to take them after the evening meal. There is an urgent need for workers in the fields near the Huangpu River. They are to be put to work first thing in the morning. If we do not get them there, the fields will not make their quota, comrade."

Fletcher straightened up. With horror, MacKendrie saw he had a rifle in his hand. It was an M-2. He shook his head back and forth, but Fletcher pointed the rifle upward, his right finger inside the trigger guard. They listened tensely.

"Where did you get that boat?"

Wang shrugged in an exaggerated fashion. "I am sorry, comrade, but I do not know. It was requisitioned."

They could hear voices in discussion. MacKendrie heard the word "inspect" and quivered, expecting gunfire to erupt in a moment.

The patrol commander said, "We are looking for counter-revolutionaries. Have you seen anything suspicious?"

To the surprise of Fletcher and MacKendrie, Wang emitted a rapid, high-pitched laugh. "Why, yes. We have Chiang Kai-shek on board. Would you like to meet him?" He laughed again, and MacKendrie, spontaneously, copied him. He gestured to Fletcher, and the chief gave out a guffaw. The patrol would think that the workers appreciated the joke.

"Enough!" The voice was annoyed. "Move on, comrade. And be sure to report anything out of the ordinary."

"Yes, comrade." Wang turned to MacKendrie and gave a nod.

MacKendrie whispered in Fletcher's ear, "They're letting us go. Go slow." He grasped the rifle, took it out of Fletcher's hands with a reproachful look, and laid it down inside the cabin. The boat moved forward, and the light on the canopy slid away.

After five minutes, Wang said, "I think we go fast now." He resumed his seat, and Fletcher raised the throttle.

MacKendrie leaned over and said in his ear, "Where'd you get the rifle, Jack?"

Fletcher didn't look at him. "Brought it on board when I stashed the fishing gear. Ordnance officer on the *Hawkins* did me a favor."

"It's against orders!"

Fletcher glared at him. "I'll be damned if I was going on this mission without a weapon."

"Cohen will have your stripes."

"He won't know."

"He would if you'd pulled the trigger back there."

"If I'd fired on that patrol, we'd probably be dead by now anyway. Better that way than capture."

MacKendrie was silent. He should have known that a man like Fletcher was bound to carry a weapon, regardless.

He checked his watch. Almost three o'clock. Another two hours before it would start getting light. He tried to determine where they were. The river was getting wider now, and Fletcher steered for the middle of the channel. At nearly four, MacKendrie pointed to the left.

"West end of Chongming Island. About twenty miles to the coast." Fletcher nodded.

The river was about ten miles wide here, but there were many more boats to contend with. Fletcher kept swerving to avoid them. Ahead to the right, the array of lights was growing. They were approaching Shanghai. MacKendrie looked at the horizon ahead. There was something indistinct about the river ahead. It took him a few minutes to realize what was causing the diffused glow around the city. Fletcher had already noticed it.

"Fog," he said.

"That's good, isn't it?" MacKendrie said. "It'll hide us."

"It'll hide us, but we've got to slow down. And fog can disappear as quick as it shows up."

Within minutes the first wisps of fog began curling around them. It was coming in thick from the south, creeping up the coast. Fletcher began easing off the throttle, and soon they were enveloped with dark gray fog. Even the lights of Shanghai to their right were little more than a dull glow. Fletcher cursed under his breath as a boat suddenly appeared in front of them, and he spun the wheel. They were just creeping along now, feeling their way. At this rate, it would take hours to get out into the open ocean.

They didn't speak. There was little sound around them, only the occasional noise from a boat or a disembodied voice. MacKendrie checked his watch. Ten till five. There was no way of knowing where they were. The fog was slowly turning from dark to light gray.

The faint buzzing of a plane reached down to the river. It flew first farther away then nearer, a single-engine model. Fletcher scowled.

"They're looking for us. Let's hope this fog holds out."

For thirty minutes, there was no change in the fog, and the plane continued to fly back and forth overhead. Then there was a subtle shift in the surface of the river. Ripples were becoming waves, and they could sense it was deeper here. There were almost no boats. They must be near the mouth of the river. The fog around them and the sky above was gradually changing from gray to white.

"Take the wheel," Fletcher said. He opened his compass and got his bearings. "We need to head zero-eight-zero. A little to port, Skipper. Little more. That's it." Fletcher closed the compass and took the wheel. The plane buzzed loudly overhead. "I'm going to put on a little more speed, see what happens." He raised the throttle, and the boat responded. The bow began to rise and fall as it rode the waves.

After ten minutes, the buzz of the plane receded to their stern, and Fletcher gave a grim smile. Then within seconds, the fog around them turned sheer white, thinned, and they burst out of the bank into the early moments of dawn. All around, they saw a flat, empty ocean. They looked astern. The fog obscured everything directly behind them and to the right. Behind and well to the left they saw the coastline, about three or four miles away. They were not very far into the sea. Ahead, a few isolated boats bobbed, none of them patrols.

"Let's go!" Fletcher raised the throttle to full. The bow rose and the boat leaped forward, cutting across the waves with a chop-chop-chop. "Yahoo!" he yelled, and MacKendrie grinned at him. There was nothing between them and the *Hawkins* now but thirty miles of sea.

The canvas canopy fluttered violently.

"It's catching the wind, slowing us down!" Fletcher shouted. He pulled out his folding knife and handed it to MacKendrie. "Get rid of it!"

MacKendrie opened the knife, plunged it through the cloth, and slashed the canopy open. Soon it was in tatters, and he yanked it off the poles and flung it overboard.

He knelt beside Wang, who looked pale in the light.

"Hold on. We'll be at the ship soon."

It took only minutes for the plane to find them. At first it circled well off to their left. Then it came in close, diving down a hundred feet above the water. It flew at them from different angles, flying over from behind, then circling around in front and buzzing over them so low that MacKendrie and Fletcher involuntarily ducked.

"What's he doing?" MacKendrie shouted.

"Looking us over. Trying to scare us," Fletcher said. "It's not him I'm worried about."

"Patrol boats?"

Fletcher nodded. "Keep a lookout to stern."

The plane gave up its sport and began circling overhead at a couple hundred feet. MacKendrie looked back toward shore. The fog and the coastline were falling behind quickly, but there was no sign of pursuit. The sun was above the horizon now, the pale light slanting back toward the coast. He looked off to the left. At first there was nothing. Then he saw a white dot, moving against the green of the coast. It appeared to be headed to Shanghai, but after a few minutes, he realized it was moving out to sea. He grabbed the binoculars and tried to keep them steady against the bouncing of the boat. Through the lenses he saw it—a large boat with an enclosed pilot house and a small deck above it, its bow pointed straight at them, plowing through the water. It was maybe four miles behind them.

"Chief! Patrol boat!" He pointed.

Fletcher looked back. "Take the wheel!" He took the binoculars and stared at it, then handed them back to MacKendrie. "They're going to catch us, but it's going to take a little while. With any luck, we'll be in sight of the ship by then."

"Can we radio for help?"

Fletcher looked at his watch. "Not yet. We don't want the ship to give away its position. MiGs could find her in minutes."

MacKendrie went back to Wang. "A patrol is after us. We're trying to get as far out to sea as possible."

Wang shook his head. "They not give up easy. We have cause them to lose face."

The chase played out in slow motion. The plane continued to circle overhead, and the patrol boat inched closer. With every mile, MacKendrie's hope grew. The sun steadily rose, and soon an unrelenting glare was all around them.

Fletcher looked at his watch. "In fifteen minutes, we'll try to raise the ship."

As if the plane's pilot had overheard him, it made a sudden dive. This time it cut directly in front of the speeding boat, no more than fifty feet above the water, flashing in front of them like a circus daredevil on a motorbike.

"Jesus!" Fletcher cried. "He's trying to slow us down!"

The plane circled for another pass, coming in from the right. It looked as if it were aiming straight at them, looming rapidly, then at the last possible second it veered, passing in front so close they could feel the draft of the aircraft an instant after it flashed in front of them. It circled around.

"Take the wheel!" Fletcher shouted. He dove into the cabin and returned with the M-2.

"Chief, you can't fire on him!"

"The hell I can't!" Fletcher shouted back, his face red with rage.

"We're in Chinese waters!"

Fletcher stared at him, then gave a humorless laugh. "I'll be sure to apologize to the Chinese embassy." He smacked the magazine to make sure it was in place, then released the safety and wrapped the rifle's sling around his left arm and wrist. He watched as the plane made for them again, coming in from the left. Without taking his eyes off the plane, he said, "I just want to scare him off."

He tried resting his elbows on the front deck, but the chop ruined his aim. He leaned against the cabin, feet spread wide, braced his left elbow against his side, and sighted the rifle. The plane was coming on quickly, headed straight for them. It was three hundred yards away. Two hundred.

The rifle erupted. Fletcher fired three short bursts. MacKendrie saw a spark as a bullet hit the fuselage. The plane pulled sharply up and left, gliding out of the boat's path and continuing to climb before circling to its left. They watched as it resumed hovering above them, like a hawk whose prey has fought back but does not want to give up.

Fletcher gave MacKendrie a satisfied look. "That ought to keep him out of our hair."

MacKendrie looked back. The patrol boat was now directly behind them, maybe two miles away. Without the binoculars, he could see details on the boat—its railings, its red flag flying from the mast.

"Hold onto this," Fletcher said, handing him the rifle. "Don't put it away. We may need it." He reached into the cabin for the microphone, clicked the transmit button a couple of times, then said, "Falcon to Hunt Master, Falcon to Hunt Master, do you read, over." Silence. Fletcher repeated the call. There was no answer. He had MacKendrie hold the wheel and checked the compass.

"We're on course."

They kept glancing behind them, watching as the patrol boat reeled in the distance between them. Fletcher kept trying the radio, only to hear static in reply. They were only a mile ahead now, and they could see activity on the patrol boat, soldiers clambering around the lower deck, while on the deck above the wheelhouse, a soldier sat waiting at the machine gun. Fletcher tried the radio once more. There was a burst of static, then a reply.

"Falcon, this is Hunt Master, we read you, over."

MacKendrie admired Fletcher's calm in his next transmission. "Hunt Master, be advised, we are under observation by unarmed aircraft, and we are being pursued by a hostile patrol. I repeat, we are being pursued by armed patrol. Our prize is aboard. When can we expect visual contact with you, over."

For a few moments they thought they had lost contact again. Finally they heard, "Falcon, we have you on radar and are proceeding at top speed. Maintain your course. Estimate visual contact in three-zero minutes."

Fletcher cursed. "We'll be shot to hell in thirty minutes." He spoke into the radio. "Roger, Hunt Master. Things are going to get hot before then. Can you supply air cover, over."

A long pause. "Stand by, Falcon, we will advise."

Fletcher replaced the microphone. MacKendrie looked back. The patrol was less than a mile behind.

"What's the range of that gun?" MacKendrie asked.

"If it's Russian, and it probably is, we're already in range. It wouldn't be very accurate. If they're going to fire on us, they've got to get closer. They'd like to capture us, but they know we're armed. They might try to knock out our engines." He looked at MacKendrie. "We can't let them get us, Skipper. If they fire on us, you'll need to take the wheel and take evasive action. Just swing her from side to side, but not in a regular pattern. Try to keep a fixed point on the horizon and keep her moving toward it, understand?"

"Got it."

The radio crackled. "Falcon, this is Hunt Master. Negative on air cover. Estimate visual contact in two-zero minutes."

Fletcher acknowledged the bad news and scanned the horizon. Suddenly sound blared at them from the rear. The patrol boat's loudspeaker poured out a stream of Mandarin.

"What are they saying?" Fletcher asked.

"This is People's Republic Coastal Defense," MacKendrie translated. "You are in violation of territorial waters. Stop and be identified, or we will shoot." He listened again. "He's repeating the message."

"At least they warned us. Polite of 'em," Fletcher said.

Minutes later, the patrol boat's loudspeaker blared again. "He says this is our last warning," MacKendrie said.

"Give me the rifle and take the wheel," Fletcher said. "When I tell you, start evasive action."

"Okay, Chief."

Fletcher retrieved an ammo belt from the cabin that held several magazines. He sat on the deck facing astern, braced himself as much as he could and readied the rifle. Just as he looked over his shoulder and said "Ready, Skipper," the patrol boat's machine gun opened up. They could hear the whine of bullets above them and on either side. Blips of spray kicked up where rounds landed in the sea.

"Warning shots!" Fletched yelled. "Start evasive action!"

MacKendrie turned the wheel right, and the boat responded, then eased it left, then made a harder left, then immediately right again. The Chinese gunner fired indiscriminately, spraying rounds in every direction. A bullet whined nearby on the right. MacKendrie wondered why Fletcher hadn't fired yet.

"That's good, Skipper! He's using his ammo," Fletcher shouted. "At this rate—"

MacKendrie heard a dull sound nearby and thought a round had hit the boat. He glanced around.

"That was close, Chief."

There was no answer. He looked back to see Fletcher lying supine on the deck, the rifle beside him. He had a surprised look on his face.

"Jack! Jack, can you move?" Fletcher moaned but didn't answer. The firing had paused, but MacKendrie knew it would start again any second. He swerved right, then left, reaching into the cabin for the microphone. "Hunt Master, this is Falcon," he shouted, feeling ridiculous at using silly code names. "We're under fire! We're under fire! The Chief is wounded. Can you hear me?"

The response was quick. "Falcon, we read you. We should have visual contact off your port bow in five minutes."

The machine gun fired. In spite of the evasive action, MacKendrie heard bullets whine and thud into the hull. He looked back to see that Wang was kneeling next to Fletcher.

"Paul! Can you stand? Can you take the wheel?"

"I will try! Help me up."

MacKendrie grabbed his hand and pulled him up to the wheel.

"Steer from side to side in irregular patterns," he shouted. "Just move the wheel a little, or you'll turn us over."

Wang nodded, and MacKendrie dropped beside Fletcher. There was a tear in his shirt below the shoulder. He unbuttoned the shirt and gently pulled it aside to reveal a puckered wound. There was little blood, but MacKendrie knew he was bleeding internally. Fletcher groaned again.

"Jack, can you hear me? Jack!"

Fletcher was panting, his face pale with shock. "Take...the rifle."

MacKendrie shook his head. "I can't, Jack."

Fletcher closed his eyes and nodded. "Yeah. Go on...Skipper." Suddenly he coughed. Dark blood began to well in his mouth and overflowed down his cheek. "Jesus!" he cried. "Help me!"

MacKendrie stared at him. A bullet thudded against the stern and another whined overhead. He reached down and picked up the rifle, then the ammo belt. He crawled to the rear, keeping behind the engine compartment as he heard the machine gun's chatter. He checked the rifle. The safety was off. He steadied himself, then in one motion rose on his knees and raised the rifle to his shoulder. The patrol boat was no more than a quarter-mile away, a fat, white target. He saw the machine gunner hunched over his weapon and the muzzle flashes.

The wheelhouse, he thought. Like the plane. I'll get them to break off. He tried to make a good aim, but the swerve of the boat and the chop made it impossible. He fired a burst, then another, but missed wildly. He crouched down, took a deep breath, then rose up again, spreading his knees apart and leaning forward against the engine compartment. He raised the rifle and timed the chop, which threw up the bow as it hit the wave. He deliberately aimed low, and just as the boat hit the wave he squeezed the trigger, spraying a burst upward. He was off to one side, but he saw the soldiers on the boat duck and take cover.

MacKendrie fired steadily, timing his bursts as the boat hit the chop. His fire was getting closer, having an effect. He saw activity in the wheelhouse. One more, he thought. He squeezed the trigger. The wheelhouse glass shattered, and the patrol boat began to drift to the left. The machine gun fire stopped, and MacKendrie lowered the rifle and yanked a magazine out of the ammo belt. As he changed out the magazine, he saw the patrol boat continue to drift. It worked, he thought, caused just enough panic to give them time. He was about to turn back to Fletcher when the gunboat suddenly veered back on course. A second later, the machine gun opened up again. Bullets whined, and spray kicked up just behind the stern.

MacKendrie glanced over his right shoulder. He could make out the profile of a ship below the horizon. It would be ten minutes or more before they were under the *Hawkins*'s guns. A burst of slugs raked the stern, thudding into the engine cowling and sending splinters into MacKendrie's face. The patrol was about a hundred yards away, and he realized that the gunner had their range now. The engines and MacKendrie were his targets. He glanced back to see Wang at the wheel and Jack on the deck, a red stain on his face. He raised the rifle and aimed at the gun deck. He could see the gunner, hunched over the machine gun, trying to follow the boat's movements. Their eyes met. Both fired at the same time.

Bullets whined past his arm. MacKendrie had the range, it was a matter of timing. Wang turned the boat left, then right. He squeezed the trigger and missed badly. He turned and shouted, "Paul! When I tell you, steer the boat straight! Don't turn!"

The boat swerved, and MacKendrie raised the rifle. The gunboat was swinging into his sights, and he held his aim steady. He shouted over his shoulder "Now!" The boat straightened, and the gunner drifted into his sight. Chop. Chop. He fired, fired again. And again. He saw the gunner jerk, fall forward against the gun, and lie still.

MacKendrie lowered his aim and began spraying the wheelhouse with fire. After one long burst, the rifle stopped, the magazine empty. He pulled it out, reached down for the ammo belt, and snapped in a full magazine. When he raised the rifle again, he saw the patrol boat was falling back. It receded slowly at first, then quickly as it came to a stop. MacKendrie looked up and saw the plane banking, turning back to the mainland. He gave a last look at the patrol boat to make sure it was not resuming its pursuit. No. It heeled about, and he saw its stern as it turned back toward China.

MacKendrie clicked on the safety and put the rifle on the deck. He crawled forward to Fletcher and shouted to Wang to make straight for the ship. He raised Fletcher's head and used his shirt to wipe away the blood.

"Jack, can you hear me?" He was weak. "Jack, the patrol's gone. We'll have you on board the ship in just a few minutes. Hang on, okay?"

"You...got him."

"Just scared him off. You'd have done a better job."

Fletched smiled. "You're...too modest for...a skipper." He gasped, and there was a wheezing sound.

"Save your strength."

"Want you...to do something...on ship."

"What is it, Jack?"

"Baptize...me."

MacKendrie smiled. "You bet I will. The whole ship's company is going to be there, too. Just take it easy. Look, I can see the ship making for us."

Fletcher motioned to see, so MacKendrie raised him up. "Bone in her teeth," Fletcher said.

"What's that?"

"Spray on each side...of the bow. Like a bone..." He fainted.

THIRTY-FIVE

MacKendrie took the wheel and steered for the ship's starboard. The ship had slowed, but it was still moving, and on the pitching seas, he had trouble getting the boat in position next to the hoist. He could see sailors on the deck shouting down at him, but he couldn't make it out. Desperate to get Fletcher aboard, he made three frustrating attempts but lacked Jack's skill at maneuvering. Finally, he matched the ship's speed and got the boat next to the hull.

A rope ladder was dropped over the side, and sailors scrambled down and jumped into the boat. One took the wheel. A basket was lowered, the unconscious Fletcher was loaded into it and raised up on deck. Cables descended, and the sailors secured them to the boat and it was lifted off of the sea. As they were lowered on the ship's deck, MacKendrie saw Cohen shouting orders. Wang was pulled out of the boat.

"Get him to sick bay," Cohen snapped, and Wang was placed on a stretcher and hustled away. Cohen looked at MacKendrie and saw his shirt and hands covered in blood. "Mac, are you all right? Are you hurt?"

"I'm all right, Harry. This is Jack's blood."

Cohen commandeered a rag from a nearby sailor and gave it to him. He ordered the sailors to secure the boat. "Don't touch anything!" he snapped. He turned back to MacKendrie and suddenly started laughing. "Mac, you did it! You pulled it off!" He was standing right in front of MacKendrie, grinning.

In one motion, MacKendrie clenched his right hand and swung it in a short arc, smacking the side of Cohen's face with a sharp sound that turned the heads of the sailors on the deck. Cohen went down hard. MacKendrie felt a sharp pain in his hand and knew he had probably broken a bone. He dropped to his knees beside Cohen and was about to hit him again when hands grabbed his arms and pulled him away. He was still staring at Cohen's face but didn't resist, and someone said, "Get him out of here." He was being pushed and pulled along, and a voice at his ear said, "This way, mister."

His mind was blank, and he followed until a door was opened and he was prodded into the small cabin where he and Fletcher had been just thirty-six hours before. His leather valise was on the neatly made bunk. He sat down heavily and felt a sudden exhaustion like he had never known. He lay down on his side. The bunk was surprisingly soft, he noticed, and the pillow felt good against his face.

A sharp metallic clank jolted him awake. "Jack!" he shouted.

Cohen was standing in the cabin, a hand on one hip, a steaming mug in the other. The left side of his face was bruised and swollen. MacKendrie blinked at him, trying to make sense of why he was back on Tinian and why Cohen was injured. Then he remembered.

Frowning, Cohen spoke in a voice that came out as a mumble. "I need to talk to you, Mac."

MacKendrie pressed his hands against his face to rub the sleep away and felt a sharp pain in his right hand that made him jerk it away. The middle finger was swollen. "How long was I out?"

"Six hours. We picked you up about oh-six-thirty. It's thirteen hundred hours now." He offered the mug. "I brought some coffee. I need you alert."

MacKendrie took the mug, gulped a long swig of the coffee, which was impossibly strong, and looked up. "Jack?"

"Still alive. Doc gives him a chance to pull through. I've talked to Wang, but I need your version. What happened out there, Mac?"

He told it briefly. Found the marsh without incident, waited all day, made it to the rendezvous point. They heard the gunshot, then Wang's transmission, asking for help.

"I don't know whether to pin a medal on you or call you a dumbass, going ashore like that," Cohen said. He wasn't smiling. "You could have fucked up more than the mission if you'd been caught."

"We were less than half a mile from him. What would you have done, left him there?"

Cohen shook his head.

He had found the house, he said, with Wang and Li and the dead man on the floor. The patrol and the ruse about being a Russian.

"That was quick thinking, Mac."

"You can thank Fletcher. If he hadn't told me there were Russians in the area, I wouldn't have thought of it. Why didn't you tell me that, Harry?"

"It was need-to-know. Go on."

"It almost worked, but the Chinese are sticklers for following orders. When the sergeant told his men to search the house, Li pushed me down and opened fire. She got three of them but took a bullet in her chest. One soldier got away. We left Li. She shot herself."

Cohen looked down and nodded.

MacKendrie told the rest of it—Wang's resourcefulness, saving them from the river patrol. How they were spotted by the plane once they emerged from the fog, pursued and fired on.

"Fletcher brought a rifle on board. M-2. He scared off the plane, which was buzzing us good. The patrol boat got closer and closer, finally opened up on us. I was at the wheel, taking evasive action, but a round hit Jack before he could fire back. They were closing in on us. I had to take the rifle."

"*You* shot back? Did you hit anyone?" MacKendrie didn't answer. "I need to know, Mac, in case there are any questions."

"I don't know if I hit anyone in the wheelhouse. Might have wounded someone. I know I hit the gunner."

"Dead?"

"I don't know, damn you!" MacKendrie burst out. He put his head in his hands.

He knows all right, Cohen thought, but he murmured, "Okay. Okay, Mac. I understand. Look, why don't you take it easy for a while. You can get some chow and get cleaned up and we'll talk more later. We're steaming for Tokyo, be there in five hours. You can call your family from there. Tomorrow we'll put you on a plane for home."

"I want to see Jack."

"He's out of it, Mac. You can see him later." Cohen put his hand up to his face. "If you ever stop being a minister, you could take up boxing. Got me pretty damn good." He put his hand on the door and glanced back. "Something tells me you wanted to do that for a long time." The door clashed behind him.

MacKendrie slumped back onto the bunk. There was a knock and a sailor carried in a tray. He sat it down on the bunk and left. MacKendrie knew he was starving and the food smelled good, but he felt sick through and through. After a few minutes, he stood and opened the door. There was no one in the passageway. Rather than making for the deck, he turned the other way. He hadn't gone far when a sailor appeared from around a bulkhead. MacKendrie asked where the sick bay was.

"Follow me, sir."

It wasn't very large, a compartment with three bunks, but clean and smelling of antiseptic. Wang was sitting up in one of them, awake. The far bunk was curtained off. A pharmacist's mate approached.

"Can I help you, sir?"

"I'm here to see Chief Fletcher."

The mate frowned. "He's unconscious, sir. Real weak. He's lost a lot of blood."

"Can I just look in on him? I'm a chaplain."

The mate was skeptical but said, "Okay, sir. Just for a minute."

He gestured to the curtained bunk. Fletcher was pale and breathing shallow. A bottle of blood was suspended above the bunk, the red line running down to his arm. MacKendrie stood silently for a moment. He closed his eyes and started to pray, then stopped. He opened his eyes again and whispered, "Please, let him live." He bent down next to Fletcher and said, "I can't baptize you while you're sleeping, Jack. I'm going to come back later. You just get better."

He went to Wang's bunk. His leg was heavily wrapped and propped up. "*Ni hao*, Paul" he said.

"*Ni hao*," Wang replied, and gestured to the bed. He said in Mandarin, "Please, be seated."

MacKendrie took up the conversation in Wang's language. "How are you feeling?"

"Better, thank you. They gave me something for the pain. But I'm afraid the leg will not get better." There was no trace of bitterness in his voice.

"Are you sure? Perhaps they can still save it."

Wang lifted a hand, the palm upturned, a Chinese gesture of resignation. "Perhaps. But life with one leg is better than death. I owe you my life."

"It's Harry Cohen you should thank." MacKendrie looked around. "He's the reason we're all here."

"Cohen did not come and get me in that house." Wang gestured to the curtain. "Your friend, he will live?"

"I don't know. I am praying for him."

A smile flickered across Wang's face. "The prayer of a righteous man can do much. James five sixteen. You see, I still remember some things you taught."

MacKendrie nodded. "You were a good student."

Wang looked away. "Good students do not ignore their teacher's lessons. I have done some terrible things."

"Paul, how did you get mixed up in this business?"

"It doesn't make much sense now."

"Cohen told me they recruited you at Pacific Reformed. Why did you agree to work for them?" Wang continued to look away. "Were you angry at the Communists?"

He looked up sharply. "The Communists? No. Not the way you mean. I didn't care who ran China." MacKendrie waited. Wang gazed at him. "I wanted to go home. I was sick of America. I was a stranger everywhere I turned, and alone. The food, the language, the customs, it was all alien. I had no family, no friends. I was angry at my mother for making me go and angry at you for arranging for me to be there."

"You thought I had abandoned you again."

Wang's face twisted. "It was because of me you had to leave China."

"No. That's nonsense. It was because of ignorance and jealousy and pride. You and your mother were used against me."

"Do you know how badly I wanted for you to take me with you?"

"Yes. I knew. I would have taken you, but Emily was against it. And the Mission Board. And the State Department. I was in agony, but it wasn't possible. You were only twelve. How could I explain all that to you?"

"All these years, I thought it was my fault."

MacKendrie put his hand to his mouth. "I'm sorry."

There was a silence, then Wang said, "I thought coming to college in America would bring us together again. But you..."

"I was three thousand miles away, with a new family."

"If I had the money, I would have gone back to China on my own. When Cohen offered me a way, I took it. I thought no one would know the difference."

"Your letters stopped. I thought you had turned away from me."

Wang suddenly leaned forward. "Pastor Ma, why did you do it? You risked your life for me, why?"

MacKendrie looked down. "Cohen said you were in danger. I couldn't bear to leave you behind again."

Wang said, "You taught us to take a life is a sin, yet on the boat…"

"I know. 'If anyone strikes you on the right cheek, turn to him the other also.' Isn't that what we taught you? It seems the teacher has ignored his own lesson. There is a word for someone like me. A hypocrite. One who wears a mask." He nodded as if he had found the answer to a question. "What must my father think of me now."

"I remember your father. He was a kind man."

"Yes." MacKendrie nodded. "Your mother, is she…"

"She is alive. She didn't know I was in China until two weeks ago. I was trying to escape from the network and—" He hung his head.

"Something went wrong?"

Wang shook his head and didn't answer.

"What will you do now?"

Wang looked up. "It seems I am destined to live in America after all. I think it will be different this time. Perhaps I could return to school. Cohen owes me that much."

"You were a good student."

MacKendrie realized the pharmacist's mate was standing nearby, watching them talk in Mandarin, a surprised look on his face. He held up his right hand. "Could you take a look at my finger? I think it may be broken."

After the finger was bandaged and splinted, MacKendrie returned to Wang's bunk. "Paul, what happened back there in the house, before I arrived? The dead man, who was he? And Li Ying?"

Wang shook his head. "I'm sorry, Pastor Ma, but Cohen has forbidden me to tell anyone."

MacKendrie frowned. "Cohen." He stood. "Tomorrow I must fly home, but we will talk again. I promise."

When Cohen entered MacKendrie's cabin later, he found him awake, sitting on his bunk. He noticed the splint on his finger. Serves him right, Cohen thought. He saw the untouched tray. "You didn't eat your food." MacKendrie shrugged. "You're gonna have to eat sooner or later, Mac."

"Maybe when we get to Tokyo. What did you want, Harry?"

"I'm going to need to debrief you about everything you saw. Especially the military equipment. Just in case Fletcher doesn't make it."

"What's the latest?"

"Touch and go."

"He wants me to baptize him."

"What?"

"Fletcher. After he was wounded, he asked me to baptize him. I intend to do that. Not that I'm worthy."

"What makes you say that?"

MacKendrie said absently, "Today I shot a man." Cohen watched in alarm as MacKendrie suddenly underwent a spasm, his face wrinkled and his voice convulsed. "My God! I, I shot another man!" He placed his hands on the top of his head and began to sob uncontrollably.

Cohen had seen this kind of thing before, the shock of battle suddenly giving way to clarity. The best course was to let it play itself out. After a few minutes, the sobs began to subside, and MacKendrie looked up, wide-eyed.

"I shot that soldier like he was just a paper target on a firing range. My God, how can I be a minister again? I'm no better than the men who killed Ulysses Brown."

"Mac, this wasn't murder. It was an act of war. You were defending your boat from enemy fire."

MacKendrie fought to get control of himself. "Enemy fire. So the man I killed was an *enemy*."

Cohen shook his head dismissively. "He was a commie. A Chinese soldier."

MacKendrie paused, breathing hard. "You know, Harry, a wise man once told me that when it comes to violence, it all depends on who's getting killed. If it's a white man, it's a big deal. A black man—or a Chinese commie—so what?"

Cohen said evenly, "Look, no one will blame you for what you did."

MacKendrie's voice rose, and Cohen almost flinched, expecting him to come at him again. "No one will blame me? What about Christ?"

"So what would your Christ have done out there on that boat?" Cohen demanded. "Surrendered? What would have happened to you then? And Wang. And Fletcher."

"Go away, Harry."

Cohen moved to the door. "Get a shower, the colder the better. I'll talk to you tonight at the base after you've had some chow and called your wife." He paused, then said, "You think you're the only guy who ever felt guilty about shooting someone? Why do you think Nathan Considine was flying transport planes?"

MacKendrie's head snapped up. "What do you mean?"

"He was a fighter pilot, remember? Had three or four confirmed kills. Told his CO he couldn't do it anymore and requested a transfer. He didn't have any guns to shoot back with on that transport." He opened the door then looked back. "I don't know much about Christ, Mac, but I thought he was big on forgiveness."

"Harry." Cohen looked back into the cabin. "Don't ever call me Mac again."

A few hours later, MacKendrie stood at the stern railing, looking back the way the *Hawkins* had come. Behind him, Tokyo harbor was coming into view. Someone was suddenly standing beside him.

"Evening, sir."

"Oh. Hello, Mister Lewis. Good to see you again."

"It's good to see you, sir." He fished in his pocket. "I promised to return this to you." He offered the letter to MacKendrie, who reached for it with his right hand only to grab it awkwardly because of the splint and bulky bandage around his middle finger.

"Thanks. You took a risk for me. I appreciate it."

"Glad to do it." They both leaned on the rail and watched the ship's wake. "I'm sorry about Chief Fletcher," Lewis said. "I heard you were with him when..."

"They called me. He took a turn for the worse. He woke up for a few minutes, and I baptized him. He called me Skipper. Then he fell asleep again and never woke up."

Lewis nodded. "That's a big compliment, sir, calling you Skipper. He must have liked you."

"I hope so. I liked him. He was a good man."

"Yes, sir." He paused. "I've got to get back on duty. Good luck, sir."

"So long, Mister Lewis."

MacKendrie turned back to watch the wake. He opened the letter and re-read it.

I wish I didn't have to go on this journey, but sometimes we are not able to choose the path that is safe and peaceful.

Slowly he tore the page into small pieces and tossed them over the railing, watching as they floated down onto the churning water and disappeared.

EPILOGUE:

BREAD OF HEAVEN

THIRTY-SIX

He was walking down a dark corridor, full of dread. There was something up ahead, a figure. A little girl, holding something in front of her. He drew closer and saw it was Priss, walking slowly and solemnly toward him. She was holding a tray, and there was some object on it. This was his daughter, but his anxiety grew with each step. Offering the tray, she said, "This is for you, Daddy." He saw it was a dead animal of some sort, bloated with decomposition and covered with blowflies and maggots. He shook with revulsion as she said, "Don't you want it?"

He backed away, turned and began running. The floor beneath him was turning to water, and it rose to his ankles, then his knees. It was harder and harder to run. A boat appeared beside him, a sleek wooden powerboat that had gun barrels sticking out everywhere. Jack Fletcher called to him, "Skipper! Climb aboard!" MacKendrie reached out to grab his hand. They were going faster and faster now, hurtling ahead through blackness without any sign of light.

"Jack, stop! We'll run aground! I'm afraid!" MacKendrie yelled, but Fletcher only laughed. A speck of light appeared ahead of them. It grew bigger, bigger by the moment, a round ball of white light, dazzling. They were speeding right into the middle of it. Fletcher reached down and flipped a switch and the guns on the boat began firing, firing all at once, firing in all directions. MacKendrie put his hands over his ears. "Stop it, stop it!" he pleaded.

The guns stopped, and Fletcher said, "Take the wheel, Skipper." He climbed onto the foredeck as the ball of light grew bigger, filling the space in front of them, displacing the blackness with an unbearable brightness. Terror filled MacKendrie to his bones as Fletcher stood on the foredeck, turned and extended his arms straight out on each side. They were racing forward, forward, into the blazing ball of light. MacKendrie was blinded. He let go of the wheel, threw his hands in front of his face and screamed, "No! No!" or it might have been "Woe!"

Something had him in its grasp, like a bird of prey. He felt its talons in his arm. He was sitting up, waving his hands in front of him to ward off the terrible light and whatever had him in its grip, but there was a voice in his ear, a woman's, one he knew...

"Jim! Jim! Wake up! Jim!"

Helen was next to him, her hands wrapped around his arm, gripping him so tight her nails dug into his skin. He gasped for breath, his heart pounding. It was dark, and he clutched at the sheets around him, still in panic, but then he saw the familiar items of their bedroom and turned to see Helen in her nightgown, still holding his arm tightly. Tears streamed down her face. "Jim," she said.

Five minutes later, they sat beside each other in the bed, neither speaking. Helen had turned on the bedside lamp, and its dim light helped him calm down. It was cold in the room, but MacKendrie was sweating. He could still feel his heart beating.

"I thought you were over those nightmares," she said. She meant it as an observation, but it came out accusingly. He didn't reply. "It's been months since you had one this bad."

"Yes."

"Jim, what if they start coming back?"

She waited a long time for his answer. "I don't know."

"Promise me something."

He turned his head to her. "What?"

"If you have another like this, you'll see someone."

He made an annoyed click with his tongue. "Helen..."

She turned violently to face him, her face white with anger. "I mean it, Jim," she said in a fierce, low voice. "I'm not going through this again with you. You won't talk to me, so you better find someone, a doctor, or... Just someone," she said with finality. "Promise me. Promise me!" she hissed, when he didn't answer.

"All right!" he retorted. "All right. If it happens again."

The tension eased, but they were both angry and couldn't sleep. Helen reached for a book on the bedside table. MacKendrie got up and walked into the living room. He lay down on the couch, staring up at the ceiling. For the first time in his life, he felt utterly powerless. He knew he could not keep the promise he just made and closed his eyes.

When he opened them again, it was morning, and Priss stood beside the couch in her pajamas. "Did you have a bad dream, Daddy?" Her eyes were wide.

He flinched, remembering her part in his dream. "Uh...it's all right, dear. I wasn't sleeping very well and didn't want to bother your mother, so I came out here to rest." He smiled and reached out to smooth her dark hair. He could tell she wasn't persuaded. She was almost eight now, an observant child. "Better go get ready for school."

He got up and went around the spacious house, lighting the gas heaters, then went into the bedroom to find Helen putting on her housecoat. They exchanged murmured good mornings. She was working full time now as a truant officer for the school district, and it was his job to fix breakfast for everyone. He washed his face and hands, donned his robe, and went into the kitchen to cook oatmeal and toast, pour orange juice, and brew a pot of coffee. After everyone left and he had the house to himself, he would leisurely read the paper, get dressed, and look over his lectures for the evening. Helen resented the reversal of roles, he knew. She once let slip something about his "laziness these days," then tried to make light of it, but she meant it, and he wondered if he were becoming lazy. He had always thought it an unforgivable vice, but he was beginning to understand that some men were not lazy as much as crippled.

There was the usual flurry of activity as they bundled out the door. They had two cars now, which MacKendrie could hardly believe, and Helen dropped off the children at school on the way to her office. "Bye, dear," he said, kissing her cheek. She offered a small smile and gave him a meaningful look.

When he returned from the mission, MacKendrie hadn't really cared about much. Helen had taken one look at him and knew something was wrong. She told the girls their father was sick and needed to rest and asked no questions at first. She made a lot of decisions, including what they would do with the small fortune he had in his pocket when he got off the plane. It was six weeks before MacKendrie felt himself returning to his senses. When she finally did ask what had happened in San Diego, or wherever it was he went, his repeated denials infuriated her. After he returned to something like normalcy, she let it drop.

Then the nightmares had started. Night after night, for four months, MacKendrie woke up yelling and sobbing, waking Helen and sometimes the girls. They all dreaded the approach of night and sleep. At his wife's frantic urging, MacKendrie went to see a doctor, but he prescribed a sleeping powder that left him groggy all day, and he quit taking it. Gradually the nightmares lessened in frequency and vividness, and then stopped, but it had left the family shaken and wary, as if a dangerous trap were sitting in the room and the slightest tremor might set it off, leaving someone caught in it.

Recently, cautiously, they began to think about the future. Helen had mentioned something to him about the ministry, and he gave a noncommittal answer. Then last night's nightmare, and he wondered if it would ever end.

About four o'clock, his head aching, he climbed in his used Chrysler sedan and set out for the junior college. It was February, chilly and drizzling. The dim light was already fading as he maneuvered the car onto the main street of Norfolk. The windshield wipers were doing a poor job of clearing the mist, and headlights made blurry streaks across the windshield. He had to slow down, but cars were speeding past, which annoyed him.

A dark pickup truck pulled up behind him. It came closer, tailing him. He tried to ignore it, but the truck inched up till it was on his bumper. A horn blared. He checked the rearview mirror but could make out no details of the driver. The horn blared again. And again. He gripped the wheel tighter. The street here was two lanes. He had nowhere to pull over. He pressed the accelerator, and the car pulled away a little. But in seconds, the truck filled the mirror again. The horn blasted his ears. His heart was pounding. It was raining hard now. White streaks flashed across the windshield. The horn sounded, louder, unrelenting—"

Without knowing how it happened, he was standing next to the truck, pounding on the window, shouting. "Stop honking that horn! Stop it, you hear?" The door opened, and a young man, lean, wearing a cap, stepped out. All MacKendrie could hear was jagged phrases—"old fucker...can't even drive...move your ass..."

He felt his fist clench, he was shouting something back, his arm was swinging somewhere in the man's direction...

The blow on his jaw snapped his head back, and he lost control. His knees buckled, and he felt his head hit something hard. He didn't lose consciousness at first. He was aware of the cold and the rain against his face. He tried moving but couldn't. He heard voices.

"Found him..." "Stand back..." "Ambulance..."

Hands were picking him up, pain shot through his skull, and he moaned. He was lying on something and it wasn't raining anymore, and he was vaguely aware of motion. I hope they're taking me home, he thought idly. Helen will be wondering about me. He swam into darkness.

* * *

Slowly he became aware of light. He groggily tried opening his eyes but shut them again immediately. Why was it so bright? Why didn't the alarm wake him up? He had to fix breakfast for his family. Squinting, he opened his eyes and tried to sit up, but pain radiated from the back of his head across his skull, and he gasped. He lay still and tried looking without moving his head.

White surrounded him. The walls, the ceiling, the floors, the cabinets. It was blinding, it couldn't be shut out. It was bone, clay, flesh without blood, a room drained of color as if someone had left open a plug in the floor and it had all run down to collect in a room below, full of laughter and joy. Children would be playing in that room, he thought, and there would be music.

The door opened and a nurse in a white uniform came in and stood by the bed. "Oh, you're awake," she said. "That's good. You had us worried there for a while. How do you feel?"

"I...don't...my head," he said.

She took his pulse. "You took a pretty nasty bump," she said. "You need to lie still."

"Bump? What... Where...?"

She smoothed the blanket covering him. "You're at Norfolk General Hospital. You've had a little accident. You just rest. I'll tell the doctor you're awake." She left.

His head throbbed. He put his hand to the side of his head and felt bandages. He explored with his hand and found the bandages were wrapped around the entire top of his head like a turban. He found the source of the pain, at the back of his skull. He could tell it was swollen and tender. What had happened to him? He remembered being cold and wet. Rain. There had been some noise. A horn. He was angry. And there was a man.

He couldn't remember what he had done, but he knew he had made a mistake, maybe a terrible mistake. Helen, he thought. Tears filled his eyes, overflowed down his face, and he began to sob. "I'm sorry," he said. "I'm sorry."

He wanted to vanish, hide somewhere, but he could barely sit up, and there was a parade of visitors. The doctor told him he had a laceration that required ten stitches to close. He also had a concussion, but luckily there had been no fracture. He had been unconscious for eight hours, and there was concern he had suffered a subdural hematoma—bleeding on the brain. "I still can't rule it out, but I think with rest you'll make a full recovery. You'll likely have dizzy spells for a while, and it could take a few months for your headaches to go away."

A middle-aged man in a dark suit introduced himself as Detective Barnes of the Norfolk Police Department. What could he remember about what happened?

Agitated, MacKendrie said there was a car...no, a truck. It was tailgating him, blasting its horn. He must have stopped to confront the driver.

Barnes said, "Passerby found you lying on the ground. There wasn't any other vehicle around. You didn't see who hit you?"

"I'm sorry, but I don't even remember getting hit." MacKendrie put his hand over his face.

The detective stood. "It's pretty clear that other driver punched you and you hit your head when you fell. If we found him, we could charge him, but we've got no witnesses, so... A word of advice, Mr. MacKendrie. Don't try to talk to someone driving like that. Just pull over. Never know what some fellas will do."

Helen, composed and unnaturally calm, had told the girls the truth, that their father had an accident and his head was badly hurt. She had tried to coach them to be brave when they visited, but when they saw him they began to cry, and he in turn sobbed in such an uncontrolled way that it brought a nurse to the room to admonish them to be quiet. Helen, eyes dry, prompted the girls to say things they had obviously rehearsed.

A whispered "I'm sorry you're hurt, Daddy." "Do they let you eat ice cream?" "When can you come home?"

He steeled himself to resume the part of their father, thanking them for visiting him and trying feebly to make them laugh. "The doctor says I will have to stay here for a few more days, and then I can come home with you. Don't worry, dear girls. They are going to make me well again."

On the third day after he woke up, Helen visited alone. She offered bits of small talk, the latest truant story, something Priss had said about school. She fell silent.

"Dear," he whispered, "the junior college..."

"I called them. They found someone to teach your classes. They heard about this." She gestured to the hospital bed. "A number of people have heard about it."

His face crumpled, and he panted with emotion. "I'm sorry." Her expression didn't change, but as he looked up at her and repeated, "Helen, I'm so sorry," she cracked. She squinted, and then her hand went to her mouth. She leaned forward and lay on his lap, shaking, as he repeated "sorry" over and over until she raised up and touched his face.

"Shh. No more." She sat down again and they didn't speak for a while. Finally she broke the silence, speaking calmly. "Since we left Kirkwell, I haven't been the best wife—let me finish! You've been so unhappy, and I don't know what to do. I suppose part of me doesn't blame you. But now, I don't know if I can..." She started to get up.

"Helen." His voice made her stop. He started trying to push himself up a little straighter and asked her to help him. When he was sitting up, he looked directly at her. "A few weeks ago, when the nightmares came back, you told me I needed to find someone to talk to. There is someone, someone who knows me straight through. I don't know why it took me so long to figure that out, and now I've made a stupid mess of things. None of this is your fault, Helen. I hope I can make you see that. I'm going to tell you a long story."

THIRTY-SEVEN

Easter fell early that year, in the midst of a March warm spell. First Presbyterian of Norfolk was a large, well-to-do church, and MacKendrie didn't feel comfortable worshiping there, but the service was grand. After the benediction, Helen helped him stand and handed him the cane, which the doctor had advised in case of a sudden dizzy spell. There had been a few of those, but they were fading, along with the headaches. Another month, the doctor said, and he could resume his normal habits. What were his normal habits these days, MacKendrie wondered.

They joined the stream of worshipers filing out. As MacKendrie waited, looking about, he saw a Chinese man with a limp approaching. The man extended his hand and gave a slight bow.

"Pastor Ma."

MacKendrie smiled and grasped his hand. "Paul. Good heavens, it's good to see you. What in the world are you doing here?"

"I was in Washington for a meeting. I was told you might be here."

MacKendrie noted that his English was improved. "I see. Well, I'm glad you came." He introduced Wang to Helen. "You remember, I've told you about Paul, how I knew him in China as a boy." She looked uncomprehending for a moment. "We worked together on that Navy project," he said carefully.

Her eyes widened, and she looked quickly at Wang, then said lightly, "Oh, that. Goodness, I worried so much while Jim was working on that." She laughed, and Wang and MacKendrie exchanged smiles. "Will you join us for lunch, Mr. Wang?"

"Thank you, but I am afraid I cannot." He turned to MacKendrie. "Would it be possible for us to talk later?"

That afternoon, MacKendrie drove to a hotel downtown. He was shocked when Wang entered the lobby on crutches, the right leg of his pants empty and pinned up just below the knee.

"Paul, your leg."

"Oh. Yes. This morning I was wearing *artificial* leg," he said, pronouncing the word carefully. "But it ah-bothers me, and I cannot wear it too long. It is nice day, yes? Perhaps we can sit outside if we do not walk far."

They walked slowly to a plaza and found a bench in the sun.

"The doctors couldn't save your leg?"

"No. The wound and tourniquet caused too much damage. It was amputated in Tokyo. I was there two months recovering. It is not so bad. I am used to it now. A little reminder of my adventures."

There was some small talk, then MacKendrie asked what had happened after they parted in Tokyo.

When Wang was cleared by the doctors, Cohen had taken him to Washington for extensive debriefing. It had taken weeks. He told them about mining stations on the river, encounters he had with the military, the names of everyone he came in contact with. Cohen was insatiable, demanding more and more information. Even the failure of mission, how Wang had been detected from the start and ultimately caused the network's collapse, was the subject of repeated interviews. Wang had asked what became of Owl. Cohen refused to say, but hinted that he was alive. Taiwan was mentioned.

He was treated well enough, but Wang began to feel like a plaything in the hands of mischievous children. At the end of three months, he declared that his debt to Cohen had been paid and he wished to be released. There was debate what to do with him. Was he in danger of being killed or kidnapped by Chinese agents? Would he turn against America? In the end, he persuaded Cohen that he was through with espionage and just wanted to be a scientist again. With the help of some altered transcripts, it was arranged for him to get into the Ph.D. program at UCLA. There were lots of fellow Chinese in the area, and he had made friends and settled into a quiet life.

Wang paused and said, "Pastor Ma, I have told no one about my time in China, but there are things that trouble me, and I have no one else to talk to about them. You would understand."

MacKendrie nodded. "Please, go on."

Wang told of his part in the network, the strain, how agents would disappear or die, the constant fear of discovery and of his chief. Then he met Li and fell in love with her, and found friendship with Juh.

"I was working in secret against the people I felt most loyal to. The chief ordered me to steal some papers from Juh, to kill him if I had to. He was going to send me back to America. I would never see Li or my mother again. I couldn't bear it."

He paused, and MacKendrie asked a question he had wanted to ask for months. "The dead man in the house that night. Who was he? What happened?"

Wang didn't look at him. "Nothing was what it seemed."

Li was part of the network, a deep operative assigned to watch him without his knowledge. His hope that she might go with him to America was impossible. And that night, as they waited in the house by the river, Juh came calling.

"He was First Bureau agent. They set a clever trap, and I fell into it. They had followed me to hunt down and kill the other agents. That night, Juh was going to arrest me, but Li attacked him, and we fought. I was wounded, and she killed him." Wang glanced at MacKendrie. "Then I called you on radio. It was Juh you saw."

MacKendrie looked at the sun slanting down through the cool air. "Something is bothering you, Paul. Is it Li's death? Or Juh's?"

Wang stirred uncomfortably and shook his head. "I am sorry they are dead, but they are not why I still lie awake at night sometimes." He told how he had discovered the plant and how an innocent passerby had been killed by bullets that were intended for him.

MacKendrie shook his head in wonder. "My God. How terrible."

"There is more. He belonged to Heaven's Way Church."

"Who was he?"

"You did not know him. He converted after you left China. But he was married to a young cousin of my mother. Yuming." Wang's voice shook, and he convulsed silently with sobs. "He is dead because of me." He shook his head and exhaled loudly. "I think maybe God will not forgive me."

MacKendrie nodded. "I have been wondering the same thing for two years."

Wang was surprised. "You have no answer, then?"

MacKendrie thought for a long moment. "I don't know. There have been so many failures. Mine, others. People dead as a result." He looked over at Wang. "God will forgive us, but that doesn't mean we get off scot-free. There's a price for our failures. We have to pay it." He shook his head. "And Harry Cohen probably sleeps like a baby at night."

"I saw Cohen yesterday." Noticing MacKendrie's surprise, he said, "Oh, yes. He is the reason I am here. He asked me to come to meeting in Washington. You are nearby, so I came to see you."

"How is Harry?"

"He says he is in line for promotion to chief of Asian operations."

MacKendrie gave a rueful laugh. "They'll probably make him an admiral before it's over."

"Said to tell you, you save his career."

They were silent for a while. MacKendrie said, "Is your mother still alive? Do you know?"

"Two months ago, I receive letter from an elder in the church. It was smuggled out of China. My mother is dead. Some sort of illness."

MacKendrie turned to face Wang. "I'm deeply sorry. I know how much you loved her. She had a hard life."

"It is all right. She believed death would bring peace."

"Yes. You say the letter came from an elder. Not Pastor Dou?"

"No. The letter said he was arrested. There is no word about him."

A gust of wind made them shiver. MacKendrie said, "Shall we go back inside?" As they approached the hotel, he asked, "You haven't married, Paul?"

Wang stopped and faced him. "Soon. She came from China two weeks ago. Yuming."

"Yuming? But..."

"Before I left, I gave Pastor Dou a message for her, told her I was responsible for her husband's death. I told her if she was willing, I would become her husband. I didn't know if she got the message, but after I arrived in California, I got letter from her. She had a way to get to Hong Kong with her young son. Wanted to know if I was still willing to have her. It has taken some time to arrange, but she is in California. Her son is a fine boy. I want to give him American name— James."

Tears stung MacKendrie's eyes, and he avoided looking at Wang. "Thank you," he whispered.

"What of you, Pastor Ma? Are you well?"

MacKendrie swallowed and forced himself to smile. "I have a good wife and two beautiful daughters. I am trying to be grateful, but gratitude is the hardest virtue to master."

"It is a task, then." He smiled. "For both of us. Our own long march."

MacKendrie nodded. "A pilgrimage."

Wang extended his hand. "I owe you everything. Please remember that."

MacKendrie took Wang's hand, then pulled him into an embrace. "I will. Please write to me. This time, I promise, I will write back."

That summer was the most pleasant the MacKendrie family could remember. They went to the beach, visited Lily and Phil on their farm, took drives through the countryside. MacKendrie was free of nightmares, and only the occasional headache troubled him. He laughed more easily, which delighted the girls, and even the brittleness between him and Helen that persisted after he came home from the hospital began to soften. One night, near midsummer's day, after the girls were asleep, he had suddenly taken her in his arms, kissed her deeply, and they had almost rushed into the bedroom to make love, the first time in months. Forgetting themselves, they cried out triumphantly as they reached the end.

As they lay in the dark, breathless, she reached for his hand. "Will it ever be the way it was, Jim?" He could tell she was crying.

"I don't know, Helen. I don't know."

After Labor Day, despondency crept over MacKendrie. There was still plenty of Cohen's money left, but no work for him. The junior college had dismissed him. His inquiries in the presbytery, even supplying the pulpits of vacationing pastors, had been politely turned aside. The girls went back to school, and Helen to work, and he idled around the house, cleaning, reading, trying desperately to fill the hours. Memories of Ulysses, Jack lying wounded, the pickup truck's blaring horn, his rage, returned again and again.

The jangling phone jolted him, and his hand shook as he picked up the receiver and quavered hello. A voice asked for him by name.

"I'm Chaplain Brooks Cofer, over at the VA Hospital. I understand you were a Navy chaplain in the war. Mind if I ask where you were stationed?"

"At a base in the South Pacific. Tinian."

"That's what I thought. I wonder if you'd mind coming over here to the VA. I've got a patient wants to talk to you."

MacKendrie had been to the VA hospital in Norfolk just once. It had reminded him of the one on Tinian, only the patients were in better shape. He located the chaplain's office and found Cofer to be a weary, balding, overweight man in a suit and tie. He had been an Army chaplain for thirty years and took the VA job after he retired. American Baptist, he told MacKendrie.

"Not as hardshell as those Southern Baptists," he said with a small smile. He folded his stubby hands.

"What can I do for you, Chaplain?"

"Well, we got a patient a few weeks ago named Alvin Leonard. He has cancer and not very much time. He was a marine, served in the South Pacific. Tough as nails. Thinks he's going to beat the disease."

"No chance of that?"

He shook his head. "Skin cancer, very advanced."

"What was his rank?"

Cofer checked a sheet. "Says master sergeant. I've visited him, and he wasn't saying much. No visitors. Got a daughter, but they're estranged. So the other day, out of the blue he says he wants to see Chaplain Mac. Who's that, I says. Well, he doesn't know the name, just he was a chaplain on Tinian. Leonard was wounded at Saipan, and they sent him to Tinian to recover. So he keeps asking me to find Chaplain Mac. I did a little digging and found there was a Chaplain MacKendrie there and figured that's his Chaplain Mac. I called up Navy HQ and they said you were right in my back yard. I figure that's a sign from the Lord you're supposed to see this man. You remember him?"

MacKendrie shook his head. "Afraid not. I saw an awful lot of men at that hospital."

"Well, Reverend, I haven't told him I found you. You're under no obligation, but it might mean a lot if you'd drop in and talk to him."

MacKendrie stood. "Of course I will."

He walked into the room to find a stocky man in his sixties, with a broad face, a short fringe of gray hair, and a downturned mouth sitting on the side of the bed in a hospital gown, a hand resting on his thigh, elbow akimbo. "You're Master Sergeant Leonard, is that right?"

Leonard said quietly, "Are you a doctor?"

"No. I'm Jim MacKendrie. Chaplain Cofer asked me to come visit with you." He extended his hand.

As Leonard took it in a crushing grip, he squinted. "MacKendrie. I remember you. You were at Tinian. You're Chaplain Mac."

"That's right. You've got a pretty good memory, Master Sergeant."

"Call me Al. Chaplain Mac. Can't believe they tracked you down. Didn't go to any trouble to get here, did you?"

"Not at all. I live in Norfolk. How are you, Al?"

"Well, they tell me not so good, but I've heard that before."

"When was that?"

Leonard regarded him. "You've probably got better things to do than listen to a lot of war stories, Padre."

"As a matter of fact, Al, I don't." He pulled a chair next to the bed.

That evening he told Helen about the conversation. Leonard had enlisted in the Marines in 1917 and was sent to France. He took a machine gun bullet at Belleau Wood and was one of fifty men in his battalion to survive. Stayed in the Corps, made it to sergeant at the start of the second war, fought his way across the South Pacific, and was hit by shrapnel from a Japanese grenade at Saipan. He retired before Korea, had lived in Norfolk for the past several years.

"We talked about the war, reminisced about Tinian. I asked him what he thought about his situation. He knows the score. He's just been putting up a front for the doctors."

"How sad. No family?"

"There's a daughter that we're sending word to."

For a month, MacKendrie visited Leonard, playing cards and talking about the ways of the military. Each day, Leonard seemed to dissolve a little. On a day when he seemed to rally, he asked for a favor.

"Two favors, really, Padre. One, I'd like to be buried at Arlington. Ever been there?" MacKendrie said no. "Damn impressive place. Lot of brave men buried there. I'd like to keep 'em company."

"I'll see to it, Al. What's the other favor?"

Leonard looked down. "I'd be obliged if you'd say a few words at the service."

"Of course I will. It would be an honor." Leonard nodded but didn't look up. "Al, is there something you want to get off your chest? Now's a good time."

Leonard stared across the room, and MacKendrie realized he was looking much farther away.

"It was on Saipan," he said. "Lot of close-quarters fighting, trying to dislodge those goddamn Jap pillboxes. We were using flamethrowers. We were inching our way up to a machine gun that was ripping our guys to shreds. Rounds were flying like hell over my head. I got to twenty yards, so close I could see 'em moving around inside that bunker. I gave a signal, our guys ceased fire, and I stood up and let 'em have it."

Leonard paused, took a wheezing breath. "I could feel the heat on my face. They were screaming, but I kept squeezing that trigger, pouring that fire in there. I been having dreams about that, Padre. I dream that after I die, I'm standing in a room and a soldier, still burning like a torch, walks in. I can feel the heat. This time it's me screaming." He took a couple of wheezing breaths. "Here's what I want to know, Padre. Is that what's gonna happen? Am I gonna see that man I—" He choked, coughed.

"Easy, Al." MacKendrie put a glass of water to his lips and eased him back onto his pillow. "There you go." He stood beside the bed, put his hand on the bony shoulder, and waited till Leonard settled down. "Al, listen to me. If you could talk to that soldier now, what would you say to him? Let's say he's standing here right now, not as you remember him on fire, but just as a man, a soldier in his uniform. You don't have to say it out loud, but what are you going to say to him?"

Leonard twitched and his mouth worked silently. He gave a gasp, then a moan, then began to breathe heavily and lay quiet. He opened his eyes.

"I told him I had to do it," Leonard said, water running down his cheeks. "I begged him to forgive me. He...he said it was okay. It is gonna be okay, ain't it, Padre?"

Weeks later, on a warm and muggy September day, MacKendrie and Cofer drove up to Arlington. Leonard's daughter and two grandchildren stood beside the flag-draped casket. The honor guard was magnificent in their ceremonial uniforms. MacKendrie kept his remarks short, telling the family that Alvin Leonard had been a man of courage and duty but also a man with a conscience who had expressed remorse for some of the terrible things he had done in time of war. And in the end, he said, he had found peace. The bugler sounded *Taps*, the rifle squad fired their salute.

Leonard's daughter curtly thanked him. Her parents separated, and she never really knew him, she said, but understood a little better now what he must have been like.

As they drove back to Norfolk, Cofer said, "That was very well done, Jim. No, I mean it. I've seen a lot of these things, seen them done badly. You have a way with it."

"Like riding a bicycle," MacKendrie said gratefully. "You don't forget how."

"I did a little asking around in the last couple months. About you," he said, glancing over, then back to the road. "You've had a time of it last two years."

"Who did you talk to?"

"Well, I talked to Reverend Land down in Wilmington. He told me all about what went on in that little town. That kind of speaks for itself. You and your family turn up in Norfolk, you're teaching at the junior college instead of preaching, and then you get yourself beaten up in some kind of roadside scrap." MacKendrie said nothing. "There's a missing piece there, Jim. Anything you can tell me about that?"

MacKendrie sighed. "I can't tell you much, Brooks. I got talked into doing a job for the Navy. Things went wrong. Someone died. I felt responsible."

Cofer nodded. "It's beginning to make sense. How are things with you now?"

"I don't know. When I was in the hospital, I finally told Helen what happened. She and I are on the mend, I guess. Physically I'm okay, but right now I'm feeling pretty useless. The presbytery thinks I'm damaged goods, and they're right. Not many churches would welcome me as a pastor."

"Have you thought about being a chaplain again?" MacKendrie stared at him. "I've been after the VA for years to get me an assistant. Just got approved. Fiscal year just started, so the position's open. Based on what I've seen, I think you'd make a fine chaplain. You interested?"

"But...what about that run-in..."

Cofer shook his head. "I don't care about that, and neither do those men in the hospital. You said you feel responsible for someone dying. We see a lot of men who feel the same way. Maybe you'd understand that better than me." MacKendrie was silent. "You think about it, brother. Pray about it."

He nodded. "I will. Sure."

Cofer let him out at the curb. As he made his way up the walk to his house, he noticed that his legs felt limber and strong for the first time in months. He walked through the front door and the air tingled all around him, as if charged with electricity. He was aware of the giggles of Dottie and Priss coming from their room, of the dust motes floating in the light slanting through the window, of the smell of Helen's stew bubbling on the stove in the kitchen. He could feel his pulse in his temples and breath deep in his lungs. Something had been released, like a hook slipping off a catch. He felt more alive than he ever remembered. Suddenly things were simple.

He called loudly, "Hello, I'm home!" It brought the girls running, and Helen appeared, surprised, in the doorway to the kitchen. MacKendrie extended his arms wide, as if to gather them in.

"I feel like taking a walk before dinner," he said. "Who wants to come with me?"

Author's Note

Like many men, I married into a family that broadened my horizons. My wife, Evelyn Worth McMullen, was the child of multiple generations of Presbyterian missionaries to Asia on her father's side, and she briefly carried on that tradition in South America. Her grandfather, the Rev. Charles Worth, was born in China, graduated from Union Theological Seminary in Richmond, and joined his father, Dr. George Worth, at the Presbyterian mission station in Jiangyin, China, as an itinerant evangelist in the 1920s and 1930s. As he tells it, he and his father were avid bird hunters.

Many years after Charles died in 1976, his daughter Julia organized his papers and had them printed for the benefit of the family. These papers included his memoir, which recounts in somewhat hair-raising detail his work during some of the most difficult years of China's extremely difficult 20th century. It also recounts his first wife's death to cancer, his service in the U.S. Navy as a chaplain during World War II, his second marriage, and his life after the war as a pastor in Eastern North Carolina. Of course, Charles was loosely the model for James MacKendrie, although I never met Charles Worth and the character of MacKendrie is entirely the product of my imagination, with a touch of my own experience as a Southern small-town pastor thrown in.

Also among Charles's papers was a curious little typewritten story that Julia jokingly called "his spy story." Titled *Call of the Cuckoo*, it spun a yarn—in first person—of joining a mission to rescue a young Chinese man working as a spy for Naval Intelligence, using a speedboat to travel up the Yangtze River. As far as the family knows, this story was not autobiographical; there's no evidence that Charles ever left the sanctuary of his church and home in North Carolina to help with what the military these days calls an extraction from hostile Communist China. Yet the story has a kind of verisimilitude that suggests Charles may have heard, or overheard, a tale of something like this.

His is a kind of *Boy's Life* version of a spy story, written in a very breezy, cheerful style without any hint of drama, danger, or possible snags that could have landed the narrator, his crewmate, and the spy in a Chinese prison, or worse. But when I read it, at a point in my life when I had time on my hands, not by choice, I thought it offered possibilities as a longer, darker story. After years of working through countless versions, *Pilgrim Through this Barren Land* is the result.

The scene of MacKendrie and Fletcher hiding in the reeds and an escape by river may remind some readers of the 1955 John Wayne film *Blood Alley*. I don't know if Charles saw that film and borrowed the idea, or arrived at it independently, but the similarity didn't occur to me until well after the book was finished.

Obviously, I owe much to Charles Worth, as the concept of the second half of this novel—the heart of the story—is his. By all accounts, he was a gentle man and likely would have been dismayed to see his protagonist turning weapons on human beings instead of ducks. I have tried to channel that gentleness in presenting MacKendrie as a man torn between his faith and desire for peace on one hand and the cruel realities of human nature on the other. I hope that in his well-earned eternal rest, he will forgive a writer's indulgences. I have been assured by his daughters, Julia Worth and

Lucy Worth, that they don't mind the alterations, and I appreciate their encouragement.

But my real thanks go to Evelyn, who was my muse through all the years of laboring on this book. As is her nature, she never complained when I spent long hours on my laptop, and her readings of the manuscripts always gave me the belief that maybe I could pull it off. In a similar vein, her brother, David Worth, gave me a good-natured kick in the pants to finally put a manuscript into print form when I thought the project was all but dead. Without the remarkable accomplishments and inspiration of the Worth family, this book simply wouldn't exist.

Our daughter, Grace McMullen, a talented artist, created the wonderful book cover, and I am not only grateful to her, I'm also proud that she chose to follow in the footsteps of her Worth ancestors as a pastor.

I am not nearly as good a historian as our son, Russell, but his keen interest in Worth family history was another source of encouragement to me.

My thanks to Cathleen Falsani and Susan Ketchin, who made helpful editorial suggestions. Also, thanks to the Rev. Steve Schaick, former chief of chaplains for the U.S. Air Force, for his advice on the protocols of funerals at Arlington National Cemetery.

I would like to acknowledge the work of The Outreach Foundation, an independent mission organization, which organized a trip to Southeast China in October 2024, on which Evelyn and I were able to see some of the locations in Hangzhou and Jiangyin where her great-grandfather and grandfather were missionaries. While there, we met many faithful Chinese Christians who gratefully acknowledged that they were beneficiaries of the labor of missionaries such as the Worths.

Finally, I am grateful to God for the ways he has tried, often unsuccessfully, to teach this stubborn heart to be silent, to listen, and to follow the way he was pointing me. Many were the times I wandered off that path, through some barren lands indeed. As the Welshman William Williams wrote in 1745, in the hymn that provided this book's title, *Songs of praises, songs of praises, I will ever give to Thee.*

About the Author

Cary McMullen is an award-winning journalist, editor, and author. A native of Texas, he worked as a computer programmer before studying at Union Presbyterian Seminary and Duke Divinity School. He served as pastor of two Presbyterian churches in southern Georgia before turning to journalism. He was a reporter for *The Cordele (Ga.) Dispatch* and religion editor at *The (Lakeland, Fla.) Ledger*. At *The Ledger*, he wrote a weekly column, *Beliefs*, that was carried by The New York Times News Service and received awards from the Florida Society of Newspaper Editors and the American Association of Sunday and Features Editors. His assignments included the national conventions of most major American denominations and reports from Cuba and Haiti. He later worked as publications editor for Florida Southern College. He and his wife, Evelyn, have two adult children, a grandchild, and two step-grandchildren. They live in North Carolina.

www.ingramcontent.com/pod-product-compliance
Lightning Source LLC
Chambersburg PA
CBHW071342300726
48976CB00006B/1738